PRAISE FOR THE WOMEN OF HOPE SERIES

Remember Me When

"In this engrossing second installment of her Women of Hope historical series, Aiken delivers a beautiful, inspirational slice of life set in 1880s Oregon.... Rich with detail, the events unfold very naturally." —*Publishers Weekly*

"Aiken's second Women of Hope novel connects nicely to the first.... The 1880 Oregon setting is accurately illustrated and the heroine's journey to renewed faith in God is nicely depicted." —*RT Book Reviews*

For Such a Time as This

"An engaging tale of duty, romance, family, and love.... I'll be eager to see what character Ms. Aiken chooses next to feature in this exciting new series." —Serena Chase, USAToday.com

"FOR SUCH A TIME AS THIS offers readers all of the elements they love in one beautifully-written Esther-themed tale. Highly recommended!" —Janice Hanna Thompson, author of *Love Finds You in Daisy, Oklahoma*

SHE SHALL BE PRAISED

Also by Ginny Aiken

For Such a Time as This
Remember Me When

SHE SHALL BE PRAISED

A WOMEN *of* HOPE NOVEL

GINNY AIKEN

New York • Boston • Nashville

FaithWords
Hachette Book Group
237 Park Avenue
New York, NY 10017

www.faithwords.com

Printed in the United States of America

RRD-C

First Edition: January 2014

10 9 8 7 6 5 4 3 2 1

FaithWords is a division of Hachette Book Group, Inc.
The FaithWords name and logo are trademarks of Hachette Book Group, Inc.

The Hachette Speakers Bureau provides a wide range of authors for speaking events. To find out more, go to www.hachettespeakersbureau.com or call (866) 376-6591.

The publisher is not responsible for websites (or their content) that are not owned by the publisher.

Library of Congress Cataloging-in-Publication Data
Aiken, Ginny.
    She shall be praised : a women of hope novel / Ginny Aiken. — First edition.
        pages cm.
    Summary: "Faith, humor, romance, and adventure blend in the third novel in Ginny Aiken's historical series, inspired by The Perfect Wife in Proverbs 31." —Provided by the publisher
        ISBN 978-0-89296-846-6 (pbk.) — ISBN 978-1-4555-7387-5 (ebook)
        1. Socialites—Fiction.   2. Husbands—Crimes against—Fiction.
    3. Oregon—History—19th century—Fiction.   I. Title.
    PS3551.I339S54 2014
    813'.54—dc23
                                                            2013019843

A book does not come about by the efforts of only one person;
a series even less. The Women of Hope series has been a
collaborative effort, and I dedicate She Shall Be Praised *to the*
two persons who've contributed the most. First, my agent, Steve
Laube, is the best an author could ever wish to have on her side.
And second, Christina Boys, my fabulous editor, is a dream
editor. Christina, you're a joy to work with. While I love to
brainstorm, who would have thought brainstorming could be so
much fun? Thanks for the ideas, the questions, and the cool eyes.
My books are much better for your contribution.

Favor is deceitful, and beauty is vain; but a woman that feareth the Lord, she shall be praised.

—Proverbs 31:30

Chapter 1

Hope County, Oregon—1883

"Miss Emma," the young man said, his voice a mixture of excited anticipation and nervous tremor. "I believe this one's mine."

Emma Crowell smiled, thrilled by the respectful, gentlemanly approach. "Mr. Walters, I believe?"

Pleasure tinted her new dance partner's youthful face. "That's me, miss. Shall we?"

She stood and slipped her own dance card into the hidden pocket at the seam of her exquisite rose silk Worth ball gown, trimmed in luscious cream Alençon lace. She then placed her hand on his to let him lead her to the center of the ballroom in Aunt Sophia and Uncle Justus's large and lovely Denver home. A moment later, the sweet, rich notes of "Over the Waves," her favorite waltz, swirled around the room.

Emma smiled, caught in the elegance of the moment; the sparkle of the crystal chandeliers overhead; the romantic music; the happy murmur of conversation and muffled laughs; the clearly smitten gentleman in whose arms she flew across the highly polished floor. Every so often, the scent of the fragrant red roses, lush in the tall, urn-shaped vases, wafted past her nose. The rustle of silks, taffetas, and velvets kept pace with the rhythm of the soaring music.

A bubble of pure happiness rippled up inside her and spilled out in a joy-filled giggle. She was having such a very splendid time during her visit to her favorite relatives. What more could a girl want? Lovely gowns—three trunks full of them, already sent home to Portland ahead of her—a doting Papa, loving aunt and uncle, invitations to party after party after party in colorful Denver, topped off by a brigade of charming gentlemen, all of whom seemed to have decided her every whim was their greatest desire. She hadn't done anything to bring them to that decision, and at times the excess of it all did embarrass her, but she wouldn't be honest if she didn't admit she enjoyed their compliments, company, and attentions.

True, it meant the other young ladies she'd met seemed to have no use for her, just as they did wherever she went. That did bother her to a greater degree than she wanted to acknowledge. Her brows drew inward, but she immediately forced her face into a cheery smile. The thought of a wrinkly forehead was enough to make her straighten her spine and remember Mama's repeated admonition.

"Unless she wants to end up looking old and dreary before her time," she often said, "a lady will always wear her most pleasant expression. And you, my Emma, are a lovely little lady."

The memory of her late mother made her falter in her dance steps. Although Mama had died eight years ago, Emma still missed her every single, solitary day. Just as she knew Papa's heart still bore the large hole Cassandra Crowell's passing had left behind.

"Oh, dear!" Mr. Walters cried, slowing a tad. "Are you unwell, Miss Emma? I didn't step on your foot, now, did I?"

"Pshaw!" She gave her dance partner her most radiant smile as he again swung them into a wide turn. "I'm fine. Just a tiny stutter of the feet. But I do adore the waltz, this one in particular. Let's do enjoy it!"

A pair of hours later, Emma's exhilaration had wilted into exhaustion. She'd danced the whole night away with a steady stream of gentlemen, and, as usual, Joshua Hamilton had penciled on her dance card two dances for himself. During an intermission, he'd led her out to the broad veranda for a breath of fresh if still chilly air—spring had taken its sweet time arriving, and nights in the Rockies still turned nippy.

While they strolled across the width of the veranda, he'd pressed her for a response to his recent marriage proposal in the nicest of ways. Papa had made no secret he viewed Joshua as a splendid specimen for his only daughter's husband, but Emma wasn't certain she was ready to settle down to the life of a proper businessman's wife. At least, not yet.

Now, she stood at the foot of the grand staircase, every so often waving her fan, more as a means to keep her hands busy than for any real need of a breeze, and bade her aunt and uncle's many guests farewell.

"Do come calling when you're in town again," Mrs. Macomb told Emma, a stiff, Rockies-chilly smile on her thin lips. At her side, her oldest daughter, Althea, shot daggers of envy Emma's way. It was said Althea had set her cap for Mr. Walters, who by now had made no secret his interest lay in Emma.

Emma wrinkled her nose. The Macomb home was one she'd avoid like the ague.

"You're too kind," she murmured. "We shall see what engagements Aunt Sophia schedules for me next time I return to Denver."

Aunt Sophia gave her a reproving look. She knew only too well how her niece felt about the Macomb women. They'd made it abundantly clear they blamed Emma for Mr. Walters's disaffection, and Emma often bristled while in their company.

"Behave!" her aunt said under her breath.

Emma beamed a beatific smile. After all, she was leaving the next afternoon. "I was only minding my manners."

Papa narrowed his gaze. "I should certainly hope so, Emma. Although...I would say we must have a brief chat in the morning—you, Uncle Justus, Aunt Sophia, and I—before you depart on your trip back to Portland. My only regret is that I won't be going with you. Are you sure you'll be—"

"Oh, Papa! Of course, I'm sure I'll be fine. I can ride in a carriage just as well as the next lady." How could he question her like this? "I'm not a child anymore, you understand. I'm all of nineteen now, and I most certainly can take care of myself. Besides, you're sending me with Reverend and Mrs. Strong. What could possibly go amiss when I have such... well, upright escorts?"

Uncle Justus laid a plump hand on Papa's arm. "Ed Schwartz, the carriage driver Reverend Strong has hired, is a decent man. He's also quite accomplished with a sidearm, and won't hesitate to use it any time he feels the need to protect his passengers. Our Emma will be safe with them."

Her father's face turned a touch pale at the mention of a weapon. "I sincerely pray you are right, Justus. She's all I have left of my darling Cassandra..."

A knot formed in Emma's throat. Papa's love for her mother was never far from his thoughts, and the loss filled his voice with sadness every time he spoke of her. She knew he saw her as an extension of his departed wife, and he'd always lavished his love on Emma. She rushed to his side and threw her arms around his neck.

"Hush, now, Papa!" She kissed his cheek and laid her head on his shoulder. "I'm fine—I will be fine. You'll see. I'll be home with Ophelia and Jedediah in no time. They'll take care of me as they always have."

The middle-aged couple had treated her as their child since the day she was born, and she loved them dearly, even if they didn't let her get away with anything. She could tease Papa into letting her have her way more often than not. Not so with the Millers.

She yawned. "Oh, goodness! I'll ask you to excuse me now, though. I'm dreadfully tired, and I'll still have a few things to see to in the morning."

"Don't forget, my dear," Papa added. "We will have that chat before the Strongs arrive."

She sighed. "Yes, Papa. We will. In the morning."

Hugs were shared all around, and, irksome discussion to come forgotten, Emma floated up the stairs. A delicious sense of...oh, adventure, perhaps danger, filled her every time she thought of her trip home alone. This would be the first time she went anywhere without Papa at her side. True, she'd be accompanied by the somewhat dour man of the cloth and his equally serious lady wife, but it still meant she'd have a certain sense of freedom. She couldn't wait.

A shiver of anticipation fluttered through her and she hurried to her room. The lovely feather bed, piled high with eyelet-trimmed green silk-covered pillows and cozy blankets, beckoned. Emma yawned again.

Sweet dreams surely awaited her.

Papa had meant what he'd said. Emma had scarcely sat at the breakfast table and sliced off the top of her perfectly and delicately poached egg before her father launched into his discussion.

"Have you given further thought to Joshua's offer of marriage?"

Emma's cheeks scorched and the tip of her nose itched. She hated blushing, but her fair red-head's complexion betrayed her only too often. "What is there to think about, Papa? He wants to marry me. You want me to marry him. I'm…well, I'm not sure I want to marry him. Rather, I'm not sure I want to marry him quite yet. I'm not ready to stop having such a— well, um…"

Aunt Sophia rushed her napkin to her lips, and Emma knew her mother's younger sister had only done so to disguise a laugh. Her mortification only heightened. She pursed her lips, buttered her toast, salted and peppered her delectable egg, and refused to meet anyone's gaze.

Papa cleared his throat. "Emma—"

"Allow me, Hugh," Aunt Sophia said.

An angel's flight would have roared out in the ensuing silence. Finally, Papa sighed. "Go ahead, then, Sophia. You are a woman, after all."

"Thank you." Emma's aunt turned her way. "Now, dear child. You do know Joshua is hardly the only young man who's offered for your hand in marriage. In fact, I do believe he's the...what? Is he the seventh? Eighth?"

"Ninth," Emma answered, her voice uncharacteristically tiny. "But why count? I've—"

"Why count?" Papa roared.

"Emma!" Uncle Justus cried.

"Why...well! I do declare..." her aunt sputtered. "That, dear child, was not the response I had hoped for."

Papa harrumphed. "I should say not."

"Indeed," added Uncle Justus, who generally agreed with his sassy, southern wife.

"A young lady," Aunt Sophia went on, twin faint lines over the bridge of her straight nose, "does not lead a gentleman on, Emma. Why...it's dreadfully cruel, you understand, dangling them along like that. Don't forget, dear child, their hearts are involved when they care for you, and it's not kind to play with their emotions. Especially when you deal with an exemplary young gentleman like Joshua. He's serious, well-educated, quite successful in business, as you should know, since he does a great deal with your father in that regard, and he does care deeply for you. He will always honor you, treat you gently—"

"Like royalty, I suspect," Uncle Justus murmured from his end of the table.

Aunt Sophia beamed at her spouse, her strawberry blond curls bobbing in a pretty fashion as she agreed with his assessment. "A young lady—you—could do much, much worse. The best marriages happen between those who have a great deal in common, and the two of you surely do."

Papa rose from his chair across from Emma, rounded the large, breakfast-laden mahogany table, and came to take the chair at his daughter's side. He placed a loving hand on hers.

"Do tell me," he said, his voice concerned. "Is there anything about the young man that makes you uneasy? Does he—" Papa's cheeks ruddied. "Does he frighten you? As a man, I mean."

"Papa!" Emma bolted upright. "That's—why…oh, dear! What a dreadful question. No, of course Mr. Hamilton does not"—she blinked furiously—"frighten me. He's completely proper and respectful. I just…well, like I said, I'm not sure of… well, of anything. We have only recently returned from London, as you well know. I haven't been back to Portland in such a long while. I don't know who's still there, what life will be like once we get there again. Oh, I don't know quite what I'm saying. Such a serious thing as marriage leaves me unsettled."

"Well, then." Papa's voice rang with a sense of finality. "Might I suggest you resolve that unsettled sensation by making up your mind about Joshua? It would, Emma, be most beneficial for me, and for Joshua, you understand, if the two of you should wed. I've gotten to know him well and he's a fine man who cares a great deal for you. I must admit, I would rest at ease knowing you'd settled down to life with a suitable and respectable husband. Please do let this exemplary young man know your decision as soon as you possibly can. I shall not pressure you any further than this."

Emma drew in a deep breath. True, Joshua Hamilton was

everything a young woman could ever hope for. His gleaming dark hair was always neatly parted and perfectly in place, his brown eyes twinkled with his gentle good humor, and his smile, beneath a full, stylish mustache, was broad, frequent, and pleasant. He stood tall and straight, and she could always count on him to have interesting things to talk about. It did give her a private thrill to stroll out onto the dance floor on his arm. All the other girls envied her his attention.

She didn't know of another man with whom she could even imagine sharing the rest of her life. That must mean the foundation for a deep fondness between her and Joshua was as it should be. Yes, he was a nice man. A kind man. They'd likely have a splendid time as man and wife.

Just like that, she made up her mind.

"I'll do it," she said. "I'll marry Mr. Hamilton. Yes, yes. He's a nice, kind man."

The three adults at the table let out surprised sounds. Papa drew his brows together. Aunt Sophia's shot up to her hairline. Uncle Justus looked puzzled.

"Emma?" her aunt said. "Just a moment ago you said you weren't ready. Now, you turn and say the contrary. Shouldn't you wait until after you've reached Portland, take the time in the carriage to think the matter through?"

Emma shrugged. "I'm sure. There's really not a whole lot to think through. I do believe Mr. Hamilton and I will suit each other quite well."

"I'm glad you feel that way," her aunt said, a hint of skepticism still on her face. "If for no other reason than that there was quite a bit of talk. Just make sure before you pledge yourself to him before the Lord."

"Talk?" Emma felt the blood drain from her face. "About me? What could I have done to make folks talk?"

Aunt Sophia, her complexion as fair as Emma's, turned rose-pink. "It was the flitting around from man to man at every event, dear child, how you kept them at your beck and call. It's a bit...unseemly. Uncaring, and some could even say it's self-centered."

She frowned. "How can that be? I'm the same I've always been. No such thing has happened before, certainly not in London."

"That," Aunt Sophie said, holding her cup of delicate jasmine tea a mere inch from her lips, "is likely because London is London and Denver is not."

"I...see." But she didn't. Not really. While she'd lived in a number of different places during her life, none of them seemed too different, one from the other. Atlanta, where she was born, had faded a tad into memories of a busy whirl of Mama's friends and evening soirées at their home that she watched from the balcony over the foyer. Then, on those occasions when their small family had spent time in New York, she'd scarcely seen her parents, what with them busy at various events every day and almost every night. She herself had had a good number of playmates from among her parents' friends.

After Mama's death, she and Papa moved to London. Grief-stricken, he had seemed inclined toward comforting, familiar things. Since his side of the family still lived in England, he'd wanted to be close to them. The years in London had been nothing if not exciting, most recently filled with a continual rush of parties and dress fittings, dances and teas, dinners and theater and...well! It had been exhilarating.

Emma had visited Uncle Justus and Aunt Sophia twice in Denver during that time for extended periods, while Papa traveled the world for his business. And she'd been at the Portland house right after construction ended, right after they'd moved in. While in Denver this time, she'd enjoyed the diversions provided by their circle of acquaintances. This year, she'd had the opportunity to take advantage of the social season itself. She really hadn't noticed anything particularly different from her life in London—except that residents of Denver spoke with a charming accent, never mind that they all said it was she who spoke with a different lilt.

On her previous visits, once Papa returned, they went together to the house in Portland. Its social whirl wasn't quite as lively, but life there wasn't especially dull, either. The western town had a somewhat rough edge to it, but so much activity was always afoot that Emma had never had the opportunity to be bored. She supposed she and Mr. Hamilton would live in Denver, though. Which reminded her, if she was now about to become a betrothed woman, her life would be filled with preparations for her wedding. Those would, of necessity, involve all the things she fancied.

She might start by considering the gorgeous clothes she could choose for her honeymoon. She wondered where Mr. Hamilton would decide to take her. Would he prefer Paris, Vienna, Venice, or Rome? Or would he fancy something more exotic? Like the Greek islands, perhaps, or...Morocco?

A thrill propelled her to her feet, the toast limp and the congealed egg by now forgotten. "Oh, goodness! I do have so much to do, don't I? After all, I have a wedding to plan. If you'll excuse me, I'll go start..."

*   *   *

"You have made me the happiest man alive!" Joshua pressed Emma's hand to his lips. "And you'll see, Miss Emma, I'll make you happy. We'll have a wonderful life together."

Emma smiled. "Why, thank you, Mr. Hamilton. I do so appreciate that promise. Surely, you must know how happy my papa is with my decision."

"And my parents will be, as well. They think the world of you."

Did they really? Had they heard the talk Aunt Sophia had mentioned? Emma's cheeks heated and she hoped the elder Hamiltons had been spared the embarrassment. Silver-haired Marianne and tall, dignified Judge Oscar Hamilton were not the sort to take disgrace kindly.

"I do hope I can keep it that way," she said in a spindly voice. "Will you be coming back to Portland with Papa? After the business trip to France, that is."

"Afraid so," Joshua said. "I would much prefer to return with you, especially now that we're engaged—engaged! That does have a nice ring to it, doesn't it?"

She nodded and smiled.

"At any rate, I'm afraid your father is counting on me. We've set things up with some gentlemen in Paris and Marseilles who wouldn't understand it if I suddenly decided not to go. But I promise I'll be back as soon as I possibly can be."

They chatted a few minutes longer about the men's trip, and then Joshua pressed Emma to set a date for the wedding. Truth be told, she hadn't thought that far ahead.

"This is all so new!" she said. "I have no idea. What do you think?"

"Me!" His eyes opened wide. "I always thought ladies put a great deal of stock in those things."

"I suppose it's different, since I don't have a mama to help me with these decisions. Of course, it must be next year. That way I'll have plenty of time, and Aunt Sophia can help, too. I'm sure it takes a great deal to put on a wedding, especially when I consider how much work it is for her to throw one of her splendid parties."

"Well, then, what do you think of...say, next June?"

"A year and a month...I'm sure I should manage to do something suitable in that time, don't you?"

He beamed. "I'm sure you will do something splendid in that time." He stood and smiled, a mischievous twinkle in his eyes. "I had planned this just a bit differently, but now that you've agreed to marry me, it's even more perfect than I thought. I came this morning with a surprise for you."

"Surprise? I love surprises! What's your perfect surprise?"

Joshua headed for the parlor door to the hall. "Ah-ah-ah! Just give me a chance. It'll only be a minute or two. Then you'll see."

Emma's curiosity itched within her. She fought the temptation to follow Joshua to the front of the house and peek out the window, but she doubted that would impress him. Such actions would make her appear almost childish. Even though she did feel the greatest urge to see what he was up to.

She hadn't expected him to show up that morning. He'd known she was leaving for Portland, and she'd let him know the night before how busy she expected her morning to be. But now, seeing that she'd made up her mind about his proposal at breakfast, she was glad he'd come, if only for a brief visit. And she was going home as a newly engaged woman, one preparing to enter the greatest adventure of her life.

She tapped the toe of her fashionable travel boot against Aunt Sophia's gleaming oak parlor floor. What could he be up to? What kind of surprise did he have? He couldn't have known she'd decided to accept his proposal before he'd walked into the parlor a scant half-hour earlier, so what could he have prepared?

Moments later, the front door opened again. She sank back into the plush velvet sofa, pretending a nonchalance she didn't feel.

"Please close your eyes," Joshua requested from just on the other side of the threshold.

Emma giggled—from excitement or nervousness, she wasn't quite sure. "They're closed."

A moment later, she sensed his presence at her side. "Now?" she asked.

"On the count of three. One ... two ... three!"

She opened her eyes. "How sweet!"

In his arms, her intended held a squirmy little dog, its curly white fur giving it the appearance of a fluffy cotton ball. Big black eyes darted everywhere, taking in its surroundings. A pink tongue darted out and took a quick swipe of Joshua's hand.

"She's a poodle," he said, wearing a tentative smile. "Do you like her?"

"Of course I like her! She's darling. What's her name?"

His smile broadened even further. "She has none. That's for you to decide. She's yours."

"Mine? What do you mean?"

"A friend of my mother's owns the parents. She and her husband brought the pair to Denver from England on their last trip to the Continent. The mama just had puppies, and I arranged to have one of them for you. I wanted to give you something, a token of my affection, so you'd never forget me even after you left. That way, you'd think of my proposal every time you looked at her."

His explanation charmed her as she took the tiny dog. "I would have thought of you even without you going to such a great deal of trouble."

"It was no trouble. Do you like her?"

"Of course . . . but I do confess, I know nothing about dogs. What do I have to do to care for her?"

"Feed her and make sure she—" He colored. "Well, you do need to make sure she goes outdoors a number of times every day. Constitutionals, on a regular basis. She . . . that is, dogs don't use privies."

Emma's cheeks sizzled. "Ah . . . er—what does she eat?"

Joshua seemed relieved to discuss anything but the dog's private functions, and they spent the next while discussing the care of Emma's new companion. It never occurred to her to think how she would transport the dog to Portland until her new fiancé was gone.

"Look, Papa!" she cried after Joshua had left. "Look what he brought for me."

Emma's surprised father gave her pointers on how to care for her new pet, adding on to what her fiancé had said, even though Papa warned her against the inconvenience she was undertaking. Emma insisted she could handle the trip with a baby animal in her care.

"How much trouble could she be?" she asked. "Look. She's so darling and tiny."

A brief while later, the reverend and his wife arrived. Emma and her luggage—the huge steamer trunk, four hatboxes, Aunt Sophia's large picnic basket to serve as a home for the dog, Emma's travel satchel, and a small leather reticule—were loaded onto the carriage. Fortunately, neither the reverend nor his wife had much luggage. Neither did the elderly other passenger, Mr. Birmingham, who slept through the commotion.

Mrs. Strong's mud-colored eyes widened more and more with each item piled higher. But it wasn't until the basket with the excited yapping puppy came out to the front stoop that she said anything.

"Surely you aren't bringing that…that creature with us, are you?"

Emma frowned. "But, of course. My…fiancé gave her to me. I wouldn't think of leaving her behind."

Mrs. Strong's eyebrows nearly vanished under the stick-stiff fringe of hair on her forehead at the mention of a betrothal, but she only sighed. "Oh, dear. That's unfortunate. I do hope she's well-trained, at the very least. I can't imagine anything worse than an undisciplined animal. Especially on a long trip in an enclosed vehicle."

Papa arched a brow, giving Emma a questioning look. "Are you sure about this?"

Emma tipped up her chin. "Yes, Papa. I know what I'm doing."

"I hope so, Princess. I certainly do."

They hugged, Emma overcome with an unexpected pang of fear.

What if—

She shook off the unwelcome sensation. "I love you, Papa. Do take care of all that business soon. I can't bear the thought of missing you for too long."

"I love you, too, my darling girl." He cupped a hand over the back of her head, bringing her close. "Are you sure you wouldn't rather come to Paris and Marseilles with Joshua and me—"

"No, no." She pulled away, tucked the handle of the dog's basket into the crook of her elbow, and smiled. "I'll be fine. I promise. And once you're home in Portland again, we'll have such wonderful fun planning my wedding. You'll see."

"May our Lord bless you, Emma," he said a moment later, a hint of dampness in his eyes. "Don't ever forget how precious you are to me. I wouldn't know what to do with myself, should anything ever happen to you."

"Don't fret, Papa, please. Do enjoy your trip. I plan to enjoy mine."

"Let us earnestly pray we all can enjoy our trip," Mrs. Strong piped up. With a huff, she gave Emma a disapproving glare as she stepped back up into the carriage.

Emma sighed, took the driver's extended hand then followed her chaperone.

The dog gave a cheery little yip.

"And please make sure your animal doesn't do that all the way out West," the pastor's wife added.

Emma figured it wouldn't hurt to take advantage of the perfect moment to commend the trip to God.

Chapter 2

Emma sighed.

Pippa, the puppy, yipped.

Mrs. Strong snorted—yet again.

Would they ever get to Portland?

The carriage hit a bump, sending Emma flying off her seat. The picnic basket where Pippa had spent her voyage followed suit, and both landed at the feet of the reverend's wife. Pippa was unharmed. The woman was not amused.

Neither was Emma.

Why *had* Papa ever thought this would be a good idea? Up until this time, she'd always traveled to Portland by rail, a far wiser and much more efficient way to get there, in her opinion.

Bouncing and jouncing over rutted ground, closed up in a box not very unlike the one where her new pet had been all this long, long while, didn't strike Emma as any way to travel. Her bottom was sore from the hard, seemingly padded-with-rocks seat, and now her knees would surely be bruised from her rough landing on the floor.

She scrambled back onto the seat with its dry, cracked leather, and set her dog on her lap one more time. Drawing a deep breath, and sending up the random plea for heavenly help, she leaned forward and peeked out. Disappointed, she plopped back down. Nothing even remotely resembling a village, much less a city, not to mention Portland, Oregon, was anywhere in sight. No, she couldn't see Bountiful anymore, the tiny town where they'd spent the night before. Rugged landscape, stark in its wild beauty, full of rocks and the rare scattered spurt of vegetation, did nothing to inspire so much as hope in Emma. Neither did the hill they'd begun to climb. All she could see was the hilly terrain cut through by the rutted road.

She sighed.

Clutching the handle of the picnic basket in one hand, she used the other to pat a loose strand of curling auburn hair back into place. She then pulled her smart silver watch from the jacket pocket of her nice amber and caramel velvet traveling suit. The ever-so-soft fabric by now looked sad and saggy, and even the black satin piping on the edges of the jacket lapels, sleeve bottoms, and outlining either side of the flat front gore of the skirt had lost its elegant luster. The lace at the neck and down the front of her buttercream-colored blouse had given up the fight nearly from the start.

Emma shifted her weight from one hip to the other, wishing there were a comfortable position to be found. Her shoulder blade pressed uncomfortably against the seat back. She wriggled. No improvement.

Her temple began to throb.

She drew a deep breath then wished she hadn't. The carriage's close quarters were dreadfully stuffy.

She pulled her watch out again. The shiny hand had moved only a hair.

"Why don't you try reading a while?" Mrs. Strong said as Emma slid her watch back. "Here's my Bible. I'm sure you can find an edifying passage to help you pass the time."

Emma gauged the size and heft of the solid book of Scripture and shook her head. "I do thank you. I certainly could do with some devotional time. However, I don't think you're prepared to hold my dog, are you?"

At the woman's look of horror, Emma smiled. "I'm sure you agree I can't hold that copy of the Good Book and the dog's basket at the same time."

That seemed to put an end to that suggestion, but it did nothing to help Emma's boredom. The long trip had grown tiresome to an extreme.

A while later she awoke from a brief nap. From the slight tilt of the carriage she could tell their climb had grown steeper, so she craned forward against the angle to peer out the side window. To her surprise, the rough road, which she again felt as the wheels jounced in and out of holes, was surrounded by tall evergreens. At that moment, she realized the air around them had grown cooler than it had felt earlier in their day's journey.

"Where are we?" she asked.

"Going up the mountains in the eastern part of Oregon," Reverend Strong answered.

"Up? The eastern part?" she repeated, disappointed.

" 'Fraid so." He had the usual bland expression on his plain face.

As though to comment, Pippa whimpered again. Emma came close to joining her, but soon recognized the cries as the blessing they truly were. They had been traveling for two weeks now, eight hours a day. Aside from their less-than-luxurious overnights and stops to change horses in odd locales, the pup's constitutionals had provided her only breaks during the otherwise dreadful, monotonous trip.

"Oh, dear!" She fought to keep the relief out of her voice and expression. "It appears that Pippa must...um...go outside again. Her constitutional, you understand."

Reverend Strong nodded absently.

Mrs. Strong pursed her lips and sniffed.

Emma pounded the front of the carriage with her umbrella, a spot right between the couple's heads, as she and the driver had agreed she should do whenever Pippa needed a stop. Moments later, the carriage halted.

Mr. Schwartz opened the door. He held out a hand for the puppy's basket. "Here we go, miss."

Emma scrambled out by way of the trim set of wooden steps the driver set up for her, more than ready to escape Mrs. Strong's judgmental stare. How she missed Aunt Sophia. While the two of them didn't always see eye-to-eye on all of Emma's ideas, her aunt at the very least listened with goodwill. The other woman in Emma's life, Ophelia, didn't agree often, but she also didn't bother with stony silences. If she objected to something Emma had concocted, she let everyone in the vicinity know, and in no uncertain terms. The chilly disapproval to which the reverend's wife had treated Emma from the very start was most difficult to handle.

"You might want your cloak, miss," Mr. Schwartz called out, holding the becoming, hunter green wool garment in Emma's direction. With the wind blowing hard and nippy all around, whistling through the thick canopy of boughs overhead, she hurried back and snagged it, grateful for its stylish cover.

Swirled in the supple wool, Emma picked her way through the dense underbrush, careful not to catch her heels in nature's carpet of debris. When she figured she'd gone far enough to remain discreetly hidden from view of the other passengers, unwilling to have them watch her dog perform her...er... functions, she opened the picnic basket, tied the rope she was using to keep Pippa under control around the puppy's neck, and then placed her lovely little pet on the ground.

Pippa pranced daintily over slender dead branches, piles of old, damp leaves, and the occasional large rock. To Emma's dismay, bits of twig and scraps of leaf clung to the pup's pristine, snowy curls as she moved, and her paws went from white to a dingy shade of dirt.

From the direction of the carriage came the sound of voices raised in agitated conversation. It appeared the men were engaged in some sort of disagreement, which surprised Emma, since the mild-mannered man of God didn't strike her as endowed with much of a temper. Mr. Schwartz, too, had been nothing if not friendly and pleasant, and the elderly Mr. Birmingham, the fourth passenger in their company, had done nothing but slumber and snore the greater part of the way.

A horse's shrill whinny pierced the forest peace.

The male voices sharpened, rang out angrier.

Emma stayed put to avoid the altercation.

"Pal-merrrrrr!" Mrs. Strong cried out.

Pippa darted deeper into the woods.

Reverend Strong answered in a muffled voice. Although his voice grew fainter as Emma followed her dog, the distant complaint of his wife's words followed her still. "Palmer Strong," the woman whined, "I tell you right now..."

A flurry of disparate sounds followed—more whinnying, more yelling, more whining, hooves striking packed earth. Though the crisp air felt refreshing after the stuffy carriage, Emma realized she couldn't stay out in the elements much longer, no matter how determined she was to avoid the unpleasantness. Besides, her presence and normally cheery nature might perhaps calm things a tad. That would only be to the good. She still had a long way to travel in the company of these people.

"Can't say the prospect appeals," she told her little dog when she scooped her up. Pippa tipped her head as though giving serious consideration to her mistress's words. "But it can't be helped, now can it?"

A moment later, Pippa objected to being stuffed in the basket again.

"This can't be helped either." Regret rang in Emma's voice. "But you just wait until we're home in Portland, little missy. Ophelia and Jedediah will simply love to spoil you."

Setting aside her natural aversion to conflict, she headed back the way she'd come. She carried on her chat with Pippa, who let out occasional yips, in her own way holding up her end of the conversation. After a while of steady marching, Emma started to question her sense of direction. She felt certain she'd now walked farther than she'd gone in the first place. Just as worry nipped the edges of her equanimity, she heard men's voices again and changed direction. This time, however, the discord was far more heated and considerably harsher than what she'd earlier heard.

Oh, dear.

"There you are!" she cried out in a cheerful voice when she crashed out into the slight clearing, watching her steps, minding that her skirt didn't snag on any brambles. "I was afraid I'd gotten lost in the woods. I didn't look forward to trudging through the wilderness for half the day, hoping to—"

Her words froze in her throat.

Horror made her eyes widen.

Fear nearly felled her.

"Well, well, well! Lookit here, Ned." A rough-looking fellow in a threadbare checked coat dragged off his ragged straw hat and clutched it to his burly chest. "Who'd a thought a body would find hisself a lady in fancy clothes out in these here woods?"

Ned, much younger but just as rough-looking and dressed in a brown jacket of equal vintage as his companion's coat, didn't respond. He couldn't; his jaw gaped, and his gaze fixed on Emma. Slowly, very, very slowly, a smitten smile oozed across his face.

"Miss..." he said in a hushed, respectful tone.

Now this was the sort of reaction Emma was accustomed to, not the sharper, bolder, more blatant stare the first man was still giving her.

Before she could gather her wits, that brutish fellow approached, his face shadowed in the dappled light of the woods.

"Now, who do we have us here, 'zackly?"

Although alarmed, Emma's instincts told her it would be unwise to let him know how his presence disconcerted her. "What have you done with my carriage? And with Reverend Strong, his wife—the others?"

He arched a brow. "Your carriage? 'Peared to me it were more the fat fellow up top's rig than nobody else's. Tobias and Dwight—"

"Don't reckon you might wanta say even a word 'bout them two 'round her, Sawyer," Ned said, his eyes never straying from Emma, his smitten smile never fading.

"Reckon you're right, boy." Sawyer donned his disreputable hat again. "Tobias and Dwight, they ain't never been easy sorts, you know. And they ain't done with these here parts yet. Mark my words." He shook his head and scoffed. "Bah! Never mind 'bout them two. What're we gonna do with her's what I wanna know."

Pippa chose that precise moment to make her presence known.

Sawyer narrowed his eyes. "Whazzat?"

Ned zeroed in on the picnic basket. "Looks to me, boss, like the lady's got herself a dog or something there."

Sawyer approached.

Fear slammed into Emma's throat. The tough character stood a good foot taller than she, and outweighed her by at least twice. Days of unshaven beard gave his face a dark, dismal, disturbing look, and his thick, droopy mustache emphasized his menace. Emma fought the urge to flee and stood her ground, chin up, gaze on his hardened expression. She waited, thoughts flitting through her head. She searched her imagination for an idea, any possible notion that might help her save herself and sweet little Pippa.

"What a fool thing to take into the woods," Sawyer said in a growl of a voice. He dropped his hand to his waist, shoved his coat open to reveal a holster at his hip as he turned to his companion. "Cain't be wasting no time on a silly woman and her dog. Not when we have us more important things to figger out. Tobias and Dwight ain't gonna just go their way. Not after all we got last night. That were worth more'n what this group here in the carriage had. And you and me…well, we have 'em all. We need to figger out what we're gonna do."

Ned gave him a careless nod, but continued to admire Emma. Sawyer followed his gaze with a frown.

Out of the corner of her eye, Emma spotted the gleam of metal at Sawyer's waist again. Sawyer was armed…and was now going for his weapon. She shuddered. Dreadful men carried guns, which, simply put, were the devil's tools, pure evil. They inspired the holders to do deadly damage to their victims. Was he really ready to—to…oh, my! To shoot her? How could she, Emma Crowell, possibly find herself in such straits?

Fighting the fear, she hugged Pippa's basket and chose to not stand and await her imminent, dreadful fate. At the very least, she would put up an objection to this…well—sin. "What, pray tell, are you doing, sir?"

Sawyer took a step toward her, one hand outstretched, the other at the butt of the gun. "Gimme that thing."

Her gut knotted ever tighter; her arms laced more tautly. "She's mine!"

The outlaw barked a laugh. "And you . . . well, missy, way I see it, you're our prisoner. Gimme it. We ain't got a use for no yapping basket."

Prisoner? Good heavens! About to call for help, she realized the man had already come too close to her and she didn't know how he'd react. She glanced at his hand still resting near his gun. A shudder shook her at the sight.

"What have you done with the others?"

"The others?" He shrugged. "That there driver of yours took off soon's Dwight and Tobias got what we wanted." He spat. "What they wanted. Driver and the old man sure 'peared in a rush to get somewhere. Reckon I might too wanna leave, what with that squealing woman in the back. Told Dwight it didn't look like no good idea to hold 'em up. I was right. Weren't as though they had them a great deal of cash in the box to begin with, and now Dwight and Tobias're gone with it all. Left us all the work, too."

The carriage had left? No, of course not. They wouldn't—couldn't—leave her here.

"You just hush there, Sawyer," Ned urged his partner. "Let's us figger what to do with the lady and her dog."

"You don't go telling me what's what . . ."

As the men carried on their silly argument, Emma's head throbbed with tangled thoughts.

What on earth was she to do now? Surely the Strongs would come back for her. But when? How would they find her? What if those other outlaws these two mentioned got back first? Quick glances all around emphasized the dire nature of her predicament. If she ran, she'd get lost in the woods—she'd almost done that while taking her dog on a simple constitutional. At that time, she hadn't been gripped by the panic she now felt rise inside her. Running was out of the question. But if she just stood and waited for matters to play out…well, Sawyer continued to fondle his sidearm.

A wild blur of foreign emotions and disjointed thoughts shot through Emma's head. Papa…Aunt Sophia…Uncle Justus…Ophelia—Joshua! Oh, dear. She hated to think she might miss her own wedding.

Wild laughter raked at her throat, but she tamed it somehow. The ridiculous notion told Emma she was more than likely hysterical, and who would blame her? But hysteria and ladylike vapors would never get her out of this nightmare. She had to pull her wits together.

Truth was, Papa would be frantic. So would Aunt Sophia and Uncle Justus. She imagined Joshua would worry, as well. She hated to put them all through the misery.

How could Reverend and Mrs. Strong have left without her? The pain that struck Emma nearly stole her breath. Papa had asked them to look out for her, and though she'd known Mrs. Strong hadn't much cared for her, she couldn't imagine abandoning the woman had their situations been reversed.

Yet they had left Emma alone, utterly alone.

While she had wanted to be on her own, this wasn't what she'd imagined it might be like. If she could escape this pair of outlaws, how would she manage in the wilds of eastern Oregon?

Still, she felt she would be safer away from them than with them. While she had been raised a genteel lady, Emma didn't see how that would mean she had to become some meek and mousy sort. Surely she had the intelligence and gumption to outwit these men, neither of whom struck her as a brilliant thinker.

Hmph! She was not about to let them do her harm, not without fighting back. And she bore the responsibility to keep her pup safe.

What could she pit against a gun? And win?

She had to think, clearly and fast, if she was to stay a step ahead of a pair of quarreling outlaws.

At that moment, to her horror, Sawyer drew the gun from the holster.

She shrieked. "Wha—"

"Aw, c'mon, Sawyer," Ned said, his voice surprisingly reasonable. "Y'ain't gonna shoot 'er, an' you know it. You know you don't wanta do that."

Sawyer fired off a glare at his companion. "What're you talking 'bout? How d'you think you know what I wanta do?" He spat a gob of spittle toward the edge of the trail. "I do want her to quit her caterwauling and carrying on. Dunno what to do with her, 'cept maybe asking her rich pappy for money in exchange. For her and that there dog, too. But...nah."

Emma, her eyes on the weapon pointed at her, fought the instinct to gag.

Sawyer went on. "You think on it some, boy. She knows we're here, and the carriage ain't. Them others seen us, too. They left, and you gotta reckon they went after the law, to tell 'em 'bout the holdup. They can finger us, even if we ain't got the loot. You want her to run to Bountiful, too, an' tell that Marshal Blair down there what she seen? You wanta go behind bars?"

"But we didn't do nothing. Dwight and Tobias are the ones that done everything. Left us behind to do the work and clean up their mess."

"Ain't no one but us gonna care about that."

Ned scratched his drab brown hair then donned a brilliant smile. "Why, then, Sawyer. There's only one thing to do. We'll just keep her with us."

Sawyer hitched up his grime-streaked, faded denim trousers, never letting go of his sidearm. "What you saying there, Ned? I look like some lady's servant to ya? She'll be asking to be done for left and right."

"Maybe she can...I dunno. Help?"

The older outlaw crossed his arms, gun now dangling at his side, turned to Emma, and arched a brow. "How?"

Emma froze. Stared. Nothing came to her.

Ned came to her rescue. Of sorts. "Maybe she can cook fer us. I'm tired of your burnt bacon and dried-out beans. My ma was a fair hand with baking pies and roasts and soups and all."

Cook? Soup?

Goodness gracious, Emma had scarcely ever even set foot in a kitchen. "Surely you must see, gentlemen, that the wisest plan of action is for you both to help me rejoin my party as soon as possible. If nothing else, help me return to Bountiful. I'm sure your gentler side understands a man is to be a lady's guardian and protector. That applies to us, if ever it did."

Sawyer guffawed. "Guardian? Don't see myself as nobody's angel, lady. And I got too much to do with protecting myself and my own what-for to hafta protect some bit a fluff what's come off a fancy carriage—with no money to her, neither."

Emma gulped when he pointed the gun at her again.

Ned stepped between them. "C'mon, Sawyer. Y'ain't no killer, and y'ain't gonna start being one now, neither. Let's think on this some more back at the camp. Ya don't need to do nothing right now."

"Makes no sense, bringing her along. Reckon she eats fancy."

Ned glanced at Emma.

She managed a weak smile and a lifted shoulder.

"Nah. I'm sure she'll eat whatever we got us to share." He sighed. "Not that there's all that much left, you know. But we can always roast mutton. We got us plenty of sheep, right? That's fine vittles, I reckon."

Sawyer stiffened. "Them sheep's not fer eating, Ned. What're you thinkin'? Them animals' money on the hoof. Get yer head on straight. She's 'nother story, though."

Ned's shoulders straightened, his jaw squared, his gaze glanced over Emma's face. He smiled, and then faced Sawyer full on, chin leading the way. "The right thing, that's what I wanta do. We're bringing 'er with us. And you're putting that there gun away now. Don't wanna shoot yer own foot off by mistake, ya know."

Sawyer glowered. "Fine, then. You want her to come on along with us, then you're the one what's gotta deal with her and her fancy ways. Not me. Not once. She's all your business from now on."

Ned grinned.

Emma groaned. "Bu—but, I don't have any other clothes! My dresses…shoes! No, no. I can't just follow the two of you, wherever you're headed. Please, Mr. Ned, take me back to Bountiful. You can come back to help Mr. Sawyer after. I at least need my trunk."

"Clothes?" Sawyer guffawed as he shook his head and holstered the gun. "Shoes? You sure do think some crazy fool things, now don'tcha?"

She breathed in relief once the weapon disappeared into the holster and the filthy coat covered it. She hugged Pippa's picnic basket closer, gaining a sense of comfort in the knowledge of the pup's presence.

Ned twisted the brim of his disgraceful hat as he spun the thing around in a circle at his waist. His nerves further showed in the high pitch of his voice as he came to Emma's side.

His eyes shined with his earnestness. "I'll take care of you, ma'am, even if I cain't be going to Bountiful myself. I'm sorry about your trunk, too." His tone struck her as...shy? Could that be? "But you can trust me," the young man added. "We're not dangerous. I promise."

Trust him? An outlaw?

Good heavens! How could he say that? Of course, Emma couldn't trust either one of them. She only had herself to trust. But until she could figure out what to do, perhaps it would be wiser to stay with them. It didn't seem she had much chance of escape now, anyway, the way Ned wouldn't take his eyes off her. What would Papa think when he learned what had happened to her on the way to Portland?

She cringed at the thought of his worry...his fear...his grief.

"Oh, Papa..." she whispered. "I should have gone with you after all."

Chapter 3

"Are you sure?" Peter Lowery said, anger doing a slow rise.

"Of course I'm sure, Pete," Colley, his ranch manager and mentor, said. "I toldja time and time again how we been losing sheep for weeks now. I don't lie. You said you believed me every time I told you."

Peter sighed. "I do believe you. I did from the start."

"Reckon you didn't want to accept it, didja?" When Peter shrugged, Colley tugged the brim of the straw hat lower, and then nodded. "Didn't want to do it either, myself, but I couldn't help but accept the truth, son. Bunch by bunch, there've been fewer sheep out there each time. Coupla dozen less by now."

Dread pooled in his gut, a sick sensation by all accounts. What would he do if he lost any more?

Colley went on. "And, sure as I'm staring right atcha, it's happened again. This time, there seems to be a bigger lot missing than any of the earlier times. I was fixing for Wade and me to do some shearing straight away, now spring's come, and I went to choose me some of 'em to start with, and I can count, you know. Been looking forward to this, seeing as how the flock's put on some good, thick wool this winter." A shake of the head followed a grimace. "We're gonna miss that wool just as much as the sheep themselves, now they're stole."

Peter needed every penny he could get for his animals and their wool. Now, more of his flock was gone . . . taken.

Stolen.

Rustled.

Life on a ranch depended on a man's animals. No wonder rustlers were seen as lower than snakes. They were hung in these parts. Livestock made the difference between survival and failure.

What was he going to do if he couldn't pay back what he owed? He glanced toward the left side of the summer camp cabin. Robby, his seven-year-old son, still lay in his bunk, sleeping securely, tucked under his covers. There was no reason for a child to rise as early as a rancher and his hands did. Today was no different. Theft was no matter for a child.

His child.

Peter wanted—no, needed—to build a legacy for his son. That was why he'd moved West shortly after he and Adele had married. He'd wanted to strike out on his own, make his own way in the world, create something of value to leave his children.

Or rather child. There wouldn't be any more children for Peter. He would never marry again.

The familiar sharp sting struck his heart at the thought of his Adele. Marriage hadn't worked as he'd hoped and expected.

Not for him—for the two of them. His wife hadn't been strong enough to cope with the challenge-filled and lonely life on the sheep ranch. She'd become ill with pleurisy. It would have taken a long day's travel to reach Bountiful's Doc Chalmers from Peter's ranch, and another day to return with the man in tow. But when the pain from her violent coughing reached the point where Adele couldn't bear it any longer, she'd demanded Peter help her return home to her mother's comfort and care rather than wait for him to fetch the doctor. He hadn't had the heart to deny her the love her large family would offer during her recovery, even though he knew travel could put her under a great deal of risk.

He'd been tragically proven right. She died before she reached Independence, Missouri.

Peter still carried the grief that came with knowing he hadn't been able to help Adele weather the pressures imposed upon her when she agreed to follow his dreams. The West had broken her, and she'd left him, and their son, to make do as best they could.

"Pete!" Colley shook his arm. "Are you hurtin' somewhere or something? That dyspepsia hitting you again?"

Peter shook his head, but didn't speak.

Colley went on. "Well, something's up with you. I been jawing away here, with you just standing there like a big old lump of cold bread dough. Not really much like you, I reckon."

Peter gave his ranch manager a wry twist of the mouth instead of a smile. Sometimes he did feel like cold bread dough. But Colley had a point. Something was up with him, all right. But no, he didn't really feel cold, not this time. This time, he wasn't about to feel sorry for himself. It was time to do something about the situation.

"Sure, I'm hurting. I've a ranch and a son, not to mention a loan to pay back. You know exactly how bad my bank account's been for a while now, and it's even worse these days. Now someone's hit me with theft again. So far, I've turned the other cheek, but my face is mighty sore from all that, and I don't think it's wrong to go get my sheep back from whoever's stealing them. Don't figure the Lord will frown on a man who sets out to try and steward what he's been blessed with."

Colley's pale blue eyes widened. "You crazy, Pete? Get your sheep back? Those animals are long gone already. Maybe halfway to Kansas by now."

"Doubt it. No one's going to try and sell sheep this time of year. They'll want to do what I'm working for, to fatten them up in the summer then go to market in the fall. And, besides, no one with a lick of sense will take them back to Kansas. Maybe they'll head for Portland or go south to California, but not this time of year. Not with a winter-thin flock."

"Sure, and that makes sense. But I figure on Kansas as the likely place they'll go just so's they can get them far away from here. Too easy to track down where the sheep really come from if they just mosey 'em over to Portland."

"You know better than that. Any rustler worth his salt has already changed the earmarks. I'll tell you again, Colley. They'll hold on to the animals and fatten them, seeing as how they're hardly worth selling right now. I feel sure in my heart I can find my sheep. It rained early yesterday morning. Remember? There's bound to be tracks in the soft ground. I'm going after what's mine."

"Who said thieves are so smart, and all? They make plenty of mistakes, son. That's how they get caught. And you!" Colley jabbed squarely at Peter's chest. "Now, you've gone and done gone mad! You can't be going after some lousy sheep rustlers who're likely armed and ready to shoot. Head on down to Bountiful. Go see the marshal—"

"By the time I fetch Adam Blair, they'll have all the earmarks on my animals changed. There'll be nothing to do. I'm not going to give them any more time. Not this time. I'm heading out right now. My mind's made up. Don't try and stop me."

Peter marched to the front door, reached for his coat, and slammed his hat on his head. "Take care of Robby for me, please."

"Whaddaya mean, take care of Robby for you?" Crisp clicks of well-worn boots followed Peter. "Don't you go thinking you're about to head out there all by your crazy self, son. You going? Well, then I'm going with you. Someone's gotta take some common sense along on that ride, and you sure lost yours this time."

Peter stopped, turned. "You're not leaving Robby here by himself. I won't stand for that."

"Fine," Colley countered, jaw jutting forward. "Don't see nothing to that. We can both of us come to our senses and stay home. We'll head on to Bountiful later in the day, once Robby's up and we can take your boy with us."

Peter shook his head. "Don't you try and stop me. I'm going. You can stay with Robby."

"Well, you sure can't shake me off like that, either. Not gonna let you do some fool thing, what with you having that boy that needs you back here." Colley rubbed a lean, leathery jaw. "Tell ya what. I'll go get Wade. He can stay with your boy. I trust him, and I reckon you can, too."

Right away, Peter started to object. Wade was young, not much more than twenty-one. But then, studying Colley, he realized he wasn't going to change his ranch manager's mind. Wade was a good solution, the only one available, and he'd proven himself generally trustworthy, too. Besides, Peter didn't intend to be gone long. Just long enough to get his property back.

"If you're coming, then let's go. Get Wade in here. Can't give the thieves any more of a head start than they already have."

They headed to the other structure at the camp, the shanty lined with numerous bunks for ranch hands, where they found Wade just rousing. No sooner had Peter and Colley related the situation than the young man stood, yanked on denim trousers, shoved first one arm then the other in the sleeves of a thick flannel shirt, tucked in his shirttails, and then hopped outside on one booted foot, dragging the other boot on as he went.

"Go, Peter," he urged as he hurried to the cabin at the edge of the pasture-rich meadow. "I won't let anything happen to your boy."

As Peter and Colley went for their horses, the younger man rushed inside and slammed the door. In his desire to make camp life easier for Adele, Peter had put up the modest but sturdy building so she and Robby at least would have the most basic of comforts during the foraging months. The lower plateau, where his ranch was located, became too dry in the summer months for sheep to find enough feed. On the other hand, the mountain meadows grew too cold in the wintertime, especially when the pregnant ewes were heavy with lambs. Like all other sheep ranchers in the region, Peter summered his flock up on the Blue Mountains' greener, lush slopes, to make sure they fattened for the fall. That was his plan for this year, and he was more determined than ever to ensure the success of the season, not just for his sake and Robby's, but also for Colley's.

His ranch manager had once owned a spread, held on to it for as long as possible. But when the plague of grasshoppers devoured all the nearby pasturage and ultimately decimated every flock in the area, the older sheep rancher had turned to Peter, who owned the adjacent land, for help. Peter had bought that land, but always kept in mind his responsibility to Colley. If he didn't make a profit, he could lose both his and Colley's livelihoods. He bore responsibility to many, owed them his best. He couldn't fail, he wouldn't let it happen.

Determination reinforced, he focused on following the marks he'd found across the meadow from the cabin, just beyond the mouth of the trail. As he'd thought, the soft earth there had retained the prints of a handful of horses, despite the flurry of sheep prints that swarmed around them. It wasn't hard to follow, at least not there. As he saddled his horse, he hoped the debris further along the mountain trail didn't obscure those prints entirely as it had the previous times.

"What," Emma asked, "is this?"

Ned dragged off his ratty hat as he followed the sweep of

her hand. "It's our home base, Miss Emma. This is where we been living lately."

" 'S enough, Ned!" Sawyer bellowed. "She don't need to know nothing more 'bout us. You brung her along with us, so, fine. She's here. But this ain't none of her business, and you know it."

The younger outlaw gave Emma an apologetic shrug. "Sorry, Miss Emma. You heard him. But it's where we're staying at these days—you, too, now."

As far as she could see, "this" was nothing more than the rocky overhang of an outcropping on the mountainside. From the looks of it, a bit of a cave hid in the shadows toward the end of the ledge. But this was certainly no kind of proper base, much less a home.

How could she have thought a carriage such a dreadful thing? This was worse. Much worse.

"Impossible," she argued. "I can't stay here. Why...where will I sleep? Where's the table for a meal? And...and..."—she blushed—"where is there a proper:...ah...well, the necessary?"

Sawyer guffawed. "That there forest out to the side of us is full of them 'necessary' trees and bushes. Go behind any one of 'em, lady. And far as sleeping goes, I reckon you can use either Dwight or Tobias's bedrolls."

Emma gaped. A tree? A bedroll?

"No," she said, her voice a mere whisper. "Impossible. I—I've never..."

"Miss...?" Ned said in a hesitant voice. "It ain't so bad in the cave toward the back. I can make sure you're safe there. I won't be letting nobody bother you none while you sleep."

She spared a glance in the direction of the darkness he indicated then shuddered and turned back to her champion. In spite of her horrid circumstances, a corner of her heart warmed. Ned was trying his best to help her, even when there was little he could do. His kindness touched her. "I deeply appreciate your offer, Mr. Ned—"

"It's Ned, Miss Emma. Just Ned. Ned Davis."

"Thank you, then, Ned. It's just...well, I've never—oh, dear." She bit her bottom lip to keep the trembling from growing any more obvious than she feared it already was. In her arms, Pippa wriggled, clearly tired of being held and in need of exercise. Then, to add injury to the indignity she'd already suffered, Emma's stomach chose that moment to let out a vociferous, unladylike growl.

"I can even take your doggie for a while," the young man added, still seeking to relieve Emma's distress. "You can rest yerself a spell. I reckon a lady like you ain't too used to walking so long in the woods."

Tears burned the backs of her eyelids, as the throb from the raw spots on her blistered feet grew more intense by the minute. "You're right. I never have gone for such a vile slog." Along with the steady pain in her feet, the memory of the numerous times she'd tripped and slid over the damp ground was imprinted in dirt on the once-lovely velvet of her skirt, her now-ruined skirt.

"I'll take good care of her," Ned promised. "You can rest."

"Nah, she cain't," Sawyer said. "She's a woman, ain't she? Way I see it, you was right, this one time. She's gotta make supper for us—like you said, help us out some. She's our pris-oner, and we gotta get to working on them sheep. You wanna sell that wool and get outta here 'fore Dwight and Tobias come back, don'tcha?"

Ned's eyes widened. "I reckon that might could be a good idea." He turned back to her. "So sorry, Miss Emma. You sure wouldn't want them two to findja here. It's best for all of us if we're gone by the time they decide to come back for what they left."

In spite of everything that had happened, Emma's curiosity was piqued. "Why? Who are they? Where are they? Why would they come back after holding up the carriage? And what did they leave behind?"

"Now, see whatcha done?" Sawyer roared at Ned. "She's got more questions than one of them sheep's got wool. You get to work shearing, and she can get to warming us up some bacon and making biscuits for an early supper. I haven't eaten nothing since sunrise, there's even less if we gotta share with her, so if she eats, she works."

Cook? Her? Could they possibly be serious?

Emma hugged Pippa closer with one arm and rubbed the filthy palm of her other hand against her skirt. She hoped her safety and future didn't depend on any kind of cookery skills—she had none. "B—but I'm your guest! A good host is supposed to serve and entertain his guests."

Sawyer slapped his thigh and laughed. "Guests and hosts! What? You think yer at some fine la-di-da mansion of some kind?"

She glared. "I can clearly see we're not, sir. But that doesn't change the rules of propriety and manners. You insisted I come here, after all."

He rolled his eyes and shook his head. "Don't know nothin' 'bout none a them rules a yours. None of that makes no never mind out here. And soonest ya larn it, soonest you'll settle in."

Emma shuddered. She had no intention of settling in anywhere near a cave in the wilderness. It was time to stop that conversational train.

"I'm afraid you're plumb out of luck, Mr. Sawyer," she said, back on the correct track. "I wouldn't know what to do with bacon or how to come up with biscuits. I don't cook, never once have."

The outlaw sputtered. "I never did hear me such a fool thing! Yer a woman, right?"

Emma tipped up her chin. "Most definitely."

"Well, then, go cook! All women's born knowing how to cook, way I seen it. They's always in the kitchen."

"Perhaps where you come from that is true, but I've...I've been otherwise occupied over the years."

Uneasiness swam in Emma's middle. Maybe excelling in her lessons hadn't been the achievements she'd always been told they were. Like the outlaws, she was quite hungry. Without a doubt, Pippa was, too. Food was the main issue at the moment.

"If you or Ned would show me how, perhaps I could give cookery a try. But I can't make any promises for that first attempt, you understand." She had the willingness, and she also had the hope she could count on the intelligence she so often had been told she possessed. Surely it couldn't be too hard to learn to cook. Could it? "I imagine I might manage to prepare the bacon if you tell me what to do, but the biscuits? I have no idea where to even start. I fear, by the time you show me and I finish, either one of you would have done it quicker and likely with a far better outcome than mine."

Sawyer gave her a measuring stare, then he shook his head, turned, and sent a dismissive wave.

"Bah!" he called over his shoulder, as he walked away. "Useless, is what I say. You go ahead and cook us a mess of bacon, then, Ned," he added when he strode past his partner. "If I recollect right, there were some beans left in that there pan from this morning, too. Shouldn't've gone sour since. Ain't that hot yet. What flour's left is in a sack back along the left wall of the cave, and the last bit from the pail of lard's down to the crick in a small jar. Be careful, and don't go wastin' none. Don't figger you're wantin' to go any hungrier'n what we are right now, are ya?"

Even though he'd just been given another task on top of the shearing duties he'd started with, Ned seemed pleased to relieve Emma from the cooking tasks. He must be as hungry as she. More than likely, he'd taken her words to heart. She had no idea if anything she tried to prepare would be suitable for human consumption.

"Wait!" she called as Sawyer picked up his pace. "I'm in dreadful need of, well, refreshing myself. Where are the facilities?"

"Facilities?" Sawyer asked, his eyes wide with surprise.

"You must wash somehow, right?" she prompted.

" 'S'right." He shrugged. "We got a bucket."

Oh, dear. "And your clothes?" Her voice came out timid and tentative. She wasn't certain she wanted to know the answer to that particular question, seeing the condition of his garments. "How do you clean those?"

"I dunk 'em in the creek from time to time, mostly when I take my baths afore I go into town." He turned to leave. "Reckon you can 'refresh' yourself in the creek once the weather's warm enough. But even then that water's right cold enough to—"

He caught himself, and, from the look on his face, Emma feared he'd been about to say something dreadfully inappropriate. Just as well he'd stopped.

What was she going to do? She wanted nothing more than to go home. London, Denver, or Portland would do just fine, but it didn't look as though she would get her wish any time soon. She looked at the filthy hole in the mountain face. A sob formed in her heart, but she bit down on her lips to keep it from escaping.

Since Ned had suggested she go deeper inside the cave, and since she really needed a moment to nurse her fear then compose herself again, she did as he'd suggested. Despite the darkness at the forbidding maw of the hole, she soon realized it didn't go especially deep.

Pippa whimpered in her arms. Emma had let her down and the puppy had relieved herself just before they'd arrived at the outlaws' hideout, so she didn't think that was the reason for her cry.

The pup reached up and licked Emma's jaw. Despite the darkness, she could clearly see the curly white dog hair, the bright eyes, and the velvety dark of Pippa's button nose. A moment later, she smiled in delight as her pet licked her again.

"You sweet dear!" How grateful she was to Joshua for the unexpected gift. It just went to show what an excellent choice for husband he was. Emma would have to make certain she especially thanked him once they were together again, seeing how much comfort the puppy was giving her.

Exhausted, she dropped down on the hard stone floor. She could hear the bleating of animals nearby.

She knew right off that Ned and Sawyer—Dwight and Tobias, too—were crooks. They had held up the carriage, after all. No doubt the sheep were stolen and they'd hidden them nearby. She couldn't remember either man coming out and saying so, but if the sheep had belonged to them, then they wouldn't have needed to hide in the dreadful little cave.

Sooner or later, they'd have to move the sheep, or the fleeces at least...somewhere. To sell them. She ran a finger over the soft fabric of her green wool Worth cloak. Hard to believe the scratchy pelt of an animal could become such lovely material.

But it could and did, all to her benefit at the moment. All Emma had to do was bide her time until the outlaws finished the shearing and moved their loot to market. Maybe she could even help them finish whatever distasteful tasks they had to accomplish before they could leave. She grimaced at the thought of cooking bacon or doing...something with lard that might somehow lead to something edible. Her imagination didn't go so far as to envision her doing anything with the sheep.

Still, she would simply have to cooperate and have them see her as an asset, somehow, always keeping clear the goal in her mind: survival for Pippa and her.

The memory of Sawyer's gun remained vivid when she closed her eyes. Yes, indeed. That was it. She knew what to do, what she had to become.

From now on, she would not think of herself as Emma Crowell, future wife of Joshua Hamilton. From now on, she would be Emma Crowell, model prisoner of a pair of outlaws left behind in a stinky cave.

A random thought crossed her mind. These didn't strike her as particularly good outlaws. After all, what outlaw went into hiding with the spoils of his crime but no food?

From outside, Emma heard Sawyer and Ned resume their near constant bickering again. She shook her head.

Who would have ever thought...?

As Peter and Colley traveled, keeping their horses as quiet as possible in the hope the thieves wouldn't detect their approach, Colley kept up a string of muttered comments.

"Mad." This was far from the first uttering of that word, but this time the objection to Peter's plan was directed more audibly toward him. "You've gone plumb raving mad, you know. This is what we got lawmen for."

Peter did his level best to ignore the complaints. After a bit, Colley decided to change the subject, though not for the better as far as Peter was concerned.

"It's Bountiful where we should be heading," the ranch manager groused.

Peter kept quiet.

"And it's not sheep rustlers you need to be looking for—"

"Colley—"

"Colley, nothing! You know you need yourself a brand-new wife, and Robby needs himself a mama. Don't even argue, son."

Peter kept his mouth shut and his gaze on the trail, but after a few minutes of Colley going on about it undeterred, Peter finally had to speak.

"I've told you"—more times than Peter wanted to count—"I'll not be wedding again."

Colley snorted—again, a frequent response, to be sure. "I hear there's plenty of single ladies down to Bountiful these days. Easy on the eyes, too. I reckon you can sweeten that sour disposition of yours some, clean up good, and rope one of 'em into marrying up with you. I'm sure a smart one will, seeing as you're decent and hardworking and sober, too. I figure the right woman'll even come on up here summers with you."

One could always count on Colley's stubbornness once a notion overtook common sense. There was no arguing, so Peter gave the only logical reply. "I have nothing more to say."

"Nope, but I reckon Robby does."

Peter winced. In the eight years since they first met, the crusty sheep rancher had come to know him much too well. Robby was Peter's greatest weakness, and Colley had figured that out in no time at all. Peter knew in the hurting part of his heart how much his boy suffered from lack of a mother.

"A woman's hand wouldn't hurt the ranch none, neither," Colley continued. "And I'd think a good one should cook some better'n I do. You might could consider that when you set out to hire more hands for the ranch. You really want for me to keep cooking for them? They might run off, thinking I'd put poison on their plates. And do you see them as the best sort of friends for a lil shaver like your Robert?"

Peter shrugged. "I suppose they can teach him about hard work and sheep ranching, instead of him wasting all that time reading Adele's old books. Likely be more helpful to him in the long run."

Colley arched a brow. "He ain't much more'n a baby yet. Needs a mama, not learning from a bunch of scruffy ranch hands."

Back when the drought hit, Peter had been forced to let go all the men who'd worked for him. With the ranch turning no profit, he'd had no means to pay them. In typical fashion, Colley had been too stubborn to listen to his urging, hadn't paid one lick of attention to any reasonable argument. "I can eat beans, bacon, and biscuits just as well as you can, and you can't run sheep all on your own," the ranch manager had said. "I'm staying with you, son, and you can't go changing my mind, so don't try."

Eventually, Peter stopped trying, grateful for the help, especially after Adele died. A few months after her death, Wade had shown up, saying he wanted to learn everything about ranching. He hadn't asked for much more than a bunk and three squares a day. Peter hadn't had more than that to offer— no more than to teach the young man the tough realities in raising sheep and whatever there was to eat at his table. He reckoned Wade had run from more than he'd run to, but in the time they'd known each other, Peter had found nothing objectionable about the fellow. Wade soon became a member of his odd little family.

"I'm not in the market for a wife, and that's the end of that, Colley. Won't do you any good to go on, but it might do us a world of good if we keep quiet and listen. We might hear something out of the ordinary. You can't really hide a small flock of sheep too well. They make a whole lot of noise, walking around, what with lambs looking for their mamas."

"Ha! True enough, and we'd'a heard them sheep if we were even close to—"

"Shh!" From a distance, Peter caught a hint of sound drifting against the blowing winds. A good amount of movement...more than the natural residents of the forest they'd ridden into would make. He also heard voices:

And, faint though it was, a lamb's baa.

Chapter 4

As he drew closer to the sound of the sheep, Peter picked out two distinct men's voices, neither of which he could identify. A scrap of wool on a dead branch at the edge of the trail solidified his determination to retrieve his property.

What would he find when he reached the rustlers? How many men were involved? Could he and Colley handle them? And how were his sheep? He wasn't as worried about the ones that had been rustled the night before, but rather the ones that were taken a while earlier. Had they been fed and watered properly? They were ready for shearing. Had their fleeces been damaged?

At his side, Colley grunted.

Peter glanced at his ranch manager. Colley pressed a finger to tightly compressed lips then jabbed a sharp chin toward the right branch of the slight fork in the trail ahead. Peter had never gone this far up the mountain, so he wasn't familiar with the path. He hoped they wouldn't have much farther to go.

He wanted his sheep back, safe and sound, pasturing in their meadow. He needed Colley and Wade busy helping him shear the flock's full coats and caring for the crop of newborn lambs.

Then he heard something he hadn't expected. A puppy barked.

"Rustlers use puppies?" he asked Colley.

Grizzled brows drew close. "I never rustled nothing, so I can't say. Like I toldja time and time again, I don't figure any of this as a good idea, though. It's not too late yet. Now we know where they are, we can head back on down the mountain and fetch Marshal Blair."

"That's crazy. It would take us much too long. We're going in."

"Not before we figure out what's happening up ahead."

"I'll go slow, and you'll figure it out fast."

Colley glared at him but said no more. Peter edged his horse forward, glad the animal had a calm, even temperament and responded to his slightest touch.

Moments later, the trees thinned a bit as they rounded the trail. A rocky shelf jutted out over the curving path, looking much like a roof above the darkened, overgrown area. Just beyond the wooded end of the trail extended a small meadow. From where they paused, Peter could see the animals that more than likely belonged with the rest of his flock. At least the rustlers had brought them to where pasture was plentiful.

"Does that look like all the ones we've lost?" he asked Colley.

His manager cast an experienced look over the small flock. "Looks about right. They didn't take even half overall, so I'd say that's likely all of 'em. Don't look like they hit any of the other ranchers yet, either. But it's early spring. Plenty of time for them to keep it up."

As they surveyed the site, they heard the angry complaints of a sheep, and noticed toward the right edge of the trail, under the rocky ledge, a rough-looking stranger. He strained hard against the large ram he'd leaned against his chest, while he held the animal's legs in a firm clasp. With clumsy, clearly inexperienced motions, another fellow jabbed away, shearing the coat in ragged strips.

The ram slithered out of the first man's clutches.

The man hollered. "Don't jist stand there!"

The sad excuse for a shearer dropped the shears and ran after the animal. His compatriot chased after him.

The ram ran in circles.

The rustlers chased. In circles.

The ram cut back, leading the two men in a silly parade.

Peter shut his eyes, hoping he'd merely awoken from a bad dream. When he opened them again, he realized his eyes hadn't deceived him. It was all too true. The two fools had stolen his sheep, and now they'd driven a superb ram to distraction.

He ground his teeth, seething deep inside. Nothing had better happen to the animal due to their ignorance.

"That fool better not hurt that animal." Furious, Colley echoed Peter's thoughts. "I'll not stand for nothing like—"

"Thought you were ready to head for Bountiful." Peter couldn't stop the touch of humor in spite of the situation. His immediate move to action had now been validated. "Are you ready to agree with me? That coming after the flock was the right thing to do?"

Eyes rolling, Colley kneed Sultan, a fiery although remarkably responsive stallion, forward.

"Wait!" Peter called in a loud whisper. "What's our plan?"

"Plan? To get the sheep back where they belong, that's the
plan. What else is there to do?"

It looked to Peter as though they'd traded instincts in the
blink of an eye. They'd seen the truth right before them, and
now Colley's earlier concern warred against the instinctive
outrage of the ludicrous scene. In the end, though, the situation did call for a healthy measure of caution.

"Hold on," Peter said. "Let's watch for a short bit, get some
idea of what they're up to—other than shearing my sheep. We
don't even know how many of them are part of the scheme."

Colley scoffed. "You didn't seem to think that mattered
much back at the camp, now did you? Besides, it don't look
like there's more'n the two of them fools butchering that wool
coat. Let's go before they ruin any more of it."

With the element of surprise on their side, and Colley's pis-
tol as well as Peter's shotgun aimed at the clumsy shearers,
Peter and the ranch manager rode forward into clear view.

Which only made the situation worse. One of the bum-
bling fools ran toward the woods, while the other sped toward
the sheep.

As Peter took off after the one headed for his animals, he
thought he heard a woman scream, "Get him, get him, get him!"

He cast a brief glance over his shoulder, but saw nothing
and no one. He resumed his chase at a full gallop. The outlaw, shorter than Colley and heavier than Peter, didn't run as
fast as his pursuer on horseback. Peter caught up to him in no
time. The man stumbled, and Peter drew his horse to a halt

and quietly dismounted. As he grasped the man's shirt collar with one fist, he dropped his shotgun and pulled his arm back to take a swing.

"No, no!" He heard the high-pitched voice again, as his captive struggled in his clasp. "Don't drop the gun. He's got one, too."

He'd never been prone to wild imaginations or fanciful notions before. He supposed the challenge of the moment could affect him in an unexpected and unwelcome way.

The rustler caught Peter with a kick to the shin. He turned his attention back to the man, and aimed his fist square at the thief's nose.

The high-pitched voice again rang out. "Oh, good! Hit him hard…"

Peter paused. Again.

He tightened his grasp so his prisoner couldn't slip away, and found and took the gun at his hip. In the distance, he heard Colley's shouts and the other outlaw's muffled responses. It sounded as though the ranch manager had things under control on that end.

His captive shook himself, but Peter hung on.

"Let's go." He swooped down and picked up his shotgun before the man could respond to his abrupt movement. He shook his prisoner and pointed him toward the cave. "Don't know what I'm going to do about all this, but I reckon I'll think about it on the way. I have to get those animals back where they belong."

The man let out yet another stream of curses, as he'd done from the moment he'd realized he and his partner in crime were no longer alone.

Peter pushed him forward.

In moments, he and Colley had the two thieves subdued, hands tied at their backs. The stream of foul words that continued to pour from the older outlaw's mouth singed the cool, spring evening air.

As Peter and Colley mounted their horses and went to herd the flock toward the trail, the younger of their two captives came to a full stop. "Wait!" he called. "We cain't be leaving just yet. We're not...ah...all of us together."

"What are you talking about?"

The younger man glanced toward the darkened area under the rocky overhang, a worried expression on his face, but he didn't speak. Peter followed his gaze, and when he didn't see anything of particular interest, he urged his horse a step toward what, on closer study, appeared to be a cave.

A dog barked inside.

True, it was the least impressive bark Peter had heard in a long time, and well muffled, too, but he had no doubt. There was a dog inside the cave. He turned to the rustler.

"I'm glad you mentioned your dog," he said as he swung down from the saddle. "I would hate to leave the poor thing out here all alone. It wouldn't live long on its own."

Still, a dog didn't explain the voice he'd heard, or thought he'd heard.

Worry pleated the young outlaw's forehead, while the older thief stopped his curses long enough to laugh out loud. When Peter spared the two crooks a final glare as he ducked into the cave, however, neither spoke. He shook his head. Why had he bothered to look back? Livestock thieves were the lowest sorts. Who knew what mattered to them besides their unlawful gains?

Moving slowly, Peter went deeper into the cave. His eyes took a bit to adjust to the lack of light. As he went, he clicked his tongue and began to call out to the dog. "Hey, there. Where are you? I won't hurt you. Come on out with us. We'll take care of you."

The dog whined, but to Peter's ears, it didn't sound like much of a herding dog, certainly no good working dog's deep bark. This one's sounded thin, spindly...maybe the animal was hurt?

He drew a deep breath, bracing for what he might find, and dropped to his knees, clicking his tongue again. If those two thieves had hurt a dog, on top of stealing his flock, why—

A small ball of white fluff tore out of the dark and ran up onto his lap.

"Oh, no!" a child cried.

A child? No...not quite a child's voice.

What had he heard? No, no. Who had he heard?

Had he found whoever he'd heard before?

The ball of fluff on Peter's lap stood on its hind paws, its small body stretched up so it could sniff his chest and chin. If he wasn't mistaken, thinking back to when he lived in Ohio, this was a rich lady's kind of pet—some fancy, French dog, playful but useless. And still a puppy, for that matter, only months old. Still, what was it doing in a cave on a mountain in Oregon with a pair of sheep rustlers? Had they stolen it, too?

Of course, the two prisoners weren't the only ones there.

"Who are you?" he called. "Come out, or I'm coming after you."

Silence.

With one arm, Peter scooped up the pup, who continued to

nuzzle and lick his chin, quite happy to be held by a stranger. Jaw set, he stepped deeper into the dark. Someone hid back there and he meant to find whoever it was. He'd see all three of them brought to justice.

He tried again. "I said, you'd best come out now."

A heartbeat went by.

Another.

Finally, with a slow, measured rustle of motion, a body took shape no more than six feet to his left. He fixed his gaze on the figure . . . then blinked. And blinked again.

He shook his head. Stared straight ahead, squinting to try and focus more clearly, certain the darkness was playing tricks with his eyes—or maybe his mind. He couldn't be seeing what he thought he was seeing. It was impossible.

This surely had to be the single most outlandish find a body could make in a cave on a forest-covered mountain.

A lady stood before him, outfitted in tired ruffles of lacy stuff down her front, a fancy fitted orangey-buff-colored jacket with a droopy black bow over one shoulder and matching black trim down the lapels, a big full skirt made of the same stuff, and a large flood of some other dark fabric draped over an arm.

Impossible, of course. He blinked again.

Nothing changed. Again.

"He-hello," the impossible apparition said.

Peter nearly dropped the dog.

The lady's dog.

Because, as unlikely as it might be, a fancy society lady did indeed stand before him at the rear of a mountainside cave.

He drew a deep breath. He was the only man he knew who

had had something like this happen to him. But he would do what he had to do, the only thing he could do.

He would take them all to his summer camp.

And he would pray.

All the way there.

Emma would never forget the first time she set eyes on Peter Lowery. Not that she'd known the sheep rancher's name at that point. She learned it a short while later.

At first, when she heard the commotion outside the cave, her heart had leaped at the thought that help had come. But, cautious and unsure of what might await her outside, she remained frozen at the rear of the cave, her hand clutched around Pippa's muzzle. She hoped the little dog didn't betray their hiding place, at least, not until Emma was sure the new-comers weren't the infamous Dwight and Tobias. If there was one thing she knew, it was that Sawyer and Ned, rough as they were, feared the other two.

She had enough wisdom to fear them, herself.

Before long, however, she realized the newcomers were strangers to her captors. She crept to the mouth of the cave, only to watch Mr. Lowery catch Sawyer and Colley chase after Ned. As soon as the newcomers had subdued the crooks, she scurried back to her spot in the back. From the hubbub taking place a few feet beyond the opening, she understood that Ned and Sawyer had suffered the same fate as she had. Since her captors had now become captives themselves, she had no idea how she might fare.

Not long afterward, Mr. Lowery's tall, powerful frame had

blocked what light came into the cave. His torso appeared as broad as the chest of Sawyer's hefty horse, and although caution undergirded his movements, he strode with ease and a sense of command. Right away, he caught and held her attention. This wasn't a man to ignore.

His wide-brimmed western hat obscured his features, but the rest of his clothes spoke volumes about him. While Sawyer's and Ned's garments had worn through at the knees and gathered abundant quantities of soil elsewhere, this man wore clean if faded denim dungarees, a blue cambric shirt open at the neck, and what looked like some kind of undergarment in a bright shade of red beneath the rest. He'd topped everything with a brown leather vest, while on his feet he wore the narrow-toed boots with the considerable heel many western men favored, since they spent so much time in the saddle.

If this fellow came with ill intent, Emma knew herself sunk. She had nowhere to go, and he had the air of someone who meant business. There was no naive youthfulness like Ned's to him, nor did she suspect the lack of smarts she'd identified in Sawyer. This man struck her as serious, determined, someone who knew his mind and would stick to his principles. From what she'd overheard, he'd come after the sheep her captors had stolen from him. He wasn't one to be trifled with.

She hoped to learn he also had a conscience. From the look of things, she had nowhere to go but with him.

Pippa seemed to like something about the sheep rancher. She'd slipped from Emma's grasp and scrambled up to greet him—the little traitor. Dread filled her gut. She had no alternative but to place herself at his mercy. She prayed for a good measure of virtue in the heart that resided somewhere within that powerful chest.

She stood, shoulders squared, when his serious tone took on a hint of threat as he called for her to come out.

All she managed to eke out was a weak, "He—hello."

Why? Why did her voice have to crack at just such a time? At the very moment when she most needed to appear strong and confident? Instead, she must be giving him the impression of a silly girl.

His attention unwavering, he shook his head a couple of times then cleared his throat. The whole time, he held on to her dog. Perhaps she should start there.

"Could I please have my dog back?"

Clearly, it was the wrong question to ask. He stumbled back, and then spun on his heel to head outside, his strides long, firm, determined. In the interest of precision, she'd have to say he had stalked out of the cave.

Oh, dear. What now?

She didn't have to wait long. At the end of yet another hushed conversation nearby, another person, this one older and squatter but garbed like Mr. Lowery, entered the cave. "Never woulda thought it possible, ma'am," he said in a raspy voice, as he rubbed a tanned cheek. "A lady like you with a coupla bums like these."

Emma decided it might be the better part of valor to keep her response to herself. He didn't seem to notice her discretion, though, since he went ahead with what he clearly had been sent to say. "We're about to get along out of here, and you can't be staying behind alone. Dunno how long it'll take us to get the sheep back to the pasture where we summer the boss's flock, but you're gonna have to make the best of it. So are we."

"Oh, dear!" She glanced down at her once-lovely calf leather boots. "More walking..."

The man shook his head and gestured for her to precede him out of the cave. "Not for you. Boss says you'll be riding his horse, even if it might could be some uncomfortable with that there"—he waved toward her clothes—"with them fussy things you're wearing. No proper riding clothes, those."

Emma shrugged and tried to catch a glimpse of the crusty cowboy's face, but the hat shielded his features remarkably well. It seemed to be the common fashion up here. "They were perfectly suitable for my trip to Portland by carriage. I never did plan to be left behind in the woods during a holdup."

"A holdup, you say?" He sounded bemused. "And the driver left after that without you? Left you at the mercy of those two out there?"

She tipped up her nose and followed him to a tree where two horses stood, their reins looped over a low branch. "Indeed."

The younger men turned away, affording her a measure of modesty, and Colley, as the older cowboy told her to call him, helped her settle onto a tall mare's back. When she was ready, Mr. Lowery took Ned's horse, while Colley and Sawyer, hands tied at the wrist, mounted their own. Ned, as eager to please the newcomers as he'd been her, had offered to help herd the sheep, promising he'd give his captors no trouble at all.

"Don't you go forgetting," Colley told him, jaw squaring into an uncompromising rocky ledge, "I have my gun. You try something on us, and I promise you'll wear the memory of your fool choice on a leg the rest of your life. You already stole from the boss here more'n once. You give me a third reason, and my gun goes off."

"Don't *you* go worrying, Colley. I'm not 'bout to do nothing that foolish. I sure do fancy my legs a whole lot stayin' right as they are. Anyway, you can trust me. I promise you."

Ned's eager expression made Emma glance down at Pippa. Mr. Lowery had returned her dog, who now sat comfortably in a puddle of crushed velvet traveling-suit skirt. Slowly, with three of the men working the sheep—two on horseback, Ned trotting on foot—Sawyer complaining, and Emma, who put up a valiant fight to stay upright on the horse, they traveled down a narrow trail, rutted, twisty, and scattered at frequent intervals with substantial broken branches.

Later, much, much later, when the sparkling stars dotted the inky fabric of the sky and the moon lent its silver gleam to illuminate the path for their odd troupe, they arrived at a large meadow where more sheep milled about. Emma sighed in relief as her horse came to a stop. She looked forward to a hot bath and a good night's sleep. As she anticipated curling up for the much-needed slumber, a breeze picked up the tumbled curls on her forehead. She shivered. A thick and heavy wool blanket on a fluffy feather bed would be an absolute necessity. Even though spring had come, they remained partway up the Blue Mountains, and night air still bore the bite of cold.

As she waited for Colley to come and help her dismount, Emma looked around, trying to orient herself.

An awful sense of dismay poured onto her, drip by drip, until it saturated her. The stark reality of her circumstances overwhelmed her. She saw...nothing. Nothing but trees and sheep. No kind of shelter anywhere. At least the cave had provided that much.

Surely this wasn't where they'd been headed.

This was...well, nothing. She realized she couldn't even see the men she had ridden in with.

Where had they gone?

"Um...Colley?" she called out. "How soon before we set out on our way again?"

"Huh?" The cowboy emerged from among nearby trees. "On our way to where?"

"Well, to...um...Mr. Lowery's sheep...place? Farm? Ranch?"

For a moment, the older cowboy didn't answer. Then he drew his felt hat off, slapped it against his thigh, and laughed. "You sure don't hail from these parts, now do you, Miss Emma? We're here. This is it, ma'am. This camp here is home for the summer months."

"Here?" Her voice went up to a shrill pitch. "What do you mean, here? Why, there's nothing here. Just sheep. And trees."

It was more than obvious to any sane soul. She couldn't stay here. Of course not. Surely, they couldn't either. There was no house anywhere to be seen. Cowboy or city woman, both needed a roof over his or her head.

"Yup, ma'am," Colley said, still chuckling. "This is it. Home for the rest of May, June, July, August, and likely a bit of September, too. And there ain't much in these parts, I'll give you that, but there's enough. Plenty pasture for the sheep, clean water for all, and the boss has himself a nice little cabin here. He built the hands a fair bunkhouse not too far, neither. You'll see."

"But...but—"

"Colley!" Mr. Lowery bellowed.

"On my way, boss," the cowboy answered then scurried away.

Emma's words died off as Colley made his way across the clearing to the shadows on the other side again. That's when it dawned on her. At the very top of Colley's head, where it had hidden under the straw hat, sat a large, tight silver-gray bun. Colley was no cowboy.

Colley was a woman!

The realization stole her breath, made her thoughts spin, and started up a horrid humming at her ears. It all conspired to leave her quite lightheaded.

Emma clutched the saddle horn, hoping to keep herself upright. She didn't relish a fall off and the rough landing that would follow. Thank goodness she'd ridden a western-style saddle. English saddles lacked that prominent feature at the very front.

"A woman...Colley is a woman." Emma's thoughts spun back to when she'd first heard him...well, her speak. That raspy voice hadn't sounded right. Now she knew why. Sure, it had a low and growly quality to it, but it didn't sound anything like a man should. It made sense now.

She watched the older woman disappear into the darkness of the trees. Who would have thought? What would make a woman turn herself into...well, that? Emma couldn't comprehend it.

From her end of the clearing, she heard Colley chase a lamb out of the woods and toward the larger cluster she could just make out in a spill of moonlight. The nearness of that many animals disturbed her, but not nearly as much as did finding herself all alone.

In the dark.

And cold.

"Hello?" she called out after a few minutes' wait. "I'm back here!"

No response came her way, as she remained on her perch atop the horse. With a dog on her lap. And she needed... um...her own "constitutional."

Since none of the men came to her rescue, even after she'd given them a handful of minutes to do so, Emma decided they'd left her to her own devices. She would have to get herself off the mountain of horse. Oh, goodness. She did not like the prospect.

While she had gone riding any number of times, in London as well as in Denver, these men—and even Colley—hadn't and wouldn't be able to provide her with a proper lady's sidesaddle. Her dilemma was immediate. Nothing nearby provided the opportunity for her to step down from this great height with any measure of feminine grace and dignity. At least the animal seemed placid enough. She hoped it wouldn't skitter away when she slid down its side.

First, however, she had to figure out what she ought to do with Pippa...ah, yes! She'd button the puppy inside her jacket. After all, the garment was ruined through and through. It didn't matter if Pippa's modest bulk stretched the velvet past its original shape. It would prevent her pet from falling, being trampled, and keep her snuggled close to Emma, should the horse shy away.

Moments later, with Pippa inside the jacket, Emma wriggled over onto her belly, legs flailing in the air, and began a controlled slither down the horse's side, bemoaning her petite stature the whole way. No sooner had she started, however, than her plan failed. She plummeted in one fast swoosh to the ground.

"Ooooof!"

She somehow managed to land with her feet squarely under her, but her knees buckled from the momentum and gave under her weight. She landed in a crumpled heap of ballooned skirt and twisted legs on a carpet of soft, damp grass. A moment later, her green wool cloak oozed down the back of her head and a shoulder to pool off to a side.

Tears of misery stung her eyes, but she refused to give in. She had to stay strong.

Pippa yelped her objection to such disgraceful treatment.

Emma scrambled upright and swiped at her damp eyes with the back of a hand. She stomped in the direction where Colley had vanished, but saw nothing of note. Where had the woman gone?

She turned, scanning the meadow, but of course, saw only sheep. As she continued to turn, her angle changed, and she spotted the mellow gleam of golden lamplight within a cluster of trees at the farthest edge of the clearing.

So that was where they'd all vanished.

A house . . . food, even.

Perhaps.

That morning, she'd been sure she had left her appetite behind ages ago. The chunk of greasy bacon Ned had offered had been inedible, and no amount of hunger made it possible to choke it down. The biscuit next to it had been hard as rock. But her stomach gave off a good grumble, as though to remind her of its empty condition. Aside from that, she was exhausted, and being left out in the cold and dark didn't sit well with her. Shoulders squared and head high, she marched toward the light, good and ready to give those scoundrels a piece of her mind.

When she drew close, she saw the outline of the cabin Colley had mentioned. Just outside the modest building, she took a deep breath, and then yanked open the door. "I do not appreciate being abandoned while you all have meandered inside to warm yourselves..."

Her scolding dried up. Instead of her companions from the trail, in the structure she found a young man she'd never seen before and a child. A sleepy boy, who sat up in a bunk and rubbed his eyes.

"Who are you?" he asked.

Pippa yipped and popped her head out the top of Emma's jacket.

The young man gaped.

The boy chortled.

Something broke loose inside Emma, and a tear finally rolled down her cheek. Would her nightmare never end?

The next morning, Emma awoke in the bunk where she'd first seen Robert—Robby, as he'd said to call him— Mr. Lowery's son. When the rancher and Colley returned after they'd marched Sawyer and Ned to the bunkhouse, they moved the boy up to what clearly had been his father's bed, built into the wall above Robby's bunk, and Emma was offered the one the boy previously had occupied.

Robby was thrilled; Emma horrified.

They expected her to sleep out in the open? In an area

where everyone seemed to come and go all the time? The cabin was nothing more than one large room with two or three doors to the outside. Anyone could walk in at any time. Besides, the child could gape down at her whenever he awoke. Not that she imagined he would do her any harm, but she'd never had to sleep with another person in the same room.

And yet, she hadn't had the heart to object. From what she came to understand, the only other structure at the summer camp was the bunkhouse Mr. Lowery had built to house his ranch hands. It would now house Wade, the young man who'd cared for Robby, Sawyer, Ned, and Mr. Lowery, himself. He was moving there to afford Emma the relative privacy of the cabin. Colley had her own tiny room in the lean-to attached to the right side of the cabin. One of the doors led to it.

The rancher was doing what he could.

When her bottom lip quivered again, she bit down hard on it. She hadn't even been able to remove her dirty, dusty, sticky, and much too uncomfortable suit. As much as she hated to climb into Robby Lowery's bed in her disgracefully dirty outfit, she didn't feel she had a choice. Colley had offered some of her shirts and denim trousers. But since she was a head and more taller than Emma, and outweighed her by a good amount of muscle, none of it would fit. And while the offer was quite generous, she must also have left her wits out in the woods. Emma couldn't envision the time or pressure that might compel her to wear men's clothes.

Unlike Colley. Evidently, that was all she ever wore.

In view of all that, Emma had, at the very least, removed her jacket.

Oh, how Emma wanted a long, hot, luxurious bath,

fragrant with the French lavender extract Aunt Sophia knew she favored, and a thick, fluffy cotton towel for drying off afterward. Instead, she'd washed hands and face in a wide bowl filled with water Colley ladled from the large kettle that hung from an iron rod over the hearth. Somehow, they managed to cook meals there, but she couldn't imagine how. There was no proper cookstove anywhere in sight, like those Aunt Sophia's and Ophelia's kitchens boasted. Just a fireplace and a rod.

So much for the civilization she hoped to find. This certainly wasn't it.

Fully awake, and in the light of day, she took a good look at her surroundings, only to have her dismay grow greater still. The structure was rough and consisted of scarcely more than four walls with some grayish-white . . . stuff crammed in between the logs, a roof, and a plank floor. Two chairs and three stools surrounded a table that looked as though someone had thrown it together from leftover floorboards and a handful of nails. More of those additional flat planks had been pressed into use as shelves on the walls. They held cooking pans, plates, cups, and a variety of other items Emma couldn't begin to identify.

A couple of fairly attractive gray, blue, and brown braided rugs lay strewn around the floor. Their rustic charm contrasted nicely with the simple rocking chair at one side of the hearth, and made it appear delicate and elegant and lovely, indeed. Clearly, the chair belonged to a woman, but Emma had yet to see any sign of female habitation besides Colley. The chair did not bring Colley to mind. There was, of course, nowhere for another woman to hide. One worth her salt would run from the place screaming. As Emma meant to do. Straight away.

What an abysmal situation.

Then again, since this was Mr. Lowery's place, and Emma would only stay here until the men helped her return to Bountiful—immediately—she didn't let herself dwell on the missing owner of the rocker for long. A huge yawn struck her and she stretched. At her side, Pippa rolled over, wiggling her paws in the air. Emma scratched her pet's belly and wondered when someone, Colley probably, would come and prepare a meal. She'd been offered, and had accepted, a hunk of decent bread and a thick slice of cold mutton the night before. She'd been so hungry it had tasted almost as exquisite as the finest, juiciest filet mignon she'd enjoyed in London.

It made sense to take Pippa out for her constitutional before Colley—or worse, the stern Mr. Lowery—walked in and found her lazing in the bed. She wasn't a child like Robby to sleep till all hours. Glad she'd stuffed Pippa's rope in her skirt pocket before she dropped off to sleep the night before, Emma now attached it to the dog, then stepped down from the bunk.

And straight into a cold puddle, undoubtedly courtesy of her pet. "Oh, dear, Pippa! You naughty girl. You've done so well this far, going outside all the time. Why would you ever do this now, inside Mr. Lowery's house...er...cabin?"

Pippa yawned.

"What's that?" Robby asked in a sleepy voice, head hanging upside down from his bunk, precisely as Emma had imagined when she first saw the bunks' setup the night before.

She looked in every direction, seeking something with which to clean up her dog's mess. "She's my dog."

"Not the dog. I can see that. I meant what you spilled there on the floor. Papa doesn't like it when I spill things. Too much lamb's wool comes in on his clothes, he says, and it can stick to the floor. Is your spill sticky?"

Sticky? "No, no." And she would clean it before Mr. Lowery or his wool were to come close, so stickiness wouldn't matter. What could she use?

Aha! Over there by the hearth. A length of plain muslin hung from a nail stuck in the wall. Emma ran across the cold floor, snagged the cloth, and hurried back to mop up the mess. Just as she finished, the cabin door opened and Colley, Wade, and Mr. Lowery walked in. They found her on her knees in the most undignified pose, swabbing away at her dog's—

"Miss Emma!" Colley cried. "Is something wrong? Did you fall?"

Her cheeks burned, and she wished she might simply melt down through the rough planks of the floor. She scrambled up and clutched the sodden fabric at her back. "No, no! I'm fine—"

"Something dripped, Papa," Robby offered.

She almost groaned, and had to fight the powerful urge to muzzle the boy, since he really hadn't done anything wrong. It was Pippa who'd erred, so Emma kept her peace.

Robby went on. "Miss Emma was just cleaning it up. I told her how you don't like sticky stuff on the floor. She says it weren't sticky or nothing—"

"Wasn't, anything," Emma murmured automatically.

Robby said, "Huh?"

The men stared.

Emma blushed hotter than before. "I'm sorry. I just meant that the correct way to say it would be 'wasn't sticky or anything.'

Mrs. Carrington, one of my teachers, came to mind. Don't ask me why."

"You had teachers?" Robby asked, his eyes wide as saucers.

"You don't?" she countered, her eyes likely as wide.

Mr. Lowery cleared his throat. "Robert lives on a sheep ranch, Miss Crowell. In the summers, he's here at the camp. You don't see a schoolhouse anywhere, do you?"

She stared down, noting her bare toes, which she curled to hide them under the filthy hem of her skirt. "I'm sorry. I didn't think about that—I didn't think at all. I just...just— oh, never mind. I'm sorry, Robby. Truly, I am. I didn't mean anything by my words."

The silence lengthened, and Emma felt worse by the second. She hadn't meant to make anyone feel less worthy, certainly not by a bit of grammatical correction. It had just burst out, a memory from her childhood. In any case, she wouldn't be here long enough for that kind of mistake to happen again.

She donned a brilliant smile. "So, then, gentlemen. How soon do we leave for Bountiful?"

As though they'd practiced the maneuver a dozen times, every one of the three men opened his mouth and gaped.

Chapter 5

Had she not seen it with her own eyes, Emma would have thought she'd dreamt the entire scenario. They all continued to stare, Robby giggled, and then, as though by some sort of sleight of hand, Colley, Wade, and even Robby vanished.

One moment they were there, the next she blinked, and . . . gone!

They had abandoned her to the sole company of the imposing Mr. Peter Lowery.

What could have been so dreadfully wrong with that simple question? Surely they understood her urgency to return. When she left Denver, she certainly didn't plan for . . . for all that had happened to her. Her destination hadn't changed; she still had to get to Portland. Especially since she had a wedding to plan. That's right. She couldn't forget that.

No matter what, Emma couldn't just stand there in the uncomfortable silence, clutching a soggy rag and staring at the grim man not ten feet away. It was time to act.

"Very well, Mr. Lowery. Now that everyone else is gone, pray tell me what your immediate plans are. I'm sure you know I need to rejoin my traveling party and reassure my loved ones that I am, although somewhat worn out by the experience, unharmed."

The rancher leaned a hip against the table, thumbs in his trouser belt loops. "I reckon you do have every reason to feel the need to return to your regular parties and other activities, but I'm afraid that need of yours is going to have to take second place to the ranch."

"But why would you do that, sir? I'm a lady in distress. Surely you understand your duty as a proper gentleman to assist me. All I need is an escort back to Bountiful. That's not too much to ask."

His jaw tightened and a muscle flexed in his cheek. "Don't you go throwing words like lady, gentleman, and distress around, ma'am. I'm just a rancher, and my flock comes first. They need to pasture up here in the meadow during the summer, and nothing—you hear?—*nothing* is going to move me away until fall comes. I even have a couple of late ewes about to drop their lambs. I can't leave."

Emma couldn't believe what she thought she'd just heard. "I'm sorry, but I believe I misunderstood. Surely you don't mean to say that you intend for me to stay out here until the fall."

He let out a humorless bark of a laugh. "That's just what I said, Miss Crowell. We're here until the fall. It takes too much to move a flock up here, and you know firsthand I've had animals stolen already. I'm not abandoning my sheep just to get you back to town."

A breath burst out in relief. "Well, then, Mr. Lowery, that

being the case, I understand your commendable sense of responsibility, sir. And of course, you can stay with your sheep. Colley can just take me back."

The rancher straightened and crossed his arms. "You don't know anything about ranching in general or sheep in particular, do you?"

Emma didn't care for the censure in his voice. "I've lived my whole life in cities. I've never needed to know about ranching, sheep, or anything else like that. I see no sin in that."

"No sin, but basic understanding on your part would help us all. We have work to do here. I can't spare my ranch manager, just so she can guide you back to town. I don't even know if the three of us can do everything that needs doing, never mind sending one of us with you. We'll get you back to Bountiful. In the fall."

Emma's eyes widened in horror. "No, Mr. Lowery, that's impossible. I can't stay here. It...it simply wouldn't be proper! I can't spend all that time...um...er—with all you men."

"Proper? I found you in a cave, captured by a pair of the most clumsy rustlers a body could ever imagine. Then, I brought you to a clean cabin with a bed instead of a dirt floor. Yet you worry about proper? Would you rather have stayed behind in that cave? Alone? Without food or real shelter from the animals out in the woods? Don't forget, Colley's here with us. She's proper."

"Well..." When he put it in those terms, she had to admit he had a point. As to Colley and her men's shirts and dungarees, time would tell about her measure of propriety.

"I suppose there are worse things," she conceded. "But, please consider this. You're a father. Do think of my poor papa. He must be beside himself with worry. Please try to understand. We're all each one has left ever since Mama died. He'll be frantic."

He blinked, a groove etched between his brows, and he swallowed hard. She took heart from the momentary flicker of weakness, but before she could press her advantage, he hardened the line of his jaw and tightened his lips.

When he spoke again, he did so in a clipped voice. "When I meet him, I'll have to apologize and offer him my regret for the stubborn demands and constraints the ranch puts on me. I can't leave until the fall."

"Bu—but...oh, I know! You now have two more men here. I'm sure Ned and Sawyer can help with the sheep while you or Colley help me back to Bountiful."

He laughed. "A couple of rustlers, Miss Crowell? I should trust the two men who stole my flock in the first place to take care of my animals? I don't reckon that makes much sense, begging your pardon, ma'am."

She had to admit, he was right. But she couldn't just surrender to his outlandish notion. Before she could come up with another line of reasoning, he went on.

"Since you're so ready to volunteer them, I suggest you try heading for Bountiful with them. I reckon Sawyer's quite handy with that sidearm we took away. I could give it back to him, and he could protect you, don't you think?"

Emma blanched. She read on his face how well he knew his suggestion was utterly out of the question. She doubted Ned would have a chance to keep Sawyer from...from whatever he might decide to do to her if the man set his mind—and his gun—to it.

"You know I can't do that." Her voice betrayed a quaver. As

Ginny Aiken

she'd thought before, she had to appeal to his mercy. "Please take pity on me. I never asked to be here, I'm so very, very sorry to be a bother to you, but I never could have envisioned my trip to Portland would involve a holdup. I hate to be a burden, and you must agree it would be far better for all if I were gone as soon as possible."

"Yes, it would be best if you weren't here, but I have no choice. I must stay, with my sheep and all my men—not two half-witted thieves—until the time is right. That won't happen until the fall. There's no more arguing to be done."

"But—"

"Save your breath, please, Miss Crowell. If you don't want to be a burden, then I suggest you make yourself useful. Everyone, and I do mean everyone here, must carry his—or her—own weight. You'll have to earn your keep while you're at the camp."

"But I'm not a sheep—shepherd—rancher..." She waved uselessly.

He lifted a shoulder. "Don't have to be. You can make yourself plenty useful in here."

She looked around the cabin. Her knees went weak. So did her voice. "Here?"

"Of course. There's plenty to be done indoors, and a woman's always best to handle that sort of thing. You can take over the cooking, the washing, and you can even give Robby some lessons, seeing as how you had all those teachers of yours. You did start right off on that last night."

Washing? Cooking?

Why did all these men try to set her to making meals? Was there something about her that suggested she had a hidden

· 78 ·

gift for cookery? She didn't think it was something folks could tell just by looking at a person.

"That, sir, would not be a good idea," she said. "Not if you and the others fancy eating. You see, Mr. Lowery, I'm very sorry, but I don't cook. I never have."

"Well, ma'am, I don't run a prison, either, but seeing as how I caught Sawyer and Ned with my sheep, I'm going to have to be their jailer until I can turn them over to Marshal Blair in the fall. Life doesn't always follow an ideal road, Miss Crowell. Real life is what you do with what comes your way, how you handle it with the gifts and grace the Lord has given you."

"Are you saying I should blame God for my situation?" How strange. "I don't see how you could say He sent the outlaws to hold up the carriage. Or that He expects me to cook for the whole lot of you."

"I don't blame God. Way I see it, Ned and Sawyer, and the other two they've mentioned, are to blame for the holdup. On the other hand, God is responsible for the gifts He's given you—me, the outlaws, Colley, Wade, and my boy, Robby, too. Each one of us is accountable to Him for how we use those gifts. It's up to us to honor Him in our day-to-day life."

Emma had been to church often enough, but she'd never heard a life of faith explained in those terms. Mr. Lowery had a most intriguing way of putting it.

But it didn't matter. "What you suggest is out of the question," she argued again. "I can't stay here. If none of you will help me back to Bountiful, then I suppose I'll have to go on my own." She thought fast. "That's it! I'll borrow a horse—Sawyer's or Ned's, since they're in jail. A buggy or wagon would also help. But I must head back. I have no other choice. My life is not here."

His shoulders shook with silent laughter. "I can't spare a horse and I promise those two won't lend you theirs, but you're welcome to walk to Bountiful—it's a day's ride, I don't know how long on foot. Depends on how quickly you walk, I suppose." He shook his head in clear bemusement. "I heard from Ned that you got lost in the woods when you took your dog for a...um...walk. Don't you think this whole mountain full of trees might prove even more challenging than a few dozen saplings at the edge of a well-worn trail?"

She hated to admit it, but he did have a point. "I can't stay." Her voice came out in little more than a whisper. "It's so inappropriate...surely you understand."

Her distress finally seemed to penetrate Mr. Lowery's stern façade. He approached.

She stepped back and sat on the bunk, covered her face with her hands.

He dropped onto one knee just inches away. "I'm very sorry, ma'am. I do reckon I understand. My wife would have been just as horrified if she'd been in your shoes, but there's not much I can do besides promise you my protection while you're in my home. I won't let anyone hurt you, and as soon as I can leave without risking everything I've worked for all these years, then I'll take you to Bountiful myself. But I can only do that once I've ensured my boy's future. It's nothing less important than that."

Something in his dark, direct gaze touched Emma. He meant it. All of it. Every single word he spoke. Could his future—Robby's future—really depend on his staying out on the mountain?

"Help me understand," she said. "What do you mean by Robby's future?"

"I earn our living raising sheep. They need to eat, and summer heat kills the grass down around the ranch. All of us who run sheep bring them up to mountain meadows to fatten them up for market in the fall. If we stay at our ranches, our flocks could starve. We'd all go belly up."

"But won't they just eat on their own?"

"Of course, and they also wander off all on their own. The land up here is too hilly to fence. And there are predators about. Not to mention those other two rustlers may still be around and could take the whole flock in a matter of hours. A flock this size needs a few people watching over it. And there's the shearing..."

To her dismay, it began to make sense. "And you personally can't leave because they're your responsibility."

"Exactly. All of it."

"But Colley...?"

"Has forgotten more about sheep than I'll ever learn."

"You need her."

He nodded.

She drew a shuddering breath. "And Wade, too..."

His answer was the first real smile she'd seen him wear. She decided she liked how it looked on him.

Immediately, she chided herself for such a bold and inappropriate thought. Her cheeks heated, and she regretted, not for the first time, her redhead's complexion. It hid nothing.

Hoping to keep his attention from going right to her surely red cheeks, she asked, "Ned?"

"If not for his thieving past, I'd think he could make

something of himself. He worked plenty hard and helped us get the sheep to the camp last night."

She sighed. "I'm not ready to take off through the woods with a stranger. Not that spending months isolated on a mountain with five strangers makes much more sense. Still, you do seem a mite more trustworthy than Sawyer and Ned."

He laughed, a hearty belly laugh that made her cheeks sizzle yet more. "Do you expect me to thank you for those grand words of praise?" When she didn't answer—she couldn't speak, she was so mortified—he went on.

"We've had some rough years around here, and it's taken all I could scrape up just to hang on long enough. In order to buy some land right next to mine, I had to take out a mortgage against my ranch. The note comes due in October. I reckon the Bank of Bountiful wants its money paid in full by then. I think I'll have it if my flock sells well. But I can't risk losing a single sheep, not even one fleece, that's how close I am. I risk losing the ranch, Robby's future, if I can't pay."

Every last drop of hope Emma might have harbored evaporated. She'd heard the softening in his voice every time Mr. Lowery had spoken his boy's name. It had to take many years of work for a man to build a profitable flock. Business was business, and Papa had always stressed how a man's word counted for much.

This businessman, this father, wasn't going to budge.

Apparently, Mr. Lowery decided he'd waited long enough for her response. He stood and turned. "I can keep you safe until the fall, and then on the way back. What I can't, and won't do, is walk away from those who're counting on me."

As he stepped away, Emma stood, too. "You've made

yourself much too clear, sir. And I—I can accept that I'm forced to stay until the first opportunity appears. So I give you my word. I'll make the very best of my stay here."

A weight seemed to drop from his shoulders as they sagged just a hint. The vulnerability in that response surprised her. And intrigued her.

She steeled herself against it. He had just appointed himself her jailer, too. True, he hadn't said it in so many words, but just as he meant to keep Sawyer and Ned under his control, he'd clearly stated his intention to do the same with her.

"Well, then," she said. "Since you've made your position so clear, I must ask you for the one thing I must have. Since I don't have a thing to wear, and seeing as my trunk was in that carriage, I must at least have a good, hot bath. Please tell me what your procedure is out here."

"Bath?" His brow furrowed as though the concept was utterly foreign to him. "We don't have a regular bath here at the camp, Miss Crowell. There's our big tin tub outside. Colley always keeps a kettle of hot water at the hearth. You can take a pail to pump cold water for mixing at any time. And I know we bought enough soap to last almost forever. Wash up all you want."

"A tin tub? Outside?" Dismay nearly crushed Emma. So that was that. Dreadful. "Preposterous, sir. And impossible."

"You said you wanted a bath." Mr. Lowery stalked out.

How had he said it? He'd suggested Emma was accountable for how she handled this new stage of her life with the gifts and grace God had given her.

So it was up to her to make the best of things. Her only problem was that she didn't have the slightest notion what those gifts might be.

*　　*　　*

"Dreadful!" Oh, the horrid, ghastly, appalling, vile, and revolting indignity of it all.

Emma fought to contain her anger and disgust as she trudged back to the cabin after being forced to use yet another tree as an—ahem!—necessary. At least the kettle of hot water was a permanent fixture in the hearth, as Mr. Lowery had said. She'd also counted a good stack of cakes of plain cream-colored soap—nothing like the sweet French-milled bars she fancied, but they certainly did the job of cleaning hands... and smelly lengths of muslin.

After Mr. Lowery had stomped out, she'd poured the steaming hot water into another, smaller pot, dunked the wet muslin, and hurried outside with the mess, a cake of soap tucked into her skirt pocket. Even though the heat had scalded her hands, she'd bitten down on her lip against the burn, dunked and dunked the rag, rubbed it with the soap, and dunked it again in fresh hot water until it smelled good and clean. When done, the fabric seemed lighter in color—maybe just washed clean of prior stains.

With the muslin spread over the back of one of the chairs, Emma stood in the center of the room, next to the table, and turned slowly all the way around, taking in every detail. She didn't know what she hoped to find, since there wasn't much to see, other than raw walls, floors and ceilings, the bunks, the hearth, the rocking chair and the... well, goodness!

She hadn't seen *that* the night before. In the farthest corner of the cabin, far away from the light that sliced in through the two front windows, Emma spotted a wooden contraption with a tall, spindly rod at one end and a large wheel at the other. Both parts were attached to a simple wooden frame. If she wasn't mistaken, it was a spinning wheel. She remembered she'd seen a similar one at an exhibition in London, and knew women in the European countryside worked them for hours and hours to turn wool into yarn.

Neither Mr. Lowery or Colley struck her as the spinning sort. Where was Mrs. Lowery?

Mr. Lowery had mentioned a wife when they'd had their conversation a short while ago. Didn't she come to the summer camp with her husband and son?

That seemed strange to Emma, even though she understood how a woman wouldn't want to endure the less-than-civilized conditions. She didn't want to be here, either, but didn't have a choice.

"*En garde!*"

Emma jumped almost a foot off the floor at the loud yell. She clasped her hands over her pounding heart, spun, and found Robby Lowery wrapped in what must once have been a woman's cape. In his hand, he held a dried, brittle tree branch like an *epée*. His hazel eyes sparkled with mischief, and his brown hair tumbled in a tousled wave over his brow.

Her breath came out in gusty bursts. "Don't you ever do that—"

The crumpling of his gleeful expression stopped her words. His bottom lip twitched and he blinked fast and hard. It struck her in that moment what a lonely life the boy must live. She didn't have the heart to crush his delight just because his sudden appearance had startled her.

"Well!" She forced a light tone of voice. "Art thou off to a duel, milord?"

Robby let out a wild whoop, spun so the cape swirled around, and leaped into another pose, his "sword" extended at the ready. He dropped to one knee before her, reminding her of the position his father had recently adopted. "I'm sworn to protect my lady's honor."

His game surprised her. The playful episode seemed unusual for a child who lived on a western ranch. Before she could ask about his unexpected form of amusement, the boy made a deep bow before her.

"Forgive thy lowly servant, milady. I have come upon thee in such a fashion as to have caused thee grave distress. It never was thy steadfast knight's intention."

Emma fought her smile. "All is forgiven, kind sir. Carry on."

"Indeed! I must be off to meet King Ban and King Bors and our twenty thousand fellowship. King Leodegrance needs rescue in the country of Ca—Came..." He paused, a fierce frown on his childish face. "Camelia—"

"Cameliard," Emma whispered, stunned by the boy's words. "You know the tales of King Arthur!"

He nodded. "Mama read to me about the king and his knights every day. I have her book, and I try to read them myself, but sometimes the words are long, and I don't know them all."

"I'm not surprised," Emma said. "It's a very old book, written with old, old words we don't use anymore."

"But it tells the best stories of kings and queens and knights and jousts and...and Merlin, of course."

The excitement on his face echoed what she had felt back when she'd discovered the wonders of Sir Thomas Malory's retelling of the Arthurian legend. "Oh, Sir Robby, milord. I do agree indeed."

His expression lit up again. She'd said the right thing.

"Can I show you my book?" he asked.

"I would love that."

As his "sword" rolled across the floor with a clatter, Robby ran to the corner where the spinning wheel sat, dropped to his knees, and opened a small leather trunk. After carefully closing it again, he returned to her side.

He held the book out to her. "Here, Lady Emma."

How long had it been since she'd last spent a few hours lost in Malory's tales of times long gone? She took the tome, hefty in its solid weight. "Would you like me to read a chapter or two?"

His eyes sparkled. "Would you really?"

"Of course." She gestured at the bunk. "Why don't you sit next to me? It is your bed after all."

Robby scrambled to one end and Emma scooted in beside him. Both leaned back against the wall. She let the book fall open on her lap to Book IV, Chapter XVI . . . How the damosel of the lake saved King Arthur from a mantle that should have burnt him. Emma smiled. She remembered the tale, one in which Arthur was given a mantle as a gift meant to do him harm. However, the Lady of the Lake came to warn him against wearing the garment lest it kill him. King Arthur turned it against the giver, who did indeed die under its effect.

Emma read, relishing the cadence of the old English, the story of intrigue, the triumph of the king.

That was how Mr. Lowery found them when he walked into the cabin. "What's this all about?" he asked.

At her side, Robby shrank down against her.

"I'm reading Robby a story," she answered, bewildered by his attitude. "Nothing strange in that."

"Robert," the rancher said, his voice stern. "Are you spending more time on those fancy tales of kings and knights?"

"Yes," the boy said into Emma's side, his puff of breath warm even through her blouse.

"Haven't we talked about this before? Didn't we decide you needed to spend more time learning about the ranch with Colley?"

This time, no response was forthcoming.

"Robby?" his father asked.

"Yessir."

"I reckon Colley has something practical for you to do. Why don't you go find her?"

A deep, heartfelt sigh warmed Emma's side. Slowly, reluctantly, Robby pried himself away from Emma and slid off the bed. He dragged his feet as he walked to the door, and as he pushed the latch, he glanced over his shoulder. Emma spotted the sheen of a tear in one of the boy's eyes.

Goodness gracious! One would think the child had committed a dreadful crime. But all he'd done was sit at her side while she read for a while.

As soon as Robby closed the door, Emma bounded upright. "Mr. Lowery—"

"Miss Crowell! Robby has a fanciful nature, as I'm sure you noticed today. There's nothing wrong with that, but it won't help him make his way out here. He must learn the practical things in life. Stories like the ones you read won't stand him well in the future. He needs to know as much as possible about ranching and running sheep."

Emma tossed the book onto the bunk, crossed her arms, and tapped a toe on the floor. "That sounds quite dreary, don't you think? Robby is a child. I enjoyed stories when I was his age."

He arched a brow. "And you've told me you can't cook. What can you do, Miss Crowell?"

Pride stung, she propped her fists on her hips. "I can speak French with a flawless continental accent. I excel at drawing and lovely watercolors. And I've been told I'm quite gifted with a needle and floss, I'll have you know. My embroidery and needlepoint tapestries are exquisite. I'm not utterly useless, sir."

To her horror, the corners of his mouth twitched. He ticked off a finger. "But you can't cook, can you?" Another digit. "Can you iron a clean shirt?" The third. "Can you patch a man's trouser knee?" A fourth, fifth, and one from the other hand. "Can you spin wool, weave cloth, train a child?"

She could do none of those things, true. But instead of letting his accusation and guilty verdict get the better of her, Emma blurted out the first thing that came to her mind.

"No, Mr. Lowery, I can't do any of those things, but I can read and write, I can sew, and, more important, I can learn. Give me a chance, and I can prove it."

The rancher gave her a measuring look. "I offered you the chance to make yourself useful here at the camp, but you answered you didn't know how to cook. Now you say you can learn."

Emma realized how strange a hole she had dug for herself. "Well, yes. I did tell you both those things."

His smile widened. "I reckon you can start to show me how well you do learn right away. If you're eager to earn your keep around here, you'll have to work. And I really do mean work.

We can't afford to carry dead wood—any dead wood. The time Colley has to spend cooking or watching Robby is time she can't spend with the sheep. Can't have that, Miss Crowell. Not when there's another able-bodied grown-up out here."

"But—"

"The most logical thing for you is to run the house, especially the kitchen. And now you've said you're quite capable of learning."

She tried yet a third objection. "But—"

"Here's your schoolroom," he said, ignoring her attempt. "And over by the spinning wheel, you'll find my wife's trunk full of women's things. Help yourself to her cookery and housekeeping books. I'm sure they have plenty in them to teach you what you need to know."

He turned on his heel and left.

How could things manage to get worse and worse as time went by? They'd been dreadful from the moment she'd taken Pippa for her constitutional in the woods.

Why did she say anything to Mr. Lowery? What had she got herself into now? And all she'd wanted was to travel from Denver to Portland. On her own.

Oh, yes. She had wanted to feel all grown up.

It dawned on Emma she'd achieved what she'd wanted, in a very odd way. She had the dreadful suspicion that life at the summer camp would have her feeling as grown up as anyone could in no time at all.

Chapter 6

Emma stood in silence after Mr. Lowery left the cabin, unsure what to do. She felt leaden, as though rooted in place, struck with an unfamiliar fear. She'd spent her life as the much-loved and well-pampered daughter of a successful businessman. She'd wanted for nothing, and had never faced anything that tested her to the core of her being, as she feared she would be by her stay here. She'd thought she knew herself, who she was meant to be.

Now, she faced a challenge so unexpected and foreign to everything she'd ever experienced that she had no idea how to even begin to confront it.

True, she rejoiced she'd been born into her particular family; she'd loved Mama, and still loved Papa, more than she could measure. She also rejoiced in the many blessings she'd enjoyed all her life, and yet, she also knew how much less many others had. She didn't think it made any sense, though, to blame her for her father's hard work and success, not even for his willingness to shower his only daughter with the fruits of that success.

It wasn't as though the family didn't share their blessings with those less fortunate. Papa regularly gave substantial sums to their church, which then used that money to serve those less fortunate and needy. Emma well knew how often she and Aunt Sophia had taken food baskets, blankets, clothes, and shoes to many, many families who otherwise would have gone without. She'd been brought up to not only acknowledge the importance of the Scripture that called one to do unto others as one would have done unto one's self, but also to live it out. She hadn't, however, seen where it might call her to reject her father's bounty.

That bounty had meant a different life from that of many others, and she was beginning to understand the enormity of that difference. Perhaps she had been spoiled and not just pampered. Perhaps she had grown into a more frivolous person than many others—maybe even most others. But she didn't feel she ought to be blamed for something she hadn't consciously chosen to do. Or be.

Emma slowly returned to the bunk. She sat gracelessly, a sense of dejection heavy and oppressive on her otherwise optimistic nature. The tears that had threatened time and time again since she'd come face to face with the two half-hearted outlaws poured out. And while she'd cried herself to sleep the night before, in that prickly, outdoors-pungent pine-needle substitute for a real mattress, those tears hadn't brought any measure of release. She wondered if any amount of weeping would. How could she feel any relief under these circumstances? Where might some manner of comfort be found?

Again she looked around, and, of course, nothing had changed. Her situation remained as bleak as it had been for a day and more. She dropped onto the bed, her face in the pillow.

She'd never felt so alone, not even after her mother died giving birth to her stillborn brother. Although consumed with grief, Papa had kept Emma at his side for months and months afterward. He'd often taken her along on his travels, even. She had for a very long time missed her mother, and still did, but Emma had never felt alone, not even during that painful mourning period. Not like she did right then. "Oh, Papa..."

But her father was nowhere near enough to hear her plea, much less answer. She had to find a way to gather her wits, to discover what she really was made of, to face her situation, and go forward to accomplish—

"What?" she whispered into the fragrant mattress. "What is it I really must do?"

No voice came to answer her question, but a tiny glimmer of gumption flickered to light deep inside her. She had wanted to be on her own. This was her chance to see what she could accomplish through her own strength and wit.

She knew herself well enough to know she was no ninny, no simpering, silly girl. True, she took pride in making the most of the looks she'd been blessed with at birth, and she always looked on the best side of everything, but that didn't mean she was an utter fool. She did have the ability to learn, as she'd told Mr. Lowery, and she'd always been told her stubborn—er...her determination was more than ample.

Just who did Mr. Lowery think he was? He'd ordered her

to work for him as though she were his employee. He'd cast down his challenge, certain she would fail, as his expression had revealed. The more she thought about it, the angrier she grew. And the more disgusted she became with the notion of possible failure.

No.

She refused.

She would not fail.

Not Emma Marguerite Crowell.

Hmph. She'd show Peter Lowery what she was made of.

At the heels of that thought a traitorous part of her began to weaken. She stood and squared her shoulders, refusing to entertain even the slightest element of feebleness. Goodness, if she was strong enough to be known as stubborn—er...determined by those who knew her best, then she must, of course, also be strong enough to succeed at just about anything she tried.

And she'd been challenged to try to run this...this... could she call it a house? No, surely not. A cabin made more sense. Or maybe it was nothing more than a rustic camp.

"Bah!" What did it matter what one called it? She only knew people lived here, including her for a number of months, and she needed to somehow run it. For her own sake—her very sanity—she had to turn it into a proper home. She knew what a proper home was. She would model her efforts after Aunt Sophia's lovely, welcoming home in Denver. She could also model them after Papa's and her own home in Portland. Ophelia knew how to make one feel at ease, and she'd succeeded there. Emma's success, of course, would depend on how much this place could be improved.

She swatted her cheeks dry of the last trails of the tears she had shed. Mr. Lowery had said his wife had books to teach the reader how to run a proper kitchen, and, one would hope, a home. With that kind of guidance, at least half of her job was already done. All she had to do now was...

"Hm...find the books."

Emma approached the trunk. She felt uncomfortable about the prospect of going through another woman's belongings. What would Mrs. Lowery say when she learned Emma had rummaged through them?

A shimmer of unease ran through her. Well, she supposed she couldn't help it. The woman's own husband had told Emma to do so. Taking a deep breath, she dropped down to her knees and opened the trunk.

"Tie 'em up?" Colley asked.

"You heard me," Peter answered. "Can't have a pair of rustlers loose around the flock. They'll have to get used to being prisoners. That's what they'll be for a good, long while after I take them down to Adam Blair in the fall."

Shotgun in hand, Colley swept the glaring Sawyer and distressed Ned with a skeptical stare. "I dunno about that tying-up part, boss. It's a long, long time 'fore fall gets here."

"Exactly. That's why keeping them subdued and tied good and hard is the best thing to do. I don't have the time to stand watch and keep a gun on them, and neither do you. You, Wade, and I already have too much work to do to waste even an hour watching these two."

"But they can still 'scape into the woods!" Robby cried,

excitement sparkling in his eyes. "They can run without their hands, you know, King Peter—er...Papa."

Peter couldn't avoid the shot of irritation that ran through him at yet more evidence of his son's love of make-believe. And Robby knew it. The boy blushed. But then, he went on.

"And then..." he frowned furiously, thinking. He crossed his arms and clamped his lips tight for all of a moment. A defiant glare and the tilt of his chin spoke volumes. "Then you, King Peter, and your faithful knight, Sir...er...Lady—um, no. Your faithful knight, Colley, will have to set off on a quest to catch them and bring them back. Can I go with you on the quest?"

Peter bit back the scolding that bubbled to his lips. Instead, he focused on the boy's initial statement. "Robby's got a good point, Colley. Make sure you and Wade tie up their feet, too. Can't have them up and walking away." He turned to his son. "No one will be setting off after these two. We're going to make sure they stay put."

"What about her?" Colley asked, eyes narrowed, free thumb jabbing toward the cabin. "You ain't gonna tell me you want to tie her up, are you? Cuz I won't tie up a lady."

Peter shook his head. "You won't have to. We're awful shorthanded as it is, and her cooking, cleaning, and doing the wash ought to help us a good deal. Plus she and Robby seem to have a lot in common. That'll help some, too."

Colley made a face, wreathing her features with more wrinkles than a body might think possible. "Ya really think she can do any of them things?"

"No. But she can read, and Adele's housekeeping books are in that old trunk. She'll learn."

He hoped.

The skepticism on Colley's face gave Peter pause. Did Miss Crowell have it in her to do what was needed? She looked as though she hadn't done a single productive thing in her whole life.

Looking beautiful wasn't productive. Pleasant? Yes. Enjoyable to see? Of course. Appealing to any man? So long as he wasn't blind...he couldn't help but notice her appeal. But deep red hair and sparkling green eyes on their own did no one any good. Neither did a woman dressed in lace and velvet. Or her love of old stories and such silliness.

Surely, Miss Crowell wouldn't spend all day entertaining Robby's penchant for flights of fancy. Peter didn't have the heart to take the book from his son, since it had been Adele's and he cherished it, especially for that reason. He did still miss his mother, even though as time drew out, Peter knew the boy's memories of her continued to blur.

Still, he feared Robby might resemble his mother more than him in nature. Adele's bookish bent had left her unprepared for the harsh realities of life on a sheep ranch.

Robby needed strength and know-how to carry on Peter's legacy.

He watched as Colley marched the two scoundrels to the rustic bunkhouse, Wade at her side. He couldn't let a pathetic pair of thieves ruin all the work he'd done since coming West. A glance at Robby, using his branch to "fence" with a tree not five yards away, reaffirmed his conviction.

He'd fought long and hard to build something of value to leave behind. As the only son in a family of five, Peter's father had inherited the family farm in Ohio, but when the War

Between the States broke out, he'd felt compelled to join the Union Army and fight for what he'd known was right. Peter remembered his father's two rare furloughs from the front line, when the older man spent much of his time in a silent haze, deep in thought. It had been especially heartrending when Captain Lowery died a few months before General Lee surrendered to General Grant at Appomattox Court House. It had never felt fair.

By that point, Peter's oldest brother, Stu, had worked the farm for years, carrying far more responsibility than most youths his age did. Their mother had worked just as hard as Stu, and while doing so, she'd instilled in all four boys the certainty of her love, respect for discipline, and appreciation for industriousness.

Peter had known the farm would provide well for Stu, their brother, Tom, two years older than Peter, and their families. Brett, the youngest Lowery boy, had always been studious and devoted to the Lord. He'd followed God's call into the ministry, and now led a growing congregation in Cleveland. But Peter had little future back home.

"*En garde!*" Robby leaped with his "sword" in hand to jab at an imaginary enemy.

Yes, Peter feared the draw that books and make-believe had for his son. Those things, while perfectly fine on their own, wouldn't do the boy a whole lot of good here on this rugged land. They certainly hadn't helped his mother. He tugged his hat off and ran a rough hand through his hair.

His dream had cost Adele her life. He couldn't, in any way at all, let her death be for a failure.

Neither drought nor grasshoppers, outlaws nor an addle-brained society belle, draped in miles of velvet frosted with lace frou-frou, as Adele used to call that sort of feminine trimming, would derail him.

He wouldn't let them.

Mr. Lowery's directions clear in her mind, Emma forced herself to overcome her reluctance and opened Mrs. Lowery's trunk. It was a plain travel storage container rather than the elegant, well-appointed case Papa had given Emma not so long ago, with all its specialty compartments and lovely dividers for her various necessities. This one was just a simple rectangular space within leather-covered wooden sides, filled with someone else's . . . things.

She found a number of books at the top, well-worn and clearly important to the rancher's wife. Robby had returned *Le Morte D'Arthur* to the trunk when his father had put an end to their reading—and napping—time, and now, she reached for that one first. Curiosity burning in her, Emma pulled out the other books, one by one. First, she brought out a lovely Bible, covered in rich black leather, its edges softened by much handling. On the cover, in embellished script, the name Adele B. Lowery had been embossed.

Odd. A Bible didn't strike Emma as something a woman would leave behind at her husband's summer camp. At least, not if the woman read it as often as the wear on the leather cover seemed to suggest.

As Emma lifted it, the Good Book fell open, and she noticed a number of notes on the margins written in graceful script. That discovery made her slam the book shut, feeling as though she'd trespassed on the other woman's most private thoughts. She would simply have to apologize once they met. She imagined that wouldn't happen until the fall.

She set the Bible to a side, and then dove back into the trunk. The next book she withdrew was *The Frugal House-wife*. She didn't much think she'd have to worry about being frugal, seeing as there was nothing but frugality around the camp. She set that one next to Mrs. Lowery's Scriptures.

Following that book, she brought out *Miss Leslie's Directions for Cookery.* That one might help, since the rancher had made clear he expected her to run the kitchen. Next came something perhaps more promising, *The Housekeeper's Encyclopedia.* While she didn't know a thing about cooking or cleaning or running a home, a housekeeper generally did. The encyclopedia might help.

The last book she found was one that nearly brought her to tears. A copy of *Mrs. Beeton's Book of Household Management* always sat within Ophelia's reach at home in Portland. If only Ophelia were near enough to teach Emma now...

Emma hugged the book close, blinked at the tears scalding her eyes, and rocked herself in place, on the floor, with knees drawn close to her body. While she was glad to have found a treasure trove of useful books, there was nothing like an excellent teacher at a student's side.

She would have no such luxury.

But before she could give in to self-pity, she squared her shoulders and returned to the trunk. A lovely, hand-made white lace shawl covered a few other items. She pulled out the exquisite piece, carefully laid it across her lap, unwilling to set it on the rough floorboards, and another book slipped out as she did so. She bent to pick it up, but when she read the notation inside the cover, she yanked her hand back as though it had been stung by a bee.

JOURNAL

That went too far. Emma couldn't imagine violating another woman's innermost self in such a direct way. She gingerly picked up the slender tome and slipped it back into the trunk, tucking it down against one wooden side. Next she placed the Bible back inside, followed by the other volumes. She did keep Mrs. Beeton's tome out. If it had been good enough for Ophelia, then it was certainly good enough for Emma.

"I'm at your service, Lady Emma!" Robby cried from the door to the cabin, startling her.

She scrambled up, heart pounding, still clutching the *Mrs. Beeton's* to her chest, and stared at the boy. "Goodness gracious, Sir Robby! You must not frighten a body by coming up behind them like that. Such a startle might give me the vapors. Give a lady a fair warning first, please."

The smug smile on his childish face told Emma the boy knew exactly what he'd done and was pleased with himself. An innocent child's prank, but goodness, it had affected her. Not that she'd ever had the vapors, but that possibility always existed.

"Oh," Robby said, his voice serious. "You have Mama's book. She used to read it all the time."

His mother used to read it all the time, hm? And Emma had found the worn Bible inside the dusty trunk, too. But she'd seen no sign of the woman other than Mrs. Lowery's rocking chair and the trunk. What did all that mean? Did she not need any of that wherever she was? She had others? Odd, indeed.

And it gnawed at Emma's curiosity.

"Sir Robby," she started, her voice warm and gentle but resolute, "where is your mama?"

The slight smile melted right off the boy's face. He lowered his gaze and shifted from foot to foot. His shoulders slumped.

Oh, dear. Something was wrong here. And she'd gone and stirred it up. But now, it couldn't be helped. She had to finish what she'd started.

In a handful of hurried steps, she came to Robby's side. When he wouldn't look up at her, Emma knelt, and she saw the tears on his cheeks. Her heart squeezed at the misery the boy displayed, especially since it hadn't been her intention to upset him.

She curved a finger under his chin and lifted his face so he couldn't avoid meeting her gaze. "Please tell me what's wrong."

A deep, shuddering breath ran through him, and Emma felt it in that minor, tender contact between them. Through the gleaming wetness in his eyes, he met her gaze.

"Mama's with the angels now."

"Oh, Robby…" She opened her arms, letting the book fall to the floor, and the boy slipped into her embrace. Emma's eyes welled up, too.

At first, she just held him with a light touch. His tears dampened the fabric of her blouse as he stood stiff while he continued to weep. But then a deep, rough sob wracked him, and he melted into her clasp. A storm of sobs followed that first painful one, and he cried in despondent anguish.

Emma couldn't help but join him. She wept for the grieving child she held, as well as for the grief-stricken girl she'd been after her own mother's death. She knew only too well how Robby felt. She wept for her situation, too, the limitless loneliness she'd felt since she realized she'd been abandoned. She wept for her uncertain future, and she even wept for the helplessness of her present.

To her amazement, she realized she also wept for Mr. Lowery, whom she scarcely knew. The loss of his wife explained to a certain degree his aloofness and unyielding stance. His struggle was as great as Robby's was and hers had been, even though somewhat different. A mother and a wife represented two different kinds of loss.

No wonder he refused to lose his ranch. He'd already lost much.

The situation also explained Robby's unexpected affinity to a book like Sir Thomas Malory's. Since it had belonged to his mother, and he said she'd read it to him regularly, it represented his strongest tie to the memory of the woman who clearly had loved him.

Emma sat after a bit, drawing Robby onto her lap. The boy curled up, and little by little his sobs diminished until they trembled to a stop. She glanced down, saw he'd cried himself to sleep, and swept the curling lock of brown hair off his forehead. As she held him, her heart felt too large for her body to contain, filled with emotion for the child, and she realized this moment would never leave her memory. Neither would her growing feelings for the youngster.

Pippa padded over to them, crept up into Robby's lap, and snuggled close to the boy.

It seemed to Emma she might be able to help here at the camp in more ways than one. Robby needed his mama, and while Emma wasn't equal to that responsibility, she certainly knew she could comfort, care for, and help the boy in ways no man, not even a father, could. Or perhaps would, since Mr. Lowery was quite consumed by the need to earn a livelihood.

Ophelia had often told her that nothing happened to folks for no reason at all. As odd as it might be, perhaps Emma had been left behind by the carriage for the sake of this child.

She sighed. Odd indeed.

Before Robby could awaken, she rose, cradled him close, surprised at how small he really was, and carried him to the bunk. There, she tucked him under the blanket and marveled at the wave of tenderness that swept over her. If this could happen to her, all but a complete stranger, simply by their shared grief, what might it be like for a mother to love a child? The mere thought moved her to tears again.

Chapter 7

As she worked to compose herself, Emma watched Robby sleep for a handful of minutes. Moments later, to help set aside her melancholy, she squared her shoulders and strode to where she'd left *Mrs. Beeton's*. She picked up the substantial tome and marched to the table, where she drew out one of the two chairs, and then sat to study for her newest assignment.

As she read, Emma didn't know whether to laugh or cry. Some of the material, since she was at a remote camp partway up an uncivilized mountain, was ludicrous. The chapter on dinners and dining included lists of dishes the likes of which she had enjoyed only at the most elegant of events in London or New York. *Mrs. Beeton* listed first courses, entrées, second and even third courses. And those menus were for dinners of twelve and up to eighteen guests. One summer dinner went so far as to suggest a menu that featured salmon and lobster sauce, perch and Dutch sauce, stewed veal and peas, lamb cutlets and cucumbers, haunch of venison, boiled fowls à la

Béchamel, braised ham, roast ducks, lobster salad, a soup, vegetables, and no fewer than five different scrumptious desserts. At one meal, at that.

Emma's mouth watered at just the idea, but she understood the absurdity of giving any of those possibilities the slightest thought here on Mr. Lowery's mountain.

Then she found a section entitled Domestic Servants. Ha! It appeared she, Emma Crowell, would be the camp's one and only domestic servant. On the other hand, she suspected the chapter on the rearing, management, and diseases of infancy and childhood might come in handy, certainly in dealing with Robby, to the best of her ability.

She continued to peruse the book until her stomach growled. Oh, dear.

She'd spent such a good, long while reading that she'd failed to keep track of time. Since she'd been charged with managing the kitchen, she supposed she needed food for an evening meal to satisfy her, Robby, Colley, and the hungry men. A quick check of her charming, flower-engraved silver pocket watch told her all she needed to know. The men would soon return and would want a hot meal on the table right away. Even if she knew nothing about preparing one. Even after she'd read bits and spots of *Mrs. Beeton*. Anxiety struck.

She tamped down the feeling. Time had come to become acquainted with the lean-to at the back of the cabin, where, after their noon meal, Colley had told her Mr. Lowery stored the camp's food supplies. The gruff but kind ranch manager had said Emma would find plenty there, since they'd just come up to the mountain meadow for the summer season, and she should be able to prepare proper meals. She'd said jars of meats, cans of vegetables, dried hams and beef, as well as a generous supply of preserved eggs, would offer sufficient variety, too.

She didn't know how to prepare any of that, but Mrs. Beeton's fat, heavy book seemed to offer directions for just about anything anyone might want to eat. And they were detailed directions, to be certain. Decision made, she attached Pippa's rope to the dog and hurried to the door. As she opened it, she heard the rustle of movement behind her.

"Where you going?" Robby asked in a sleepy voice.

"To find something to make for supper."

"Can I come with you, Lady Emma?"

"Of course, Sir Robby. Maybe you can tell me what you'd like to eat while we look through the supplies."

He scrambled out of bed, stomped into his boots, and trotted by her side as she rounded the cabin. "I really, really like chicken and biscuits and beans," he said, his chatter a welcome respite from the constant, smothering silence of the woods. "'Specially when the beans have lots and lots of 'lasses. Mmm..."

She didn't remember having eaten beans with molasses before, but rather with onions and butter, but she supposed one could prepare things in a multitude of different ways. As she'd glanced through the different sections of Mrs. Beeton's book, she thought she'd seen something about beans taking ten to fifteen minutes to cook, which would be most helpful to her, since she didn't want to be late with the meal. She hoped to find the beans in the lean-to without much searching.

"We might be able to have beans," she told Robby, "but I don't know about the chicken. I don't see chickens here in the yard, and I wouldn't know what to do with one even if you did have them."

"Colley does know. She takes the chickens—they make lots and lots and lots of noise—and then she twists the heads all the way around. The necks break and...well, that's it." Ghoulish humor brightened his expression. "I reckon you can cook 'em up, then."

The notion of twisting a chicken's head until it broke turned Emma's stomach. She couldn't see where any amount of hunger would ever force her to reach that desperate decision. She hoped Mr. Lowery didn't expect her to do...that to a poor, innocent, undeserving bird. No matter how much she enjoyed the lush flavor of roasted chicken.

"Yes, well," she said. "We can do without having to resort to such a distasteful action just for a meal, right? I'm sure we'll find some other nice thing to eat in the shed."

When her eyes adjusted to the darkness, she realized the lean-to was even more rustic than the cabin, perhaps closer to flimsy and rickety. The small structure had a packed, swept dirt floor, and multiple shelves lined three of the walls, like the section of the cabin closest to the fireplace. All the shelves sagged with jars and cans of food. Stacked at the very back, Emma saw large sacks labeled "coffee," "flour," "sugar," and "beans." Some unidentified wooden barrels and a pair of tall crocks stood in the farthest corner. A number of stout tins nearby had white labels that identified their contents as lard.

More of those neat paper labels with not-as-neat writing told which of the many glass jars contained what preserved meats, while the many tins of vegetables bore bright-colored wrappers. In seconds, Emma found a supply of jarred chicken meat.

"Look, Robby! Here's your chicken. We're partway to a supper."

"C'mere, then," the boy said, grinning. "Let's get beans from the sack. Colley keeps a jar of 'lasses in the kitchen. One of flour, too. For the biscuits, you know."

Ah...he meant mealy haricot-type beans, rather than the green broad bean variety, of which she could see many tins. On the basis of what she recalled from skimming through the *Mrs. Beeton*, Emma was willing to cook the beans—for fifteen or so minutes, as she remembered. She handed Pippa's rope to Robby with strict instructions to hang on tight to the dog, hurried back to the cabin, picked up a bowl for the beans, and returned to scoop out a good amount for supper.

Inside again, Pippa was happy to jump up onto the bunk and curl up on the pillow as soon as Emma freed her from the rope. Comfortable in her soft perch, the pup watched every bit of activity, her dark eyes fixed on Robby. Robby, however, paid poor Pippa no attention. He wouldn't leave Emma's side. Not that she really wanted him there; she didn't want him to witness any disaster she might stir up. True, she didn't plan to create a disaster, but trouble could always happen. And often did.

Emma spread everything out on the table.

"Remember the flour for the biscuits," Robby said.

She did indeed, but she had already begun to feel overwhelmed. "One thing at a time, please, don't you think? Perhaps I should put the chicken to cook first. And then we could place the beans over the fire."

He nodded and smiled. "Fine. And then I can help you stir things with my wooden spoon, right? I have a special one, and Colley lets me do that when she's making supper."

As far as Emma could see, that wouldn't be too much trouble. "I'm glad you want to help. But we do have to beware of that fire, you understand. How about if you fetch me a good pan for this chicken first? I brought in two large jars, since we have four hungry men, Colley, and the two of us to feed."

She had no idea how much a man might eat, but the individual jars, while stuffed full, didn't seem to have too much for six adults and Robby. At least, it didn't seem too much to her inexperienced eye. Since she couldn't guess on quantities, Emma decided to make a large batch of beans and a good stack of biscuits to make sure the meal would satisfy all those appetites. She hoped it all turned out simply delightful. Edible would do fine, as well.

Her stomach growled.

Robby giggled. "You're hungry, too, Lady Emma!"

"Oh, yes. And from what you said, I gather you're ready to eat, aren't you?"

The boy handed her a navy-blue enameled kettlelike pan with white speckles, deep and with a thick-wire handle attached from side to side. Then he rubbed his belly. "Mm-hm."

Emma caught her breath and studied the two jars of preserved meat. Tin lids covered the wide mouths, secured to the glass containers with screw-on zinc caps. She twisted off the first one...and confronted the tight seal of the flat metal part. It clung to the glass with a stubborn strength she hadn't expected. She couldn't pull it off, even after the pads of her fingers had turned red from her efforts.

"I need to check something in your mama's book," she told Robby, as she hurried to the table where *Mrs. Beeton* lay waiting—she hoped—to provide guidance, pan and jars clutched tight. How was she supposed to open the container without breaking it and spilling everything if the lid didn't yield? Was there a special trick to it?

But when she rifled through the book, nothing jumped out at her to offer the information she wanted. She suspected those other women she'd thought about earlier, the ones who hadn't been blessed with the kind of life Papa had provided for her, would know how to conquer the obstinate jar. She'd never felt so ignorant in her life.

"Lady Emma?" Robby asked. "What's wrong?"

"Um...I'm looking for something—"

"But what about the chicken? I'm hungry."

Straight from "the lips of babes and sucklings..." She needed to open the jars.

Closing *Mrs. Beeton*, she confronted her task again. This time, she tried to pry off the lids with her fingernails, only for one to surrender before the lid. She turned the container around and around, holding it up for a better look.

As she studied the container, it made a long, slow sucking sound and sticky liquid oozed out from between the tin and the glass, right onto her hands. "Oh-oh-oh! I—it just—oh, dear!"

The contents continued the thick seepage as Robby giggled again. Emma held the jar over the enamel pan. A second later, the resistant lid gave way. All the contents plopped down. Through her fingers.

The boy laughed out loud. His chortles and peals of

laughter were so cheery that they were almost worth Emma's embarrassment and discomfort. Almost.

She still had a lid to fish out of the gelatinous globs in the pan. And she needed to wash her hands. The pinkish-beige stuff didn't look like any chicken she'd ever eaten. She hoped its appearance improved with cooking.

"Lady Emma! That was so funny! Your face ... the chicken surprised you, didn't it?"

And how. "It did, Sir Robby, I must confess."

"You going to do it again?"

Heaven forbid. "I hope not. Let's see how this other jar goes."

She hastily rinsed her hands in the water Colley had poured into a pitcher for her earlier in the morning, when Emma had wanted to wash up a bit. With a touch more skill this second time around, she used a knife to fight off the tight, sealed lid. Nothing, however, could have stopped a repeat of the sucking sound followed by the plop into the pan.

It sent Robby into another fit of mirth.

Spoon in hand, she tried to stir the mess, but gave up her efforts when she realized nothing much would help break up the blobs and lumps. Except perhaps the actual cooking.

She hoped.

Cooking. Hm ... she glanced at the hearth. An iron rod ran across the very front of the opening, with S-shaped iron hooks hanging from the rod. She supposed that was how Colley hung kettles over the coals, but didn't know if they would do anything for the chicken, since the coals were covered with a white powdery haze and didn't feel particularly fiery. On the other hand, the hearth did still put out heat, even this much later. Colley had lit it in the morning, cooked breakfast on the strange, three-legged, flat pan-topped iron…thing, and left the coals to continue to warm the cabin. Emma had appreciated the extra warmth, since spring mornings seemed to come in chilly, and days still ended in cold nights up on these mountains.

With hope in her heart, she hooked the handle of her kettlelike pan on one of the S hooks.

She gave her hands a sweeping clap, a sense of accomplishment within her. "There! Now on to the beans."

"I put them right here, Lady Emma." The boy pointed at the bowl on the table. "And the 'lasses are up there"—he indicated the second shelf—"plus the flour for the biscuits, too."

She gathered the two containers and brought them to the table. Thank goodness for Robby. She'd be lost without him. "What about a pan for the beans? What does Colley use?"

The boy's brows drew close as he concentrated. "Not sure, milady. Sometimes I seen her—"

"I've seen her," she corrected.

"Good," Robby answered. "Then you know."

Emma chuckled. "No, no. That's not what I meant. Your papa has said I should help you speak properly, and I was just correcting you. The right way to say that is to say 'Sometimes I've seen her,' not 'Sometimes I seen her.'"

"Really? Sounds the same to me."

"There's a difference. I've seen her means that you have seen her. 'I've' is short for 'I have.'"

He shrugged. "All right, then. I have seen her use two different pans to make beans. Sometimes she uses a big, deep pan with a heavy lid, but sometimes she uses the spider."

Robby pointed at the flat pan on three legs where Colley had cooked breakfast. So it was called a spider. Emma supposed the three legs looked a bit like the bug itself, although the contraption did lack five additional legs. Regardless, she would use it, since it already stood in a corner of the hearth, close enough to the coals that it should prove simple enough to scoot it over the ones mounded higher toward the center. She imagined more coals meant more heat, and the beans should cook quicker with more heat. That way, she could have the meal ready to serve the men as soon as they walked in the door.

Emma picked up her bowl of beans and walked to the spider. She tipped the crock to pour them out, and the clanking of the hard beans against the iron rang out in the room. When she figured she had enough in the pan, since the bowl had been fairly full, she returned to the table again. Time for the 'lasses, as Robby called the sweetener.

After she added a large quantity of the thick, strong-scented dark syrup to the beans, she put that jar away, and returned to the hearth, a long-handled scoop in hand. A deep, black kettle full of hot water gave off wisps of steam where it hung at one end of the iron rod across the fireplace. Filling her scoop a couple of times, Emma transferred sufficient water to the spider to make sure the molasses dissolved and the liquid covered the beans.

After another good stir, she returned to *Mrs. Beeton* to see if she could solve the mystery of turning flour into something as tender and flaky as a biscuit.

"Whatcha doing?" Robby asked, perched on a stool across the table from where she sat.

"Trying to learn about biscuits."

"Biscuits? In Mama's book?"

"It's a book about cookery."

"Oh." He scratched his head. "Colley don't—"

"Doesn't."

He smiled. "Doesn't. Colley doesn't use a book to make biscuits. She uses flour and water and salt and that thick, white stuff in the tin pail and...and..." He frowned. "Can't 'member what else she might could use."

It was good enough for Emma. So far, the boy hadn't steered her wrong. "Well, then, shall we gather our ingredients here on the table, Sir Robby?"

She grabbed the largest bowl off the shelf, piled in the salt crock, snagged the pail of lard from where it sat close to the door, and returned to the table. "We can start by mixing these."

The flour whooshed up into a puffy cloud when she dumped it into the thick, yellow earthenware bowl. She coughed as it tickled her throat. "Oh, my goodness!"

Robby laughed again. "Lady Emma! You're so funny."

"I must admit, I've never aspired to be funny, Sir Robby, but if it's to your pleasure, then I'm happy to oblige."

"And you talk some funny, too."

"We'll fix that opinion as we go along," she said. "You'll see."

He plunked his elbows on the table, quite content to watch her efforts.

Salt. Hm...biscuits needed salt. How much? As she went to check *Mrs. Beeton*, her stomach growled again. Robby covered his mouth with both hands to keep from laughing out loud. But his eyes twinkled above his fingers.

"Yes, Sir Robby, I'm hungry. Aren't you?"

He nodded, hands fixed in place.

Emma figured it might be a good idea to check her pocket watch. It was close to five in the afternoon, and she suspected the men wouldn't be gone too much longer. Her research in Mrs. Beeton's book would have to wait.

She dipped a hand in the gray crock full of salt and poured a quantity of the seasoning into the palm of her hand. Most folks liked salt. Filling the well in the center of her hand gave her a good mound. She dumped it into the flour.

For the lard, she used a large wooden spoon to measure out a big lump of the white stuff, which plopped into the middle of the dry flour, creating another poof. Then, armed with her trusty water scoop, she retrieved some from the hot kettle at the hearth, poured it into her bowl, and began to stir.

The resulting substance was thick and hard to mix. At first, it felt crumbly and stiff. Emma added water. Then it seemed thin. She poured more flour into the bowl. Bit by bit, she came up with something that looked possible to her. The whole time, Robby kept up his chatter.

Emma listened with less than half her attention. Her mind was on her next step. What would she use to form the biscuits? How did one bake them? She'd seen Ophelia bake before, but that was on the family's huge black Excelsior iron stove with its oven door on the front. Here, on a hearth, she saw no logical substitute for the oven.

Not that she would have known what to do once she put pats of the blended fat, water, and flour into an oven, had she had one available. And she really hadn't had anywhere near enough time to search *Mrs. Beeton* for instructions.

When her hands were sticky with chunks of dough, when the table was snowed under a flurry of flour, when the front of her ruined skirt and the wilted lace of her blouse were not only floured, but also smeared with smudges of the lard, Colley marched in. The door banged shut. "Afternoon, Miss Emma—"

Her footsteps came to a complete halt.

Robby's chatter died.

Emma's middle knotted, and her hands shook. She didn't speak.

Colley did. "What in the name of goat's gizzards happened here?"

Emma, certain the best way to handle this kind of situation was to present a strong, confident stance, stiffened her back, squared her shoulders, tipped up her chin, and gave Colley a brilliant smile. "I've been making supper."

"She made chicken and beans, and now she's making biscuits."

"Looks to this body like she's made a mess more'n anything else." Colley marched to the table, her booted steps clomping loudly in the small room and, after dragging off her hat, peered into the bowl. "What in thunder is this, Miss Emma?"

Proud of her hard work, Emma smiled again. "As Robby just informed you, it's the biscuits."

Colley's pewter-toned brows rose to almost her hairline. She studied the unevenly mixed ingredients, and then glanced at Robby, who nodded with great enthusiasm. "You don't say."

Robby nodded even more. "An' I helped Lady Emma, Colley. We made supper together."

The ranch manager rubbed the back of her neck. "Well, Miss Emma, I'm feeling a mite starved, I must confess," she said. "Let me give you a hand with them biscuits and dishin' up. The boss is bringing in them two rustlers. Him and Wade had to untie their feet so's they could walk on over from the bunkhouse, and they'll all be right hungry."

It struck Emma as unusual to have the outlaws tied by the foot, but she wasn't about to argue. She still had the biscuits to bake. "Oh, yes, Mrs. Colley, what do I do to bake those biscuits? I see you don't have a proper cook stove anywhere."

The ranch manager chuckled. "See that there tin contraption over next to the fireplace? That's a tin kitchen. It's an old-fangled thing a body uses to bake when she don't have herself a cook stove. Makes right fine biscuits, too, missy. You'll see. Let me have that dough you made up there."

Relieved, Emma surrendered the bowl. She couldn't wait to wash up and get the sticky bits off her fingers. She went to the pitcher and poured water into the wash basin. She rubbed her fingers over and over again, and with a bit of determination, plus a cake of plain, cream-colored soap, the dough finally melted off.

"Wha...Miss Emma!" Colley cried. "What is this?"

She spun around, a length of cotton toweling in her hands. Just then, the door opened again and Wade strode in, followed by the two outlaws and Mr. Lowery. Her gaze flew back and forth between the newcomers and Colley, who stood at the hearth, staring at the beans in the spider. She scooped up a spoonful then let the beans drop back down to the pan, the round pebbles slithering off the wooden bowl of the spoon and plopping into the liquid with glugging sounds.

It didn't look anything like any beans she'd ever eaten.

"Miss Crowell?" Mr. Lowery asked, frowning. "Do you not have our supper ready yet?"

She met the rancher's gaze. "The chicken should be done. And the beans . . . well, they must be about to be ready anytime soon. They've been cooking for a while now, and the cookery book I used said beans generally take between ten and fifteen minutes to cook."

"What?" Mr. Lowery said.

This time, Colley's eyebrows disappeared under the hair that had loosened around her forehead. "It couldn't have!"

Sawyer guffawed.

Ned looked puzzled.

Emma's middle quaked. Something had gone dreadfully wrong. And she knew it began with the beans that looked anything but right.

Colley set the spoon down on a nearby shelf. She approached Emma, concern on her mature features. "You weren't playin' pretend when you told the boss here you didn't know how to cook, now, were you?"

"Why would you think I'd do something so silly as pretend?" she asked.

Colley tipped her head, as though mystified by her own foolishness. "I figured all women knew how to go 'bout fixin' something simple to eat. I reckon I was wrong."

"What about our supper?" Mr. Lowery asked in a tight voice.

Emma didn't dare look at him. He sounded cross. And he hadn't struck her as especially cheery even once since they'd met.

"Ahem!" Colley cleared her throat as she gave the beans

yet another stir. "Looks like I'm going to have to cook these down real low, all the way overnight. Hate to throw this much good food away, otherwise."

"What?" Mr. Lowery sounded horrified. "We can't afford to throw out food. What has she done?"

Emma went on the defense. "I only—"

"Well, Pete," the older woman started, pouring the beans into a huge black kettle on short, nubby legs. "She says she did tell ya she didn't cook. Cain't fault a body for tellin' ya the truth."

Emma gave Colley a grateful smile.

"Yes, but I did tell her where she could find the information she would need."

Colley barked out a laugh. "Them's books, Pete. Ain't the same's knowing what you're doing, nor nothing like having someone with you who does to show you how. I reckon a body can learn from them books of Miss Adele's just fine, but that might could take a whole lot a time. Not just one day or so."

"I don't recall where sitting around and reading Adele's books is part of earning her keep," Mr. Lowery countered, crossing his arms, brow furrowed. "It's clear to anyone who's got eyes that those beans are nowhere near where anyone's going to be eating them. Maybe tomorrow, but sure and it won't be tonight. And we all still need supper."

"True enough," Colley answered. "I'm going to figger what I can make do with, and come up with something tasty—"

"Filling," the rancher cut in. "Gotta fill a number of bellies here, Colley. Worry about tasty later."

Robby's dismay radiated from his every feature. "Papa!"

"We can do both, son," Colley said in a conciliatory tone. "Let me make us a mess of gravy for that canned chicken Miss Emma's been cooking, and see what the good Lord and I can do to help this doughy batter turn into biscuits." She turned to Emma. "How's it sound to ya if you help me put this meal on the table for us? You can do some watching. Reckon that should make it some easier next time you try your hand at a meal."

"You mean tomorrow, Colley, right?" Mr. Lowery said in a voice as inflexible as the iron bar across the front of the fireplace. "You have shearing to do, and those two ewes are about to birth their lambs any moment now. Can't be having you hold her hand through the making of every meal."

Dread swam in Emma's middle. He wasn't about to ease up on his decision, was he?

Colley arched a brow. "Let's see how we get us through tonight's supper, now, Pete. My belly's cozyin' right up to my backbone, it's so empty, an' I reckon yours might could be, too. Tomorrow's time enough for us to take care of tomorrow."

While Colley's description of her hunger struck Emma as a tad inappropriate, Emma had to fight to stifle her nervous laugh. The ranch manager had described her own appetite to perfection.

"How can I help you?" she asked Colley.

"Seein' as how I figger anybody might could think of the green, string kinda beans 'stead of the regular kind when looking quick through some book, how's about you fetch us a couple of cans of 'em from the shed?"

Emma nodded and scurried to the door, more than eager to redeem herself. Anybody could fetch a can...or two.

But when she returned, she could hear Colley's and Mr. Lowery's agitated voices, even before she opened the cabin door.

"Gotta tell ya, Pete, this ain't one bit like the man I know you to be. Never known ya to be cruel, and holding that little girl to them kinda rules ain't all that kind. Not her fault she ain't never lived on a ranch, you know."

Gratitude etched a slight smile on Emma's lips.

"Haven't said it's her fault, Colley," the rancher answered. "But I can't risk Robby's future on account of a silly woman who can't even figure the basic difference between two kinds of beans. She's here now, and it's time for her to leave behind the kind of life that never did make any sense even back where she came from. Time to be good for more than her fancy clothes, storybooks, and, I suspect with good reason, breaking foolish men's hearts with her silliness."

Emma gasped. Why . . . he was accusing her of the same sort of thing a number of the jealous girls and their mamas did back in London and Denver. How dare he? He didn't know her one bit.

Then Colley answered. "Miss Emma ain't Adele, Pete."

"I know that better than anyone." Mr. Lowery's voice came out rough and harsh. "Looks to me like she's likely much worse. She's the kind who expects everything done for her. She can't even do half of what Adele could. My wife couldn't handle the land, but she did run a house—well, too. And I know you remember her cooking. Never once did you or I have any kind of complaint. You just saw Miss Emma Crowell can't do that, even with Adele's cookery books to help."

"Time, Pete. Time's what she'd be needing."

"Time and money are the two things I don't have, Colley. There's too much at stake here. What good does a silly girl like that do a man like me? She could cost me everything I've worked for. Miss Crowell strikes me as utterly useless, and I can't carry useless out here. She's really going to have to come up with the what-for and work like you, Wade, and me. Nothing else will do."

Chapter 8

By the time she sat at the table for supper, Emma had no appetite. Eating became a battle. Tears burned her eyes, blurring her view of whatever Colley had concocted out of Emma's unsuccessful efforts and put on everyone's plate. The knot in her throat blocked every bite she tried to swallow.

To hear someone discount her as utterly useless had struck a devastating blow. This was the second time Mr. Lowery had spoken so poorly of her without knowing her especially well. Was that how everyone saw her? All those ladies in London and Denver who'd snubbed her? Was that the reason they'd showed no willingness to befriend her? Had Emma merely fooled herself when she'd thought they were all consumed with envy?

When she managed to rein in her ragged emotions, she noticed the strained air in the cabin. The room struck her as filled with a tension she'd never experienced before. Pleasant conversation and happy laughter had accompanied the meals she'd shared with family and friends—no, no, no! From what Mr. Lowery had said, she now had to view those people as mere acquaintances.

Emma had no friends.

A pang close to bitterness speared through her.

If anything, she felt lonelier than before.

None of the others showed even the slightest interest in her, so she soldiered on, trying to eat the food that for the most part refused to go down. After a bit, however, she began to register some of what was going on. Robby's voice came through the fog that had surrounded her, and the constant stream of his typical chatter made her smile. She'd become quite familiar with his tendency toward constant conversation during the afternoon they'd just spent together.

Now, the little boy seemed intent on garnering his father's attention. Unfortunately, his father appeared, if anything, more uncommunicative than she'd seen him in the brief time since they'd met. The most Mr. Lowery offered in response to Robby was when he let out the occasional grunted comment.

Every so often, Colley did exercise herself enough to pipe up. "Ya don't say?" she murmured on a couple of occasions, then resumed her silent consumption of the mound of food on her thick, white china plate.

The two rustlers remained as silent as Mr. Lowery and as focused on their food as Colley.

Emma just stared at her still nearly full plate. How Colley had so quickly pulled the various elements of the disastrous dishes into something that resembled a meal, she still didn't know. It would appear it took more than the sum of lard, water, salt, and flour to make biscuits. In the time she'd worked at Colley's side to get the food done, the older woman had made sure Emma understood the need for a small amount of both sour milk and soda powder—leavening, she'd called it. Never, ever would Emma forget that detail again.

Where the milk had come from, she didn't know. Perhaps they had a cow hidden somewhere around the camp. There was, after all, an overabundance of darkened forest beyond the cabin door.

"...and Lady Emma says she has one like Mama's book at her own house, too," Robby told his father.

She winced. A glance at Mr. Lowery revealed a muscle tight in one cheek and deepened lines across his forehead. He shot her a glare then turned to his son again, disapproval loud in every inch of his posture.

But before he could scold the boy, Emma squared her shoulders and conjured the brightest smile she could. She would do all she could to spare the boy the pain of learning his great interest in books meant nothing more than a disappointment to his father. She couldn't imagine how it would have felt to know Papa felt that way about her and something that mattered to her. Especially if it had as strong a tie to her mother.

"You know, Sir Robby," she said, well aware her words would increase the rancher's dislike, "I've visited a number of splendid castles in the British Isles."

The child's attention turned to Emma. "Really?"

"Indeed." Although she felt the weight of Mr. Lowery's disapproval as an almost palpable thing, Emma couldn't bear the thought of the man bruising his child's interest in history or literature any further. Surely there was much to value in matters of education, as she'd been taught since childhood.

She launched into a spirited and detailed description of various locales she'd visited across Great Britain while she and Papa had lived in London. Robby soaked it all in with a rapt expression on his face. As long as he showed interest, Emma kept talking. "And the queen—"

"The queen?" Robby asked in a voice hushed with awe. "You've seen a real queen?"

Emma fought to keep the corners of her mouth from quirking up into a broad smile. "I have. There are events in London that many folks attend where Queen Victoria appears. She's a very serious lady, I'll have you know, and busy."

Of course, Robby wanted to know everything she could tell him about Her Majesty, the queen. Descriptions of Buckingham Palace also enthralled him.

When she couldn't think of another thing to say, Emma fell silent. That's when she realized everyone's attention was fixed on her. Except Sawyer's. He let out a snuffling snore.

Heat rose from her throat, through her cheeks, and to her hairline. She'd never intended to take over the conversation, but she supposed she had.

"I'm sorry." Her words came out in little more than a whisper. "I didn't mean to go on this long. I only wanted to tell Robby some things I knew he'd enjoy."

"Maybe if you'd given him a list of sums to practice then he might have learned something that would do him good," the rancher countered. "Don't see where stories of castles and queens and palaces will help him any."

Emma glared at the man. "We will certainly focus on mathematics, sir, since that is your wish, but I'll suggest to you the boy also needs a solid foundation in literature, history, and a passing knowledge of the events that take place around the world these days. It's a pity you don't have the benefit of a good newspaper here at this camp."

A deep sigh drew her attention to Ned. Uh-oh. The young man wore a dreamy expression, focused on her, and a silly smile tipped up his lips.

No-no-no! Over her recent past, Emma had become the regular recipient of that sort of attention. Any number of young men had declared themselves charmed by her presence, even though she hadn't gone out of her way to...well, charm them.

Not much.

She hadn't.

Not really.

Fine, fine. She hadn't been excessive. Or mean-spirited.

Of course, it pleased her to know she was a charming person, but she didn't work to charm every man she met. Besides, that had been then, this was now. Now she had to face a host who clearly wanted no part of her presence, while one of that host's prisoners seemed to have fallen prey to her charms. Without her wanting him to do so.

She had to find the wisdom to handle the situation well.

Emma couldn't remember when she'd needed wisdom as much.

Mr. Lowery, a look of displeasure on his rugged features, shrugged, then nodded. "I reckon if you give your word, then I'll have to take it. Just see you don't give my boy any more crazy notions to waste our time on. He needs to learn what he'll need to run a solid sheep operation."

A sharp retort popped to Emma's lips, but she bit down on

it. After exerting a moment of control, she sat up straight and crossed her arms. "In that case, sir, perhaps you ought to consider seeing to the boy's education yourself. Since you seem so very particular as to what he learns, why, then, wouldn't you be the person best suited for that specific job?"

He pushed back his chair and stood. "Are you suggesting you'll take over my work with the sheep while I teach my son? Can Colley and Wade expect you ready to shear fleece in the morning? How about helping birth a lamb or two? We have some late ones about to be born."

"Oh, no!" Ned said, his expression perking right up, his dingy blond hair dropping over his eyes in a thick curtain. "Miss Emma, she don't need to be doin' that, sir. She's . . . she's a lady. And a lady like her shouldn't hafta get herself dirty with sheep. Please let me do it for her."

Emma winced.

Peter snorted. "I'm not setting you loose, Ned, and you know it. Not until I hand you over to Marshal Blair in the fall. Even then, I doubt you'll be any much looser than you are here."

Ned's expression turned to one of pure dejection.

Emma felt awful. Ever since she'd met him, Mr. Lowery had seemed to relish displaying a very rigid side to him. While she wasn't ready to champion any outlaw, she also saw no reason to scold Ned for his attempt at kindness. But she couldn't worry about Ned right then, much less wonder about the rancher's reasons for his attitude. She had to do whatever she could to keep Robby from feeling as poorly as the young outlaw clearly did.

She followed Mr. Lowery's lead and stood as well, determined to champion Robby's cause, no matter how foreign the venture felt to her. Robby mattered. She knew only too well what life was like for a child without a mother's tender, gentle attention.

"You know your suggestion is nothing less than foolish," she told Mr. Lowery, chin up, gaze level. "I know even less about ranching and sheep than I do about housekeeping."

The thought of the imminent births, however, did stick out in her mind and intrigued her more by the passing minute. She forged ahead.

"On the other hand, I wouldn't mind learning about your animals, especially the babies. I assure you, I do learn—given the opportunity. It's simply not reasonable of you to expect me to accomplish it in one afternoon with a couple of books. Which, I suspect, you knew only too well when you commanded me to do so."

She felt a measure of triumph when he averted his gaze and his dark-tanned cheekbones turned a burnished red. She'd made her point. Still, his words had sparked a glimmer of interest within her. "Could I..." She squared her shoulders and took a firmer tone. "I would like to join you and Colley when the lambs are being born. Could I, please?"

He hadn't expected her request. He met her gaze, surprise on his face. "I won't have you distracting us at such a crucial moment, Miss Crowell. We can't afford to lose even one ewe or lamb."

"I wouldn't distract you, sir. Observing from a reasonable distance is all I would like to do."

"You are a distracting nuisance by just you being—"

"I reckon it's right about time we get after washin' up after this here supper we've done gone and had us...somehow." A fierce frown wreathed Colley's leathery face in lines and furrows. "How 'bout you and Wade get these two good-fornothings back to the bunkhouse, Pete? I'll take care of things here, and then come on out to meet up with ya afore I git back to my bedroom and hit my bed."

The rancher looked ready to object, but then, with another unhappy stare for Emma, he turned to Wade and jerked his head in the direction of the two outlaws.

Wade scurried to the hook on the wall where he'd looped the ropes that had secured Sawyer's and Ned's hands, did his job, tugged to make sure the knots wouldn't give way, and then nudged the men toward the door. Mr. Lowery stood as straight as one of the massive trees outside the door and studied the barely-glowing embers in the center of the hearth. When the three others reached the door, he turned to his son.

"I'll be back to read to you in a bit." Then, with the briefest of nods for Emma in an apparent attempt at civility, he opened the door and left.

Emma released her tension in a huge gust of a sigh.

With a glance over her shoulder, she noted that Robby had made his way to his mother's trunk and was rummaging, most likely for the Malory book. She smiled. Once she and Colley had finished cleaning up, she would read for a while. Mr. Lowery could certainly continue where she left off.

She turned to Colley, who was pouring steaming-hot water into the deep, wide basin where she'd washed her face and hands earlier that day. "Is he always such a dreadful curmudgeon?"

"Cur-mut-chon?" Colley scratched her head near the tight bun on top, making the silver knot jog only the tiniest tad, then shook her head. "Dunno 'bout that word, but he is sore-headed much of the time."

Oh, dear. "That means I can expect quite a bit more of…" She gave a weak little wave. "That."

Colley struck her as reluctant to answer, but then, after shaving some curls of the bar of soap into the steamy water, she shrugged. "Been mostly that way since his missus died. Hit him real hard, I tell ya."

Emma tried to steel herself against feeling too much sympathy for the grumpy widower, but the memory of Papa's suffering the first few years after Mama's death melted her resolve. "I understand. No, I truly do," she insisted when Colley seemed to disbelieve her. "I lost my own dearest mama when I was ten, and Papa…well, he had such a time back then. They loved each other very deeply, and he seemed lost without her."

"I reckon that's a good way to put it, then, miss. Pete, he puts me in mind of a lost sheep, you could say, bellowin' and hollerin' for someone to come find it. He's making the same kinda noise, but he won't git himself down to Bountiful and find himself a new ewe. That's what'll put 'im to rights, all right."

Emma blushed. "I do think that's a mite too much for you to tell a practical stranger, Colley. All I can say is that I'd like to go home as soon as tomorrow morning, but Mr. Lowery has made it plain he won't permit anyone to help me. And so, since I'm stuck here until he changes his mind, I'd like to make my stay as least unpleasant as possible."

The ranch manager gave out a bark of laughter. "That there sure and was the tightest knot of words a body could ever tie together to just say you ain't none too happy stuck out here with a bunch of sheep, some unshined-up men, and me."

Again, her cheeks heated. "Oh, I don't think I said that—"

"No, ma'am. You didn't, but you sure wanted to." She grinned. "I do get the gist of what you meant. Most women-folk I've known don't much cotton to this kinda life out here, neither. Mrs. Lowery fought a fierce fight against the lone-liness, the weather, and the long, long hours of work every single last day, but it still got her but good. He took it hard, losing her."

Again, she braced herself against the rush of compassion for the man who'd shown her mighty little of it. Well, he had offered her a roof. And food…which she had to make—heaven help them all. "At least she could cook."

Again, Colley laughed. "So will you, if you want to learn. Way I see it, it's up to you, missy. Cookin' up a plate of vittles don't take too much, you just have to make up your mind to do it."

Emma understood what Colley was trying to say in her gentlest way. It would be a matter of determination. And sin-cere desire.

She bit her bottom lip. To be honest, she didn't have any interest in spending time bent over the hot hearth, making bacon and beans and biscuits.

Colley marched to the door. "Back in a minute, miss."

"Where are you going?"

"We need us some cold water. Can't be washing up dishes with that there water what's right near boiling. And every-thing needs a rinsing with clean water, too."

After Colley closed the door, Emma heard the soft rus-tle of Robby's voice. When she turned to check on the child, she realized he was slowly sounding out Sir Thomas Malory's old-fashioned English. Although she saw no harm in it, she feared his father wouldn't be happy with him—or her—if he returned and found the boy with all his attention on the collection of tales.

"Robby, I think this might be a good time to change into your nightshirt. Your papa's likely to come in soon to say goodnight, and you won't want to not be ready."

The boy looked from Emma to his beloved book to the cabin door and back to her. "Reckon you don't want me to not be ready, Lady Emma. He don't like my mama's book."

Sadness weighed down the narrow shoulders and Robby kept his gaze on the book. Emma couldn't bear the raw emotion she saw depicted on the sweet, boyish features, so she let the grammatical error pass. She hurried to his side, sat, and slid an arm around his shoulders.

"But I do," she said, her voice soft and crooning. "And I'm here, aren't I? We can read a bit once you've changed and washed up. There's also time tomorrow for reading...and the next day, too."

When he looked up at her, her heart ached for the lonely motherless boy.

"Are you gonna be staying with us, then?" he asked, a hint of toughness to his expression. "Mama didn't stay."

What could she do? What could she say?

"Oh, Robby. I'm here now. Let's not think about the future, since we need to get through right now first. The future will have plenty of time of its own."

She could see her response hadn't satisfied him, but she refused to tell him an untruth. She couldn't bear the thought of building hopes she had no intention of meeting. She was going home. As soon as she could figure out how.

He didn't move, didn't speak, but kept his gaze on the tome on his lap. Emma feared she might have said something wrong, something that could have hurt his feelings—the farthest thing from what she'd intended.

"How about if you only think about one thing? How about a change into your clean nightshirt?" she suggested again. "That way, you'll be ready when your papa returns. He did say he would come read to you tonight."

Robby lifted a shoulder. "Sure, he did. But—"

"Ready for them dishes, Miss Emma?" Colley asked, punctuating her words with the slap of the door in her wake. "Here's the cold water so's no one's burning any fingers."

She glanced at Colley, but stayed right by the boy. "I'll be right there. I'd just like to make sure Robby gets ready for bed."

"Reckon he's as ready as he's likely to get," Colley answered as she tipped cold water into the basin of hot. "And he's always ready to argue with his pa so's not to hafta do any sleepin'. Ain't that right, Robby?"

Emma let a frown creep on her face. "But a boy needs his sleep, Colley." She turned to Robby. "You want to grow up big and strong like...like your papa, right?"

The boy finally reacted again. He nodded, very tiny bobs of the head at first, but then they grew firmer. "Yes."

"See, Colley?" She spun, and then realized the woman had known all along what she was doing. Her pale blue eyes, the color of a fresh, spring morning sky, twinkled with clear evidence of a hidden good nature. "Oh, you! You knew, didn't you? How do you know me so well so fast?"

"Not near so hard to do, Miss Emma, as trying to figger out them two so-an'-sos what kidnapped you. What were them two fools thinkin'?"

Emma gave it a momentary thought then faced the boy. "Please change out of those clothes, Robby. I imagine there's a clean nightshirt somewhere here in this cabin for you to put on."

"Nightshirt?" the boy asked. "What's a nightshirt? 'S it different from a regular... um... day shirt?"

It was Colley's turn to blush. "Since his ma went home to Jesus—"

"She's an angel, Colley," Robby said. "'Member?"

"'Zactly. When his ma went to be an angel with the Lord, why, Pete and I kinda stopped frettin' 'bout things like nightshirts and such. He's been sleepin' in his—uh..."

Emma held out a hand, palm toward the ranch manager. "I see. Do you or Mr. Lowery have a clean shirt we can borrow then? If I'm going to see to Robby while I'm here, then we're going to start out right. And it's right for a boy to change into a proper sleeping garment."

Although the older woman turned to head back out of the cabin, Emma thought she spied the start of a grin bracketed by all those wrinkles and creases on her weathered face.

She told Robby to wait to see what Colley would bring, and then went to the basin of tolerable hot water, cooled by the half-empty pail of cold. She dunked tin plate after fork after heavy china mug in the soapy liquid, scrubbed, and then rinsed and dried. By the time Colley returned, a red-and-gray checked shirt over an arm, she had almost everything ready to store.

The ranch manager praised her far more than her effort deserved. Emma rolled her eyes. "Please, I should hope anyone can see where a plate's not clean, wash it, dry it, and stack it with others. It doesn't take much to do this. Now cooking...?" She shrugged.

Colley chuckled. "You're a right interesting lady, Miss Emma, I'll say that 'bout you. Reckon you keep all them folks 'round you a-hoppin' all the time." She held out the shirt. "You can do this, and I'll store the dishes for ya. These old bones of mine are tellin' me they can sure do with some sleep, and straight away now."

Robby didn't seem happy to change clothes then wash his face and hands, but Emma didn't brook any argument. This was the proper way to go to bed, and for however long she had to stay here, those things that were up to her would be done right.

Something Colley had said came back to Emma. "Did you say that Sawyer and Ned kidnapped me?"

Colley nodded.

Emma shook her head. "They didn't kidnap me. Not really. They and some other crook-friends of theirs—from what I've heard them say there were four to start with—held up the carriage I was in. That's it. I'd gone into the woods with Pippa, seeing as how she needed her...well, her constitutional, when they held up the other passengers. I think as soon as the driver saw an opportunity to escape, he took it, and fled. I walked up, and don't know who was more surprised, them or me."

Colley sputtered in outrage. "What kinda lousy fool of a

man goes off and leaves a lady like you all alone in the woods?" She clicked her tongue against her teeth. "Purty sad substitutes for real men, them two are, too."

Emma remembered Ned's kindness toward her, his efforts to shield her from the difficulties of her situation. "I can't speak for Sawyer, since he does frighten me, but I suspect Ned's not nearly as bad. Perhaps you could give him a chance and he could choose to do right."

Colley opened the door, now that she'd finished her post-supper chore. "Hmph! I'll hafta see 'bout anything like that. Dunno as I can trust a fellow like him, what with him takin' the boss's sheep an' us findin' him with them."

"Give him a chance," Emma urged. "I have a...an intuition about him. I think you'll be surprised."

The older woman snorted. "Tomorrow's a different day's what I say, missy. Lord bless ya both so's you both do sleep well."

"Good night, Colley. I hope tomorrow's a much better day."

"So do I." She closed the door to her room.

Robby had watched and listened, and had yet to change out of his day clothes. Emma started him along the process, but moments later, Pippa gave an intense little cry. Emma had come to recognize that particular sound, and knew her pet gave her but a scant minute or two to act before she did what puppies do.

"Please continue," she told the boy, hurrying to tie Pippa's rope around her neck. "I'll only be a short while. Pippa doesn't dawdle."

The evening had grown nippy by then, and Emma hoped

the pup did indeed take care of her needs fast. She shivered, wishing she had her wool cloak along with her. She didn't want to leave Robby alone for long. She did not want to have to face Mr. Lowery again, either, especially with the boy unready for bed, but she supposed a final encounter for the day could not be helped.

"Hurry, Pippa!"

For a change, however, Pippa did dawdle. She sniffed and burrowed her nose between twigs and around rocks, and then behind a branch or two. Finally—finally—she found the right spot for her needs, and moments later, Emma led her back to the cabin.

As soon as she walked in, she fought the urge to make a face. Mr. Lowery had returned and was seated in his late wife's rocker. He'd pulled the chair close to Robby as the little boy lay snuggled under his covers already, looking down from the top bunk. The resonant rumble of the rancher's voice made a surprisingly pleasant backdrop as she untied her dog, stowed away the rope, unlaced her boots, and took a seat at the table.

Only when she stopped bustling did what Robby's father read register.

"...'Moreover,'" Mr. Lowery cleared his throat. To Emma, it seemed when he resumed his reading, he did so in a louder voice. "'Moreover the Lord saith, because the daughters of Zion are haughty, and walk with stretched forth necks and wanton eyes, walking and mincing as they go and making a tinkling with their feet:

"'Therefore the Lord will smite with a scab the crown of the head of the daughters of Zion, and the Lord will discover their secret parts.

" 'In that day the Lord will take away the bravery of their tinkling ornaments about their feet, and their cauls, and their round tires like the moon, the chains, and the bracelets, and the mufflers, the bonnets, and the ornaments of the legs, and the headbands, and the tablets, and the earrings, the rings, and nose jewels, the changeable suits of apparel and the mantles, and the wimples, and the crisping pins, the glasses, and the fine linen, and the hoods, and the veils.' "

Although he didn't look her way, not even once, she had the horrid feeling he'd read those harsh words for her. No, not for her. Emma felt certain Peter Lowery had read fire and brimstone Scriptures directly *at* her.

In that very second, she decided to find her way home.

Chapter 9

She blanched.

Peter saw it out of the corner of his eye. He closed his Bible, satisfied he'd made his point. Perhaps that would encourage Miss Crowell to make a serious effort to do her part. It wasn't his fault she'd been abandoned in the woods by her traveling companions. It also wasn't his fault he couldn't just up and take her back to Bountiful any old time, either. He bore responsibility to his men, his son, and his wife's memory.

That was the single, solitary reason he didn't hoof it to town for no practical reason other than to get rid of the burden Miss Crowell and the outlaws represented. Yes, she was a burden. He'd seen the way not only Robby, but also Ned, and even Wade looked at her. Sawyer? Oh, he looked at her, too, only in a different, more dangerous way.

Not that Peter could fault any normal man for admiring Miss Crowell. Sure, she was the prettiest thing he'd ever seen. All that red, curling hair—even when in a messy tumble—caught a man's eye and didn't let go. Her green eyes sparkled with her every thought and emotion. And when she got mad...who-eee! Those eyes blazed, her cheeks colored right up to a bright rose, and even the curls on her head quivered with her anger.

He had to fight a grin whenever she bristled.

A quick glance showed her silent, biting her bottom lip.

Peter shrugged. At least she wasn't arguing right then.

No matter what, he wanted nothing to do with her. He had no patience for frivolous women. Emma Crowell had proved to him she didn't have a single bit of usefulness to her. She wasn't even built to endure the hard work, weather extremes, and harsh realities of this raw, wild land. This land where he'd put down his roots...the land he'd come to love...the land where he belonged.

It seemed no matter how hard he worked to keep his land, he found nothing but trouble—or troublemakers. He thought of the two sheep rustlers. Or were they really wool rustlers? They'd begun shearing the sheep rather than taking off with the animals to try to sell them. He supposed wool was easier and more lucrative to sell than winter-thin sheep. At least he'd been able to find the rustled animals and get them back where they belonged. He just wished he hadn't had to bring the thieves with them.

Then there was Miss Emma Crowell...she posed a number of problems. A truly decorative woman would never be of any help out here or even on a ranch. Peter knew he could fight his tendency to let his gaze stray toward her more often than it should, but he didn't know how the other men would handle their reactions to the pretty butterfly among them.

Even now, the image of Miss Crowell's dark auburn hair, shiny with its rich red lights, leaped to life in his thoughts. True, she'd tried to tame those long locks into a braid that morning, but her efforts hadn't really succeeded. That hair seemed to have a life of its own.

Just like the owner.

Where the rogue notion came from, Peter didn't know. But it wasn't the first time it had popped into his head, and he reckoned it was true enough. She had a lively personality, all right. He'd tried to tamp down her sparkle, but it seemed she just got right back up again and kept on going. Somehow, no matter how many chores he gave her—even the challenge of Robby's schooling—deep in his belly, he knew she would find time to encourage the boy's silly pursuits.

On the other hand, Peter wouldn't soon forget the excitement in his son's eyes when he had walked in and found them head-to-head over the book. The excitement that had faded in his presence.

A pang of an unaccustomed feeling seared through him, its hit so strong it forced him against the chair's back rails. At that moment, he almost—almost—wished he could bring that same light into Robby's eyes himself. But in no way could he ever imagine reading foolish nonsense to his son. Still, the odd emotion lingered.

Was he...could he be jealous of Miss Crowell?

He stole another look at her. She still sat at the table, stick-straight, her lips clamped tight and her shoulders stiff. Hm... perhaps his words had achieved their desired effect.

Perhaps they'd done more.

Much, much more.

An unintended more.

Peter shifted in discomfort and glanced at the boy. He'd fallen asleep. At the very least, tonight he'd been lulled into slumber by the Lord's Word, not the book of make-believe.

But what good did the particular passage you read do Robby?

Even more uncomfortable in the wake of the thought, he stood. Out of the corner of his eye, he saw Miss Crowell glare as she watched him move. Her head tipped up in the defiance she seemed to display any time she disagreed with him. Clearly, his attempt to instruct her with biblical wisdom had not been a success.

He took notice of the charged air in the room. Miss Crowell was not pleased.

Peter shrugged. They did have a whole summer to make progress on that score. Neither one of them was going anywhere. "Good night, ma'am."

"Indeed, sir." Her words came out icy and clipped.

It would appear he had a mighty long way to go.

Heading for the door, Peter forced himself to relax. As long as he didn't lose his ranch, he could handle anything, even a silly society lady who didn't think too highly of sensible ranch living and hard work.

He prayed she at least had enough common sense to respect God's Word some and take it to heart.

Walking and mincing?
Tinkling feet?
Haughty?
What a nasty man!

After Mr. Lowery left, Emma continued to stare at the tiny wisps of smoke that still curled every so often from the ashes on the fireplace hearth. She could no longer see red embers through the thick coating of silvery ash, but the smoke told her they were still there.

Maybe it was the misery that made it hard to see much.

Emma leaned forward and laid her face in the palms of her hands. Her tangle of curls cascaded forward, bringing to mind what an utter mess she must look like by now. Her hair had become a nest of knots. She had no comb, no brush, and each time she worked to untangle and braid it with her fingers, it only stayed in the plait for a short while. The wild curls fought against any kind of restraint.

Her clothes...well, they were beyond ruined. She wanted a clean change of garments, but she didn't see how that would be possible anytime soon. The thought of spending months imprisoned in these filthy rags was almost more than she could bear.

But a bath...oh, goodness. That she truly needed. A pail of cold water mixed with kettles of hot sounded dreadful. On the other hand, her skin felt uncomfortable. Her arms and legs and back itched. At times, it was all she could do to keep from scratching like the tiny monkey she had seen when Papa took her to the Central Park Zoo in New York a few years before. One way or another she was going to make the tin tub Mr. Lowery had mentioned work for her. Only thing she had to figure was how she would avoid bathing outdoors. No matter how much she itched, she had no intention to ever bathe outdoors. Under no circumstances.

She stood, stretched, and walked to the bunk. "Wanton

eyes. Hmph. Absolutely not. I am not some...some floozy, Mr. Peter Lowery. I will show you."

Determined not to cry herself to sleep again, Emma lay down. Although she wasn't one given to prayer at the drop of a hat, the sight of Mr. Lowery reading Scripture to scold her had awakened something restless and sad inside her. She could, however, remember having heard something about nothing being impossible for God back when Mama insisted on attending church every single Sunday.

"God? Seeing as he seems to be on such close terms with You, could You please tell him I'm not a criminal like the other two? Nor am I a floozy, as he called me."

She rolled onto a side, and a wave of exhaustion swept over her. Her eyes felt heavy and gritty, and before she gave it much thought, she'd fallen asleep.

She didn't stay that way for long. Strange dreams filled her night. Disjointed images had her jolting awake over and over again. Finally, when she was nearly in tears from frustration, she again dozed off to a dreamless slumber.

Morning came much faster than Emma wanted. Robby shook her shoulder and her aching head told her right away she hadn't rested half enough. "Oooh..."

"Miss Emma! Colley's here. She says you said you wanted her to show you how to make breakfast."

She almost gave in and groaned. The amount of movement it took to just rub her eyes made her feel as though her whole body might break into dozens of tiny pieces, she was so tired and sore. She wasn't used to this sort of life, of course, and her muscles were objecting in the most unpleasant way. Almost as nasty as Mr. Lowery's very pointed and mean-spirited Scripture reading—

Mr. Lowery! The very thought of the judgmental man made her scramble out of bed and straighten her clothes as best she could. When she gave up, frustrated by the futility in the effort, she pulled her hair forward and began to braid again.

"'Morning, Colley," she said, finishing up the end of the braid. "What're we making this morning?"

"Flapjacks." The older woman gave the contents of a large yellow ware bowl another good stir. "And bacon."

Emma had now eaten bacon at every meal since the outlaws had taken her to the cave, even when she'd made the chicken, since Colley had added bacon to the beans. It seemed as though it was all folks out here wanted to eat.

The door burst open and Ned rushed in. "I'm here! With the fresh water—" He stopped, stared at Emma, that silly smile widening across his face. He swiped his frayed hat off his head, the pail of water in his other hand sloshing over. "Good mornin', Miss Emma. Hope you did rest yourself well last night."

Emma had to stifle her quick, true, but unhappy response. She felt as though she hadn't slept at all. "It was a long night."

Colley harrumphed.

Emma sensed the ranch manager was fighting a laugh, and at her expense, no less. She felt her cheeks warm. *Don't let it get the best of you, Emma.*

"So, Colley," she said, "how can I help you this morning?"

"The flapjacks are pretty much made already, an' I'm gonna

be fryin' 'em straight away, but you can slice up the bacon. Good knife's on the shelf, and the slab a bacon's—"

"In the lean-to," Emma said with a smile. "I saw it yesterday when I was out there. I'll be happy to fetch it for you."

She began to don her boots, but Ned hurried past her to the door. "No need to go an' trouble yourself none, Miss Emma. I'll get that bacon for you."

"That's…" His presence in the cabin suddenly registered. "I thought Mr. Lowery had put Wade to watch you and Sawyer. How is it you're here instead?"

Ned shuffled his feet, spun his hat around in front of his middle, stared off past her shoulder. "Well, miss, I…well, I told Miz Colley, here, I'd be much obliged if she'd be willing to let me make myself helpful to her. I know I can, really, I do. Then she gone an' told Mr. Lowery she'd be seeing to me if the boss'd let me come on along with her. An' then, why, I'm just trying to help you now."

Emma sent a questioning look to Colley, who gave her a quick nod. "Very well, then, Ned," Emma said. "You get the bacon, and I'll get the knife. We'll be done much faster."

"Good!" Robby cheered. "I'm hungry."

"You're always hungry," Colley answered.

Emma stepped close to Colley, not wishing to alarm Robby with her question. "Are you sure Ned should be trusted to go out alone? I mean, I know what I said and I don't think he's pure evil, or anything like that, but he did steal your sheep."

"I reckon that boy there is just needin' hisself a mite of sensible learning from a body what knows some. Reckon he fell in with the wrong sort, if that there Sawyer's anything to go by."

Emma found the knife on the shelf, then returned to the table, ready to try her hand at slicing meat. "Don't you wonder how they wound up partners?"

" 'S just what I mean, missy. Don't look right to me, some-how, and I'm ready to give him a chance. He might could make something right and good of hisself while he's here stuck with us."

"I did mention it to Mr. Lowery, but, of course, he paid me no mind." Emma shook her head. "He's dead set against me, and I don't know that there's much I can do to change his opinion. I didn't ask to be left in the woods, you know."

"Naw, Miss Emma, you didn't." A wise and serious light deepened her gaze. "But then he didn't go and ask to be left a widower with a lil shaver, neither."

She felt the mild rebuke despite Colley's bland tone. "I do understand, Colley, but I would hope he understands a mite how difficult this is for me, too. I'm here, all alone with a group of men—and you, of course—I don't know…and that's not right. Not for a lady. And I do promise you, I am willing to do everything I can so I don't become any more of a burden than necessary."

Colley's smile tilted up one side more than the other. "I reckon I can take you at your word. Mr. Lowery, why, he might could take you a mite longer to bring 'round to your way of seein' things, but he'll come 'round. He's not so hard-headed that he'll keep refusing to see."

"We shall see, won't we?"

The cabin door opened, and Ned rushed in, carrying a huge slab of smoked bacon. Emma glanced at the knife she'd retrieved from the shelf. She really hoped she could do this right. She didn't want to give the rancher any more reasons to dislike her.

The next few minutes went by peacefully as Colley mixed up a fresh batch of biscuits. It seemed the men ate them at every meal, too, no matter what else appeared on the plates. At the table, Emma concentrated on slicing even strips of the streaky meat. Robby kept up his chatter, and Ned sat across the table from Emma, his expression as silly as ever.

His blatant admiration was difficult to handle. Had she really basked in that sort of attention before? It was growing uncomfortable, indeed.

When she had sliced a good stack of meat, she turned to Colley again. "I'm ready. Is the...um...spider ready?"

"Sure. I'm using the big skillet for the biscuits."

Emma spread out the bacon on the hot spider, and then, curious, hurried back to Colley's side. "Is that where you make the flapjacks, too?"

"Watch."

The older woman poured the thick mixture onto a strange, flat iron disk hanging by a thick wire handle on an S hook from the iron rod across the fireplace. As the mix hit the hot, greased metal, it sizzled and spread. Small bubbles formed one by one on the surface, and then, when it all looked a bit dry around the bubbles, Colley used a long tool with a flat paddle at its end to flip the flapjack over onto the bubbled side.

"See, missy?" Colley asked. "That's all there is to it."

"And to make the mix you're cooking?"

"Eggs, buttermilk, sugar, flour, baking soda, and a pinch of salt."

"Same as for biscuits, then."

"That's right, Miss Emma," Ned piped in. "They're kind of the same, 'cept different. Biscuits and flapjacks, they're close. Only difference is y'aren't wantin' to put no eggs in biscuits, and then the flapjacks, they're...uh...wetter."

Emma turned. "You cook?"

"Nah," Ned answered, looking bashful. "Just that Sawyer and Dwight always need a hand here and there, so I helped and seen 'em make food. I can help you learn some, too."

His hope-filled expression reminded Emma of Robby. He didn't know how to cook, but he insisted he could help her learn. An interesting—if ludicrous—proposition. "I suppose we can all learn from Colley."

"You're all going to learn what?" Mr. Lowery asked from the open doorway.

Emma started. She hadn't heard a sound. "Oh! Ah...good morning, Mr. Lowery." With a pair of long-handled metal tongs, she flipped over the strips of bacon, not wishing to give her unwilling host any more reason to object to her.

Ned spun to face the rancher. "Mr. Boss—oh!"

SPLASH!

In his enthusiastic effort to greet Mr. Lowery, Ned moved too fast, and hit the bucket of water he'd brought in earlier. The entire thing seemed to explode in a large wave of glistening wetness, bathing everything in its path. Unfortunately, Mr. Lowery's boots and legs were in that path.

"What—?" The rancher was not pleased.

"Oh-oh-oh!" Ned lost all color from his face. "I... am...er—"

"Here," Emma said, running to Mr. Lowery's side, cotton

towel in her hand. She dropped down on a knee, and swished the cloth over his boots, then did what she could with the other puddles of water on the wooden floor.

While she realized Mr. Lowery was anything but pleased with this latest disaster, at least it hadn't been one of her making. Out of the corner of her eye, she saw Colley fighting a laugh. Robby lost his battle. The boy laughed and laughed, and Emma tried with all her might not to follow his lead.

Ned, on the other hand, offered the most inventive stream of apologies Emma had ever heard. When her rag became so soaked all it did anymore was slosh the water from one spot to another, she stood, holding the fabric carefully, and went for the door. She came to a complete stop, face to face with Sawyer, who stood in the doorway. The look on his face made her feel dirtier than ever, if possible.

"Excuse me, Mr. Sawyer. I must take this outside."

He paused for a second longer than Emma thought proper, all the while staring at her in that way that made her so dreadfully uncomfortable. Just as she was about to turn and go back to the table with the drippy cloth, he stepped aside, but only enough for her to squeeze by past him, holding her breath so as not to touch him. To her disgust, her arm made contact. She shuddered and he laughed, only too aware of how much he'd bothered her.

She ran. She wasn't too clear where she was going, but she knew she wanted to get as far from the vile man as she could. Behind her, she heard his hateful laughs, and despite her better judgment, she cast a glance over a shoulder.

The last thing she saw was Mr. Lowery grab Sawyer by the arm and shove him back toward the bunkhouse. Perhaps she wouldn't have to face him again when she returned for the meal.

When she returned. She had to gather her wits about her before that could ever happen. The incident with Sawyer, as brief as it had been, had shaken her up more than she could have imagined. Then again, she didn't think she ever could have imagined such treatment before meeting a ruffian like the thief.

When she reached the edge of the woods, she stopped. A few steps away she saw a fallen tree and made her way over the carpet of fallen leaves. She had run out of the cabin barefoot, hadn't noticed any sensation on her feet as she'd run, but now that she'd slowed down, she'd begun to feel the painful reality of the forest floor.

She collapsed on the felled trunk, her filthy skirt whooshing into a puddle around her. The streaks of dirt on the once-lovely velvet made her feel worse than they would have had she noticed them at any other time.

Emma burst into tears.

It seemed she had cried more in the past two days than she had in all the years since her mother died. And yet, she just couldn't seem to stop. She sat and sobbed, her heart aching so much she feared it would have fractured into a million shards had it been possible in some way. Her situation seemed hopeless, and she saw no way to make things better. How could she do this? How would she ever find the strength to cope with Mr. Lowery's disapproval; with Ned's unwanted adoration; with the pressure of unexpected responsibilities; with Robby's loss and loneliness; how would she ever cope with Sawyer's repulsive stares?

How? How was she going to make it through this disaster? "Dear God…please help me. Now."

"Hey!" Sawyer bellowed as Peter turned to leave the bunkhouse. "You cain't jist go an' leave me trussed up like a chicken here. I'm hungry."

Peter's rage grew. "Perhaps you should have thought of that before you went and treated Miss Crowell like that. She's not some…woman of ill repute, for you to look at her and try and rub yourself all up against her."

"Ah…that weren't nuthin'. I was just having a little fun with her, she bein' so silly, an' all."

"She may be silly, but she's a guest here on my land. You, on the other hand, are a prisoner. I'm sure as sure can be that she's never been treated with such disrespect, and you knew exactly what you were doing. A man, a real man, would care for and protect a lady."

For a moment, Peter paused. He sounded quite like something out of the book of tales his son so loved. But before he could ponder that, Sawyer let out a humorless chuckle.

"Now here y'are sounding jist like the lil lady herself," he said, then cackled again. "She were wantin' Ned and me to be her guards and…and—oh, I don't know. Maybe you're jist tyin' me up in this bed so's you can have her all to yerself."

The taunt hit Peter in his gut. How disgusting. "I'll have you know, I have a whole lot more honor than to be considering my guest in that way. You sit here, think about your sins, and when we're done with our food, I might find someone willing to bring you something to eat."

"Sins..." Sawyer laughed again. "Jist bring me that food. We'll see how you go on and do being 'round that lil lady up to your house. Let's jist see how you do."

To his horror, Peter felt the strangest urge to smash his fist into Sawyer's leering face. As much as he had no patience for Miss Crowell, he also had no tolerance for a fellow who would dishonor a woman after he'd just offended her. After a silent plea to his Lord for strength, he was able to shut down the urge and walk out of the bunkhouse. He headed back to the cabin, speaking to his heavenly Father the whole way.

"Lord, I always reckoned You knew what You were doing, but I confess I have no idea what You might be up to with this woman. The rustlers...well, I just can't take them to town right now, and I figure we can watch over them until it's time to go to market in the fall. But her? Can I really keep her safe out here? What else can I do with her, Father? You know I can't leave my flock unprotected. I owe Robby my best. And Colley, too. Sure, she sold me her spread—fair and square and all that, even—but I don't want to let her down. She's trusting me not to let it go, especially not if it happens just on account of my not doing all I could."

He fell silent, unable to come up with anything further to say. What was there to say? Miss Crowell was a beautiful, refined lady, and they were a bunch of rough and tumble men—and Colley—on an isolated meadow partway up a mountain. None of them was blind, all could see how beautiful she was. Or could be, once she cleaned up some. But he realized that wasn't her fault.

The lively cascade of auburn curls came to mind again. He smiled.

None of the crazy situation was anyone's fault. Except maybe Sawyer's and Ned's. Although, truth be told, he wasn't certain how much blame anyone could rightly put on Ned. He was young, barely more than an adolescent, and so far, Peter hadn't seen enough smarts to the youth to consider him particularly wise. He'd likely hitched his fortunes up to those of men he thought exciting.

Lawlessness wasn't exciting. It was just plain wrong.

As was Sawyer's treating a lady, any lady, in such an inappropriate way. Even a lady who had a vain streak wide as the West's open spaces, and was unlikely to have ever done a thing of true worth in her life.

She still didn't deserve such treatment.

And she was Peter's guest.

It was up to him to make certain she never suffered such shameful treatment again, not while she was under his care and protection. He had told her he'd do that because it was the right thing to do, the only Christian way to act.

A vague twinge struck him. Some would also say it was the courtly, gentlemanly thing to do. What one of Robby's and, yes, even Miss Emma's, knights would do. He set the notion aside as soon as it appeared.

As he headed toward the cabin, he saw movement at the far edge of the woods. A glimpse of the by-now familiar, orangey-gold velvet garments revealed Miss Crowell's location. As much as he didn't want to spend much time with her, he knew he owed her an apology.

And a promise.

He made his way to her side. As he came closer, he took care for his boots to crunch debris on the ground loudly enough to alert her to his approach. The moment she realized he was nearly at her side, she bounded up from the log where she'd sat, the soggy rag she'd used to wipe up the floor plopping to the ground.

"I'm sorry, Mr. Lowery. I—"

"No, Miss Crowell. Allow me to offer my apologies. First off, you really didn't need to clean up the mess on the floor. I'm sure Ned is more than capable of doing at least that, and with the way he wants nothing more than to please you, he'd have been right pleased if he could have done it instead."

"But—"

"Please. I'm not done. I...er..." He felt his ears getting hot, a sure sign his face had turned the color of flames. "I must also apologize for not keeping Sawyer under much tighter control. What he did, how he behaved toward you, was wrong, and I won't have such shameful treatment of a lady at my place. I take full responsibility for keeping him away from you for the rest of the time you're my guest."

Clearly, his words surprised her. She blinked. "You can't take the blame for that man's boorish behavior. Why, he's nothing but a brute. And a thief, you know."

He chuckled. "Oh, believe me. I do know. But—"

"No, sir, it's my turn this time. Sawyer's to blame for Sawyer's actions. Not you. I do appreciate your offer to keep him away, but that might not be possible. The man does need to eat—oh!" Her eyes narrowed and she frowned. "Now, you don't mean to starve him, do you?"

"I've half a mind to—" At her look of horror, he backtracked a bit. "I'm not serious, ma'am, not serious at all. Just making a joke, and probably not at the best time. No, one or the other of us will take his meals to the bunkhouse from now on."

"And you mean to keep him there all the time until the fall?"

"If that's what we must do."

"Surely you don't expect him to just stay there like an obedient schoolchild, do you?"

"I don't expect anything from him, good or bad. We'll tie him up, and pray for the best."

"You'll likely have to leave someone at his side to make sure he doesn't set himself loose."

"If that's what it takes, then that's what we'll do. Right?"

"That's dreadfully wasteful, sir. Especially since you've told me you can't spare a man to take me back to Bountiful. If you could, I think it would make far more sense to send that person to escort us back. But since you've made it clear that's quite impossible, at the very least, you could put Sawyer to work. Both him and Ned. They're able-bodied, if not particularly bright. I'm sure you, Colley, and Wade can use their help with the animals, and keep an eye on them while they work. I'll help with Robby. And the cabin."

He crossed his arms and his lips twitched at the corners. He fought the smile, seeing as he doubted she'd appreciate his laughing at her. "You're still telling me you're a quick learner, aren't you?"

She tipped her head up in that way he was coming to know as typical of her, full of bravado, determination, and more than likely, not much more. He fought another smile.

"Why, yes," she said. "I now know how to make flapjacks, biscuits, bacon, can warm up all kinds of tinned and jarred foods, and I absolutely have learned mealy haricot beans must be soaked at the very least overnight before setting them to bake."

"Quite a lengthy menu there, ma'am." When she sputtered in indignation, he raised a hand to stop her. "Colley's said the same about Ned, how he could help out, and I let him come to help this morning. But next I know he's dumping a bucket of freezing water all over my feet. Don't know as I'm ready to repeat that experience."

"It was an accident, Mr. Lowery. You are dreadfully stern, and can make even a gaslight post jumpy. I fully sympathize with poor Ned, if you must know."

Had she just called him frightening? "I'm not stern."

"Ha!" She crossed her arms and stared him square in the face. "I'll have you know, you're the...the sternest man I have ever met. You have not been a welcoming host to me, you can't even understand your own son's need to be a little boy, and...and...then there's poor Ned. I suspect you scare him to bits, too."

He'd never been called scary before. Certainly not to his face.

Was he? Really?

Lord?

The weight of her glare got to him. He couldn't hold her gaze any longer, and his hunger reminded him he hadn't eaten in hours. He cleared his throat. "Well, Miss Crowell. This has been a mighty interesting conversation, but I reckon we've wasted enough of my day already. From where I stand, it's right about time to go eat."

"See?" she asked, holding her ground. "It appears you

didn't like something I said, perhaps something you didn't know quite how to take, and you sped right back to your stiff lord-of-the-manor posture. Stern. Yes, I do indeed mean stern, sir."

And she recoiled right into the stiffest way of talking he'd ever heard. He didn't dare mention it, though, otherwise they might spend the rest of the day and into the night outdoors.

Peter turned toward the cabin. "Well…er…I'll have to consider what you said, but what I said holds true, too. Time's running by, and I need to eat. It's time we head on back inside."

"You will consider what I said?" she asked, insistent.

"I said it, didn't I?"

"You did, and I'll hold you to it. I promise you, Mr. Lowery. This conversation's not over, but rather only interrupted. We will have many, many opportunities in the next few months to talk again."

He fought the groan that rose to his throat. Groaning in her presence, right to her face, would not be a good idea. Not at all. "We'll see."

"Oh, we will, indeed, sir."

He would have given just about anything he owned then to be able to load her up on the wagon and drive her down to Bountiful. He suspected Miss Emma Crowell rarely ever forgot a thing. Especially not when she believed she was right about the matter.

From the way she continued to glare at him, she was certain she was right. She had not even a shred of a doubt he was a stern man. And who knew? A lot had happened to him in his life.

She just might be right about him.

He gestured for her to step ahead of him toward the cabin. "After you."

Peter feared this wouldn't be the last time he'd have to let her step ahead, while he followed in her wake. Heaven help him, seeing as he didn't think he could help himself when it came to his fiery red-haired guest.

Chapter 10

"Time to get to work, Robby," Peter said once they'd finished eating. "Wade, you can take a plate to that... that—to Sawyer. I left him tied up in the bunkhouse. Make sure you take Colley's shotgun with you. Wouldn't want him to be getting any ideas."

Colley nodded. "Guess we still got us plenty of shearin' to do, eh, boss?"

"That we do." Peter glanced at Emma, but she seemed busy with the dirty breakfast dishes. At least it didn't take much know-how to wash up. He didn't think she could get in too much trouble with pots and pans, dishes, and soapy water.

"Aw, Pa!" Robby put on a mule-headed expression. "I wanta stay with Lady Emma today. Can't I stay and help her?"

"Really, Mr. Lowery, I don't know nothing 'bout sheep," Ned said, nodding, his eyes wide and eager. "I can stay and help Miss Emma, too. I'm fair strong, and can carry the water for her—it gets right heavy, you know. She's a fine lady, and shouldn't hafta bother herself with that kinda work. I can clean some good, too."

Over his shoulder, Peter caught sight of Miss Crowell's dismay at the young outlaw's offer.

"Oh, dear me, Ned," she said before Peter could speak, wearing a kind smile on her lips. "That's so generous of you, but really, I'm fine. I can do all those things Colley and I discussed quite well, I'm sure. If I do need help, why, then I'll go fetch one of you gentlemen to come to my rescue."

She turned her snapping green eyes on Peter. "What you really need to do, though, is help Mr. Lowery. He's kind enough to house you—and me—and he's feeding all of us from his supplies. I suspect he, Colley, and Wade can certainly use another pair of hands with the sheep. And surely they'll teach you all you need to know to help them."

To Peter, she looked as though the words she ground out from between her even, gritted white teeth dared him to reject her suggestion. He fought a grin. She was one fascinating woman. And perhaps not quite so bad as he'd thought from the start. Time would, of course, tell.

In a defiant corner of his head, he still hated to agree with Miss Crowell. After all, she was the fluff-headed woman who'd managed to get herself left behind out in the woods by her party. But she did have a point. "I reckon we should do like she says, Ned, and get to the sheep. Colley and I can use the help. You can show us you're speaking truth when you tell us all you need is a chance to prove yourself trustworthy and a good worker."

Robby gave a small hop in excitement. "See, Papa? You need to get out to the sheep." He put his palms together in a gesture of pleading. "Pleeze! Can I stay with Lady Emma? You said she should learn me my lessons, didn't you? We can do that after she's done with all that Colley's told her needs doing. And like Ned's gonna help you, I can too help her. That way she can finish faster, get more done. See? See?"

"Sure, I see." Irritation caused him to frown. "I told you—" Peter caught himself. She'd said he was stern. And he'd doubted her. Now, here he was, scolding his son in a stern voice. Maybe she did make some sense.

He cleared his throat and tried again. "Look, son. I reckon we should let Miss Crowell do just what you said, handle what all Colley's told her to do. She's assured me she's quite capable and an excellent learner. She's got herself some proving to do, herself."

He again fought a smile when she stuck her fists on her hips and her green eyes shot fiery darts of anger at him. Before she could voice the retort he knew was dancing on her lips, he went on. "We'll let her get through her chores, while you and I get through the ones out in the barn. Then, if Colley, Wade, and I don't think we'll need you with us after that, you can come in and work on your lessons with her."

The boy let out a deep, heartfelt sigh. "All right. If I really hafta."

This time, Peter was helpless against the smile. He turned away so his son wouldn't see it. "You do."

As he held the door open for Robby, the boy dragged his feet, making his displeasure more than clear. With as little as Robby cared for the work around the camp—or the ranch, for that matter—and as little attention as he paid to the chores he did do on his best day, today's attitude held no more promise than usual. Still, Peter knew his responsibility toward his son. It was up to him to prepare the boy for the future.

He chose to ignore Robby's contrariness. "Come on, son. We have a lot of cleaning out to do."

"Manure," the boy said with disdain. "Yuck. Why can't Bossie do...well, do all that out on the meadow during the day? Why's she hafta wait until she's in the barn to do it? We wouldn't hafta clean up if she did do it out there."

Peter again chose to ignore the complaint. Instead, when the two of them reached the barn he and Colley had built in a sheltered area at the other side of the clearing, he pointed to the large iron hooks where he kept the tools. "Take the manure fork, Robby."

"Yuck." But the boy did as asked.

Peter led the way, the second manure fork in hand, and the two of them started raking the mess out of the cow's stall. He'd always been a stickler for cleanliness, seeing as he'd seen many a good animal sicken and die when the owner didn't bother with basic, decent care. And he needed Bossie's good, rich milk, not only for the sweet butter Colley churned from the cream, but also for the milk Robby needed to grow strong and healthy.

He'd wondered if he should have brought some chickens up the mountain, but the last time he had, he and Colley decided never to try it again. The animals had given them far more trouble than the good eggs and tasty meat they'd provided had been worth. Colley had assured him she'd preserved enough eggs to last through the summer. And she'd put up plenty of chicken last fall.

He'd helped his ranch manager stock the food supply

lean-to when they'd first arrived less than two weeks earlier, and he'd seen proof of the fruit of Colley's kitchen efforts. They did have a good measure of eatings out there.

A quirked-up grin tipped his lips as he dropped the manure fork and picked up the shovel. It would be a fascinating experience to see what Miss Emma Crowell could do with all that bounty. Miss Emma, the woman who'd never done anything.

But who had plenty to say, anytime, and at all times.

When he had the pile of animal droppings mixed with straw at the door of Bossie's stall, he leaned the shovel against the support post and went for the wheelbarrow. He and Colley had found a good patch of ground that got just the right amount of sun and shade, and they'd been spreading out the rich manure there. At the end of last summer, they'd turned over the earth and manure, and would do the same this year. By next spring, they reckoned they'd have the perfect place to plant themselves a good garden. That's when, at least for part of the summer, they'd have good, fresh—

"En garde!"

Peter groaned. Robby had grown distracted and was back to his make-believe. And he needed his son's help—well, needed was perhaps too strong a word. He wanted his son to want to help, he wanted the boy's enthusiasm, which, it always seemed, was reserved for his flights of fancy. Adele had encouraged them, and after she'd died, Robby had found great comfort in the memories of his mother's fairy tales. Now, as unlikely as it might be, Peter had found a woman in the woods who was partial to the same kind of silliness.

Who would have thought such a thing possible?

"Hie, ye worthless knave . . ." the boy hollered, then giggled. Peter turned. "Robby—oooof!"

When he'd stepped toward his son, he hadn't noticed where the boy had left his manure fork, and he'd stepped on the tines. That had sent the thick wooden handle flying straight up, and it had smacked him right across his hip and caught his ribs. The tool packed a wallop, but he still considered himself fortunate. The tines could have pierced the sole of his boot and caused a wicked injury to his foot. That would have curtailed his ability to work to such a degree that his hopes of turning that much-needed profit would die a painful death.

"Son! Stop that foolish nonsense straight away, and come right here, right now." Oh, yes. He sounded stern. And he'd better. Things could have ended far, far worse.

Robby, his expression downfallen and his demeanor crushed, sidled up to Peter. "Yes, Papa?"

"Do you see this fork?"

"Yessir."

"It's the one you used, right?"

"Yessir."

"And what did you do with it when you were done?"

At that point, the boy looked around Bossie's stall, the small cavern of barn, up at the rafters, and finally down toward the floor. He frowned.

"I don't 'member putting it down there . . ."

"Could it be, son, you were so busy thinking on that Lords and Ladies nonsense that you just didn't exactly put it anywhere? Just let it drop where you'd been standing?"

Robby's cheeks turned rosy. "Maybe."

"And was that a good idea?"

He shrugged, digging a hole in the dirt floor with the toe of his boot. He didn't speak.

Peter crossed his arms. "I just stepped on it."

"Oh!" Concern drew a tiny furrow between his brows. "Did it break?"

"Break!" He couldn't stop himself, no matter how Miss Emma's voice rang in his mind. "No, it didn't break, Robby. That fork's made of solid-forged iron and the handle's of good, hard oak. It'll take much more than me stepping on it to break it."

Robby's frown deepened. "But then, if it's not broken, then—then why are you so angry?"

"Because when I stepped on it, it flew up and the end of the handle walloped me in the belly..."

Robby laughed too hard for Peter to continue. His explanation died off a slow death. His scolding flew right into the explanation's grave.

After all, if Peter took a step back from his irritation with Robby's fanciful nature, he had to admit the moment had been somewhat humorous. It would have been even funnier for the child if he had witnessed his father's expression when the handle had smacked his ribs.

Thank goodness Miss Emma hadn't been in the barn to get a gander at his embarrassment. Something told Peter her hilarity would have been greater, and more pointed, than his son's. Perhaps more deserved.

He blushed.

"Yes, well..." What more was there to say? Well, he could explain about the tines, but the moment had passed. It was something he would not forget to bring up again at the boy's bedtime. Safety was crucial around the sheep operation.

He let out a deep sigh. "Go ahead, son. Go back to the cabin. I'll finish shoveling this muck into the wheelbarrow and take it out. But, and I do mean this, you do need to help Miss Emma, and you must do your lessons, too. I don't want to come in at noon and find you've done nothing but play make-believe."

Disappointment dimmed Robby's excitement. "But, Papa, what about when we're done?"

The boy did have a point. No matter how much it bothered Peter, since he felt it encouraged his son's lack of focus on the things that really mattered, he couldn't just say no without any rhyme or reason to his refusal.

He nodded slowly. "But only after all the chores—and lessons—are done. I can't have anyone not doing their part. I can't be taking up any more slack, or cleaning up any more messes made by others. Rosie and Sunnybelle are about to birth their lambs, maybe even tonight, and I have to check on them regularly."

"Can Lady Emma and I check on the sheep?"

Robby loved the animals, but more as pets and playmates than for the profit they would provide. The boy knew nothing about lambing. Neither, of course, did the indomitable Miss Emma. But it wouldn't do to squelch the boy's interest in the animals, not when Peter wanted to foster Robby's focus on ranching matters.

"Well, we'll have to see how things go with the chores and the lessons."

Robby's eyes lit up again. "Really? When we're done?"

"Only after you and Miss Emma finish your work. And only

after you and she finish making supper, and have it ready to serve. And don't go asking Miss Emma about all that book nonsense, I don't want her filling your head with any more of it."

"It's not nonsense, Papa. Lady Emma says it's lit-rat-chewer."

Inspired by the boy's pronunciation, it was all Peter could do not to make a disparaging comment about Miss Emma's opinion, but he didn't think it would help.

Robby scampered off, his high spirits in graphic contrast to his earlier unwillingness to work in the barn. Every day they had the same conversation. Peter knew he had to find a way to change his son's attitude. Only problem was, he didn't know how. And now, not only did he have to battle Robby's natural tendencies, but he also had to battle the influence of his high-falutin' educated guest.

For the first time since they'd met, he acknowledged what he'd tried to avoid. Miss Emma was not only beautiful, but she was also glamorous and very, very appealing. To males of all ages.

Including him.

Perhaps most especially him.

As contrary as she was—or perhaps because she was—she had an unexpected appeal that shocked him.

And, to a certain extent, horrified him as well.

Heaven help him.

Emma was sorely tired of a solid diet of bacon, beans, and biscuits; she had been from the start of her nightmare. She supposed she wasn't suited for a life on the edge of Nowhere,

America, and yet she knew a lean-to full of a respectable variety of foodstuffs was just around the corner. She intended to make good use of its contents.

Shortly after Colley, the men, and Robby left, she slipped on her ruined boots and hurried to the storage shed. There, as she surveyed the contents, images of dishes she might want to eat flew through her thoughts. A particular favorite, as well as her dear aunt's face, crystallized in her memories.

It wasn't an elaborate delicacy Aunt Sophia had set out at one of her feasts that made Emma think of her table. Instead, the simple chicken croquettes served many times while she'd visited her aunt's home struck her as near to ambrosia at the moment. The light cream sauce the cook would place alongside made more delectable, and a salad had always been a perfect accompaniment. Her mouth watered.

Emma remembered seeing a cream sauce mentioned in *Mrs. Beeton*, but she had yet to find any fresh vegetables anywhere in the lean-to. It was, of course, spring and gardens hadn't yielded anything yet, but that didn't diminish her longing.

To make matters worse, and although she'd eaten well at breakfast, her stomach grumbled at the thought of the familiar, pleasant fare. She shook off the homesickness, since she could do nothing about it. With shoulders squared, she snagged a pair of jars of chicken meat off the shelf then headed back inside. She set them on the table and went to fetch Mrs. Beeton's book. Surely the extensive tome held the secret to the perfect croquette. She laughed.

"Not necessarily the perfect croquette," she murmured, "but at least directions on how to make an edible one."

She flipped through pages of hints and instructions, and

soon she located the section she wanted. "Hm...shallots? No. Didn't find any of those out there. Butter, flour, salt, and pepper—those I have. But...pounded mace? What is that?"

The only kind of mace she knew was the kind King Arthur Pendragon had used to scare Merlin the first time they met. But one used that mace to do the pounding, it wasn't anything one pounded. It didn't strike Emma as something one would use to make chicken croquettes. Would she need to beat—pound—pieces of chicken to a pulp to concoct croquettes?

No, when she reread the list, she saw the chicken itself wasn't to be pounded, but instead the mace was described as pounded. A pounded...weapon? That didn't make any sense, but she didn't have a clue what the recipe might mean.

Perhaps it wouldn't matter if she ignored that pesky detail. She would, though, ask Colley about mace once the ranch manager came back after working the sheep.

"What else...?" Oh, yes. Sugar, roast fowls—well, cooked, jarred chicken—eggs, bread crumbs—bread crumbs? Biscuit crumbs would be more like it. And then white sauce, too. "White sauce..."

Since she hadn't seen anything labeled as such in the shed, and since Mrs. Beeton hadn't seen fit to provide a recipe in her substantial tome, Emma would have to rely on milk. There was some left from breakfast. Even though milk wasn't lush and thick as the white sauce she knew, she figured, one way or another, she'd make it do.

With an unexpected sensation of industriousness settled upon her, she tied on the rough white apron Colley had given her and began to hum the chorus to "Over the Waves," her favorite waltz. She set to chopping chicken with a wicked-sharp knife—Mrs. Beeton said to mince it, but Emma wasn't sure she'd know what minced versus chopped chicken might look like.

On the other hand, since she did know her vocabulary, she guessed that running the chicken through the flour would be dredging it, as the cookery book said to do. As she covered the pieces with the fine flour, she grimaced. She didn't think Mrs. Beeton had intended for her to also raise a floury cloud, but so far, it couldn't be helped, and so she continued to follow the recipe.

Emma melted butter; didn't fry shallots she didn't have; dumped a cloudy mound of floured chicken into the buttery spider pan; stirred the lumps that immediately formed; added salt, pepper, and skipped that pounded mace; stirred in sugar—not pounded, as Mrs. Beeton also requested—and trickled in a thin stream of rich milk.

She stirred the odd-looking concoction, her arm straining against the thick stuff in the pan at the edge of the open hearth. She had to be careful not to let a spark catch her skirt.

Stir...stir...stir. "Oh, dear..."

The mixture in the spider only got worse—and harder to stir. In moments, it became a large, lumpy blob with rivulets of unincorporated milk around it. How she was supposed to add beaten eggs, and then turn it all into rolls to cover in bread crumbs and fry? Those lumps swimming in drips? She couldn't see it.

"Lady Emma!" Robby ran in and came to a complete halt at her side. "Whatcha doing, Lady Emma? Can I help you? Can you be a lady and I be a knight now? Can we read, too? Can we? Please?"

She glanced from the iron spider with the bland-looking blobs to the boy's excited expression, and she didn't know how her mortification let her force herself to stand beside her latest failure of a meal. "Well, Robby—"

"Miss Emma!" Ned slammed the door, and ran to her side, an expression not unlike Robby's on his somewhat older features. "I reckoned you'd be needin' some strong arms to help you out right 'bout now. 'M I right, ma'am?"

Emma hated to admit it, but leaning over the spider while trying to stir the sorry-looking start—and perhaps end, too—of the croquettes had proved harder than she would have expected. She was quite petite, and her arm didn't stretch out long enough to afford her a reasonable distance from which to maneuver the ingredients in the pan without her skirt getting too close to the coals. It didn't take her long to consider her response, but Ned was quicker than she.

"Here, Miss Emma," he said. "Let me do that for ya. You can...can...well, you can do whatever a lady like you likes to be doin' this time of day."

Emma wiped her heated, damp forehead with the apron hem then faced Robby. "I do believe your papa said something about lessons, right?"

"Aw...do we—"

"Hafta?" she asked, imitating his enunciation and tone. "It's have to, and yes, Lord Robby, we do have to do our lessons."

As she retrieved his mother's Bible, Emma heard Ned clear his throat. "Er...Miss Emma?"

She paused. "Yes?"

"I did heered from Missus Colley—um...Colley, that

you're from that there place, English, an' that you're like to do some strange things, an' this here...ah...food might could be from English, too, but...what am I s'posed to do with it to help you? What're you fixin' to make us for supper tonight?"

Emma blushed up to her hairline. She stared down at the contents of the spider, and had to agree they looked anything but appetizing. They didn't even look edible, if she were honest. Puddles of milk bubbled here and there, and in the middle of the pan, the mound of flour-dredged chicken had consolidated into what resembled plaster at the best, and perhaps looked more like one of the mountains among which Mr. Lowery had located his camp.

"Well, Ned," she began, opting to soften the truth as much as possible, "I suppose Colley also told you I don't have much experience in the kitchen. What you see there is further evidence of my inexperience."

Ned looked puzzled, but didn't speak.

She drew a deep breath and continued. "I tried to follow the recipe, but..."

His eyes widened. "A recipe?"

"Yes. I have a book with directions for different dishes. Recipes."

He shook his head. "A recipe made that?"

Robby approached the spider then looked at Emma. "Is that supper?"

She cringed at the worry in his voice. "I'm sure it'll look much better once I'm—ah...it's done."

Robby gave her a doubtful look then walked toward the trunk in the corner. Emma thought she heard him say, "I hope so."

"Sure thing, ma'am," Ned said, drawing her attention back from the boy to the food in the spider. "But...what's that you're fixin' to feed us? Sure, I don't rightly know much 'bout cookery, but I do know me some."

Emma dreaded answering. The contents of the spider looked like nothing she'd ever eaten. "Croquettes," she said in her most subdued voice, then followed Robby to the trunk.

"I see." The skepticism in Ned's voice made Emma blush hotter. "Don't reckon I ever had me none of 'em."

"Oh, Ned. They're supposed to be lovely fried rolls of bits of chicken, but I'm afraid I made a mistake"—surely more than one—"while following the directions."

Ned doffed his hat and scratched his head. "Cain't be fryin' that up, Miss Emma. Is that milk?"

She nodded, biting her bottom lip to keep it from quivering.

"You go dropping that milky stuff into hot lard, and whoo-eee! Hot fat'll go spittin' out everywhere, and you'll likely be burnt. Dunno what you'll be doing with this stuff, but I sure can stir it right up for ya. After that, ma'am, you'll have to figger the rest all out."

Oh, dear. Even Ned was ready to abandon her. He'd go so far, but only so far.

A half-hour later, Emma finished putting Robby through an exercise of Scripture reading, and then spelling words she chose from among the verses. She then curled up with the boy and his favorite book in the bunk and launched into another of Sir Thomas Malory's intriguing tales of adventure. Ned nudged the spider away from the coals to the outside edge of the hearth, pulled up a chair close to the bunk, and sat to listen. The longer she read from *Le Morte D'Arthur*, the more enthralled he grew.

After a while, however, an uncomfortable niggle started up in a corner of Emma's mind. The men and Colley would soon be back. They would rightly be hungry, and would expect a substantial meal. What did Emma have for them?

She glanced at the spider and shuddered. The congealed contents looked dreadful.

Ned's efforts had incorporated the puddles of milk into the mountain of floured chicken, so they were no longer a concern, but by now it all had flattened into a gray-beige plateau. Emma didn't think she could break off chunks to form into the regular shape of a croquette, much less dunk them into beaten egg and roll them in biscuit crumbs. The chicken plateau looked firm—no, not merely firm. It looked solid.

As she debated her options for the fast-approaching meal, she heard movement behind her. Before she could turn around, she heard Robby yell.

"*En garde!*"

CRASH!

Emma spun to find Ned sprawled out on the floor, sputtering, blinking, and blushing a bright red.

She had learned the boy kept a steady supply of tree branch "*epées*" squirreled away around the cabin. Unlike his father, she saw no harm in his play, even though the occasional shout did catch her off-guard. Apparently, it had startled Ned even more.

"What in the name of tarnation was that there hollerin' all

'bout, Robby?" the erstwhile rustler asked. "And what-fer you wearin' a lady's wrap for?"

"I," the boy said in a haughty, serious voice, "am Lord Robert, Sir Ned. A knight of the realm."

"How c'n a boy be a night? Night's comin' on right quick now, but..."

As Robby launched into his child-styled description of knights, ladies, and Arthurian Britain, Emma tried to squash a smile. Ned, however, looked fascinated. The loveable child stole deeper into her heart. Before long, Robby asked her to help him teach Ned to fence.

"Please, Lady Emma," the boy asked. "Sir Ned must know how to fence. How else is he gonna 'fend a lady's honor?"

Ned shook his head. "Never did hear just one stick called a fence, nor sticking 'nother person with one of them sticks, neither."

Robby ran across the open space of the cabin, dragged the trunk away from the wall, rummaged behind it, and came up with another twig *epée* in hand. He held it out, and she grasped it.

"Really, now..." For a moment, she contemplated refusing his invitation to play, since she needed to turn the chicken into supper, a feat she doubted even Merlin could accomplish. But the prospect seemed so dreadful that she set aside any thought of responsible behavior. She surrendered and joined the boy.

She took what to her mind must surely be some sort of fencing stance, held up the branch, and made her expression grim. Robby followed her lead, bracing himself before her, his weapon raised at the ready.

"*En garde!*" he bellowed again, then lunged at her, "sword" extended.

Emma leaped back to avoid being stabbed by the twig, spun, felt her skirts swirl around her, and then returned the attack. "Aha! Take that, you knave!"

They whirled and jabbed and yelled and laughed. Before long, Ned reached out for Emma's sword. "Please, Miss Emma. A lady like you oughta do...um...lady things. This looks to me like men's work. I'll fence Lord Robby for ya. For yer honer, Lady Emma."

"Prepare to die!" Robby cried as Emma passed her weapon to Ned.

And that's how Mr. Lowery found them.

Chapter 11

As if they'd been the three blind mice of old ditty fame, Emma, Robby, and Ned scurried apart when Mr. Lowery walked in.

"What is going on here?" he asked, his words terse, brusque, deadly quiet.

Robby's wide-open eyes and pale face revealed his distress.

Ned looked around, perhaps seeking escape. None was to be found, since Peter stood in the doorway, and none of the cabin's windows was large enough for him to fit through.

Even the usually calm and docile Pippa reacted. She darted around, trotted from the hearth to the bunk, bounced up on the pillow, glared at the newcomer, all the while yapping and barking without pause.

"Pippa, hush!" Emma cried as she sped to the hearth. Her heart galloped in her chest, blood pounded in her temples, breath caught in her chest.

A quick glance revealed the chicken dinner as glutinous,

rocklike, and inedible as ever. Her time had run out. She had nothing to feed the men. Or Colley.

Worse yet, she had nothing to feed Robby.

Dear God. Help! What should I do . . . ?

She felt she should offer Peter an explanation, to tell her unwilling host how she'd begun to prepare a dish, how she'd taught Robby a list of vocabulary words, how she'd read to the boy and Ned—

Oh, dear. Perhaps mentioning the reading material she and Robby enjoyed wasn't the wisest thing to do. Emma decided to keep her peace and picked up the spoon Ned had set down. With great reluctance, she stabbed at the chicken mixture. To her horror, the spoon bounced back from the rubbery surface.

Through the rushing in her ears, she heard Mr. Lowery send Robby and Ned outside to fetch Colley. When the door closed behind them, she set the spoon back down and very, very slowly inched around to face her fate.

"Is that our supper, Miss Crowell?"

She swallowed hard. "That was my intention."

His brows crashed together over the bridge of his nose. "Was? Your intention?" He shook his head. "What is your intention now?"

Emma felt as though she were living in one of her history studies books, as though she were facing a fate not unlike Marie Antoinette's when she looked at the rioting mob. She had no suspicion a decent man like Peter would ever consider the notion of murder, but she knew her host viewed her in the same light as the French had their ill-fated queen.

She held her head high. "I, sir, intend to serve supper."

He glanced at the spider. "Supper."

Emma stiffened her spine. "Indeed."

"Tonight?"

"Of course."

He shot another glance at the pan, shook his head, and then headed toward the door. "Then I suggest you get back to working on it. It doesn't look one bit to me as if you've come up with anything any of us has ever eaten. Or will."

She blushed. That, at the very least, was true. "I will do that."

"We are hungry, you know."

At his terse words of judgment, her bottom lip quivered and her voice quavered. She had to gulp down hard to keep from admitting she was guilty as charged. "I do know."

With her words hanging in the cabin, she reached for the sharp knife again, determined to fashion something out of the contents of the pan. Fortunately, the man left the cabin once she did. But before she got too far, the cabin door opened again, shattering the deafening silence. Colley paused in the doorway long enough to run her boots across the cast-iron scraper there, an unexpectedly attractive item. Its graceful cast-iron scrolls and curlicues led Emma to suspect it had been one of the late Mrs. Lowery's purchases.

Colley's arrival had Emma wishing she could hide all evidence of her failed attempts. The no-nonsense older woman struck her as eminently capable, as though nothing she'd ever faced had bested her. Emma, on the other hand, aside from the success she'd achieved in her schoolgirl days, seemed unable to accomplish anything of significant worth.

That is, anything other than stealing gentlemen's hearts.

But that wasn't an accomplishment that could help her one bit in her current, peculiar predicament. She sighed, noting the quivery hitch in her exhalation.

Before Emma could speak, Colley stomped inside, dragged her hat off her head, and slammed the door behind her.

"Let's see here, now," the ranch manager said, her raspy voice light with what struck Emma as bottled-up humor. "What kind of pickle have ya got yerself into this time, Miss Emma?"

The comment stung straight to the heart, but she knew it came without condemnation. The small smile on Colley's weathered face was warm, and kindness radiated from her expression. Emma shrugged.

"I'm making supper."

"I do recollect hearing something just now 'bout time spent with that book the boss doesn't much fancy, some sticks, Ned, Robby...and you. But nothing much was said 'bout fixin' to feed none of us." She shook her head, and the large bun at the crown of her head scarcely budged. A strand of pewter-toned hair did slip down over her forehead. "I reckon I can give you a hand with fixin' us up some kinda supper. Let's take us a gander at what-all we're dealin' with here."

Emma didn't know whether to cringe or to hug the woman and the hope she'd brought along with her. She blinked hard, over and over again, and watched Colley march to the spider, stare at the chicken, jab at it with the spoon, and then turn to face Emma and shake her head. She hooked her hat on a chair stile then went to wash her hands. "Now, then. What were ya after dishin' up for supper for us?"

Heat filled her cheeks. "Croquettes."

"Croquettes?" Colley spun to fix Emma with a dumbfounded stare. She gestured toward the hearth with a hand dripping suds. "I ain't had me any croquettes in an age an' a half, but I sure as shootin' don't recollect 'em looking anything like that."

"Well, no, ma'am," Emma answered, mortified. "I know croquettes are lovely little rolls of bits of chicken, not this..." She blinked again. "And I followed the recipe. I really did." She thought back over her efforts. She frowned. "Well, I didn't know what on earth a mace—pounded, no less—had to do with a croquette, but I can't see where that would make it all turn out like that. And there was no white sauce out in the shed or here on the shelves, so I used milk instead—it is white and creamy. I can't imagine how skipping a handful of minced shallots might have that effect on the mixture..."

Again, Colley's lips twitched at the corner. Emma appreciated the older woman's efforts to keep from laughing, especially since she herself saw nothing humorous in her dilemma. "I do need to have something to serve for supper. And I can't serve this as it is."

"That you cain't, missy." She turned and dried her hands off on a length of cotton towel. "Come on, now, Miss Crowell. Let's see what we can wrassle up outta that mess you've gone and made today. We sure cain't be throwing out every try that don't work out right, now can we? We'd cost poor Pete his whole ranch and then some."

Emma bit her tongue to keep a defense from spilling out.

"Years ago," Colley said, "back in San Antonio when I was a little bit of a girl, my mama got mace—for a right dear price, mind you—so she only used it for some few special times. It's a spice, and I reckon they do pound it into a powder, but it sure ain't nothin' we need to make us a tasty dish."

In spite of her mortification, Emma joined forces with Colley, and before long they'd salvaged the concoction she'd made. They cut it into more or less rectangles, broke up left-over biscuits into small crumbs, dipped the rectangles in beaten egg, rolled them in the crumbs, and then fried them in deep, melted sweet butter. Colley even showed Emma how to make a cream sauce from butter, flour, and milk, and with onions added to improve the bland taste of Emma's chicken creation. When the men came back inside, none of them would have known the neat, golden pieces on the big plate had started life as total failures if Peter and Ned hadn't seen their first incarnation.

Perhaps by the time she returned home Peter and Colley would no longer view her as a failure. The urge to prove her-self capable grew to where it consumed her every thought during the meal.

Later, as everyone finished the more than acceptable dish she and Colley had cobbled together and offered their grunted compliments, Emma studied the faces around the table. At that moment, she reached a decision. The overwhelming urge had now turned into a firm goal. She would prove to everyone she was no one's notion of a failure. No need for Colley to run in and rescue Emma in the future. Somehow, she would succeed.

Somehow, she would learn to give proper meals to these folks from her kitchen.

Ginny Aiken

* * *

How Colley had turned the ugly mix in the spider into something that tasted as good as those chicken things had, Peter would never know. He did, however, know they all would have gone hungry if he'd left Emma to her own devices.

He strode out toward the barn to have a last look around as he did every night. He checked on the cow, the horses, and then looked out over the open meadow where he could make out the occasional sheep wandering toward the pond. As he often did, he waited for a cloud to pass so the gleam of moonlight would dance on the water's surface. It never failed to bring to mind the words of the twenty-third Psalm.

"The Lord is my shepherd," he whispered. "I shall not want. He maketh me to lie down in green pastures: he leadeth me beside the still waters..."

The ancient words had grown real when Peter had learned more about the animals he'd chosen to raise. In this rugged land he'd realized sheep would go without water for periods of time, on occasion even die, if the source ran briskly, if it grew agitated, since that kind of unrest tended to frighten them. A still pond, on the other hand, a peaceful spot from which to drink the life-giving liquid, was a different matter. It was up to a good shepherd—in Peter's case, a rancher—to lead his flock to a peaceful source so they could quench their thirst.

His caring for his animals struck him as like the Father's love that offered His children peaceful respite. His word said in the twenty-second chapter of Revelation, "a pure river of water of life, clear as crystal, proceeding out of the throne of God and of the Lamb..."

Peace...something he'd come to long for more and more

after coming out West. Peace...a gift from God. Peace... something he still hadn't fully grasped, but continued to seek. Peter would always treasure the closer glimpse his flock had given him into the Father's love for His flock.

A horse's whicker broke into the quiet of the night, calling him to the barn. Right off, he thought of the plucky Miss Emma Crowell, who'd come and shattered whatever measure of peace he'd achieved while working toward his goals.

Would he be able to return to even that flimsy layer of calm while he was stuck with her through the summer months?

Peter sighed. He wasn't sure he really wanted to examine the answer to that question.

As usual, Emma took Pippa out for a constitutional after she'd fed her pet that night. Colley had chased her away, saying she could finish drying the dishes from supper, but Emma should be the one to care for her dog. As before, Peter returned to the cabin before Pippa finished her business in the woods. By the time they slipped inside again, he'd taken his place by Robby's bed, the black leather-bound Bible in his large hands. His deep voice rang out in the cabin as he read the poetic Scriptures to his son.

Poetic they might be in written form, but in Peter's voice, they could and had become weapons. Emma braced herself for what she feared was sure to come. She didn't have long to wait.

"'...She seeketh wool, and flax, and worketh willingly with her hands,'" he read. "'She is like the merchants' ships; she bringeth her food from afar. She riseth also while it is yet night, and giveth meat to her household, and a portion to her maidens.'"

Emma had to wonder if his pause, right after the statement about feeding a household, was due to a need for a breath or to a need for emphasis. A glance at the drowsy Robby told her that Peter's readings certainly would not do any good to a child who needed sleep.

Or, as irritated as he'd made her, to her.

He resumed his reading after a handful of seconds. "'She considereth a field, and buyeth it: with the fruit of her hands she planteth a vineyard. She girdeth her loins with strength, and strengtheneth her arms. She perceiveth that her merchandise is good: her candle goeth not out by night. She layeth her hands to the spindle...'"

As his words trailed off, Emma felt his gaze turn toward her. Unlikely though it might be, she felt its weight as though it had been a heavy anvil on her head. Her temper had risen steadily, at the same pace as his reading of his indictment continued, but this latest pause struck her as even stranger than the earlier one. Before she could come up with an adequate question, his voice rang out again.

"'...and her hands hold the distaff—'"

The door burst open, cutting off any further reading—or any question she might have posed. "Hey, boss!" Wade cried out, somewhat out of breath. "Colley says to hurry. Ewe's about to birth that lamb, she says."

The men ran out, for which Emma was duly grateful. She doubted she could have controlled her fury much longer. The gall of the man! To scold her using something so...so sacred as God's Word.

She shook her head. Peter Lowery wasn't her father. How dare he discipline her in such a nasty way? Why didn't he come right out and take her to task? Face to face? He'd had no qualms before.

Standing, she began to pace the length of the cabin, thinking of things she wanted to say to the disapproving rancher. Before long, though, she stopped. It wouldn't do her any good to let her temper get the better of her. Peter would likely continue to correct her night after night without end. He'd made no secret of his disapproval. She doubted she could ever change that. Instead of chasing after something futile, she had to keep her mind set on what mattered. She had goals—to prove herself at the very least capable of basic tasks and to get back home where she belonged as soon as possible.

She also had a little boy who needed a woman's loving care.

She glanced at the bunk. Robby hadn't budged. He'd fallen asleep during his father's condemnations, and not even the slamming door had disturbed his sleep. She shook her head. How could Peter think scolding her would teach his son matters of the faith?

As she stood there, unable to come up with a satisfactory answer to her question, something else came to her mind. She still wanted to witness the birth of the lamb. She'd mentioned it to Peter before, and he hadn't come right out and told her no. She should be getting ready to follow the men to the barn instead of worrying over her latest encounter with her unwilling host. If she gnawed any longer on her irritation with him, she'd miss the intriguing event. She should come up with an argument persuasive enough to convince Wade to stay with Robby in the house, since Pippa, as much as the dog loved the boy, was no one's idea of a responsible caretaker.

She wrapped herself in her green wool cloak and slipped

outside. She hurried in the darkness, headed toward the faint hint of light burning in the barn. A cool breeze pierced through the warmth of the wool wrap, making her pick up her pace.

Inside, Emma was greeted by earthy scents. The spicy tang of what she assumed must be the straw bedding she could see inside the five stalls, and perhaps animal feed of some sort, reached her nostrils, and she was surprised by how pleasant it seemed. She'd always assumed a barn would smell of dreadful things. Underlying the grassy smell was the musk of animals, something she'd grown familiar with while she learned to ride.

A warm welcome drew her in, and she stepped closer to the stall. The scene before her intrigued her, as foreign as it was to her. Wade stood to a side, watching Peter and Colley, who crouched just inside one of the smaller stalls. They were so preoccupied with the ewe lying on the straw bedding that they didn't notice Emma's arrival. She hoped to keep it that way.

She sidled up to Wade. "Are you needed here?" she whispered, stunned by her audacity. She'd never been so brazen in her life.

He blinked. "Dunno, miss. Boss might need me to fetch him something. I always help with the lambing."

"But you're not needed, right? Not unless something happens."

"I reckon you could put it that way."

She drew a deep breath and searched deep for a measure of courage, the brazenness that had begun to flag. "Then there's something I would appreciate you doing for me."

The ranch hand's expression brightened as the light of

admiration glowed in his gaze. "How could I help you, Miss Emma?"

"Well, you see...I spoke to Mr. Lowery about watching the birth of the lamb, but since it's nighttime, Robby's asleep in the cabin. I don't think it's a good idea to wake him, do you?"

Wade dragged off his hat and ruffled his brown hair as he considered her question. "Well, no, ma'am. I reckon the boss wouldn't particularly like that one bit. But...I dunno what you can do, seein' as you're wanting to be two places at once."

"No, not really. I'd like to stay here to watch something I've never seen before." She took a gulp of air for the courage that again wilted. "I would need you to keep an eye on Robby for me."

When his gaze flew to Peter, a frown on his forehead, Emma hurried to add, "Not for long, you understand, just enough for me to see the birth. Then I'll run back to the cabin and fetch you. Colley and Peter—er...Mr. Lowery won't even notice, I'm sure."

Wade's frown deepened. "I dunno 'bout that, Miss Emma. He don't go 'round missing much of what goes on. But I reckon he can't get too hot under the collar if I go watch his boy."

She smiled. "That's right. It's to care for his son." And she could have her way, too.

"He'll likely not be happy," the ranch hand said, "but I can see where a body'd want to see what's happening on the ranch where they're staying. See? This isn't something to take lightly. It's something special to see a life the Lord's made come to a start."

A thrill ran through Emma. She didn't know quite why she wanted to witness the birth of the lamb, she only knew she did. "Thank you, Wade. I do appreciate your help."

"Sure do hope the boss appreciates my doing it, too."

Emma winced as he walked away, dreading the moment Peter realized his ranch hand had left and she'd stayed in his stead. She wouldn't be much help in the event that another pair of hands was needed.

After Wade left, she stepped closer and closer to the stall, until she could clearly see the shorn ewe lying in the straw. She also saw the gentle way Peter touched the animal, even as she heard his soothing, tender words.

Very different from the man she'd come to know.

"Here she goes again," Colley whispered, as the animal raised her head a bit and the rest of her body tensed, straining mightily against some unseen force.

"Easy, easy..." Peter murmured, his hand light on the distended belly. "It won't be much longer, now. You're doing fine..."

Who would have thought? What a change from the stern ranch owner she knew to this gentle...what? Was he a shepherd? No, surely not. She'd always heard those who raised sheep called ranchers out West. She supposed, though, in a fashion, that was exactly what Peter was.

"A shepherd..."

She only realized the words had slipped out when Peter and Colley swiveled and pinned her with questioning stares. They spoke at once.

"What—"

"Is Robby—"

Emma hurried the rest of the way in to just outside the stall. There was no need to stay a discreet distance away now that she'd been found out. "Robby's fine. He was sleeping soundly when I came outside. And I sent Wade to stay with him, so he's not alone."

A thunderous frown lined Peter's face. "Why would you just walk out on a sleeping child?"

Colley snickered.

The rancher shook his head. "Worse! Why did you send my ranch hand to play nursemaid to my son? Robby is your responsibility. I need Wade here."

With another soft chuckle, Colley turned back to the ewe, shaking her head.

Emma squared her shoulders. "We discussed my desire to watch one of the ewes give birth earlier, if you'll remember. I'm here to do just that. I wouldn't dream of leaving a child alone in the night. That's why I asked Wade to please sit with him while I'm gone."

To Emma's dismay, Colley's shoulders shook with mirth. Clearly, Peter didn't much care that his ranch manager had laughed at the situation, so he turned to her.

"We'll be needing a bucket of warm soapy water right soon here," he told Colley. "And some clean cloths to dry off the lamb."

Although the older woman gave Peter a strange look, she did as he asked, and left the barn. "Ain't like this is the first lamb I helped birth..."

Without a word, Emma knelt just outside the stall. Unexpected peace settled on her as she took in the sight of the animal before her, felt the warm presence of the man nearby, heard the soft whicker of a horse in one of the other stalls. Perhaps she had missed more than she knew in her regular life. "Please let me know if there's anything I can do to help you with—"

"Hush!" His request was more absent than pointed, and Emma realized he'd fixed his attention on the ewe again. The animal raised her head, gritted her jaw, let out a guttural grunt from deep in her throat, and her every muscle strained hard again.

She leaned forward.

Peter laid his hand on the animal's side. "Easy."

The ewe's immense effort struck Emma as so great that she felt compelled to help her, to do anything to ease her struggle. But was there anything she could do? It didn't appear there was, since Colley had left to fetch needed supplies, and Peter just sat at the animal's side, his only movement those gentle touches to the ewe's abdomen.

To her surprise, the calm assurance he exuded helped ease Emma's sense of urgency somewhat, even as it seemed to encourage the ewe in her travail. That composure brought her a measure of respect for the man.

Seconds later, the animal's strain let up, she lowered her head down a touch, and eased back onto the bed of straw. As she took her rest, she seemed to prepare for the next bout in her labor.

The silence in the barn began to disconcert Emma, especially since Colley had yet to return. The only ones in the structure, aside from the horses and the laboring ewe, were Peter and her. She grew unsettled.

When she was about to burst out with some inconsequential

chatter, the ewe raised her head and let out another of her rough grunts. Emma was coming to know the rhythm of the animal's labor pains, and she felt she could go with their ebbs and flows until the lamb was born. Peter seemed enthralled by the event, and likely didn't register her presence at his side anymore.

Then, when she least expected it, the ewe's straining grew harsher and Peter leaned closer, blocking her view. "Here we go, girl," he said, a touch of excitement in his voice. "I see your lamb, now. Easy...easy."

Emma's heart kicked up its beat, and she found herself praying under her breath. Before, she hadn't been one to spend much time pleading for heavenly assistance, but in this sweet-smelling barn, as she watched the miracle of Creation played out before her, she gained a new appreciation of God's gifting. She wanted nothing to go wrong, nothing to keep the valiant mother-to-be from ending her efforts with a hearty and healthy little one at her side.

Peter shifted closer as he reached out to the ewe. As he moved, Emma saw what his hands had stretched out for. Even though he hadn't yet touched it, she could see the lamb. As the infant protruded from between the ewe's rear legs, its forefeet and nose showed through a clear membrane. An odd emotion caught hold of Emma, and she was helpless to keep tears from welling up.

The ewe strained once again, and Peter grasped the little feet that poked out through the membrane between the first three fingers of one of his large hands. With the other, he cradled the small head, his tenderness causing her heart to swell even more.

With firm, sure motions, he held the tiny new life in his hands, his voice crooning to the mother. To Emma's surprise, she realized he'd lulled her, too, into a sense of peace she doubted she otherwise would have felt at such an eventful moment, or any other moment, at that. The ewe continued her labor, her effort nearly continuous by then, all the while Peter exerted the gentlest of pulls on the infant to help ease it into the world.

Birth.

New life.

God's Creation.

A drop of moisture slipped onto Emma's lips, and only then did she realize she wept at the wonder of it all. Awe at the reality of what was happening before her, of the promise of a future existence, washed over her. Images flew through her thoughts, inspired by the lessons she'd been taught her whole life in church.

She'd accepted what she'd heard, but hadn't spent much deep thought on the teachings. Superficial, indeed. Right then, however, in Peter's small barn, as Emma watched the miracle of birth, she caught a glimpse of the much more awe-inspiring, more unfathomable miracle of Jesus' birth.

The new lamb, not yet fully into the world, couldn't yet breathe or live on its own. It would remain a part of its mother until it drew that first life-giving breath. The notion impressed upon her as never before mankind's need of the Father. God the Father had breathed the breath of life into Adam, the first man, and continued to do so with every new creature on earth. Emma had never felt so small and humble in her life.

Emotions she'd never experienced wracked her, and she

breathed a prayer of thanksgiving. She would never regret coming out to the barn to watch this lamb be born.

The ewe's body gave another massive heave, and just like that, the rest of the lamb's body slipped out into Peter's hands. With a large finger, he wiped across the tiny nostrils, clearing away the thick moisture visible there. He laid the newborn in the straw right by its mama's head, then picked up a blade of the straw bedding, and with it tickled the animal's nose. The little one shook its head. A snuffly sneeze burst out.

The ewe nudged her offspring with her nose, sniffing, acquainting herself with her infant, and then began to vigorously lick the lamb. She appeared quite intent on cleaning it of all sign of the birthing process.

"Emma," Peter said, his voice husky. "There's a piece of clean towel hanging from a hook outside the stall. Could you please hand it to me?"

Clearly he hadn't forgotten her presence in the barn. Emma scrambled up and let her cape drop to the ground, thrilled to be able to participate in the blessed event, even if in such an insignificant way. A moment later, she found the rough-woven, much-washed cotton, grabbed it, and returned to her prior post.

"Here."

Without turning in her direction, he reached blindly behind him for the cloth. Emma grasped his hand, the large hand that only moments before had held a new life, and placed the towel there. The moist warmth of his work-roughened skin gave evidence of the event she'd just witnessed, and moved her more than it likely should. Admiration filled her. Those hands had helped that lamb ease its way safely into the world.

Her view of Peter Lowery shifted. She counted the moment as yet another one that changed her life. How, she couldn't say.

But change it had.

As the realization struck, Peter glanced back.

Their gazes met.

And held.

Chapter 12

Birthing a lamb had never felt like such an intimate experience before. Peter had always recognized the Creator's hand in all phases of life, but as he'd felt Emma's presence at his back, as he'd listened to her hushed breathing, as he'd sensed her amazement, he'd viewed an otherwise mundane lambing in a new way.

He'd watched and helped deliver dozens of lambs by now. Usually, it was Colley with her practical, sensible demeanor who kept him company, especially during the touchy ones, as this first-time mama's birthing had been. Tonight, Emma had brought him a different way of thinking about what he did day after day after day. Pride and humility mingled inside him, contrary though the two emotions were.

As he found himself caught in the web of her tear-filled green gaze, Peter couldn't help but acknowledge once again the wonder of life. God held it all in His magnificent, all-powerful hands. Even when loss and pain invaded, the Father had a way of bringing hope back into His children's lives. The trick was in recognizing it when it came.

He let out an odd hiccup of a laugh. Funny how it took a frivolous society miss to remind him of that.

"Thank you." The roughness in his voice caught him by surprise. Not only that, but he realized unaccustomed dampness had risen to his eyes. Just as had happened to her. He could still see the moisture spiking her eyelashes and making the many shades of green flicker in the lantern's light. How a woman like Emma could raise within him such a peculiar response to something so familiar, he'd never know. Peter just knew Emma had come into his life like a wild storm, and nothing had felt the same since.

The red-haired storm nodded and gave him a small, tentative smile. Something told him this was the true Emma Crowell, the one few ever saw. The socialite with her fancy airs was a part of her, true, but a part he suspected she'd grown used to displaying over time. This emotional woman, the one who'd held his son close to her side, who'd read to him until they'd both fallen asleep, this one who'd let herself be moved by the simple miracle of new life, was the woman he suspected few ever saw.

Why he should feel so honored by that realization, he also didn't know.

Oh, yes. Emma Crowell was trouble. Peter feared the danger she posed was greater than that posed by the threat of ruin in the fall.

He couldn't let himself fall under her spell.

She couldn't be any further from the kind of woman he needed. He couldn't let his attention wander toward her any more than it should.

To that end, he shook his head to free himself from the effect she still had on him.

Colley marched into the barn again, destroying the magic of the moment he and his uninvited guest had shared. "Here y'are. Brought ya the warm water and soap, plus the scissors, tincture of iodine, and more clean cloths. That there lamb sure is one pretty little girl, now, isn't she?"

All Peter registered was Colley talking about a pretty "she," and he couldn't help but nod. While Emma's hair still displayed that wild quality, no matter how tightly she tried to plait it each day, it didn't detract one bit from her looks. She was still the loveliest woman he'd ever seen.

As much as he'd loved his wife, and as pretty as she'd been, he knew in an objective way that Emma outshone her like no other woman he knew.

When he realized he hadn't answered his ranch manager, his irritation grew. At the source of his distraction, of course. Time to pay attention to his business again.

The ranch. His animals. The lamb. "Looks right healthy, too."

"Good thing, I'd say."

From the corner of his eye, he saw Emma sit back into the layer of straw, twin dabs of red on her cheeks, the dampness in her eyes only making them shine brighter still. She scooted a hair sideways, letting Colley into the stall closer to his side.

A surprising sense of loss struck him, but he pushed that aside and focused on the newest member of his mercifully growing flock.

With the ease of expertise, he and Colley cared for the two animals, and once the stall was clean again, he prepared to leave the barn. It was then he realized Colley must have forgotten the pail of warm water for the ewe to drink. She would need plenty of liquid in order to produce the amount of milk the newborn would need.

"We need another pail of warm water," he said. "And molasses."

Colley made a face. "Silly of me! I up and forgot the other one back at the cabin. I'll be right back, Pete. Don't you worry none. And give me them dirty rags. I'll take 'em out with me."

With a final look to make sure the lamb was suckling properly, Peter stood, ready to head to the bunkhouse for some much-needed sleep. He realized Emma still sat on the cushion of straw, wearing a tender expression, seemingly unable or unwilling to drag her gaze away from the occupants of the stall.

He couldn't stop the grin. "There's nothing more to see."

She blinked, then looked up at him. "What do you mean?"

"The lamb is born. Now, the ewe will raise her. Just like all the other sheep do. And they need to get their rest. It's best for the lamb if they're not disturbed for the next couple of days. It lets the two of them grow close, like a mama and lamb should."

She pursed her lips and her eyes snapped. "Are you making fun of me, Mr. Lowery?"

His mouth twitched as he tried to keep from smiling. "I reckon it's past time you called me by my given name."

"Fine." She stood. "But should they really be left all alone? What if something goes wrong? Who'll help the poor little thing?"

"Right now, the best help the 'little thing' can have is attention and lots of milk from its mother. The two of us sitting here and talking will only distract them. They really need to sleep. So do you."

"Sleep?" She looked surprised. "You really think sleep is possible? After…" She gestured toward the sheep. "After this?"

He had to laugh. "I don't know about you, Miss Emma, but I know I sure can sleep. I need it. A full day's worth of work and then some will be waiting on me when the sun rises. I'm sure Robby'll be up before you know it, too. Then there's all those meals you'll be needing to make, right? We're all waiting on you."

Indignation turned her face the color of fresh-cooked beets. "Oh! Oh-oh-oh! How dare you?"

He raised his hands in a gesture of innocence. "What? Mention what we all know? That you can't cook? There's no shame in that." At her surprise, he shrugged. "I've come to think you did have a point. It isn't your fault you never were taught, but I reckon you can learn while you're with us, can't you?"

"As if you've given me a choice!"

"I don't have a choice, either. I found you, whether I wanted to or not. I could hardly up and leave you out there." He lifted a shoulder. "I'm not one to hurt anyone, even by not taking action, by walking away and not doing something to keep them from being hurt. My faith doesn't have room for that kind of thing. And I'm not ready to be an inhospitable oaf, once a body's on my land."

"I'd say an oaf is just what you are. Why, I've been working mighty hard to learn, and I've been working with Robby to teach him his vocabulary, too. We've been working on improving his reading ability, I'll have you know."

His humor faded some. "About that reading…"

She crossed her arms. "Are you about to protest over the reading matter? Because if that's the case, sir, then I'll have you know we did our lessons using the Good Book before we ever touched *Le Morte D'Arthur.* By the time you came back to the cabin, we'd finished. I gave you my word, and I kept it. We only read from the Malory after I'd put Robby through his lesson."

Skepticism made him arch a brow. "Were you teaching Ned some kind of lesson, too? I never asked you to teach my prisoner anything, you know."

She squared her shoulders. "He didn't take any part in our lesson. But there wasn't much for him to do in the cabin. He simply sat and listened while Robby and I read. Then…well, then Robby wanted to play, and I, sir, saw no harm in letting a child entertain himself. It was innocent play, after all."

"Innocent play you knew I wanted you to avoid."

She shook her head, and the dark auburn curls flew loose from the bounds of her braid. "I couldn't do that. It's something he enjoys because it reminds him of his mother. I could never take that away from him. I can't say I see your reason to do so, in fact."

He narrowed his eyes. "It didn't look to me like you were recollecting my late wife when I walked in. You were neglecting your work and cavorting with the man who stole from my flock."

She gasped, horror blazing in her expression. "Cavorting? I wasn't cavorting with Ned! Not at all." Her arms punctuated her words with firm, wide gestures that set her richly colored curls to dancing over her shoulders. "When you walked in,

I'll have you know, I was in the process of handing Ned the sword—er...the branch, so that he and Robby could play. I was about to return to my supper preparations."

The thought of the contents of the spider before Colley had stepped in made Peter laugh. "And a fine supper it would have been, had I not sent my ranch manager in to save it, right? Seems to me your efforts do more harm than good. It didn't even look like food."

Her eyes grew huge. Peter knew he'd gone too far. He'd let his fears, worries, and irritation push him to where he'd wounded Emma.

Without another word, she swooped down, caught up her cape in her arms, spun on her heel, and fled the barn. As she ran away, the silence of the night grew thick, uncomfortable, and troubling.

While he hadn't wanted Robby to waste his time on useless fairy tales, he also had never wanted to wound anyone as he just had hurt Emma. As guilt swelled in his heart, the door opened again.

"What in tarnation was all that about, Peter Lowery?" Colley asked, shaking her head. She plunked down the bucket of sweetened warm water in a corner of the stall, closed the door and latched it, then clapped her hands free of straw. She turned her blue eyes on Peter. "Well?"

"Ah...that was Emma."

"I ain't gone blind, all of the sudden, you know. I saw it was Emma right clear when she flew by. Now, what kind of forest fire was she runnin' from, Pete?"

Shame heated his face, so he shrugged. "She wasn't running from any fire."

"And of course, y'ain't foolin' me none, neither. What did you go and do to that lil girl?"

Peter couldn't make himself meet his ranch manager's gaze. He also couldn't find the words to confess his cruelty toward a guest in his home. He knew Colley would take to that truth no more kindly than she had to whatever her no-nonsense mind suspected.

Of course, she suspected the truth. That he'd lashed out as he'd done before. Only thing was, his criticism had been worse, it had gone deeper this time. This woman who'd helped him so much after his wife's death had come to know him better than anyone else ever had. She knew he'd hurt Emma and, as she often did, she was going to hold him accountable. He wasn't ready for that, he never was.

With a glare in her direction, he gave an abrupt wave of his hand, snagged the lantern hanging from the iron arm on the wall, and stalked outside.

"Hey!" Colley yelled her objection. "It's dark in here."

"Go to the cabin. Emma has no idea what she's doing." She'd never find her way back. He had to go and find her himself. If he had to apologize, and he did, he'd do it right to her face. He wasn't about to do it twice.

He'd worry about Colley once his "guest" was safe again.

"Women!" He shook his head as he headed into the wooded darkness. His swinging lantern sent fantastical, misshapen shadows into the trees. Robby—and likely Emma, as well—would view the shapes as "dragons" for a knight to slay.

"Bah!" He'd never understand any one single woman, much less the whole lot of them.

Men were much easier to figure out. They focused on more

concrete and practical things. Like finding a distraught guest on a chilly spring night lit by only a sliver of a moon and a small lantern in his hand. Before she got lost in the woods.

Again.

In the scant light, he paused to look around. To his surprise, he saw no sign of the fleeing woman. How could that be? She hadn't left his side that many minutes ago.

Where could Emma Crowell have gotten herself to in such a short time?

At least there was no snow on the forest floor. Emma gulped fast bursts of cold, evening air into her lungs, enough to keep her going, going—where?

She pulled up short, panting, her legs aching from the sudden hard sprint. She had no idea how far she'd gone. She only knew she'd given it her all, just so she could get away from any more critical, judgmental, detestable, insufferable, hurtful comments. And from Peter. Maybe she should just keep running until she went all the way down the mountain and came to flat ground. Surely she'd get to Bountiful—or some other somewhat civilized place—sooner or later.

Anything to avoid Peter Lowery for the rest of her life.

Even though she'd run out of steam, she continued to march away from the direction of the barn, the camp, and that...that lout—oaf! That's what he'd called himself, and she might as well use the term. And to think she'd been so impressed by him just moments before he'd opened his mouth. But now, when she thought back over the time she'd spent in the barn, she realized the ewe had been the one who'd done all the work. All Peter did was to catch the newborn lamb after the ewe birthed it.

True, he never said anything to suggest he took credit for what Emma had witnessed. And the event had clearly moved him. They had exchanged that meaningful look...

"No!" She was not about to let herself be lulled into a sense of comfortable companionship again when it came to that man. He'd gone and ruined a truly nice moment by mocking her, by insulting her, by ... by ...

By reminding her of her own failings.

Slowly, her steps came to a stop. No matter how hard she'd tried to flee from the truth, it had followed her. She didn't have to run from Peter to know in her heart that she'd failed to learn anything that made her useful. If she'd never been separated from her traveling party, maybe things would have been different. Maybe she would have been able to stay in her oblivious state. Maybe she wouldn't have needed to know any of the more practical things of life. But her life had taken that turn.

And it had made her see herself in a different way.

Yes, of course, she could learn. Given adequate time and a bit of help. But she didn't want either at Peter's camp. She'd much rather hurry home where, in the privacy of Ophelia's comfortable kitchen, Emma could become the older woman's apprentice.

Very well, then. Time had come to gather her gumption, as Ophelia often said, and head back to civilization. She took a step, but had to pause. Which way was Bountiful located? Portland? Other folks? Anything?

She turned, first one way then the next. The dark of night

lay heavy on the woods, making them impenetrable and menacing. She couldn't even tell which way she'd come. Oh, dear.

Whereas anger had been her overriding emotion only minutes earlier, a sense of foreboding appeared in a corner of her heart. It was one thing to run from an overbearing man. It was altogether another to run aimlessly in the woods.

In the pitch black.

At night.

Alone.

"Oh, goodness." A sinking sensation left her a touch queasy. "I couldn't have gotten lost that soon. It's not possible. I just have to look more carefully, trace my way back."

But when she tried to look down toward her feet, to search for her own immediate footprints, she could see not even a hint of her recent flight. Not only was it dark, making it more difficult than necessary to identify something as minor as the mark of a shoe, but the forest floor was also littered with leaves and twigs and who-knew-what-else, a cushion that sprang back to disguise any impression.

Had she ever known what direction she should take to reach Bountiful? Even on that day she'd first found herself lost on this mountain, she hadn't had a clue where the town was located. She'd wandered around with Pippa, following voices to that small clearing. Now, she couldn't hope for voices to guide her. Everyone was back at the camp. Even her little dog.

A sob caught in her throat.

She would rather move forward than go back.

The sooner she found her way back to town, the sooner she'd be in Papa's loving embrace again. And once there, she could send for her pet. Her determination back as a beacon, she set off to her right, since she'd seen nothing to draw her in any one direction more than another.

"Lord?" Her voice seemed to echo much louder than she thought the puny murmur should have. "I know I haven't paid You the kind of attention You deserve in the last few years. I also know You showed me something powerful tonight in that barn—ouch!"

Her ankle twisted when she stepped on something, more than likely a fallen branch since it felt as though it had rolled beneath her weight. Emma reached down and rubbed, well aware it would smart the next day. But she couldn't stop and nurse an ache. She had to keep going.

She hurried, hoping to come out of the woods sooner. "And then," she said, resuming her conversation with God, "it was quite foolish to run out into the dark with no idea which way I should go, just because Peter irked me with his comments. It's because it was true, what he said. It seems as though that's how I've been, like a child, tumbling from one adventure to the next, but Papa's always been there to tell me it's all right when something's not gone right."

She kept walking, the moon not giving her much help through the tree-thick forest. A branch scraped her cheek. "Ooooh!"

She fought against the sting, rubbing her cheek, hoping she didn't wind up with an ugly scar. "Please, do help me, Lord."

The depth of the silence continued to stun her, and she walked on. Soon, however, the reality of her loneliness had her chattering to God again. "I guess a life of little-girl adventures becomes a more serious matter when one is grown up and still falling into those adventures. Especially if one gets lost in the woods. More than once, at that. I need help to get... somewhere—"

"Well, well, well." Sawyer materialized before her out of the stygian black. "Looky what we have us here. It ain't 'specially nice out here by night. I figgered y'ain't never done much that ain't not nice in yer life, missy."

Emma ignored him and continued walking, her gaze fixed ahead and just to the right of Sawyer's shoulder. He stepped out of her way, then matched his pace to hers, walking at her side.

After a few silent minutes, he seemed to draw closer. "So, missy. Where ya headin' to?"

She sidled away, but didn't slow down. "I needed some air."

After a handful of steps, he tipped his head toward her and again came closer than she wanted. She stepped away, yet again.

Then, with what seemed like a smile in his voice, he said, "Wouldn'ta thought you'd be out and about in the middle of the night."

She didn't respond. She just wanted to get away from him and closer to folks. Regular folks.

"Don't ya wanta be cozy-like in one a them beds in Lowery's cabin?"

She didn't like the way he made his words sound...dirty. She thought of Mrs. Hepplesmith, her watercolor instructor, the most prim and proper woman she'd ever met. She fashioned her tone after the lady's instructional approach. "One of the ewes gave birth tonight, Mr. Sawyer."

The rustler again matched his steps to hers, ever closer to

her side. "I heered something 'bout some animal in the barn. Didn't pay much mind though."

Mrs. Hepplesmith...Mrs. Hepplesmith, she repeated soundlessly, hoping the woman's starchy demeanor would affix itself to her own. "I chose to spend a while in the barn watching the lovely event, but then—"

Emma caught herself before she revealed too much. It wasn't in her nature to not be amiable, but the longer he walked alongside her, closer and closer with each step, the more anxious she became. She didn't want to encourage him. *Please, Lord, help!*

Then something occurred to her. She pulled up short. "What, pray tell, are you doing out here, sir? I understood you'd been confined to the bunkhouse, that you've been kept tied to your bed all this time."

In the meager light that filtered through the trees from the slivered moon, she saw Sawyer give a one-shouldered shrug. "I found me an old china cup. It broke right quick, and I used it to saw through the rope 'round my feet. Dinnent cut myself as much there, on account of my socks, as when I tried to get my hands loose."

A glance revealed hands still secured at his back. "I see."

She marched on in silence. It gave her some comfort to know his hands were bound. And he couldn't have retrieved his weapon. Her initial fear now began to turn to irritation as he kept up with her.

No more than twenty paces later, her discomfort grew even more acute. It was absolutely not a necessity for Sawyer to have narrowed the distance between them quite this much as they'd passed through the thick stands of trees. The trees didn't grow that close together. Clearly, ignoring him was doing little to discourage him.

Once again, she came to a full stop, this time perching her fists on her cloak-draped hips. "Do tell, Mr. Sawyer, sir. What do you plan to do now that you've freed yourself?"

"I ain't rightly freed myself yet."

She rolled her eyes and sighed. "I can see that, sir, but you're no longer Mr. Lowery's captive. What is in your future now?"

"Future?" His voice rose in outrage. "Lady, all's I'm after is gettin' this blamed rope off my hands. I ain't thinking of no future past that. Mebbe then I'll think on finding me a good glass of sour mash—"

"Understood!" She didn't want their discussion to go down any such path. She knew she would immediately regret that. "Once you are freed, then what? I don't recollect any . . . ahem! Sour mash, sir, anywhere in these woods."

He shot her a sideways glance. "When I've my hands back, why, then I reckon I can head for that Bountiful place you talk so much about. Hear say there's a fair hotel there, with good cooking. Should find me some way to win myself a pocketful of money at that new saloon I heered they built theirselves. Poker's big there, too, I hear."

Distaste filled her. "Hm . . ." But then the more important point of his statement struck her. "You're headed to Bountiful, you say."

"Mm-hm."

"You know how to get there?"

"Well, I ain't rightly said, now, have I? But it can't be too hard to find the way. Man's gotta go down these mountains no matter what he does. Then I reckon I can figger which way's east. I know the south a right bit better, but I heered east is where the town is, so that's where I'm heading."

"Funny you should say all that, Mr. Sawyer. I'm headed to Bountiful, myself. But I don't know which way it's located, much less how to find my way around this mountain."

His walking slowed. He tipped his head, studying her for long moments. "And, you're wanting...?"

Rescue me, Mrs. Hepplesmith! Then she realized how silly the stray notion was. The only help for her right then was standing before her in the shape of the highly untrustworthy and fully disreputable Mr. Sawyer. But what choice did she have?

None, if she wanted to head home to Papa. Mr. Lowery had said it was a day by horse, but it couldn't be that much longer on foot. If they left now and didn't stop, perhaps she could be in Bountiful by tomorrow evening. Surely she could manage to tolerate Mr. Sawyer's company for that long.

Emma squared her shoulders. "Well, sir. I'm asking your assistance. I must return to civilization so that I can notify my father as to my whereabouts. I absolutely know he must be frantic by now. I know he'd be quite happy to make any help you offer me well worth your while."

"Ya sure do talk some funny." Sawyer shook his head. "Worth my while, huh? Ya don't say?"

"Indeed." Swallowing her misgivings, and desperate to get home, she thought of an old saying. In for a penny, in for a pound. She drew in a deep breath then lurched forward with her words. "I would like to suggest that you help me return to Bountiful. I promise Papa will offer you a respectable reward once we're back."

She could see him mulling over her offer.

He rubbed his chin against his shoulder, and the friction made a strange, raspy sound. "See, I figger it's like this. I reckon I could use me some dollars, seein' as how I been left behind without a thing to show for all the work I done. And then, that Lowery fella goes an' ties me up. Like a hog, I tell ya."

Emma kept her peace.

Once again, Sawyer studied her in silence, his gaze a heavy weight as he raked her with those piercing, dark eyes. "If that's the case, why then, I figger you got yerself a deal here, missy. But, seein' as we're pardners, now, untie my hands."

She drew in a harsh breath. She hadn't thought that far ahead when she'd made her offer. Sawyer unfettered didn't strike her as a wise proposition. On the other hand, she certainly didn't relish the thought of the enraged thief if she refused to help him free himself.

Would he be as likely to wreak the same havoc with his hands tied as free? He could run as fast as she, if not faster. He could then knock her to the ground...and then? What could he do?

On the other hand, with full use of his hands...

Which alternative was the lesser evil?

She feared she knew the answer to that, but she also could see the ire rising in his expression as she took her time to consider his request. Anger in Sawyer didn't strike her as particularly beneficial to her, regardless of whether his hands were bound or not. And he'd hardly help her get to Bountiful if she didn't release him.

In the end, she sent up another brief prayer, then nodded. "Very well. I'll see what I can do."

He let out a growl. "Wrong! What you'll see is that you can and will untie my hands."

"I'll do my best, Mr. Sawyer."

"Mr. Sawyer-this! Mr. Sawyer-that! My name's Sawyer Smith, missy. Jist call me Sawyer, a'right?"

Emma bit her bottom lip, then gave another, smaller nod. The thought of touching the man repulsed her, but the thought of infuriating him any further—no! She shuddered, but made her choice.

"Turn around, please." She hated the tremor in her voice. Sawyer was the sort who'd take advantage of even the slightest sign of weakness. "It's quite dark, and I can't see well at all."

She began to work on the knots, which had been tied by someone with experience and strength, neither of which she had. Gnawing on her bottom lip, she concentrated, tugging at the rope with her ragged fingernails. Her awkward position didn't help the matter, and her frustration grew.

His impatience grew at the same pace.

And then, when she was about to give up in defeat, an especially strong tug loosened the knot. Moments later, Emma had Sawyer freed.

"Ah-ha!" He rubbed his wrists, shook his hands, and rolled his shoulders.

Then, before Emma realized what was happening, he grabbed her by the shoulders and plastered himself on her. He smashed wet lips on her face, dragged them down toward her mouth.

Emma pulled back, horrified. The wetness on her cheek turned her stomach. The stench of the man, sour sweat mixed with something sharp she couldn't identify, was overpowering.

She gagged as she fought to wedge her fists between her body and Sawyer, fighting to get in a punch or two, but without much power to them they did little good.

Oh, dear God! This wasn't supposed to happen. Help me!

With all her strength, she repeated her plea, with all her might, the sound reverberating against the surrounding trees. "HELP!"

Chapter 13

"HELP!"

Peter thought he'd imagined Emma's scream until another came on the next breeze. Half of him wanted to believe his mind had played tricks on him, but his other half knew better.

"Colley!" he cried. "Get back to the cabin. Send Wade out here then stay with Robby. Something's happened to Emma."

Without waiting for his ranch manager's response, Peter took off in the direction of the screams. He prayed a third one would ring out again, to give him a better sense of which direction to follow, but the silence grew deafening.

"Lord, please!"

Where had she gone? And what had she stumbled into out there?

Guilt was not a man's best companion. He hadn't recognized the worth in her efforts. Even after she'd tried more than once, he'd teased her about her lack of expertise, practically mocking her attempts. He now understood her urge to flee from him.

Peter didn't think she'd gone anywhere in particular, but rather, that she'd rushed out, clearly desperate to get away from him.

The overwhelming sense of remorse drove him to move faster. "Emma!"

His voice echoed off the trees in waves. It came back at him with haunting emptiness. He knew, though, the forest wasn't empty. Emma was out there. And she'd called for help.

"Mr. Lowery!" Ned cried, rushing up to his side. "Mr. Lowery, sir. You gotta come—now. Sawyer's gone!"

"What?" His thoughts spiraled down the worst path and made him sick. "We had him tied up. How could that be?"

"I found this," the younger outlaw said, holding a white shard in the light cast by the lantern. "Looks like it might could be a cup or a plate or something. I reckon he broke it, see? Found it right by his bed."

The sick dread in Peter's stomach curdled into pure worry. He remembered the way Sawyer had rubbed up against Emma, the leering looks he'd sent her way, the fear she'd revealed in her pretty green gaze. Meeting up with that—that animal in the dark forest would no doubt provoke screams like the ones he'd heard. His urgency grew.

"Come on, Ned. I need your help." As hope bloomed on the young man's face, Peter raised a finger. "I warn you. You must do what I say. There'll be consequences if you bolt. I will find you, no matter where you run."

"I ain't dumb, Mr. Lowery, sir." Ned's voice rang out in

earnest if somewhat out of breath from trotting by Peter's side. "You're a right fine sorta man, an' Sawyer's not. I ain't sure I wanna come up an' find him in the dark, myself. Never know what that snake might could do a body, you know."

The blood drained from Peter's face. "Come on. Emma's out here. With Sawyer loose now . . ."

He didn't have the strength to finish the thought.

It didn't look as though Ned wanted him to waste time either. "Let's us be movin', then, Mr. Lowery. There ain't no time to let go wastin'."

Peter set off again toward where he thought he'd heard the cries, Ned at his heels. But that didn't strike him as productive. "You go that way." He pointed back toward the clearing. "Stay on the edge of the road. I'll call you when I find anything. And you can—"

"I'll call you when I find that good-for-nothin' Saw—"

"*HELP*—"

The cut-off scream sent ice through Peter's veins. "Let's go!"

His boots pounded the ground as he ran toward the cry. Ned followed, only a pace behind. As he ran, however, Peter caught what sounded like someone approaching. He hoped it was Wade. He had no idea what they'd find when they reached Emma's side, and he wasn't sure how reliable Ned would be.

Peter cast a glance over his shoulder, but saw nothing. He kept running, the spring-cold air cutting in his lungs like a knife. He'd never forgive himself if Sawyer hurt Emma.

"You see anything, boss?" Wade called out of the dark.

"Nothing yet. But we heard her yelling out this way."

"I heard her, too."

The three men pushed their way through the underbrush, darted between the trees. Fear tightened the knot in Peter's gut.

Another cry tore the night.

"There!" he called to his two companions. "We're closing in. At least we're not moving blind anymore."

Heart racing, he braced his forearms before him, using them as a fence against the whipping of the branches in his way. He prayed he and the others weren't too late, for Emma's sake.

Step after step, heartbeat after heartbeat, Peter prayed for light, for the sun to rise soon, for them to find Emma.

Emma's nightmare began in earnest when they landed in a tangled heap in a bed of debris on the forest floor. She tried to roll away, but only brought Sawyer fully on top of her, pinning her against the side of a felled tree. One of his legs bound hers to the old trunk, and Sawyer let out an unholy cackle she took for his sick laugh. She bucked and jerked her shoulders from one side to the other, doing everything she could to dislodge the foul creature from on top of her.

All her fighting did was present him with the opportunity to grab her cloak at the neck and drag one half to a side. She feared she knew what was coming, and she let out another scream. "Help!"

Sawyer slapped his mouth full on hers. A fist grabbed the neck of her lace-trimmed blouse, twisted, and pulled. Horror filled her when she heard the delicate fabric give in a sickening rent. Cold assailed her neck, her chest, and even the top of her bosom, bared by the edge of her corset cover.

Dear God, no!

Fear unlike anything she'd ever imagined filled her, and while she recognized her own vulnerability, she refused to give in to what felt like the impending inevitable. She refused to surrender.

With what had to be the greatest spurt of strength she'd ever produced, she wrenched her arm free from between their tangled bodies and clawed at everything she touched. She knew she'd struck success when Sawyer cried out like the animal he was.

"Why, you...ya think yer too good for the likes of me—"

Again he latched his repulsive mouth to her, this time landing blindly on her brow. She grunted with her effort to dislodge him, snarling with frustration at her failure to escape her attacker, no matter how dogged her fight.

His rough handling, the evil twisting of his expression, made Emma fear for her life. If he carried through his carnal intent, he would rob her of her sanity. Then, if the vicious violence in his actions went through to the end she feared, surely he wouldn't give up until all her fight was gone. And that would only happen when...

When her life was done.

But she still had fight in her. She arched her back, pulled her chin toward the sky, and gave out another scream. "Help—"

He clamped his dirty hand over her mouth. "Shut up!"

Whimpers of pain rose in her throat and came out in guttural sounds. Tears burned her eyes. But she refused—

"GET OFF HER!"

At first, Emma thought she'd imagined Peter's command, but when the pressure of Sawyer's body lifted from atop hers, she opened her eyes and looked right into the sheep rancher's storm-dark ones. At that moment, not only were his eyes dark, but his enraged expression evoked a gale.

Unaccountably, while she knew help had arrived, tremors set off from within her core. "How...?" Her question died when Peter landed a blow to Sawyer's gut. The outlaw bent double as his breath whooshed out, yet he still managed to kick out. As he did, his heavy boot clipped Peter's shin.

The rancher grunted in pain.

Emma's tremors grew. Soon, her body quaked out of control. Tears poured from her eyes and down her temples, where the dead leaves on the forest floor caught them all.

The men continued to battle, but she knew Sawyer wouldn't fight fair.

He hadn't thought to deal decently with her.

"Go on, Emma!" Peter yelled, his hand still clenched in the fabric of Sawyer's shirt. "Get back to the cabin."

Emma didn't know if she could move, much less find her way back, but she knew she couldn't stay where she was. With shudders still wracking her, she sent up wild, formless prayers.

"Lord...the sunrise! We need light..."

As she tried to move, she felt weaker than before, fought for a breath...then knew no more.

Drawing his arm back, Peter landed a punch on Sawyer's jaw. As he wound up again, he got the wind knocked out of him. Sparks burst before his eyes, and he gasped for air, furious he hadn't seen Sawyer's arm. Bent over, gasping, he tried to draw in air, but the outlaw took advantage of his momentary weakness. Sawyer stunned him with a blow to the side of the head.

On his way down, Peter used his last bit of strength to fling Sawyer toward the ground. He heard the crash as his head spun, his lungs burned for lack of air. He tried to cling to consciousness, his mind on Robby, but in the end, the dark rose up, and he felt himself drown in the pain.

When Peter opened his eyes, the slightest hint of gray peered through the lowest boughs of the nearest evergreens. Dawn wasn't far off. Fortunately, he'd be able to get a better idea of what he faced with the increasing light. All he remembered was the fight with Sawyer and going down, to his shame and vexation.

Emma!

He rose to his elbows, needing to see if she'd left safely, as he'd told her to do, but the movement made his head swim. He fell right back. "Ooof!"

From somewhere to his left, he heard a soft, "Owww!"

"Emma!" he called. "Wh—why are you...still here?"

Silence.

Then the rustle of underbrush.

Finally, "Because I...I had"—shock cut into Emma's words—"the vapors! For the first time ever, I'll have you know, Peter Lowery. I'm not some silly, simpering—NO!"

Her horror-filled shriek made him ignore the shattering pain in every inch of his body and the stunning pounding in his head. He rose in one shaky motion, swayed as he tried to stand, but his determination lent him the will to struggle on. He felt weaker than the lamb that had dropped the night before, and his stomach gave a sick lurch. Still, worry for Emma made him force his eyes to focus. What he saw explained her scream.

And nearly had him echo it with one of his own.

Not ten feet away, he saw the outline of a man lying on his back. The grayish light cast over the trees to the east allowed him to make out the features, and he recognized Sawyer. The way the outlaw lay sprawled—head at an unnatural angle, fingers clawed at his own throat, eyes bulging, tongue protruding, one leg bent at the knee, the other jutted straight out—told him they needn't fear Sawyer would hurt Emma again.

On the other hand, it was clear Sawyer had met an untimely and violent death. Someone had strangled him.

Murder.

On Peter's land.

As he stared in horror-struck silence, a foreign sound began to pierce his nightmare rush of thoughts. A moment later, he realized the high-pitched keening came from Emma, where she stood near Sawyer's corpse, her green eyes open wide, fixed on the man who only a short while earlier had meant her harm.

Without warning, she fell silent and turned to meet Peter's gaze. An odd, blank expression overtook her features. As abruptly as she'd faced him, she turned back to Sawyer, and shuddered right away. Then her shoulders rose with a rough breath and she trembled. She shook her head.

He took a step toward her, not sure what he meant to do, but pain sliced through him, and his leg gave out under his weight. He let out a loud moan as he fell to the ground again.

Emma spun toward him, this time seeming to register his condition. "Oh. Oh!"

To his mortification, she flew to his side, one hand clenched in the wool of her cloak to keep it closed at her throat. "Peter! What's wrong? And what happened to"—she gulped as she dropped down to her knees at his side—"to Sawyer?"

Gritting his teeth, Peter met her frantic gaze. "My leg. I must have injured it when Sawyer and I were fighting."

"He's . . . dead, right?"

Peter stole a glimpse in the direction where the outlaw lay felled. "Looks that way. What happened to him?"

"What do you mean, what happened to him? You're the one who pulled him off me. Surely you must know."

Her outrage sounded sincere. "You didn't see how he wound up dead?"

"No!" She sniffed. "How dare you ask me such a thing? I already told you, I had my very first case of the vapors when I tried to stand after you dragged him off me—for which I greatly thank you, of course."

Peter blinked. She was able to think of manners at a moment like this? She'd scarcely escaped Sawyer's clutches, she'd fainted, Sawyer had died, and unless he was much mistaken, he himself had somehow broken a leg. Yet she still managed to put courtesy first?

"I ask, Emma," he said, squeezing each word through the pain that made him queasy, "because he walloped me in the gut and knocked me out. By the time I could breathe enough again to come to, all I heard was you. Then I saw him there. Dead."

"Well, I don't know how he died. I can assure you I didn't do a thing to him. On the other hand, before I fainted, I saw you hit him."

"I only landed a couple of punches. They weren't near enough to kill him."

"Very well, then, Peter, who killed him?"

Silence fell between them as a greater glow of light lightened the canopy of the trees above them. "I don't know, but someone did."

Only then did it occur to Peter that they were alone in the woods. He, Emma, and Sawyer. And yet, when he'd come upon the beast accosting her, Ned and Wade had been right on his heels. Hadn't they?

Where were they?

Why had they left?

Was one of them guilty of the crime?

Chapter 14

"NED!" Peter bellowed. "WADE!"

Emma started at the unexpected yells. "Why did you do that?"

"I don't know about Ned, but I doubt Wade would have just up and left me, seeing as I was fighting Sawyer." He shifted, and Emma saw him wince. The pain seemed to carve brackets on either side of his mouth. Before she could think of a way to help, he went on. "Wade could well have gone back for a shotgun. Ned knows—knew—Sawyer better than the rest of us. He might have had a better reason to run than anyone knows."

"I suppose it does make an odd kind of sense. So...what do you intend to do?"

He closed his eyes, as though by turning his attention inward he'd come up with a solution. Emma could see none. They were still out in the woods, on their own, with Peter injured and Sawyer in need of burial. Oh, and a killer to identify. Not to mention bring to justice, no matter how repugnant the deceased had been. Murder was murder, a sin.

She shuddered at the memory of Sawyer's evil face.

Rising up onto one elbow, Peter met her gaze again. "You do realize I need help, right? I can't walk back to the cabin by myself. I just took one single step, and you saw what happened. My leg wouldn't hold me up. From what it feels like, I reckon it's broken."

From his expression, she thought he wanted to say more, but instead, the effort to speak even those few words appeared to wear him out. Sympathy filled her as she read pain and irritation on his features. Frustration, too. She didn't blame him. She supposed she would feel the same if she'd broken a limb confronting a monster.

"I can help you back to the cabin," she offered, even though she wasn't quite sure how she would manage.

He let out a humorless chuckle. "You can't possibly think you can carry even a part of the weight I need help with, can you? Still, I do appreciate your offer. It was kind. But we can't leave. Not yet. We have to do something about him."

Emma kept her gaze fixed on Peter's face. She couldn't bear to look at Sawyer again. "Of course we do, and I did think of that. On the other hand, we can't just stay here, either. We need to see to your leg."

He gave her a brief nod. "I'd say we don't have long to wait. I trust Wade's on his way back."

"I hope you're right." She fell silent, but her thoughts didn't stop. "Sawyer's dead, right?"

"Clearly."

She pressed a hand to her throat. "Well, I know I didn't kill him. Did you?"

Peter snorted. "You know I didn't kill him, Emma."

"That's what you tell me, but he did steal your sheep, didn't he?" She waited until he nodded—reluctantly. "And you were quite furious about the theft, right?"

"I had every reason to be mad. I've worked hard to build my flock. It doesn't sit well with a man to have his work stolen like that." He fell silent. A white line appeared around his clamped lips. Then he shook his head. "I know what you're trying to say, but you're wrong. Sure. Yes, of course, I was furious, and I went after them, but—"

"Is she all right?" Wade ran up, clearly distraught, a shotgun at the ready. "What did that Sawyer do to Miss Emma? Where is he? Tell me! Where is that pig of a—"

"You can put it down," Peter said. "Sawyer's dead."

Wade shot him a questioning look, but didn't put down the gun. "Dead?"

"Take a look."

Dawn had finally arrived, and soft light sifted down between the trees. The hush of the forest seemed deeper than ever, especially in view of all that had taken place the night before. Still unwilling to view the reality of Sawyer's death again, Emma kept her gaze on Wade's expression as he looked where Peter indicated. His face turned a sickly shade of putty, and only then did he lower the shotgun. "But..."

"Did you do it?" Peter asked his ranch hand.

Emma gasped at the blunt nature of the question. She supposed, however, as Wade's boss, Peter had every right to demand a response.

"I took off as soon as you pulled him off of her," the younger man answered. "I reckoned you had Ned with you, here, and the both of you could help Miss Emma. But if things did go bad for you, I wanted to be able to—well...I reckon I don't need this anymore." He gestured with the gun, then lowered it to his side. "I did want to warn Colley what was happening."

"So where is he?" Peter asked.

Wade frowned. "He, who?"

"Ned, of course."

The ranch hand shook his head. "Dunno, boss. He didn't come back to the cabin with me. Like I told you before, I reckoned he'd stayed behind to help you with Sawyer." He looked around. "Reckon now he didn't, huh?"

"I dinnent help none," Ned said, his shaky voice scarcely above a whisper, as he crept out from behind a hefty tree. "But I dinnent do nothing to Sawyer, neither. I set off after you, Wade, a short bit after you left. Weren't no reason for me to stay here, what with Sawyer all furious, an' all that. I got to know all 'bout Sawyer, an' all's what he can do a body when he gits it in his head to do it. But when I headed back for the bunkhouse, I got lost. Been walking round for a long while since. Just heard ya running back, and now talking here. I followed all them sounds."

He approached Sawyer's body. "Fella really is dead, ain't he?" He shook his head, pale around the flared nostrils. "I dinnent kill him, but I cain't say I'm surprised he got himself killed. Ain't many what liked Sawyer much, you know."

Emma's head felt leaden with so many different thoughts to sift through. She rubbed her forehead, where her headache had worsened with each passing moment. "Please explain this to me," she said. "If I didn't kill Sawyer, and Peter didn't kill him, and neither Wade nor Ned—"

"Then who kilt Sawyer?" Ned asked, bewildered.

No one answered. No one had to.

Emma's heart began to pound. Was there really a killer among them? Or had someone materialized in the woods and committed the crime?

She could see similar thoughts ran through the others' minds, but she wasn't sure who she could trust. She wanted to trust Peter, and she doubted there was any true malice in Ned, but she didn't know Wade, and . . . and—well, really. What did she know about any of these men?

In the growing silence, she squared her shoulders. "It would seem to me, gentlemen, we have a decision to make. We can't all stay out here, but we can't all leave, either. Who will stay with Sawyer, and who will see to the undertaking duties?"

At first, all three men kept their peace, then, as her patience began to wane, they erupted into vigorous discussion.

"I—"

"Yes—"

"No—"

At any other time, Emma might have forced herself to come up with the necessary patience to sort out what the men had to say. As it was, she just wanted to return to the cabin. Shelter, food, and Robby's and Colley's welcome faces struck her as the most wonderful of treats right then. Since it looked as though none of her motley companions were ready to quit their arguments, Emma stood, rolled her eyes, and marched off in the direction that seemed the most likely to lead to the cabin.

She had only taken a few steps when Peter called out. "Hey! Where are you going?"

She glared back over a shoulder. "I'm tired, sore from fighting Sawyer. He has made my clothes nothing more than rags, and I am in desperate need of a bath. If any of you is interested, I'd love an escort, especially since I easily could get lost again."

Both Wade and Ned rushed to her side.

"I'll help you—"

"Don't rightly know the way—"

"Enough!" Peter yelled. "Yes, Emma, it is a good idea for you to return to the cabin. I need to get back to have Colley see to my leg, too, but we can't just leave Sawyer's body out here like this. We need to bury him. It's the Christian thing to do."

Out of the corner of her eye, Emma saw Ned blanch and Wade turn to a side. Peter looked no happier than the others about the prospect, but he also looked resolute. He went on.

"Take her with you, Wade. Go to the cabin for the shovels while I wait here."

The two younger men let out loud objections.

He cut them off. "Stop! It's decided. I'll wait here for you both to come back with a couple of shovels. We have to give this man a decent burial. We'll figure out what happened once that's taken care of. And believe me, we *will* figure it out."

A wave of profound relief washed over Emma. She was glad to leave the scene of the attack, the scene where Sawyer had breathed his last. True, she felt a twinge of regret, since she wouldn't be there when Peter and the two others buried him, strange though it seemed, but what could she say about a man who'd made such dreadful, sinful choices? She could, of course, and did indeed, hope Sawyer had repented, even at that last moment. She prayed he'd taken advantage of God's offer of mercy.

After they took a pair of wrong turns on their return, Wade led them into the meadow. While upon arrival, Emma had despaired of her fate at landing in such a rustic place, when they at last burst through the woods into the clear sunshine and safety, she knew the greatest sense of peace she ever remembered experiencing.

"Well, look at you!" Colley exclaimed when Emma walked into the cabin, cloak clutched tight to her heart to maintain some kind of modesty. "That single big button at your throat ain't near enough, now is it?"

She shook her head. "My blouse . . . Sawyer—it . . . it's torn."

Colley narrowed her eyes, clamped her lips tight, then turned back to the hearth.

That's when the scent of bacon mingled with that of fresh-baked biscuits penetrated Emma's senses. The by-now-familiar richness of the simple food made her realize how hungry she was. The thought of the grand dinners she'd eaten in some of the world's greatest cities paled in comparison to the plain meal. Satisfaction now moved to a place of greater importance in her thoughts than elegance and delicacy and beauty for the sake of those things alone.

"It's nice to be back," she said, her words full of the wonder and appreciation she'd won the hard way.

Colley chuckled. "Ain't much, but a body don't really need much, ya know?"

Emma shrugged. "I'm learning."

"Good!" She met Colley's gaze, serious and direct. "Pete...?"

She understood the unasked question, but then noticed Robby stir in his bed. "He still has...something to see to, about Sawyer. After the other two help him, they'll all be back."

The older woman didn't bother to hide her worry. "Is the boss well—"

"Lady Emma!" Robby cried from the depths of his bunk. He launched himself at her, arms outstretched, a beaming grin on his sweet face. "I missed you this morning when you wasn't—"

"Weren't," she said, automatically correcting him.

His grin widened. "Weren't! Yes. I missed you this morning when you weren't here. I was afraid you'd disappeared, you'd left me like—" The child stopped and turned away.

A pang of sadness struck Emma's heart, well aware that she would one day leave, and he would again experience loss. Certainly, it wouldn't be the same as the loss of his mother, but she knew they'd built a close attachment between them. She would grieve their parting, herself.

"Oh, I am still here," she said in a breezy tone. "You can't rid yourself of me that easily."

He looked around, alarm dawning. "Where's Papa?"

Oh, dear. She couldn't quite tell the child all that had happened. "He's still out in the woods, waiting for the men to bring some...um...things he needs out to him. He'll be back once they're done, but he's hurt his leg."

Colley turned again. Worry had drawn parallel lines on her forehead. "How bad?"

Emma met her gaze. "He feels it's broken, and he'll need your help to set it as soon as he gets back."

The ranch manager's concern eased only a touch. "Done it before. Ain't much to settin' a bone, long's it's a clean break."

"I wouldn't know what a clean break would look like," Emma said, "but I'd like to learn what you do to fix one."

In Colley's company, the tension had begun to dissipate from her shoulders. Only then did Emma feel again the uncomfortable, scratchy sense of being...well, unclean. She imagined she could smell Sawyer's sour odor clinging to her and all she could think of was washing it away. The memory would take longer...Besides, this was the first time the men hadn't been near the house, and the opportunity for privacy, as unfortunate as the cause was, was too rare to pass up. "I know I spoke to Peter—er...Mr. Lowery about it before," she said, "but other matters interfered. It's time for a bath. I can't put it off a moment longer."

Colley scoffed. "Afraid you'll have to, missy. There's things to be seen to, an' I'm the lonesome one to do it all."

The older woman turned back to the hearth, stirred something in the spider, and then gestured with the hand that held a wooden spoon. "Hand me three plates. I'll dish up for us so's I can git back out to them sheep. I'll pack up some biscuits and cold bacon for the men."

Emma noticed the grime on her skin as she reached for the dishes. "About my bath, when...?"

"We'll worry about such oncet the men are all back home. Safe an' sound, missy."

That put an end to that request. Emma did understand, even though her discomfort and her difficulty with the ruined blouse made her miserable. She grudgingly was learning she had to take some things in stride. She'd just have to do her best with the pitcher, soap, and basin. "I understand. And, please, do go on back to your work outside. I promise you, I can get the food ready for the men to take on their way back to Peter. Why don't you just see to yourself, so you can get to the sheep sooner?"

"Well, missy!" Surprise brightened Colley's expression. "I reckon y'ain't half bad, after all! You might could do, with a little learning of your own. You really might."

The comment struck Emma as high praise, especially when she realized Colley was putting together a biscuit and some bacon on her way out. Moments later, the ranch manager was gone.

Emma washed her hands and face in the basin then bustled around the kitchen, taking comfort in the work that kept her thoughts too busy to stray. She soon had a reasonable meal packed for Peter and the other two. She kept an eye on the bacon over the coals, while with a fraction of her attention she kept up her end of a conversation with Robby. When Wade returned, she handed him the biscuits and bacon she'd wrapped with the clean towel and an empty molasses jug she'd filled with fresh water.

She waved off the ranch hand's gratitude. "Hurry back to Peter," she said. "And please be careful. It's dangerous out there."

Wade nodded, and then left with Ned, who sent a longing last look toward the cozy hearth. Even a day earlier she wouldn't have caught its meaning, but she'd learned a lot overnight. She understood.

Emma kept up with Robby's chatter, listened to him read to her, first from the Bible and then from the Malory, and took care to prepare an evening meal. While he'd worked on a list of sums, she'd pored over Mrs. Beeton's recipes. Nowhere, however, did she find directions for anything with dried beef, of which the lean-to contained vast quantities. Tough as leather, the stuff didn't look as though a human tooth could tackle it. On the other hand, dried meant just that. Someone somewhere had dried it. Logic suggested she rewet it. Nothing would be lost if she failed in her effort; she could always serve eggs, bacon, biscuits, and leftover beans to the men. On the other hand, if the dried beef became edible, she could try one of the stewed beef dishes from the cookery book.

With Robby peering over her shoulder, Emma poured boiling water on the dark, hard strips. After a few minutes, she jabbed one with a fork, and saw where the tines made an impression.

"Patience," she murmured.

"'S'that what we're making for supper?" Robby asked. "Patience?"

Emma laughed. "I think that's the menu for a long while to come, my valiant knight!"

By the time the men returned, Emma had a creditable meal ready. While her biscuits weren't anywhere near the fluffy, mouth-melting treats Colley could whip up in minutes, they also weren't rock-hard. The meat had softened, as she'd hoped, and she'd cooked it with some sad-looking carrots, some onions, and a handful of potatoes. She'd poured a jar of gravy she'd found in the lean-to over everything, and had tasted the concoction over and over as it stewed, if only to make sure it would be tolerable in the end.

She'd refused to fail again.

"Supper smells right close to ready," Colley said when she walked in.

Emma nodded, but said nothing more in view of the men behind the older woman.

Wade and Ned stood just on the other side of the cabin door, one on either side of Peter. Together, they bore the taller man's weight with a long arm wrapped around their shoulders. The injured sheep rancher held up his left leg at an awkward angle, bent at the knee.

Colley took over. "Git me a straight piece of wood," she told Wade. "Flat as you can find it, too. Need to keep this leg as still as possible for it to git back to where it works right again."

Ned seemed to have become Wade's shadow, and the two left in a hurry to fetch the wood for Colley. When the cabin door closed behind them, the ranch manager turned to Emma. "I keep a stack of clean flour sacks out to the barn. We're needin' some of 'em in here now so you can start tearin' up strips to tie the splint to his leg."

Eager to help, Emma hurried back with the rough but clean cotton fabric. As much as they'd differed when she first arrived, Peter had come to her rescue. He'd saved her from a foul fate at Sawyer's hands. As stern as he could be, he had also proved himself a decent man.

She'd known from the start how hard he worked, too. Perhaps there was much more to admire about the man than she had thought at first. She studied him through lowered lashes. Although he had a broken leg, he'd taken time and explained to Robby how his injury would heal before he'd let Colley start on the splint. He had to be in considerable pain, but he'd chosen to first set his son's mind at ease.

In spite of his dislike of Robby's much-loved British legends, he was a loving father. Yes, it did appear there was much more to appreciate about the man who'd rescued her than she'd first thought. She'd do whatever she could to help.

A sense of shared purpose settled over them. Emma tore fabric. Colley cut Peter's denim pants leg up near his knee to reveal a swollen, purple mess in the midshin area. As Colley prodded and pressed, Peter lost all color on his face. He clamped his mouth shut tight, and it was clear how much even the gentle examination hurt.

"Should be fine once we git it nice and straight again, and tie it up good and tight here," Colley murmured as she reached for the stack of strips.

"Fine, huh?" Peter ground out. "I wouldn't call it fine. It's clear you're not the one with the broken leg."

Colley tsk-tsked and tapped his shoulder. "Had my own share of broken bones an' things over the years on our own spread." With gentle hands, she adjusted his sore-looking leg a fraction. "A body don't raise sheep for fifteen years without gettin' a scrape or two."

She adjusted the flat, narrow board Wade had brought inside.

Peter grunted.

Emma winced.

"You know," he said through gritted teeth, "this is a far sight worse'n a scrape or two."

"You hush, now." Colley knotted a strip of cotton and handed it to him. "Here. Like midwives do for women in labor. Go on an' bite down on this, if ya cain't stand the pain. I know it's gonna hurt, an' I'm real sorry, but it cain't be helped, Pete. Gotta set it, so's to save that leg for ya."

Grim-faced, he ignored the rag. "Do what you have to do, just get it done."

Emma turned to Colley. "Please tell me how I can help. It's the least I can do—"

"I'll let you know," the ranch manager said. Under the older woman's direction, Emma helped support the injured leg until Colley was satisfied with its position on the splint. As Colley tied the strips around the leg and the board, sweat beaded Peter's forehead and his upper lip. Sympathy filled Emma, and her respect for the man grew.

As did her guilt. If not for her, this wouldn't have happened to him.

At the height of Peter's misery, Emma realized he'd spent the whole time in silent prayer. He let out a rough breath, squared his shoulders, and whispered, "Oh Father . . ."

Mercifully, Colley finished doctoring soon, and Peter, pale and tired, had been eased back onto the pillows Colley had piled on the bunk. Wade and Ned had been happy to help.

A short while later, Emma served the long-awaited evening meal. Anxious, she waited for a verdict on this latest attempt on her part.

Peter stared at the plate of food on his lap. "Looks and smells like a fair improvement on your earlier efforts." He met her gaze, eyes narrowed. "Or are you passing off Colley's cooking as your own?"

She gasped. "How dare you! That, sir, would be lying, and I'm not about to start doing that. Besides, I have a witness. Your son can tell you how the meal came about."

A fair attempt at a smile on his lips, he turned to Robby. "Well, son, how did the meal happen?"

Robby launched into an earnest discussion of water, the lean-to, gravy, lard, flour, and various spills. "And that, Papa, is how she came to give you that big plate of patience."

Peter's gaze flew to Emma, who blushed to her hairline, remembering what she'd said.

He chuckled.

This time, however, Emma felt no condemnation, even when the others joined in.

By the time they were done eating, not a morsel was left. While nothing about it had been elegant, the food had been plentiful and substantial, and it had tasted quite good, even to her discriminating palate. The others wasted no time in praising her efforts, especially Peter.

"Have to hand it to you." He smiled. "You did learn to make at least one meal. Let's see what else you do, seeing as you said you could learn."

Emma wasn't about to let him dent her sense of accomplishment. She crossed her arms. "I can and will learn, as I promised, but there is one thing I already knew before I came." She gestured toward the grimy cloak that protected her modesty after the lacy blouse's unfortunate end. "A person needs to be clean, and I am anything but clean. We spoke of baths before, and I insist on one tonight."

He frowned. "But—"

"No, sir! I waited patiently until a better time," she said.

"And there is no more waiting. That better time has arrived." She turned to Wade and Ned. "You will bring in the tub Mr. Lowery mentioned. Don't forget the bucket in the lean-to. I'll need your help to fill up the tub, and the bucket will make it quicker. I'll take care of the hot water."

The two young men swapped looks, as though to say she'd lost her mind, but they didn't argue. Peter didn't either, but he looked doubtful. She suspected he was ready for her to fail again.

Emma returned to the hearth to fill every available container with water. She meant to have her bath, and she meant to have hot water for it.

As they waited for the tin tub, Colley washed plates, pots, and glasses. Peter leaned back in the bunk, an expression of slight amusement on his usually serious features. Robby sat next to his father, curiosity burning in him, as his dark eyes followed her every move.

Somehow, Emma feared, something as basic as a bath could backfire. But she remained determined. In light of all she'd learned in the short time she'd been at the camp, she decided she could do much worse than to follow the example of the man who'd braved having his broken leg set in the crudest of circumstances. She turned to God.

"Oh Lord," she whispered as she checked the steaming water. "I need that bath. And I need clean clothes. I don't know how I'm going to make it happen, but the God I met in church growing up should. Peter turned to You, and even though a bath isn't the same as a broken leg, I do need help. Especially, now that it's not just Robby, Colley, and me in the cabin...I don't know how I'll make this work. Please help me..."

Once again, she refused to fail.

She would have her bath.

And, if she had anything to say about the matter, so would every other member of Peter Lowery's household.

Except, perhaps, the new invalid.

He would have to see to his ablutions himself. But clean they all would be.

The time to do things the proper way had come.

Chapter 15

A tin tub, a small boy, two women, three men, and a tiny cabin.

A recipe for trouble, and not one found in *Mrs. Beeton.*

As Emma waited for the water to heat, she turned the situation over in her mind. No matter how she looked at it, she had a predicament on her hands. She'd made such a fuss over the need for baths that she didn't see how she could back away from her demand, even though she'd identified a few problems. Especially not now that she'd sent the men to fetch tub and bucket, and in view of the quantities of water she'd pumped and set to heat. And then, the additional water they would need to still fetch for so many baths.

As soon as she had finished with the washing up, Colley had made herself scarce. Emma suspected the older woman had gone to the barn, where she would enjoy the company of the animals she loved. She also feared Colley knew there might be a bit of a disagreement—or more—in the cabin, and she hadn't cared to be present for that.

"Explain your plan to me again," Peter said when only the two Lowery men and Emma remained in the cabin.

"Very simple," she answered, determined to see this through to the end. "Baths are important. The time for baths has come. We will bathe."

The cabin door burst open. With a great deal of banging and clanging, Wade and Ned got the tin tub inside, and then set it up a few feet in front of the hearth. It looked enormous in the small room.

With the tub in position, Emma could no longer escape the truth. How were she and Colley, two women, going to bathe in a cabin full of men? Wade and Ned could easily be sent to the bunkhouse, but Peter was injured, Colley had said he shouldn't move, and at the moment he lay on Robby's usual bunk—

"Aha!" The solution to the predicament burst into her thoughts fully formed. "Please carry the tub to Colley's room. She and I will need our privacy, gentlemen."

She hoped Colley didn't object to her presumptuousness—at least, not too strenuously. Emma had, after all, chosen to invade the older woman's sanctuary.

Out of the corner of her eye, she caught the surprise on Peter's face. He hadn't expected her to come up with a solution. But she had begun to glimpse how resourceful she could be, something she'd never realized before her fateful trip to Portland. She'd had no need for that resourcefulness before. She liked the Emma she was coming to know.

Now, if only that Emma could figure out what she would wear after she took off her filthy, torn clothes, and had the bath she so wanted....

She Shall Be Praised

To buy herself additional time, she turned to the two Lowery men. "Robby, you're first."

He opened his mouth as wide as the mouth of the kettle of
boiling water. "Me first? Why?"

Why? Oh, dear. She couldn't very well tell him all the reasons why. Not with his father lying right beside the child.

"Why...um...oh, yes! Because you're the smallest of us
all. And children need baths to be healthy. It would appear
you've done without one for too long already. And you need
the least amount of hot water for proper cleanliness. It'll take
less time to heat enough for you. While you bathe, I'll heat
more."

Robby didn't argue with her odd logic, but from the
twitching at the corners of Peter's mouth, Emma knew she
hadn't fooled him. He might not have figured out precisely
everything that troubled her, but he knew she didn't have
everything planned out as she'd said.

Think! She needed an answer, and soon.

When the men set the tub in Colley's tiny room, the metal
contraption dwarfed the area. But the room had a door that
closed, a luxury that allowed the bather a measure of modesty.

Emma required privacy. No matter what.

"Here's a length of flour sack to dry yourself, and a piece
we use as a dishcloth," she told Robby.

"Dishcloth?" he asked, horror-stricken. "I'm no dish, Lady
Emma."

She fought a smile as she reached up to the top shelf on
the wall by the hearth. "Oh, indeed. I do agree. But the cloth
will help you do the job right. Here, take this bar of soap,
and please make sure you use both, cloth and soap, especially

around that neck and behind the ears. And don't forget your hair. Not that you'll wash that with the dishcloth, of course, but you see that you wash it too."

The boy's bottom lip protruded like a shelf, and his eyes resembled a thunderstorm about to burst. Still, Emma wouldn't budge, and the father wouldn't speak. She wished Peter would say something to encourage the child, but she realized her host was testing her. And fighting yet another laugh.

"This will work," she assured the father as the son dragged himself into Colley's room, one of Wade's shirts trailing on the floor behind him. It was the smallest piece of men's clothing they had found on that short a notice. The boy had refused to wear one of Colley's shirts to bed, even though the garment was clean and identical to the one Wade brought to share. Emma smiled at the memory.

"Colley's a lady, and I ain't," he'd said.

"Am not," Emma had corrected.

"Are so."

"I," she said, fighting a laugh again, "am indeed a lady, but you are not. The correct way to say it is 'I am not.' Please repeat it the right way."

He'd sighed, but complied anyway. "I am not a lady. An' I won't wear ladies' clothes."

Emma had decided it would be far less trouble to send Wade for one of his shirts than to argue any further. Now, armed with an adequate, manly shirt, and after they'd emptied the bucket, the kettle, and two other pots into the tub, she chased the boy toward the bath. He slammed the door as he stepped into Colley's room.

Emma covered her mouth to muffle her laughter. She wasn't

quite sure why Robby objected to a bath, since she found bathing one of the most enjoyable activities, but his reaction had been funny.

A moment later, she heard the clapping. She spun, her cheeks blazing, and caught a glint of admiration in Peter's eyes. She froze.

"That," he said, "was almost worth having a broken leg."

"Are you sure it was only your leg you injured?" she asked. "I'm afraid you must have hit your head as well."

"Oh, Sawyer did knock me out, but that doesn't take anything away from this moment. Robby does not like his baths, never has. Don't reckon many little boys do, seeing as I didn't when I was his age. You just did something I doubt any of the rest of us here could have done that easily."

His compliment pleased her, especially when she thought back to his many harsh critiques. "I wouldn't be quite so ready to celebrate so soon. I'll wait until he comes out, all clean and shiny." She pointed. "That door is closed. There's nothing that says he's in there and busy with that cloth, as I told him to be."

Peter let out a hearty chuckle. "Good for you! I did wonder if you'd think enough like Robby to figure that out. Let's wait and see."

"It strikes me your leg might not be in as much pain as before by now," she said. "Did Colley's doctoring help?"

"It's not comfortable, but it has reached the level of passable. I reckon in a day or two I'll be well enough to—"

"Oh, no! No, you don't." Emma wagged a finger at him. "I heard Colley say you couldn't walk on that leg for quite a spell. You don't want to undo all the good work she did. She says it must stay still so it grows back straight."

He shrugged. "I can't afford the time away from the sheep. It's no different than leaving the camp to fetch you to Bountiful. I have work to do. I'll be fine after a day or so."

"I don't see how your presence on the meadow will fatten your flock any better than if you take the time to heal. I've found Colley a most sensible woman, and her advice seems sound. Besides, since you are in that condition on my account, why, there will be no hurry involved." She tamped down the rush of guilt. "You will let your leg recover properly."

He frowned, but not for long. A moment later, the twitching at the corners of his mouth started up again. "Are you fixing to be the one to make sure I don't move? Because I'm much larger than you. I don't reckon you could stop me, once I set my mind to heading back to work."

"Perhaps not alone, but I'm sure Colley will help me."

"Colley will help you what?" asked the lady under discussion from the doorway. "What all are you settin' me up to do now?"

"Do?" Emma asked, mischief in her smile. "Nothing to do; but I do believe you might want to know your patient is in quite a hurry to return to his flock. He objects to resting his leg, since he says he'll be fine in a day or two."

"Izzat right, Pete?" Colley strolled to the bunk. "You thinkin' that leg's gonna hold ya up in just a coupla days? Cuz I don't reckon it will for a longer while than that, seein' as I've had one of my own, and doctored up more'n my share of broken bones."

He shrugged. "More than likely it will set up quick. It won't feel none too good, but it should work."

Colley shook her head. "Ain't fixin' to let you give it a

chance to leave you lame for good." She bent and picked up his boots. "Takin' these old, smelly things out to the barn with me now. You can go after 'em oncet your leg's healed."

Well aware of the condition of the ground around the cabin, the barn, and the bunkhouse, with all the rocks, branches, uneven bumps, and holes in the often soggy, muddy surface, Emma doubted any sensible soul would try to brave it on his bare feet. She'd learned that lesson herself the hard way. Now it was her turn to fight a laugh, so she turned away from Peter and busied herself with the next batch of heated water.

"Give a holler when you need me to fetch them other two fellers fer their baths." Humor colored Colley's words. "Don't look like either one of 'em's gonna be any happier'n Robby about it. Like little boys, all of them, I tell you." On her way out the door, she paused, sent Emma one of her broad, genuine smiles. "Reckon I was right about ya all along, Miss Emma. You will do fine, after all. You will indeed."

Emma didn't dare turn to see how Peter took Colley's validating word. She stayed in the kitchen corner, fussed with perfectly arranged items, moved a mixing bowl one inch to a side on the nearest shelf.

Peter chuckled. "I'll bide my time. You might have outsmarted my boy, but you won't outsmart me."

"All that matters at this time is your leg." Emma swallowed hard, turned, met Peter's gaze, her heart full with the realization of what he'd done for her. "I could never forget you were injured because you came to my rescue. I can't thank you enough for what you did. If you hadn't, Sawyer would have—"

"Please, don't think about it another minute. I couldn't have lived with myself if he'd hurt you while you were here, at my camp. Any man would do what I did. I'm glad you're not hurt."

In the past, she might have taken the easy way out by letting the conversation die right then, but nothing like this had happened before. What this man had willingly done for her was nothing to take lightly.

She approached the bunk. "I'm truly sorry, Peter. You never asked for any of this. I landed here because of nothing you did. Now you're hurt because of me—"

"Shh!" As he struggled up into a better sitting position, his gaze remained clear and direct. Emma couldn't miss the sincerity there. "Who's to say I wouldn't have had to face Sawyer even if you hadn't been here? He had been stealing my flock, remember? I don't reckon he would have stopped all on his own."

Once again, the thought crossed Emma's mind. Had Peter killed the rustler? She couldn't say what might have happened between the two men after she'd fainted. They had still been locked in a fierce fight when she'd lost consciousness. In the heat of the moment, Peter might have gone ahead and exacted his own justice.

He crossed his arms. "I wouldn't waste time thinking on that, if I were you. I didn't kill that man. I was furious, and you know it, but I also know God reserves vengeance for Himself. I won't say it isn't mighty hard for a man to back away, and I won't say I didn't want to get in a few licks for myself, but I did keep my head straight enough. I didn't kill him. He's the one who knocked me out."

Emma wanted to believe him, especially since the better she came to know Peter, the more she appreciated him, and the more she found to respect and admire. But she hadn't seen what happened, and in the end, one of the two men had wound up dead. It hadn't been Peter.

BANG!

Robby flung open the door to Colley's room. "I'm done," he said. "And I did use your dishcloth." He held out the drippy piece of cloth. "But I ain't no dish to wash with none of them cloths again."

His wounded dignity was such that Emma didn't have the heart to correct his grammar. "I do believe you're properly ready for bed now."

"Bed, too?" His outrage was priceless.

"Perhaps not right away," she conceded. "The rest of us still need our baths."

In the end, she won the battle of the baths. First Colley, then Wade, and then Ned took their turns in the tub. The men had protested, saying a lady should go first, but Emma still needed time and insisted. As the minutes sped by, she grew more anxious. Would she have to don a pair of Colley's trousers for the simple sake of cleanliness? Her cheeks heated.

The possibility was too scandalous for her to entertain, but she feared it might come to that. It was unlikely that Colley might have a simple skirt or dress hidden somewhere among her things. Even if she did, anything that belonged to the ranch manager would be far too large, since Colley was five or six inches taller than Emma, and outweighed her by a good twenty pounds or more.

Emma sat at the table, her hands clasped tight in her lap, mulling over her situation. She wanted no one to see her growing uneasiness. While she sat and fretted, Peter and Robby chattered about the new lamb, they prayed, and before long, the child fell asleep tucked in close at his father's side. Not much later, Emma noticed Peter had followed suit, a slight smile on his lean, tanned face. Peace had settled in on the cabin for the night.

Emma's heart warmed at the sight before her. Tears welled up in her eyes. The love between Peter and Robby was undeniable and familiar. She'd grown up with that kind of love, and she treasured it, even more now that she'd faced hardship, now that she knew Papa was suffering because of her disappearance.

While she no longer hated Peter's summer camp, nor did the thought of spending any length of time there make her desperate, she did still feel the urgency to return to her father's side, to ease what she was sure had turned to grief. The more she thought of her father, the more Emma realized the love of her aunt and uncle, of the Millers at the home in Portland, and especially of her dear Papa, was all she truly missed.

The parties and the gowns, the attention and the elegance, the travel and the luxury and all those other things she'd loved before had lost their luster. She'd faced the horror Sawyer had meted out, and she'd fought him with everything she had. Well, yes, she had indeed needed help, and Peter had offered it, but she had also learned not to give her trust quite so easily in the future.

During the short span of time since she'd set off from Denver, Emma had also discovered the satisfaction of using her determination and wits to conquer a challenge. She'd gone from scarcely setting foot in a kitchen, to having served a meal to a trio of hungry men. And they'd enjoyed what she'd served. Now, at the end of the day, as she sat and waited her turn at some soap and water, she had the privilege of witnessing the love between a father and his child. She saw between the two Lowery men what really mattered after all.

Nothing in the trunk she'd missed so much at the start of this experience had any true worth.

She'd learned so much in such a short while . . . but she suspected God still had a great deal more for her to learn.

This episode in her life, as frightening as it had been, had given rise to something else inside her, something more than a shift in her attitude. An ache she never had experienced before now made its presence known in a deep, secret corner of her heart. As she watched Peter and Robby, the ache grew and mellowed and became a part of the new her. In the love they shared, Emma recognized how much she wanted someone to love like Peter loved Robby, like Papa loved her.

Yes, she did want to marry, and all the rich gifts such precious love brought with it. The want began to feel more like a craving, and she realized it came from the need to love as her father had loved her mother, even after Mama's death. She wanted to love as the man before her had loved the woman whose trunk he still kept.

She wanted to be loved like that in turn.

Strange how she'd come to discover that about herself as she sat in the most rustic of homes, as she waited for her turn to soak in a crude tin tub, as she longed to wash with a bar of plain lye soap and a dishcloth borrowed for a bath. It amazed her to see what really mattered to her now that she'd been stripped of all she'd known a handful of meaningful days before.

Armed with yet another sample of Colley's seemingly endless supply of clean flour sacks, Emma went into the makeshift bathroom, anticipating the moment she would sink into the modest quantity of warm water. The gas lantern lit the room with a warm golden glow, and as tiny as it was, she still felt as though she'd walked into a palace.

For the first time since she'd left Denver she was completely alone, in a spot where she could close the door, where the rest of the world would leave her alone. And yet, all she could think about was soap and water.

Emma smiled as she unbuttoned the cloak. While she couldn't wait to be done with these ruined clothes, it was the memories she wished she could shed as easily. Harder still was going to be replacing them. She should have spoken to Colley about it already, but she hadn't wanted to give Peter any more reason to laugh. She supposed she would have to put the rags back on until she came up with a plan. She'd run out of time.

And she was in a hurry to get clean.

As she began to remove her torn blouse, a knock came at the door. "Who is it?" she asked.

"Colley. Open up, there, Miss Emma. I have somethin' here for ya you're gonna be happy to see."

Curiosity piqued, she grabbed the ripped edges of the

blouse and opened the door. Colley slipped inside, an armful of cotton calico leading the way.

"Here ya go, missy," the older woman said, holding out the garments. "They're the clothes the old missus kept here for her summers. Pete never got 'round to getting rid of all her things, and I reckon it's just as well you put 'em to use after these years. Especially, seein' as how well you done so far with that there cookery book of hers."

Emma's eyes grew huge. "I couldn't possibly wear Mrs. Lowery's clothes. It wouldn't be right. We have to think of Peter and Robby. The memories—"

"It was Pete what sent me here with 'em. As much as you'd want your own clothes, he knew you had nothin' with ya, an' he knew, too, how much stock you were puttin' on this bath. Cain't say's I blame ya. I like my soap and water, too."

She knew Colley was trying to set her mind at ease, remind-ing her how much she wanted to bathe, and being practical as always, but nothing could distract her from the truth. Those were the clothes Peter's wife had worn, the garments Robby's mother had used when she'd fed him, rocked him to sleep. Emma had already stepped into enough of the late woman's jobs. She couldn't also step right into her clothes. Would she even feel like herself if she did? And which self, which Emma, should she feel like?

There was no means for one to turn back the clock. She doubted she could ever go back to her previous life, where she enjoyed luxuries without giving them any thought or appreci-ation. Was she ready to see herself even more as the new Emma she was becoming?

And would Peter view her differently when he saw her in those clothes?

"Don't you have an old skirt or dress I could borrow?" she asked Colley.

"Ain't worn one of 'em for years, going on eighteen or twenty of 'em. They don't work too well fer a woman working sheep on a ranch with her man."

Emma's curiosity grew. Colley had a husband? Why had she never mentioned him? But the shuttered expression on Colley's face didn't invite questions. She chose to let the other woman speak her piece.

"Ain't never oncet thought Pete would get past losin' Adele," she said. "It means somethin' he's told me to git these things fer ya. I wouldn't turn 'im down, if I were you. It's right high praise, I reckon. An' he's a good man." She frowned, her gaze on Emma's, and more stern than she'd ever seen. "Now don't ya go thinkin' nothin' wrong 'about the fella. He's as fine as a man comes, and he's only thinkin' of helpin' ya while yer here. Always wants what's best fer all of us here. He takes his responsibilities serious-like. Pete ain't nothin' like that there Sawyer, ya know."

Emma gasped. "It never even crossed my mind, Colley. I think only the best of Peter. Why, if it weren't for him, Sawyer...well, I would be the one with the injuries, and they wouldn't be something as simple and innocent as a broken leg."

The older woman shuddered, clamped her lips into a tight, thin line, and let her gaze dart away. Emma didn't blame Colley. Even the thought of what might have happened had Peter not shown up when he did was more than she wanted to remember.

She tried again. "It's not anything against Peter. I just feel quite awkward in another woman's…life. I'm already teaching her son, cooking for him and his father, caring for her home…I—I don't know."

Colley tsk-tsked and slammed her fists on her hips. "Now you tell me here, missy. Do ya or do ya not want that bath? Cuz I reckon if ya do, there's not much to be done 'bout it. That"—she waved at Emma's blouse—"ain't nothin' you're gonna be wearin' 'round here. An' that there skirt…well, it's right filthy, beggin' pardon, of course. This ain't like none of them big cities yer used to. We do practical things 'round these parts. You need clothes. Here's clothes."

"I suppose there's not much more I can say, is there?" She reached out for the clothes.

Smiling broadly, Colley stuffed them into Emma's arms.

"Now take yer bath while I dry my hair. We still have us a coupla things to do tonight, you and me. Before we get some sleep, that is. Don't be dawdlin' too long, either. Mornin' comes 'round right quick."

"Do? What do we need to do tonight?"

Colley gave a one-shouldered shrug. "Ya'll see soon enough. Let's not waste any more time."

Moments after Colley walked away, Emma disrobed and stepped into the still-warm water. As imperfect as her surroundings were, the water felt lovely and lavish, and if she closed her eyes, she felt quite pampered as the warmth eased her sore muscles. She didn't remember ever appreciating a bath as much as she did right then. Not when she'd bathed with the most extravagant of French-milled violet-scented soaps and the most opulent gardenia-fragranced oils, or even

Ginny Aiken

the soothing lavender extract Aunt Sophia always had waiting for Emma's enjoyment. When she dried off with the humble flour sack, she enjoyed the clean sensation as much as she'd ever enjoyed the most exquisite of Turkish-cotton towels.

Bliss, in the form of a bath, didn't need extravagance.

Soap, water, and a clean cotton flour sack did just fine.

Chapter 16

Self-conscious in another woman's clothes, Emma tugged the too-long sleeves of Adele Lowery's simple, flowered cotton calico dress up from her wrists. The much-washed fabric felt soft and comforting against her warm, fresh-scrubbed skin and helped her overcome her nervousness. She didn't look her elegant best. The garment's former owner had been a taller, more robust woman, so it didn't fit as it should; it never would. As it was, the skirt trailed on the floor behind her as she walked.

It looked as though dress alterations would be part of her new schooling. She saw how all the hours spent with needle in hand, even if it had been for petit point embroidery and various kinds of tapestry work, would now come to her rescue.

Still, the ill fit didn't diminish her gratitude. She realized Peter had set aside the sadness he surely still felt from the loss of his wife in order to help her in her moment of need—yet another moment of need. She had to let him know how much she appreciated this latest generosity on his part.

When she reached the bunk she saw the peaceful, relaxed expression on his face, heard his soft, deep breaths, noticed the easy, loving way he held his son close, and didn't have the heart to wake him. Despite his quick-to-irritate tendencies, Peter Lowery was a good man.

The yearning she'd identified earlier in the evening yawned large inside her again. She experienced a pang of envy for the woman who'd first worn the dress draped clumsily over her own frame. Adele Lowery cast a long shadow, years after her death.

Something in Emma urged her to strive to match the late woman's influence in her own life, not try to fill that shadow. She could never be Adele, and she couldn't imagine trying to become a copy of the other woman, either. Instead, she wanted to become what the other woman had become, to be Emma, the real Emma, the one God had made her to be, and to live her life that way within her own world. Her misadventure in the woods was proving a challenge she never could have imagined, but one she doubted she would ever regret.

She knew she'd already become a stronger woman for it.

A stray thought reminded her that Adele Lowery had broken here in this rugged land. Perhaps Emma hadn't put together a realistic mental image of the other woman. Imperfections were normal, a truth that made her smile for her own sake.

As she turned, she noticed Colley in a chair she'd pulled up close to the hearth. The older woman stroked a silver hairbrush through her thick, waist-length steel-colored hair, and paused a time or two to ease apart the occasional tangle with work-roughened fingers. The lush ripples and waves came as a surprise to Emma, who'd only seen the ranch manager's hair pinned up into the large, severe bun on the crown of her head, where it anchored her well-worn hat.

That night, as the no-nonsense ranch manager sat by the fire, all that beautiful hair flowed like molten metal over her shoulders and back. Emma spotted a glimmer of the beauty Rosaline Colley had once been. Her features, although covered by weather- and sun-tanned, leathery skin, still displayed a grace Emma hadn't noticed before. The woman's eyes, a soft sky blue, wore a fringe of dark lashes, and when Emma gave them a closer scrutiny, revealed a sadness she hadn't perceived before. With the usual manly plaids and cotton denim fading into the background, the woman herself seemed to step to the foreground, almost as though a mask had been removed. It occurred to Emma the mask had been Colley's intent all along.

While still lovely at her age, the ranch manager must have been a gorgeous woman in her younger years, one blessed with a feminine loveliness and appeal she worked hard to disguise. Emma had to wonder…

Colley sighed.

Emma approached, keeping her steps quiet so as not to startle her. But as usual, the older woman was one step ahead of her. She turned in the plain wooden chair and met Emma's gaze.

"Why?" The word flew out before she could give it half a thought.

"I reckon ya ain't forgotten Sawyer yet, have ya?"

She shuddered, but didn't speak.

"This land of ours here is right pretty, I reckon," Colley

said, her words measured, clipped, emotionless, "but it sure is tough in many ways, wouldn't ya say?"

Emma nodded, seating herself near the fire where she began to dry her own hair.

Colley snorted. "I'll tell ya, it's more like a church social these days compared to what it was when I came up to Oregon. Back then, even a woman had to fight just to make it day to day. This"—she waved a hand down the front of her torso—"helped cut down on the fightin'."

A faraway expression, not a happy one, came into Colley's eyes, and Emma felt as though she might as well not have been in the room. Still, she kept quiet to let the other woman have her time with her memories.

Moments later Colley sat taller, still shielded by the silver curtain of hair, and continued. "Papa, he came to California back then fer the Gold Rush." She chuckled. "Didn't find hisself much of anything that glittered in that dirt, so he quit pannin' after a while and set off to wander some. But then, when he met Mama—she'd lost her first husband, my father, a Mexican man—he reckoned he'd found in her all the glitter he'd be needin' anytime soon. She was one true Spanish beauty, and he'd'a done anything fer her, didn't matter what, he loved her so much. They ran my real father's store fer years, and they turned a good trade there, the two of 'em and my brothers, too."

"You were born in California?"

Colley shook her head. "Nah. Papa went to California to look fer gold, but he found Mama in Texas, an' that's where he wound up. Had him no gold, but instead had Mama, a whole lot of love between 'em, and a passel of young'uns to raise, some from her first marriage, including me, then some from the two of them. I was one in the middle there, and had a big head of stubborn on me back in those times."

"Then how did you end up in Oregon?"

Colley gave her a crooked smile. "Followed my new papa's footsteps. Fell in love soon's I met me a good-lookin' young man with dreams of land and his own ranch in his black eyes. We married up and rushed right out to claim us some land. But it didn't end up quite like we dreamed, after all."

Emma looked up, fascinated by Colley's tale. "What happened?"

"War happened." Colley's features took on a hard cast. "David had 'im what he called 'his moral duty' to the country, the Union, he said. Had to do what he thought was right. Couldn't face his children otherwise, he said. Never did get to face 'em again in the end."

Colley turned her gaze to the red coals in the hearth, shoulders slumped, a figure draped in long-lived grief. When she straightened her spine, she didn't look away.

"Yeah, that's how it went. In the end, he didn't face his children," she repeated, voice empty of all emotion. "Died on a battlefield in Virginia, an' I had me four little ones to raise by myself, more sheep than I knew what to do with, an' more land than a body can ranch alone. Did as best's I could fer as long's I could. The drought and them hungry grasshoppers a few years back did me in at last. Sold out to Peter when I couldn't do more, and hired myself out, seein' as how he needed help."

"Your children wouldn't help?"

She shrugged. "Three girls wanted nothin' to do with the ranch. Begged and begged me to send 'em off to my brother an' his wife in San Antonio. All of 'em's married up now. Have me a wagonload of grandbabies, down there, too, but I had no one to run sheep with here. Sold it all out to the best man I knew. Peter's done a right fine job, too, even as hard as things've been."

Colley had clearly skipped over a lot. "I don't mean to be curious just for the sake of curiosity, but...you said you had four—"

"Son's gone."

The way she spat out those two meager, hard words told Emma the confidences were over for the night. There was more there, but Colley either couldn't make herself return to the events or simply didn't want to. Emma suspected the older woman held her pain too deep and too raw even years after her loss. She respected her choice.

In short order, Colley twisted all that wealth of steely hair into the usual coil on her crown, stood, and then returned the chair to its spot at the table. "Come on," she told Emma. "Let's be gittin' ya to bed."

Emma started toward the bunk Robby had been using since she arrived.

Colley shook her head. "Nah. Wouldn't be proper fer a lady like you to share the open cabin with Pete sleepin' here now. You take my room while he's hurt up like that. It's only right. I'll do fine fer myself on that top bunk."

The offer stunned her. "Oh, but I couldn't take your bed. You work too hard, and you need your rest."

"Nah. Wouldn't be right."

"There's nothing improper about a woman watching over a little boy and his injured father."

Colley grimaced. "Hmph! I know that an' you know that, an' he knows that. But others won't. I won't be havin' neither one a you bein' tarred like that."

"Who would ever find out?"

"May as well stop right there, Emma. I ain't about to change my mind. Folks is folks, and they're always curious. Things have a way of slippin' out when you ain't watchin'. Go on ahead to my room oncet Wade and Ned take that tub outta here."

"But—"

"But no. Done is done."

Those words left Emma no doubt there would be no further argument. Somewhere deep in a corner of her mind, she recognized Colley had a point. She never knew how, but gossip always did have a way of getting out, even when those involved never told. She remembered the various lives she'd seen ruined just because of a loose-lipped comment never intended to hurt.

"Thank you, then," she said. "I'll go fetch the men."

She hurried out before Colley could object, clutching close her too-long skirts so they wouldn't trip her. She wanted to help in any way she could, if for no other reason than to show her gratitude. She knew how much the ranch manager and Peter continued to do for her.

At the bunkhouse, she knocked. A familiar yapping inside responded. "Pippa! What are you doing—"

When Wade opened the door, the white ball of fluff pranced forward to greet her from right at his side. "Miss Emma!"

he cried, smiling. "I'm surprised to see you here. How can I help you?"

She bent down and scooped up the dog. "How did Pippa end up here?" And how had she failed to notice her pup's absence from the cabin? Oh, dear. She was turning into a poor owner in spite of herself.

The young ranch hand shrugged. "I like dogs, and she followed me. I reckoned you were busy with other things. She's no trouble, ma'am. Kinda like having her here. Keeps us company."

"Oh, goodness." Pippa licked Emma's chin, and she held her pet just far enough away to give her a scolding stare. "You've turned into quite a little traitor, now, haven't you?"

"Nah," Ned offered as he ambled out to the door from the darkened depths of the room. "She's jist one friendly little doggy, Miss Emma. She likes everybody, way I seen it."

"Likes the sheep, too," Wade added, then chuckled. "Looks some like a lamb sometimes."

She patted the pup's small head. "That curly white hair, right?"

He nodded. "Don't reckon the boss'll be shearing her. Hafta wonder, though, if that dog hair would spin into yarn like wool does."

Emma shuddered at the thought. Dog hair garments didn't quite appeal. "I don't think we should ever think to put it to the test. And I don't think it's wise if we chat away half the night, either. Colley and I are done with our baths, but the tub needs to go back outside. We would appreciate your help with emptying it."

The men hurried to the cabin with her and removed the tub. Emma again tried to thank Colley for the use of her bedroom, and once again the older woman shrugged it off.

"Part of bein' a ranch manager is managin' things 'round the place. I can solve this with lettin' you use my room. That's all it is."

But Emma knew otherwise. She'd seen the expression on Colley's face when she went to retire at night. The room was her refuge, and now it would be Emma's. With Pippa held secure in one arm, she closed the door behind them and shut out the glow of the big lantern in the cabin's main room.

She slept as soon as the pillow cushioned her head.

No man in his right mind ever wanted an injury. Peter was no different, especially since he considered himself to be quite sensible and right-minded. Still, he hadn't thought through all the things he wouldn't be able to do while stuck in the bunk.

"Help me to the table," he'd asked at breakfast.

"You can eat off yer lap in bed," Colley had answered. "That leg ain't moving long's I'm doctorin' you."

He'd looked to the other men for support, but neither Wade nor Ned had wanted to buck Colley's decision. Peter couldn't blame them. With him indoors, the ranch manager was responsible for the work at the camp. If either argued on his behalf, who knew what kind of chore Colley would assign the argumentative worker. She was a force to be reckoned with.

Then, there was the matter of Robby's lessons. While

he had been willing to teach his son, it wasn't an activity he particularly enjoyed. He would much rather spend his days outdoors, working with the flock, mending tools, repairing buildings. And, since it had been something Adele had loved to do, it brought to mind too many memories. But from the moment Colley had finished hog-tying him, his son had stuck to him like a burr to a man's sock. He loved the boy too much to hurt him by pushing him away.

"Pleeeeze!" Robby asked. "We did sums already, an' I read Scripture, too. 'Sides, you promised, Papa. Please read to me about King Arthur and his knights."

Out of the corner of his eye, he saw Emma fight a smile. He never wanted to encourage Robby, but he also didn't want to crush his spirit. He feared if he made it too great a choice between the ranch and the book, the boy might choose a life of study far from the legacy Peter had worked so long to achieve.

So he read. In that overdone, old, old language.

At the same time, Emma, much to his surprise, worked with needle and thread to adjust Adele's old dresses to her shorter, more delicate frame. He never would have expected that from the silly, useless girl he'd found in the cave.

He had to admit she'd surprised him with the meal she'd made. He'd never thought she would take up his challenge, much less succeed. And that morning, according to Colley, the grits, bacon, and eggs had all been made by their guest. The biscuits Emma served, while not quite as fluffy as Colley's, had been edible, especially since she'd tucked butter in the opened middles, then drenched them with honey she'd found in the shed.

Wade had gone on and on about how good the meal had been.

Ned had stared at Emma, his calf-eyed look rubbing Peter the wrong way. True, the two young men were close to her age, and were likely ready to find a girl to settle down with, but they struck him as wrong for her.

Wade had nothing to offer a wife, seeing as he was Peter's employee. And Ned...? Why, Ned still had to face the sheriff for the rustling he'd done. Surely Emma wouldn't fall for the excessive and obvious devotion both men showered upon her.

Way he saw it, she needed a stronger, more level-headed, more mature man. Someone more like him, not that he could ever see her in that way. Aside from the differences in their natures, she belonged in a city, while this was his world. And no matter how much she learned, Emma didn't belong here.

Much less with either his ranch hand or his prisoner, and Peter felt certain she knew it, too. And yet, she was kind and friendly to both. Peter had seen no sign of interest on her part, but at the same time, he'd never seen her act rude or push either away.

No one could miss Ned's determination to try to help her, nor could anyone ignore how the young outlaw merely made more work for her in the end. It was humorous, but at times, like when he'd dumped a bucket of water on Peter's boots, irritating as well.

He could chuckle at the memory, now the moment was well in the past. On the other hand, he still had a great deal of work that needed doing, and he was laid up.

"Ned," he'd said after breakfast, "I need you to help Colley today. You're strong and young, and she can use you to hold the sheep while she shears."

The shearing would keep the outlaw out of the house, since there was so much to be done still.

"And Wade, you can go back to work fixing the winter damage on the barn roof. Be careful out there. If you need help, fetch Colley and Ned. I want no one else hurt. It's bad enough with me like this."

In that fashion, Peter established a new routine, one he didn't much care for, since he was still bound to the bunk. He did, however, appreciate watching Emma as she went about the various chores Colley assigned her. Time crawled by, and observing his guest's activities became his only pastime.

She handled the laundering Colley assigned her quite well, even though the flour sacks his ranch manager took so much pride in didn't end up quite as white as when the older woman did the wash. At the end of laundry day, Emma looked much the worse for wear. She didn't argue when Ned offered to take Pippa for her last evening constitutional. With the dog back inside, she stumbled off to Colley's room scant minutes after she'd set the last washed bowl on the shelf.

Then, while she yelped a time or two as she worked on her sewing project, in less than a handful of days Peter noticed how much better those old dresses of Adele's fit her. He didn't dare compliment her on her handiwork, afraid she might realize how much time he'd spent studying her every move.

When he caught himself anticipating Emma's next chore, he knew he had to do something about his preoccupation or he'd lose his mind. She was too attractive, too determined, and too hard-working for him not to notice. And to like. But that kind of response had no place in his situation. It didn't fit within his plans.

This new Emma he was coming to know felt dangerous indeed. This Emma had a number of qualities he couldn't help but admire.

It would suit him much better if she irritated him again, if he could find a challenge she couldn't meet.

A week after he'd been forced to take up life as an invalid, Peter lay in the by-now-hated bunk and mulled over his predicament. It never would have struck him that he'd wind up liking his guest a touch more than he should. He needed to get back to work, to get away from Emma's humming, to evade the enticing scents of her mostly successful cooking, to escape the lulling pull of her voice as she read to Robby. Colley couldn't baby him on account of the leg a moment longer. The splint would have to do to keep the break in the bone from leaving him lame.

As he was in the process of thinking out the argument he planned to use to persuade his ranch manager, the blamed woman herself came back indoors.

"Don't reckon you figgered out yet what yer gonna do with all that fleece I sheared, now we got those holes in the barn roof. Damage is worse than we thought and repair work's goin' much slower with just Wade." She slapped her dusty hat against her leg. "You cain't be heading into Bountiful with that leg like that, and I cain't be leaving Wade all alone with them sheep. What's in yer head right about now?"

"Don't reckon I've thought much about it," he said. "We'll just have to keep it clean and dry as possible until we go down to market in the fall. We'll sell it then."

Colley cast a glance toward the corner where Adele's belongings had sat, unused, since her death. Peter feared he knew what she was thinking, and, for the first time in a long while, deep pain didn't come with dread at the mere thought. This time, he acknowledged his great sadness and sense of loss, but didn't experience the wrenching grief that had stolen his breath away for such a long time. He also identified a wistful wish for the love that only lived in memories these days.

He sighed. "What's running through that head of yours, then?"

"I reckon ya know."

"You're thinking I should spend my time in your jail here spinning some of the wool into yarn, aren't you?"

She let out a bark of laughter. "See no jail 'round these parts. Just a fella resting up like he should." Shaking her head, she dragged a chair near the bed. "Funny how a body doesn't have to say a word when things make sense. I know yer not a lady, and I know it was Adele who did the spinning, but ya did tell me yer mama had ya learn how to do it, too. And you know it makes fer easier storing when ya got yerself yarn than when ya got yerself fleece."

"Fast-talking me isn't going to do it, and you know it. I hate spinning yarn. It's a pity you don't like it any better than I do—"

"I'd like to learn," Emma said. Peter had forgotten she was in the cabin, busy with supper preparation. She went on. "I've been curious about that spinning wheel. I think it's a lovely piece. If one of you would teach me, I'm sure I could learn."

Colley looked from Emma to him and back to her again. "Well, then, there ya go." She stood, clapped the hat back on the roll of hair on top of her head, and crossed to the door. "I'll be back for supper."

"That's it?" he asked. "You won't offer to help Emma?"

Colley cackled. "Don't reckon I see nothing wrong with yer two hands, Pete. It's yer leg ya broke, right? Ya can teach her to spin, since ya were saying how ya hated feeling useless fer so long. Go ahead, an' make yerself useful now."

Echoes of the slammed door seemed to go on and on in Peter's head. Not only did he not enjoy the tedious exercise of spinning wool into yarn, but the large wheel in the corner also brought its share of hard memories. Adele had loved to spin and had spent hours in the quiet, rhythmic venture. She'd said it filled her with a sense of peace and accomplishment that satisfied in particular at the end of a long, busy day.

Now, Colley wanted him to pull out the lovely, graceful wheel, one that in his heart and mind only spoke of his late wife, and place it in the hands of the woman already wearing Adele's clothes. He hadn't had the heart to burn it up for firewood after Adele's death, but now he wondered if he shouldn't have. Had he done so, he wouldn't be faced with having to teach Emma to use his dead wife's wheel.

How? How could God ask this of him?

"Well," Emma said as she dried her hands on a flour sack towel, giving him no further time with his question. "Supper's minding itself, and I'm ready to learn. Where's the wool?"

Peter frowned. His uninvited guest was not a woman to be put off when she set her mind to something, as he was coming to learn. "Last I checked, the only carded wool is in a sack, more than likely in the barn. Colley's the one for you to ask."

Emma gave him a quick nod. "I'll be right back then. I'll

help you sit up if you need me as soon as I return with the wool."

It was only too clear she wasn't about to let him use his injury as a way to escape his apparent fate. Between her and Colley...he had to wonder who was in charge of his sheep operation anymore.

By the time he'd propped himself up into a full sitting position, Emma had stepped back into the cabin, a full, clean flour sack stuffed with wool in her arms. "Colley says this is all she took time to card. You should start by teaching me to spin since she told me this is ready, and then, once we're done with it, you can show me how to card—whatever that might be."

"Carding the wool is what you need to do to prepare the fleece you sheared for spinning it into yarn. We'll see how you do with spinning before we think about getting wool ready to card, never mind carding it."

Her warm smile appealed to him more than it should, especially since it came about from his agreeing to do something he didn't want to do. His irritation with his easy susceptibility grew.

Gesturing toward the wheel, he said, "Let's get to it, then. Bring it over and pull up a chair."

Emma did as asked, expressing surprise that it wasn't as heavy as she'd expected. Then, once seated, she sent him a mischievous grin. "It sounds to me as though you're ready to take some kind of punishment Colley has handed out. I promise I won't make this as bad as that."

The twinkle in her gaze made him realize how churlish he sounded. "I'm sorry. I have never cared for spinning. It was something my mother liked while I grew up, and Adele—my late wife—learned from her. I prefer the animals and the land. That's why I came out West."

She leaned back in the chair and studied him. Her scrutiny made him the slightest bit uncomfortable, as her green eyes seemed to reach deep inside him, to see his likes and dislikes, his dreams and wishes, his failures and flaws. He didn't much like that loss of his usual protective walls.

"I saw you with that ewe the other night. I don't doubt it was your love of animals that drove your wish. But I don't think it was the only thing that brought you here. I think you felt the need to test yourself, to prove to yourself you had it in you to do whatever you set your mind to."

He shrugged. She'd hit the target full on.

"I'm not much different," she said. "At least, I'm learning that about myself. I decided I did want to learn to cook, and I'm making progress—I haven't poisoned any of you yet, right?"

He only dignified the comment with a snort.

She giggled then went on. "I also decided to use my skills with a needle and alter these dresses myself. I think I did a fair job of it, and with practice, I could outfit myself in time. Now, I've decided to learn to spin."

He couldn't argue with a thing she'd said. A grudging sense of admiration struck him. Again.

As she sat and waited for him, he pulled a puff of wool from the sack. Her eyes gleamed and she continued to smile, her anticipation almost something he could touch. He remembered Adele's wistful wish for more women who would learn to spin, now that many bought their yarn ready-spun from the mercantile. She'd always hoped for others to keep the ancient art alive. It struck him as odd that a woman who'd grown up in Emma's situation might be one to catch the interest. At least, she'd be interested for the moment.

"Like Colley said," he started, holding out the wool, "this is already carded. Carding's what you do to untangle and clean the shorn wool. When you first shear the animal, the fleece still has bits of dirt and seeds in it. You don't want that in the mix when you spin."

"We are going to card wool later, right?"

He sighed. "From your insistence, I'm thinking I have a good deal of carding in my future."

"Just enough to teach me. I'll take it over once I've learned."

He just shook his head. "Fine. I'll show you how to sort and wash the wool, then the carders and how to use them later. As I said, Colley took care to prepare all this."

"Good. I want to learn it all."

"Then let's get started." He held out the rounded tuft of wool again. "This is called a sliver or, more correctly, a rolag. That's because after she carded it, Colley rolled it up on itself to get it off the card."

Peter spread the end of the rolag in a fan shape across his palm. He picked up the short end of yarn left on the spinning wheel's bobbin and continued with his lesson. "This is called a leader. It's a short piece you always want to leave attached to the spindle after you remove the last quantity you spun. You use it to start your next batch."

He bent in closer to the wheel, but then realized it had also brought him closer to her. The nearness made him intensely aware of her, something he didn't want. She already took up too much room in his thoughts.

But it couldn't be helped. He didn't know how to teach her to spin, other than for both of them to stay near the wheel. He'd known what was what straight from the start. This had not been one of Colley's better ideas. He should have flat-out refused. Now, it was too late, and Emma was much too close.

He cleared his throat. "To start to spin, you have to join the carded wool and the leader. To do this, I'll twist them both a bit to the left." He demonstrated, and nearly groaned when she leaned closer still.

Spinning. You're spinning wool. Think how much you hate it.

He continued. "Once I've twisted them together, I hold the spot where I joined them between my left thumb and forefinger. With my right hand, I give the wheel a clockwise turn and start to treadle."

And there, he ran into yet another hurdle. For his good leg to reach the treadle, he had to sit up, closer still to Emma. This time, though, his shoulder grazed hers. The light touch took in her warmth, and it occurred to Peter he hadn't been this close to another person, aside from his son, since the day he'd hugged Adele good-bye and helped her onto the train back East.

A yawning hole opened up inside him, and he realized how much he missed that human closeness, the simple squeeze of a hand, soft fingers against his cheek, a tug on his hair. The sudden need for that kind of tender, intimate companionship stunned him, stole his breath, and left him reeling from the gut-deep realization of his loneliness. He sensed the years spread out before him in the same way...

Why? Why did it have to be the most impossible person he knew who would lead him to that point? And why now?

Spin, spin the wool...

Without another word, he set his foot on the wooden platform and set the wheel to turning with a simple up and down pressure. Emma stared at his hand, clearly fascinated by the way he turned a cloud of fibers into smooth, sturdy yarn. He could sense her interest growing, and he remembered Adele's excitement when his mother had taught her to spin so many years before.

Echoes of his life swirled around him, and he found himself fighting an intense internal battle. He couldn't stop the clock now any more than he could have cured Adele on his own. If he'd had his choice, his wife never would have fallen ill and would still be the one using the wheel. Instead, here he sat next to a lovely, distracting stranger who stared at him as though he'd conquered the greatest army, simply because he knew how to turn animal hair to yarn. A woman who made him stare into his future and find it lacking.

She looked up from his hands, her green eyes dancing and sparkling like the brightest shooting stars the western night sky had ever known. "That is marvelous! I'm so impressed by you, that you can do something like this..."

Peter found he couldn't tear his own gaze away from hers. The moment lengthened, and he again recognized how much danger Emma posed for him. Still, he didn't look away, but instead soaked up her admiration as his land had soaked in the moisture once the rain had broken the drought.

A man could get used to being looked at like that.

He could risk too much just to hear a compliment like hers.

He could lose his fool heart and not even mind, on account of a woman like her.

It occurred to him then he'd come close enough to the distracting Emma that if he moved all of an inch or so to the left he'd find himself within kissing distance of his unwanted guest. Still, if she was so unwanted, then why did he, at that moment, want most to bridge the gap and kiss her?

Why did he feel his drought was at the point of breaking?

Chapter 17

Every evening that followed the spinning lesson, Peter watched Emma hurry through her chores, take Pippa out for her last constitutional of the night, and then march straight to the wheel. At first, what she spun onto the bobbin looked like a mass of knots strung together by a thread from a spider's web and fell apart from little more than a passing look sent its way. Not what anyone would even think to use to knit or weave a single, useful thing.

But again, with that determination he was coming to know, she kept up her efforts, and in a shorter number of days than he'd expected, she began to fill the bobbin with a respectable beginner's yarn. Each new batch looked better and better to his fairly critical eye.

That night, she followed her routine again, and now sat at the wheel, working the wool into yarn. It would appear she, too, knew how much progress she had made, since, after a glance toward him, she took her foot off the treadle and brought the soothing whir of the wheel to a stop.

"Well, Peter." She pointed to the bobbin. "What do you think?"

He felt himself blush, certain she'd caught him staring at her. At least he could blame his fixation on his interest in her progress, not something he could do any of the many other times he found himself following her every move. "That looks right even and strong," he said. "Do you knit?"

She shook her head. "I've always preferred petit point embroidery. The colors of the silk threads are so lovely, and the patterns so intricate and charming. Why, you can make a complete picture, like an artist paints with oils, out of nothing besides needle and thread. But, I must admit, unless one is making a tapestry to upholster a chair cushion, and that does take an eternity to make, then I don't see any practical use for all those pieces that took up so much of my time. Will you teach me to knit?"

He laughed, relieved. "Oh, no. That I can't do. I've never picked up a pair of knitting needles, not once in my whole life. You'll have to turn to Colley for that. I reckon she can teach you to make some of those socks of hers. Maybe you'll learn to make them where they aren't quite so scratchy."

She arched a brow and crossed her arms. "Now that I've spent some time with wool and yarn, I would have to wonder if the scratchiness comes from the quality of the wool itself, since that would seem to make a great deal of difference in the yarn."

How dared she? "Are you questioning the quality of my product? I'll have you know, I raise fine Merino sheep. They produce good, tasty meat, and their wool is strong and long-fibered. We shear about twelve pounds per ewe. An excellent yield—"

"Goodness! I didn't think my simple comment would set off a lecture on the merits of your flock."

"And why not? I have plenty of reasons to feel right good about my work. Up until those years of drought and the grasshopper plagues, I had no trouble getting fine, healthy animals to market, and selling them and their fleece for fair sums."

"How long ago was the drought?"

He told Emma how it had been five years earlier, right around the time Robby was toddling around the ranch, when the weather turned dry and harsh. The land became an endless expanse of dust. The next spring, while young shoots braved the conditions to work their way up through the soil, bathed by the few welcome spring showers that fell, swarms of hungry grasshoppers descended on the area and left nothing but memories of the hints of green. After those years and the hard hit from the loss of his wife, he'd almost sold out.

"I'm glad you didn't," she said in a soft voice, careful not to wake Robby. "I don't know what would have become of me if you hadn't been up here with your flock this year. I'm so glad you came and rescued me from that cave."

Her comment shouldn't have pleased him such a great deal, but it did. He shrugged, not wanting to let her know just how much it meant. "Someone would have been here. I would have sold to another fella with the same dreams. No one would just up and leave his animals and his ranch."

"But whoever you sold to might not have cared what became of me once he'd found me."

"Well, you're right about some other fellas," he answered, mischief bubbling up in him. "My conscience wouldn't have let me be if I hadn't done right by you, no matter how irksome you might be at times. And here I thought you found me harsh—stern, I recollect was the word you used. Maybe that other fella would have had fewer of those stern words for you. You might already be back at Bountiful, owing to that other fella, too."

She didn't snap back at him straight away, but rather gave his half-jesting words careful thought. "I must confess it hasn't been a real hardship here for me. Different? Oh, indeed. But it hasn't been nearly as dreadful as I first feared. If it weren't for Papa, I think I wouldn't be so distressed, since everything here is so...interesting. But Papa must be heartbroken by now, and so full of sadness, too. I fear he thinks he's all alone."

The love for her father rang deep and sincere. Peter had fought her insistent pleas to return to Bountiful from the moment he'd found her because of the demands of his ranching life that asked so much but also could give back such a good existence. His reasons had been and still were valid, seeing as how he was a father and had taken on responsibility for everything around him. But now that he'd come to know her better, he realized how much she truly ached for the way news of her loss would have affected her father, and the grief he must continue to feel.

"I'm sorry, Emma."

She met his gaze. "I think you are. Thank you for that."

"Please think how much more it will mean to your father when you return. His joy will come as an enormous relief."

Her smile looked a mite crooked. "And all of this came to be, just because I felt the need to prove how much of an adult I'd become. It was my first time to travel without him at my side."

His brows went up. "I've often wondered what kind of father would send a beautiful young woman like you on such a long journey West all on her own."

At first she gaped, and then she glared. "Nothing of the sort, sir! Be careful what you say about my papa. He sent me with Reverend Strong and his wife, who were headed to Portland as well. They're friends of my uncle's family in Denver, and they're a perfectly sober, proper, and serious couple, too. For him to even let me do that much, I'll have you know, I had to beg and beg. I assured him many times I could indeed care for myself, that I was no longer his little girl."

Peter tried but failed to keep the knowing smirk off his face. "And now that you've been through all these...experiences...how well do you think you can care for yourself on a journey to Portland?"

Although she blushed a bright rosy red, she also bolted upright as though she'd been jabbed by a pin. "I'm doing quite fine for myself these days, I'll have you know. You've even said so, yourself."

It was his turn to give her words careful consideration. "I'm happy to see your experience with Sawyer has left you no scars."

Emma shuddered, and for a moment he almost regretted his comment. The attack had happened, as had Sawyer's murder, and no one had mentioned the event since, not even Emma. He'd waited, hoping someone would let something slip that he could grasp, but nothing. It was Emma who surprised him most. She was the one who'd been attacked, and she was the one who chattered all day about every last little thing, likely just to keep her ears from growing lazy on her head. And still she'd said not a word about the attack. Had she been able to just forget it all? What did that say about her? Did it mean she knew more about the outlaw's death than she'd let on? That it didn't bother her on account of that knowledge?

He waited out her silence.

After a bit, she shut her eyes tight then shook her head. "I have tried hard to forget that man. And what he was bent on doing to me. But at the oddest moments it all comes back. At those times, I make myself think of something much better, of going back home and seeing my father again, of reading to Robby, of playing with Pippa out in the sun. Other times, I go to *Mrs. Beeton* to find a new recipe to try, or I'll work harder to spin a better yarn. I find something to do—anything—that takes more time and thought than simpler, more thoughtless things might."

Her words caught him by surprise. "Is that why you've worked so hard since that night?"

"It's one of the reasons. I haven't lost my mind or any such thing to wish for an experience like mine with Sawyer, but I learned a great deal that night, about myself and about . . . well, about God. I called out in prayer, and then . . . there you were, and—well, we know what happened after that. But while you were injured, I was not. I know God heard me cry out to Him. He protected me. Now, I'd rather think and try to understand why you would have to suffer the pain Sawyer meant for me."

He shrugged. "I don't know, but I'm glad it happened that way. I'd much rather put up with a broken leg than try and put you back together, had Sawyer gotten his wish. I'm just waiting to see how God will turn all this into something to the good."

Her eyebrows shot up. "To the good?"

"Scripture says, 'And we know that all things work together for good to them that love God, to them who are called according to His purpose.'"

"I have heard that, but…"

"But we will have to see how He takes that moment and then works something good out of it for all of us who do love Him."

"I grew up at church every Sunday, and I heard many verses during all that time, but I know now I didn't pay as much attention as I should have." She smiled. "I must have learned enough to know to call on God when I had no other hope. I suppose deep inside of that action is a form of love. I'll have to work on my understanding of it…"

"That might be the best of all the work you do. You can always trust Him when you reach the point where there's no one else to trust."

She sighed and grimaced. "I suppose I must admit to you, of all possible people, that wasn't my finest moment. I never should have trusted Sawyer even so much as to walk with him to the cabin door, never mind consider, if only for a few crazed, furious minutes, he might be someone I could count on to see me safely to Bountiful."

He thought back on the moment when he'd realized Sawyer had died. He supposed he, too, had refused to come to terms with what had happened, since he couldn't make himself mourn the man too deeply. Still, no matter how great a sinner a man might be, none should have to face death by another's hand. That was up to God, who called His children to cherish life, to never kill.

Someone had killed Sawyer.

Since he hadn't done it, it had to have been either Ned or Wade. While Peter didn't feel about Ned the same way he cared about Wade's fate, he was coming to have a soft spot for the inept outlaw. He'd never known a man with a less criminal nature than Ned, never mind his lack of smarts and cunning. Peter doubted the young fella had the wits to pull off a misdeed on his own. Without a doubt, he'd fallen in with the wrong sorts. And yet, just like Wade, the would-be sheep rustler had fallen under Emma's bewitching spell.

Had either of them killed Sawyer to protect the woman they wished to win?

Emma's soft voice broke into his thoughts. "I haven't let myself dwell on it, even if the thoughts do come up many a time. I know someone must have done it, and only a certain number of us are here. But I can't see anyone I know doing such a thing."

He gave a humorless laugh. "You couldn't see Sawyer turning on you the way he did either."

"No, I suppose you're right. I didn't like him, but...no."

To his dismay, he couldn't shake the nagging thought he'd missed something, something that didn't quite fit.

He took hold of the splint and eased his leg up onto the bunk again. The relief from the discomfort he'd ignored while he'd spent all that time talking to Emma was such that a heart-deep sigh burst out from him uninvited. He'd held the leg out at an odd angle from his body, seeing as he couldn't bend or move it in any normal way. But lying about in bed during a conversation with a lady hadn't seemed right, certainly not proper. It did surprise him how easy it had been to talk, just talk to her.

Too easy, he reckoned. Too easy for his own good.

"There's not much more to be said about that night, Emma, so I'll just say goodnight."

She gave him an odd look, but didn't answer. She stood, stored the spinning wheel in its corner, tucked the chair she'd used back in its place at the table, and then stepped to the door to Colley's room. She opened it, and only then did she speak again.

"I can never thank you enough for what you did that night for me. If you hadn't come after me, regardless how much I'd irritated you, if you hadn't fought Sawyer off me, I...I—"

"Don't." His heart felt squeezed with the mix of emotions the memory brought up in him. To think of such a lovely, delicate woman debased in such a way by a brute like Sawyer was more than Peter could stomach. "I've thanked God more than once that He led me to you at that moment. I don't know if I could have faced myself or my God if you'd been harmed because I'd behaved in a terrible way since the day we met."

"It wasn't your fault. It was Sawyer who made his choice."

"But it was my fault that I chose to speak to you in a way that made you run away from the barn. For that, I will always be sorry. Please forgive me."

"I did, right from the start."

Her words warmed a spot Peter hadn't realized held a chill. "That means a whole lot."

"Goodnight, Peter. I'm glad we talked tonight."

With great reluctance, but also with total honesty, he said, "So am I. Goodnight."

As soon as she closed the door, Peter dropped back down onto the pillow. What was that woman doing to him? How had she torn down his defenses in such a way that he was having heart-to-heart chats with her? And why had she moved into even his dreams of late? Wasn't her constant presence in his home and his days enough?

His cabin rang with her voice and her laughter at all times. His son sang her praises morning to night. His crusty ranch manager thought the world of her, and his ranch hand wanted to woo her. It would seem Emma Crowell had taken over every inch of Peter's life in only a matter of a very few short weeks.

What troubled him most was how easily she'd done it.

Stern? Him?

Hah! Not around her.

Maybe his words had been thoughtless and hurtful, but, him? Stern? A stern man wouldn't be fighting his every stray thought to keep it from flying right to her.

Colley came inside for the night. As she stood in the doorway, scraping her boots, with a satisfied grin turning her weathered face into a pleated wreath, Peter realized he'd been had. Up until a short time after Emma had invaded the camp, his ranch manager had always been in an all-fired hurry to make her way to her room after a hard day's work. Ever since his injury, however, Colley had made herself scarce until right around Peter's bedtime.

Who would have thought he'd have to fight a denim- and flannel-clad matchmaker as well when it came to keeping his heart intact?

At first, Emma had been reluctant to do much more than take Adele's Bible out of the trunk to reach inside for something else. But after the night Sawyer died, she'd gone straight to the trunk and retrieved the leather-bound book. She'd wanted to explore the matter of God answering, specifically her prayer. Of course, she'd always heard it said that the Lord listened, and she'd also heard, all her growing-up years, that He delighted in giving His children good things, but she'd never experienced such a direct response to a plea. She'd seen her family's many blessings as God's way to answer prayers for provision and protection.

She'd begun to read random sections, but soon found herself consuming chapter after chapter, if only to learn what would happen next in the biblical tale. But what she read weren't stories like one of those in *Le Morte D'Arthur*. Oh, sure, they were full of just as many fascinating characters and multiple twists of plot, but the Bible stories made her think, they kept her pondering the reasons why they'd turned out the way they had. Each time, she came back to one simple answer. It had always been as a result of the Father's touch. Just as had happened with her.

At the same time, she'd read bits and parts that made her think of situations she hadn't handled well or even sections that brought other people's actions to mind. Peter seemed to feature prominently in those recollections, especially when she read through the brief collection of thirty-one chapters of Proverbs.

A few days after the evening she and Peter talked so openly about that dreadful night, her mischievous side stepped up. Later that night, after supper had been cleaned away, after Colley had run off to the barn, and after Ned had taken Pippa for her walk, silence reigned in the cabin. In anticipation of her plans, Emma kept an eye on Peter. When she saw him reach for his Bible, a smile turned up her lips.

"Time for a bit of Scripture," he told his son, who'd sat quietly on the floor and played with a pair of wooden railroad cars he loved.

"I think," Emma said, surprising father and son, "that it would only be right if I took my turn reading Scripture at night. You are injured and recovering, after all, and it might even help you rest easier. Maybe you'll sleep sooner, as well."

He snorted. "All I do is rest these days. I don't need any more of that. What I need is a full day's work to wear me out good." He eyed her with curiosity then. "But I can't deny you a chance to read the Word. Go ahead. It should be good to take turns."

She fought the urge to grin. "I agree, especially since I've become quite fond of the book of Psalms. And I've learned a good many bits of sound advice from the book of Proverbs. How about if I start with a Psalm?"

"Excellent choice."

Emma read, filling her words with the best intonation for the particular passage. Before long, Peter seemed to relax, his eyelids lowered a bit, as though he were listening with his attention on his own application of God's Word. Robby, as usual, fell asleep before more than a couple of verses were read.

Oh, yes, indeed, Mr. Peter Lowery; two could very well read the Word.

"Now," she said, "for a Proverb or two." She quickly flipped pages and came to the passage she'd earlier marked. " 'The wise in heart,' " she read from the sixteenth chapter, "'will be called discerning, and sweetness of speech increases persuasiveness. Understanding is a fountain of life to him who has it, but…'" She slowed for mischievous emphasis. "'But the discipline of fools is folly—'"

Outraged sputtering cut into her words. Emma ignored it.

She continued. "'The heart of the wise teaches his mouth, and adds persuasiveness to his lips. Pleasant words are a honeycomb, sweet to the soul and healing to the bones.'"

"I am not a fool—"

"Oh, dear," she said, again ignoring his indignation, trying to keep from laughing. Of course, she didn't think he was a fool, but those lectures straight from his Scripture readings still rankled, and she thought, since he was injured at the moment, a touch of his own medicine might do wonders indeed. "It is late, and I'm so tired. Robby fell asleep right away, didn't he?"

She set up the usual ruckus dragging first the spinning wheel to its corner, and then the chair to the table, making it quite impossible to catch Peter's objection. It was a good thing Robby always seemed to sleep so deeply, or she surely would have woken the child. "I'm sure I'll do the same, no sooner than my head touches the pillow. It is so quiet and peaceful here at night that I've had moments of the most interesting discernment when I retire." She scooped up Pippa, who'd faithfully followed her every step. "Since getting lost in the woods, I've come to deeply appreciate the wonders of a bed and a pillow."

Finally, at the door to Colley's room, she came to a halt in her chatter. "Well, Peter. It has been a long, satisfying day. Goodnight. I hope you sleep well."

And she closed the door to the continuing, one-sided debate. Only then did she let herself giggle at what she'd just seen. One very annoyed rancher had been dosed with his own tonic. She wondered what effect it would have by the time the morning dawned. There was only one way to find out.

Ah, yes...sleep was welcome, indeed. Emma's daily chores left her tired at the end of the day, tired but satisfied with her efforts.

She curled up under the fluffy quilt, Pippa at her feet, and closed her eyes. She'd discovered a number of pleasant qualities to the camp. Not the least of which was a decent, upright owner, even if he had an overgrown sense of his own importance at times. She respected Peter a great deal, which only made the last few minutes the more enjoyable for the challenge she'd returned.

Even though she'd grown to respect and even like Peter, Emma hadn't been able to shed the discomfort she felt from being observed at all times. Of course, she couldn't really blame the man. He was stuck in bed; she worked in the cabin. There wasn't much for him to look at in the space. But understanding his situation didn't relieve her anxiety. Especially since she suffered his observation as a critical stare. As mild a parry as her Scripture *riposte* had been, she was glad she'd made the point the night before, as evidenced by his loud objections.

She didn't think she could ever find anything to do that might not meet with his objections. It was hard to tackle chores with dread, fearful she'd never live up to his exacting expectations. And she cared. No matter how often she told herself it was foolish to feel that way, she did care what he thought of her.

Yet another reason to leave.

The sooner the fall came, the better.

His judgmental scrutiny was only one of the reasons she'd come to appreciate, if not love, laundry day. Because of the need to hang the clean items to dry, she had every reason to spend time in the lovely outdoors. She no longer found the woods quite as ominous as she had when she'd first wound up lost on the untamed mountain. At least, she didn't during the daytime. At night, in the shadowy murk, the whoosh of the winds and the unfamiliar sounds still made her scurry as she saw to her needs—and Pippa's—and then hurry back to the safety of the cabin.

The horror of Sawyer's attack in the dark hadn't faded.

But this day was sunny, and armed with her basket of clean clothes, she went outside as usual, followed by Robby.

"Lady Emma! Shall we joust today? What say you?"

Emma knew the child's playacting still rankled his father, especially in the close quarters of the cabin. Fortunately, on laundry day they could play outdoors. Peter was still in bed, per Colley's staunch orders. Emma suspected he could get around if he were to try with the help of a cane, but she wasn't prepared to argue with the formidable ranch manager, any more than Peter was.

"As soon as I have the laundry hung on the rope," she answered.

Robby's eyes sparkled even more. He cheered. "I'm going to find us each a good, sturdy lance, then."

Emma took little time to hang the clothes, and Robby even less to return with a pair of adequate lance substitutes—leafless branches he had found inside the edge of the woods. If for no other reason, she was thankful for the abundance of "weapons" the forest provided the child.

"Are you ready?" he asked, as soon as he'd handed her one of the sticks.

"Of course."

The battle was launched. He danced from foot to foot, lunging at her with more enthusiasm than accuracy or grace. Pippa bounced around them, barking. Robby's cries were matched only by his chortles of glee, and Emma made certain he could land more blows than she did. His pleasure made her heart swell with joy, which made her realize how much he meant to her. She couldn't understand how his father could deny himself, and the boy, that delight she gained from their games.

As the thought occurred to her, the man himself appeared in the cabin doorway, as though summoned by her wandering mind. She hadn't seen him stand since he'd broken his leg. If Colley saw him...

"Peter!" she yelled. "What are you doing out of bed? Colley hasn't given permission for you to put weight on that leg yet."

His thunderous frown gave her pause. As it registered, she remembered the stick—the lance—she held aloft. In a gesture as inconspicuous as possible, she lowered it, brought it to her side first, and then slipped it behind her back. Once there, she dropped it, wishing she could persuade herself he hadn't noticed.

But he had. And he wasn't pleased.

"Robert," he said in that implacable voice, "have you checked in with Wade or Colley today? Have they told you what chores they need you to do?"

Out of the corner of her eye, Emma saw the happiness vanish from Robby's face. He lowered his gaze to the ground at the same pace he lowered his "lance."

"No, sir," the child said "I meant to go after we were done—"

"In a ranch," Peter said, his words clipped and edged with the weariness of frequent repetition, "we work first, play later. Go find out what you need to do, then do it. We'll have us a long, meaningful talk once you've finished."

As soon as the boy had gone a few feet away, Pippa trotting along beside him, the rancher turned to Emma. "I do believe I've told you not to indulge him with all those fantasies. Why do you insist on going against the one thing I've insisted you do? Why must you fight me?"

She tilted her chin up in the air. "I have yet to fight you, sir. And I have found myself in need of making a choice. My alternatives are few—two, as a matter of fact. The one you prefer would have me stifle all the joy out of that little man of yours. If you're of a mind to do so, then suit yourself. I will not do that to any youngster, much less such a wonderful, bright, engaging young man."

"But I am his father!"

"Indeed! But not his jailer, I would venture. On the other hand, how about a killjoy? A spoilsport, perhaps?"

As she spat out the questions, her courage grew, as did her determination. The child needed to be...well, a child at this point in his life. Sure, he could also take care of his share of the chores, but that was, of course, his share, a child's share.

Before Peter quit sputtering in indignation, she went on. "Have you lost sight of reason? Have you lost your mind? I would have thought the loss of your wife would have been enough to mourn, but it would appear to me that you've decided to lose the love and affection of your son, too. Perhaps his company, as well, if in a few years' time you haven't changed your ways."

His face turned an alarming shade of red. "You have no right—" As he clearly sought more to say, he stepped outside and marched toward Emma, his steps uneven. "I'll have you know, I love my son. He can be assured of my affection at all times. I do not agree that to love a child a man must put aside the need to teach him—aaagh!"

As he stomped up to Emma, he stepped on Robby's forgotten lance, and the injured leg collapsed. Horrified to see a tall, strong, proud man fall, she flew toward him, arms extended, determined to catch him, break his fall, keep him from further injury.

While she was much smaller than he, when his bulk struck hers, his momentum halted. She wobbled, unable to fully bear his weight. As she held him for that brief moment, his stunned gaze met hers. Her arms burned with the strain of holding him, but in the end, there was nothing she could have done. She wasn't tall enough, strong enough, to keep them from toppling over. As she lay on her back staring up, all she saw was the angry brown eyes, the tumbled dark hair, the vast expanse of cloudless blue beyond, and at the edges, the tips of the evergreen branches aimed at the sky.

Emma fought for breath, but pinned beneath Peter's larger body she could only gasp, stare . . . and notice he was doing the same. Only a scant whisper away, she also noticed the gold flecks in his brown eyes. The warmth there reminded her of the night the lamb was born, the night he'd come to her rescue, the night he'd fought to protect her from a monster. The gentle, courageous, decent man she'd witnessed in action seemed to overshadow the outraged father, and her irritation melted away in soft waves of sensation. It would appear his anger toward her vanished as well.

Before she realized what was about to happen, he let out a rough breath and brought his lips down to hers. Oh, yes. He did have a gentle touch, indeed, and he knew how and when to call it into play. Peter kissed her, tenderly, but with a heated intensity she'd never experienced before. It stole what breath she had left, her strength, all thought of consequences. He deepened the kiss in slow, even measures, and she lost herself in the heady whirl of her senses.

But it was his tenderness that overrode her reason.

In that one vivid, emotion-packed moment Emma realized she'd only been a girl until then. She'd played at feelings, at romance, at adulthood, at growing up. It had taken a man to show her how naïve she'd really been.

It had taken Peter Lowery to kiss her like the woman she'd longed to be.

Chapter 18

A corner of his more reasonable mind screamed in self-defense. "*No, no!*"

The rest of him, the man enthralled by the woman, sent out a louder roar. "YES!"

In either case, Peter found himself lost in the sweet tenderness of Emma's lips. He hadn't meant to kiss her, but when he'd wound up on top of her, those splendid green eyes staring at him, her lips parted, her breath soft against his face, he'd felt as though he'd fallen—yes, fallen—not to the ground but under a spell. A spell the enchanting Emma Crowell, herself, had woven around him.

He hadn't been able to help himself, just as he hadn't been able to help himself when she'd kept herself busy in the cabin. She'd captured every bit of his attention, left him too captivated to resist her appeal.

Thoughts spun in his head, but they seemed to disappear

behind the veil of sensation. Emma's warmth, her sweet gentleness, her timid response all served to steal his sanity—

"PETER!"

The panicked scream barely pierced the haze of his passion. With great reluctance, Peter eased up on the kiss, his eyes focused on hers again. He heard the cry one more time, from somewhere near the cabin.

"Peter!" Wade called. "Where are you? It's Robby!"

At the sound of his son's name, Emma seemed to awaken as though from a dream, and, hands on his chest, pushed against him. She made a strangled sound in her throat, then wriggled her shoulders, kicked her legs under him. He pulled farther from her tempting lips, splayed his hands flat on either side of her shoulders.

"Pe-ter!" This time, Wade's irritation broke through, and Peter reacted. He eased his torso up from hers. "It's Robby!"

"I'm here!" he managed to croak out as he tried to gain his feet.

Unfortunately, he wasn't fast enough. That was how his ranch hand found them, with Emma on her back on the ground at the edge of the forest, him on top, his arms framing her, their bodies pressed flat one to the other. Her lips were reddened and puffy, and no one with eyes to see could fail to note she'd just been kissed. Peter's embarrassment knew no bounds. He imagined hers would be worse.

To his amazement, she sprang into action. "Get off!" She pushed—again. "What's wrong with you? It's about Robby."

Wade ran up, and then pulled to a halt. "Oh!" He blushed. "I...ah...didn't see you, miss. I'm...uh...sorry—"

"Don't bother with that!" Emma said.

Peter scrambled up, Wade's words finally registering. "What's this about Robby?"

The horror in Wade's eyes struck a matching fear in Peter. "Oh, boss," his ranch hand said. "I don't rightly know how it happened, but one moment I seen the boy on the corner of the barn roof, and the next, why... he—he's falling—"

"Where?" Emma demanded.

Wade faced her, and if anything, turned redder still as he waved to the ground where they'd sprawled only moments earlier. "I'm so sorry, ma'am—"

"Stop!" she cried with a dismissive wave. "Robby. He's what matters. What happened?"

"He fell, Miss Emma. Dunno how he got there, but straight off the barn roof..."

Before Wade had the words out of his mouth, Emma was already pelting toward the barn. Sudden anxiety and panic struck, and Peter found himself frozen to the ground. And yet... it was the mortification that overwhelmed him. Emma had responded like... well, like the mother the boy no longer had. He, on the other hand, Robby's father, had acted like a lusty adolescent boy, more intent on and dazed by a pretty girl than focused on the son who counted on him. He'd failed. Again.

"Well," he bit off the word, "what are you waiting for, Wade? Let's go to the boy."

Wade's bewildered expression told Peter more than if the man had complained about his churlish response.

He sent a panicked prayer heavenward as he jolted himself out of his self-absorption. He started toward the barn. His leg kept his pace maddeningly slow, and he berated himself as he limped along as quickly as he could.

He hadn't controlled his feelings, not around Emma, and certainly not now, in the face of his son's emergency. His sense of inadequacy as a father grew. What kind of man was he? He'd failed to protect the wife of his youth, the mother of his son. Now he'd failed to protect Robby. He'd let his focus stray toward a pretty-faced girl who'd never make a good and proper wife for a rancher like him. Worse yet, he'd acted like little more than an animal, like nothing but an uncivilized man, one who'd surrendered to his baser, physical drives. Was he any better than Sawyer had been?

Shame and guilt threatened to bring him down like one of the trees around him as he and Wade reached the barn. He thanked God when he saw Emma crouched at Robby's side, gently touching the boy's legs, arms, his torso…his head. A scant second later, he let out a guttural groan when he saw the flow of blood on the boy's forehead.

He stepped toward them. "Emma…is he—"

"Oh, Peter…" She shifted toward him. "He…he's not, but…"

Tears poured down her cheeks, fear and dread mingled in her expression. She didn't have to say any more. He understood.

He knelt awkwardly at their side, and saw what she'd tried to express. His son lay on the ground unconscious, wounded in ways he couldn't know right then. One thing, however, he did know. The boy had struck his head in the fall. If Robby didn't come to, there was no telling what the outcome would be.

Peter couldn't bear the thought of another loss.

Not Robby!

"Let's go," he urged Wade. "Get the wagon ready. I need to get Robby to Doc Chalmers in Bountiful. I'll bring Emma and you get Ned. He should come, too. The marshal will know what to do with them. You and Colley will have to manage things here yourselves until I can come home again. Robby comes first."

"But, boss. There's too much to do here—"

"I know." His stomach roiled. But there really was nothing to think about. Between the ranch and his boy, his choice would always come down on Robby's side. "I know better than anyone what all needs doing here, but it can't be helped. Robby needs the doc, and I won't let him wait for one of us to fetch him here. And it's past time Emma went back. She's said it often enough." And he now knew she'd been right. He had to put himself as far away as possible from temptation. "This is the time to do it."

Emma gasped, covered her mouth with her hand. Then, without a word, she stood slowly. "I'll go fetch my cloak and some blankets for Robby."

To Peter's surprise, the woman who'd begged time and time again to be taken back to Bountiful didn't appear glad to be getting her wish. Instead, she looked stricken. Surely her intense but odd response was on account of the boy's injuries, right?

She couldn't possibly have any interest in staying.

He glanced up briefly from his son and watched for a few seconds as she ran off. She cast glance after glance behind her. It would have taken a great deal of persuasion to convince him she'd only looked at his son, since a time or two those green, green eyes seemed to look straight at him.

He didn't know what her actions might mean, but he had Robby to think of right now.

This wasn't the time to ponder the possibilities.

Emma's heart ached to where she feared it might shatter into a million tiny pieces. As she gazed at that small, still body, as she watched the blood flow from the deep, open gash on Robby's high forehead, grief and guilt mingled inside her. She never should have allowed herself to roll on the ground with—much less kiss—the child's father. She'd been assigned Robby's care. Yet she'd failed...

... failed at the most critical task she'd ever attempted.

Unwilling to waste another second, she ran into the cabin, gathered up her cloak, just about her only belonging, together with a quilt and a pair of pillows for Robby, and then hurried outside again, as ready for their trip as she would ever be. A final glance back ripped a sob out from deep inside her.

Craziness, pure craziness! She would miss the rustic home... its residents even more.

Tears scalded her eyes. She wanted nothing more than to get help for the innocent victim of her irresponsible, wanton behavior. And she had been wanton. She couldn't deny she'd liked being kissed by Peter. A secret, newly discovered part of her wanted him to kiss her again.

But reality couldn't be changed. She should have been watching Robby.

The heat of shame flooded her cheeks. While she had grown fond enough of the camp, and especially of its residents, she couldn't bear even the thought of facing Peter again. She couldn't stand the thought of meeting Colley's almost uncanny, perceptive stare. And she couldn't imagine facing Robby, the child she'd let down with her careless—and if one was to believe Peter—rebellious refusal to listen to what he called reason.

But this wasn't the time for recriminations. There'd be plenty of opportunity for those later on. This was the time to get Robby to the doctor, the time to care for the child she'd come to love. Time to do what she should have been doing in the first place.

As she ran to the barn, arms overflowing, she realized Wade had wasted no time either. By the time she arrived, Peter's horse had already been hitched to the serviceable buttercream-painted wagon. As the rancher picked up his seemingly broken child, she caught sight of tears on the strong man's cheeks.

Inside her chest, her heart felt squeezed, and she would have given much to run to his side and comfort him, encourage him. But she didn't have that right. She was nothing to him, nothing but the woman who'd failed his son.

She had to do her best to help him...them.

At the wagon, she rose on tiptoe and dropped the cloak and bedding onto the wagon floorboards. Before Wade could offer help, she scrambled up inside, sat on the hard wooden bottom, and held out her arms for the boy. "Here," she told Peter. "I'll hold him still while you get us down to Bountiful."

Every inch of Peter Lowery broadcast his reluctance to relinquish hold of his son, but there wasn't much else he could do. He couldn't guide the horse while he held his child.

Misery deep within her, she tried again. "Please..."

She saw the anguish on Peter's face as he placed Robby on

her lap, in the tender way he eased a dark curl off the boy's brow, in the way he winced when that touch came close to the open wound.

Emma pulled her wits together. "It can't be good for that to stay like that. We need something for the bleeding—"

"Here!" Colley yelled, running toward them. "Wade said the boy was bleedin' somethin' fierce. You hafta put this clean flour sack bandage on the gash then press down on it. And you press hard, missy. You hafta keep it from bleeding any more'n it has to."

She recoiled. "But pressing hard will hurt him. Look how deep that is."

Colley punched her fists onto her sturdy hips and glared up at Emma. "If you don't do what I tellya, poor kid's gonna bleed out. That'll really hurt 'im, don'tcha think? Ain't gonna be doing much recovering without blood, is he?" She paused. "Ah . . . but you're scared, ain't ya?"

Emma nodded, the tears pouring down her cheeks again.

Colley clamped her lips tight and shook her head. "Don't you be scared, Miss Emma. You hafta be strong for 'im, for 'em both. Peter here wants to be with his boy, but he has to handle the horse. And him with that broken leg and all. You hafta do the right thing. Push hard on that bandage. It's nice and clean, and the boy needs ya to help 'im until ya get to Doc Chalmers's. Ya hear?"

Something about the insistence in the older woman's rough voice pierced right through Emma's fear. She found herself drawing strength from Colley's urgency. And she remembered . . . she remembered the night Colley had revealed all those details of her life. The memories made Emma feel once again weak and silly and useless in comparison to the remarkable woman, and she knew she never wanted to feel that way again. She wanted to feel strong and capable and an asset to—to anyone.

For that to happen, Emma had to draw on her own strength and courage, especially at that moment. Not for her sake, but rather for Robby's sake. And Peter's. She swallowed hard and did as she was told.

Ned ran up to the wagon. "Miss Emma! Miss Emma! Y'almost fergot yer doggie. I brung her for ya. Here she is."

He dropped Pippa inside the wagon, and the little white pup trotted up to Robby's side, stared at his face for a moment or two, licked his dirt-streaked cheek, and then curled up at the boy's feet. The two of them had become great friends in the short time Emma and Pippa had spent at the camp. If— no! *When* Robby came to, he'd be glad to have Pippa at his side.

But then, when Emma and her pet were on their way home to Portland again, why, the boy would surely miss the animal's companionship. Still, she couldn't let herself think that way. She had to think only of helping Robby recover from his wound.

The trip down the mountain meant almost constant bouncing and jouncing over the rough, rutted trails. The hard bottom of the wagon offered her no comfort, especially since she held Robby across her lap. While she had brought the quilt and two pillows with them, she'd used the much-folded blanket to provide the softest bed possible for the injured child. The pillows cushioned him on either side.

As frightened as she was, she did what Colley had told her

to do. She kept a firm pressure on the flour sack bandage, and while she fought back the mental image of the wound, her thoughts kept returning to the frightening sight. Her curiosity bit at her, so much that by the time they'd traveled for an hour or so, she could no longer resist. She lifted a corner to check on the gash.

Scant seconds after she eased up on the pressure, the blood beaded up on the raw edges of the flesh. Immediately, the deep cut bled again. Colley had been right. Emma had to keep that pressure constant, all the way to town.

Up front, sitting high on the simple bench, Ned and Peter rode in absolute silence, neither man breaking the agonizing hush. Emma didn't remember the trip from Bountiful to where she'd taken Pippa for her constitutional having taken this long. She must have dozed off for longer than she remembered.

Even though the silence grew more awkward by the minute, she preferred the discomfiture to any conversation with Peter. She couldn't make herself meet his gaze. The memory of their kiss lived too vivid in her thoughts, and made the embarrassment too great for words. Perhaps it was best for her to return to Bountiful.

"Oh, goodness!" she said under her breath. *Perhaps?*

No, no. Of course it was best to return to town, to return to her normal life. Indeed. Papa needed to know she was fine. She couldn't stay away even a moment longer than necessary.

But if that was the case, then why did she feel sudden emptiness at just the thought of leaving? After all, she'd wanted desperately to leave no sooner than she'd arrived.

Emma didn't belong at the camp. She didn't. That wasn't

the life for her. Her life was back in Denver, in Portland, at Papa's side, or...oh!

Mr. Hamilton. Joshua Hamilton.

Her...fiancé.

First she went hot. Then she went cold.

She...she'd actually forgotten the poor man! How could she have? And after he'd given her the dog she loved so dearly, just so she wouldn't forget him. What kind of woman did that make her? That she had scarcely thought of the man she intended to wed in those first days after the holdup, and then...nothing. She hadn't spared him a single, solitary second after that.

Was she such a fickle-hearted fool? First, she'd accepted a man's proposal. Then, she'd wound up on this mountain where she'd thought only of herself and the hardships she'd encountered.

She hadn't thought of Joshua's worry and grief.

Oh, goodness gracious. Hardships?

Hah! Hardly.

All she'd encountered was a way of life different from the one she'd known before. Hardship was what Colley had experienced, what Peter had gone through to carve out a life in a new land, to build a ranch, to create a heritage for his son, even after he'd lost the woman he loved.

And here she'd thought it a hardship to be rescued by a decent, God-fearing man, who'd taken her to his home, where his equally decent ranch manager had shown her how much a woman could do. She'd also learned how easy it was to love a child, one you hadn't birthed yourself. In the meantime, she'd learned a number of skills she'd come to appreciate.

She was no longer the Emma who'd left Aunt Sophia's house in Denver all of...how many weeks ago had it been?

Emma shook her head at her own silliness. It didn't matter. She'd lost track of time while she became a brand-new woman; she'd stopped counting days. At the current moment, however, what really mattered was the child on her lap...and the man who'd made her look at herself and see her own flaws, her lack.

A pang of sadness struck her heart, and she bit her bottom lip. How could she not have known how frivolous she'd been? How foolish of her.

She had a lot of hours left until they reached Bountiful, a lot of hours to think about the girl she had been, the woman she'd become, and the one she would continue to grow into.

And that long ride gave her a whole lot of time to pray. She'd never keep growing if she turned away from the God she was coming to know.

"Oh Lord...don't leave me now..."

"What have we here?" the white-haired woman said as she opened the door. When she saw Robby in Peter's arms, she gasped. "Oh, no! Doc! Come down here right now. Hurry, you hear?"

Emma twisted her fingers, her anxiety growing worse by the minute. The lady's reaction was alarming. What if...?

No! She couldn't let herself contemplate such a thing.

"What in tarnation, woman?" a rotund gentleman with only a ruff of graying brown hair around the lower hemisphere of his head appeared on the stairs. "I told you I needed some sleep earlier, what with that McGarvey baby taking so everlasting long to birth last night, and today—"

"I'm sorry to come here at such a late hour, Doc," Peter said. "My boy's had an accident. We need you."

The doctor's eyes opened wide. "Never you mind a word I just babbled there, son. And the hour makes no never mind. Come on into my office straight away."

Emma knew she didn't have the right to follow, but no power on earth would have kept her from Robby right then.

"Put him over there." The doctor indicated the leather-covered examination table. "From what I can see, he'll be needing stitches. And some more than that, too, I reckon, but let's see to stopping the bleeding first."

Peter lowered the boy onto the brown leather. Worry carved lines on his brow.

"It's quite deep," Emma murmured, fearful for the boy. "And it has bled a great deal." She stepped closer to the physician. "Is there anything I can do to help?"

The doctor looked her over. "Thank you, kindly, miss. I do appreciate your offer." He crossed the room to the washstand and scrubbed his hands. As he dried them, he cast a glance over his shoulder. "My wife usually helps, seeing as she's trained in nursing the ill. But, go on now, and tell me this. Who do I have the pleasure of talking to? As pretty as you are, I'd remember if I'd seen you before. I don't reckon I've had the pleasure of making your acquaintance."

"I'm Miss Emma Crowell," she said. "From London, Denver, and Portland."

The doctor's salt-and-pepper eyebrows rose as he crossed to the examination table and lifted the flour sack bandage from

Robby's forehead. "You don't say? And you're in these parts because...?"

Emma took a deep breath and squared her shoulders. "Well, sir, a number of weeks ago I was on my way home to Portland after a visit to my auntie and uncle in Denver, when I was the victim of a holdup. A band of outlaws stopped our carriage—"

"Well, I'll be a ten-toed rooster..." The doctor dropped Robby's bandage back in place after a close scrutiny of the swollen, split flesh. "Everyone here in town's heard all about you by now, I reckon. The reverend and his wife were beside themselves, distraught about your fate out there in the wilds and at the mercy of thievin' outlaws. That poor driver, we couldn't stop him from punishing himself over your loss. I mean, we all of us here in town thought you were a goner, what with outlaws not being known for taking kindly to meager pickings when they strike."

As he talked, he picked up the gas lantern on his desk and brought it close to Robby. He lifted each of the child's eyelids. When done with his examination, he set the light back in place, and then walked to a glass-fronted white-metal cabinet in the corner. He reached inside, evidently for supplies.

He kept up his end of the conversation. "So...Miss Emma—Crowley, you say?"

"Crowell, sir. Emma Crowell."

"Miss Emma Crowell it is, then." He crossed the room, his steps crisp against the highly polished wood floor. "Tell me all about your adventure, missy, while I sew up this boy."

Peter cleared his throat and shifted from foot to foot. "Is

that all you're going to do for him? Sew him up and talk to Emma?"

The doctor stopped, his last step echoing in the heavy silence. "There's not a whole lot a body can do for him until he comes to but to keep him right comfortable, clean up his wound, and suture it up, son. And pray." He pinned Peter with a serious stare. "Pray a whole lot. Your boy needs the Great Healer to show up soon and heal him right quick."

When he returned to the examination table, he held a small brown bottle in one hand and a couple of other items in the other, one of which was a shiny silver needle. Emma's stomach lurched. The thought of that cold, sharp metal piercing Robby's skin was too much for her.

Before she could brood too long over what was about to happen, the physician spoke to her again. "Tell me about that there holdup, missy. And how it is you came to wind up here at my house with Peter tonight. I say none of it makes much sense to me."

As Emma recounted her experiences, she grew aware of a presence at her back. A glance over her shoulder revealed Ned, pale, lines of exhaustion on his lean and youthful face, concern in his muddy brown eyes. She gestured him closer.

The doctor noticed. "Now who might this be?"

Ned grimaced, spun his hat a full circle before his stomach with his big hands. "I'm one of them fools what held up Miss Emma's carriage," he said, shame in his droopy shoulders and morose face. "I've asked forgiveness, sir." He shrugged, resignation dawning on his features. "I ain't no fool. I reckon I'll be havin' me some time with the law, pretty soon now."

Doc Chalmers turned to Peter. "Well, son, seems to me you've had your bonnet right full for a spell now, haven't you?"

"Bonnet?" Peter tipped his mouth up into a twisted half-smile. "I reckon I would agree, Doc."

"Seein' as there ain't much you can do here, Pete, hovering over your son, and all, why'n't you head on over to the boarding house and fetch Adam Blair? He can handle your male guest here better'n I can."

Peter looked at his son, immobile on the examination table. "But Robby—"

"There ain't one blasted thing you can do for your boy right now," Doc Chalmers said, his voice kind, his expression full of compassion. "Best thing for both of you is for you to keep yourself busy until he wakes. And like I toldja already, pray."

"But—"

"Go, Pete," Doc urged. "Go fetch Adam Blair."

With reluctance in his every move, Peter headed out of the doctor's office. The sound of the slamming front door echoed through the silent house. At her side, Ned sucked in a breath. Emma shivered, then turned her attention back to the still figure on the table.

"Could I stay here with Robby?" she asked the doctor. "It doesn't feel right to think of him all alone. He is a little boy."

He studied her a moment, then nodded. "You come with me, Ned. Let's fetch the lady a decent chair here. Looks to me like she's likely to sleep by the boy, and there ain't a body what will talk her out of it. Might as well get her comfortable, and all."

Ned opened his jacket, revealing Pippa hidden inside. "Here, Miss Emma. I kept her safe fer ya, but I reckon you'll want her to keep you company. You and Robby, I mean. He does put a great deal of stock on that little dog of ya's, doesn't he?"

Tears filled Emma's eyes, and she wasn't sure if they were of gratitude for the young outlaw's kindness, or of sadness at Robby's plight, or...or...she didn't know. And she didn't dare look too closely at the cause, since she feared it might have more to do with the man who'd just walked out than she wanted it to.

"Thank you," she whispered. "You're a good man, Ned. Remember that."

"Aw, Miss Emma. You don't know nothing 'bout me—"

"I know enough. It's you who doesn't—yet. I'll be praying for you."

That made him uncomfortable, but he didn't argue against prayer. Emma was glad. She would indeed pray for him, and she would insist someone step up to help him before...before she left. A sob broke in her throat at the thought of her imminent departure.

She turned and walked to Robby's side, her steps halting. How she had come to love this child so much in such a short time, she'd never know, she only knew that she did. And she wanted the best for him. The best would have to start with restored health. She would do anything to help him. She wanted the doctor to know that. And Peter, too.

She cuddled her dog close, seeking comfort, but finding less than she would have thought. Ever since the night Sawyer attacked her, she'd thought of Peter every time she'd needed strength, reassurance, and yes, comfort, as well. A dog didn't have the same effect, no matter how dear.

It frightened her. She couldn't come to lean on him, to reach for his solid, dependable presence, even if only from a distance, even if with nothing more than a look. He was beyond her reach.

Besides, even though she'd somehow, inexplicably, failed to keep their engagement at the forefront of her thoughts, Emma was promised to another man. She sighed. Yes, yes, yes. A man she'd only too easily forgotten since the moment the rancher had found her in the woods.

She had to examine that phenomenon.

But she didn't want to.

The men returned to the office carrying an upholstered chair between them. "Here we are, Miss Emma," Ned said. "Nice and soft, too. I checked."

The doctor chuckled. "I'll have you know, he did just that. Wanted to make sure it was good enough for you, young lady. Even after I assured him it would do quite well."

As the men left, she settled in, the dog in her arms, a prayer on her lips. In the shadowy dimness of the room, since the doctor considered the lowered lighting better for Robby, the minutes seemed to fly by. Before she thought it possible, the front door opened again. Hushed male voices sounded in the entrance hallway. She heard Peter introduce Ned.

Emma stood and went to join the men.

"...I found her in a cave with the two of them," Peter was saying as she approached. "Couldn't leave her and that excuse for a dog of hers where they were, now could I?"

"No," Emma said, head held high. "You weren't about to leave me there"

The marshal nodded to her acknowledgment, then turned

back to Peter. "You say you caught two of them. Where's the other man?"

"He's dead," Peter said evenly.

The marshal raised a brow.

"Did you tell the marshal what Sawyer tried to do to me? That he..." Emma faltered, afraid she couldn't go on. But she knew she had to. The law had arrived. It was the right time.

"Someone killed Sawyer out there in the woods," Peter said before she could speak. "And we don't know who."

Chapter 19

In short measure, after filling in the marshal with the briefest of details about the night in question, Peter found himself facing off against Adam Blair, not something a sensible man ever wanted to do.

"I will not have you drag both Colley and Wade away from the camp," he said, digging in his heels. "I've fought with everything I have to get back to where I was before the weather and those blasted grasshoppers nearly ruined me. It looks as though I might turn a profit this fall and pay off the loan to the bank, but only if my flock is in top shape. It's bad enough for me to be here instead of at the camp, but Robby's life comes first. My ranch hand and manager won't be coming down to town until the fall."

Adam crossed his arms. "I ain't one to stand between a man and his livelihood, Peter, but you just told me I have to deal with a murder now. You can't expect me to just sit back and let things go for your convenience, you know. I'll send my new deputy, John Griffith, on up to your land. I figger he can watch your sheep a coupla days for ya."

Peter scoffed. "We can barely manage the three of us, and now you're telling me one lonely lawman's going to take care of things up at the camp by himself. How long's he been raising sheep?"

"Well, now, of course, he hasn't been raising sheep. But all he'd have to do is make sure they don't go wander off that there meadow of yours, right? I mean, they eat pasture grass, and there's that pond for water—"

"There's more to it than watching them graze. And can he shear? All by himself?" Peter asked. "It's been slow going with all that's gone on, and we still have a couple of head that need shearing."

"No, can't say he can do that, either."

"Then it's final. Colley and Wade are staying put." He shook his head. "I couldn't see my way clear to spare one of us for bringing Emma to town when I first found her. And the only reason we're here now"—he glanced at the door to the darkened examination room, then cleared his throat—"the only reason I came to town is Robby. I'd do anything for him."

He paused as his emotions threatened to break him again, but he called up his determination and stiffened his backbone. "I see no need for you to rush to lock up whoever's killed Sawyer if it means risking my ranch's future for it. Sawyer's dead. Nothing's going to change that, and it's been a couple of weeks since he died. It can all wait a while longer. You can try the guilty party in the fall."

"That isn't one bit the way the law works—"

"How about this?" Peter offered in a more conciliatory

tone. "How about you ride up to the camp and do your questioning there? You could do a decent investigation that way."

Adam let out a bark of a laugh. "Let me get this straight. You can't spare your hands, but Bountiful's supposed to spare the sheriff."

He shrugged.

The lawman shook his head. "That's not the way it's going to be. I can't leave. It's my job to protect the town. The law doesn't wait on you and your needs out to the ranch. This is a murder I have to investigate here."

"If that's your final word, then that's the way it is. If you won't go up to talk with them, then you can wait until September, seeing as how it's all waited this long. I can't—won't—leave my son, and they won't be abandoning his future, my life's work, so as you can ask your questions, either—"

"Gentlemen!" Emma cried out. "I'm certain we can resolve this matter somehow." She turned to Doc Chalmers, who'd been watching the exchange with an amused expression on his weathered face. "I suspect you know everyone around these parts, right?"

"Of course."

"Well, then. You'd be the one to know who might need a job, even if it would only be for a handful of days. Do any strong, reliable men come to mind?"

The doctor rubbed a hand over his bald head. "There's always folks who could do with some decent work. Only thing is, are they the ones who'll be willing to do the work."

Peter coughed. "Now, wait a minute, there—"

"Don't you go twisting your trousers there, son," Doc said. "Didn't say I don't know any fellows who could do you right. I know me a few. Give me a couple hours to see if they're available still."

He didn't like this plan one bit, but he wasn't about to leave his son's side. Neither was he willing to leave his sheep uncared-for. "Let me know what you learn, then."

"Sure thing, son," the doctor replied, as he headed back toward Robby. "I reckon Stephen Moore's two boys are grown enough now and might be wanting to make some extra money. I'll see if Livvy Whitman knows what they're up to these days..."

"Seein' as how Doc fixed that right up," the sheriff said, "I reckon I better catch me some sleep. I'll be having me some questions for all three of you soon enough. And as for you"—he turned toward Ned—"you'd best be coming along with me. You and I have us a holdup to talk about."

Still uneasy, Peter realized there was nothing more he could do. He surrendered to the inevitable, and spoke a brief farewell to the lawman and Ned.

They left, and as soon as the door closed behind them, Emma turned to follow the doctor.

"Thank you," he said.

She stopped, a puzzled look on her face. "For what?"

"For coming up with a solution there."

She gave a dismissive wave. "That was nothing, but, of course, you're welcome. I could see both of you were too intent on your own perspective to find a way out of the situation. I just made a simple suggestion."

"But it worked. So, I take my hat off to you." He mimicked the motion although hatless.

She gave a quick bob of her head and smiled. "You're quite welcome, Peter. I'm thankful I could be of help."

With that she turned back toward Robby, and the flurry of emotions that had stormed him out on the yard by the cabin returned. Who would have thought that first night that Miss Emma Crowell had it in her?

Not he.

It was no wonder she continued to surprise him on a regular basis. He was learning every day how much more there was to Emma than he'd first thought.

"Well," Adam Blair said a few days later as he sat in the Chalmers's tidy parlor, palms spread out on his knees. "I need me many more answers than I'm getting here. Don't figger any one of us is going anywhere until I get 'em, either."

Peter frowned. They had been talking for well over an hour, maybe two. "I need to see my son."

Adam shrugged. "Boy's in the other room. That's the reason I decided to do this here at Doc's place. So's you could look after your boy. Go ahead. Take some minutes to do what you must. We can all have us a drink of water, I reckon. I'm parched from talking so much."

"Interrogatin's what I'd call it," Colley muttered under her breath.

Peter shot his manager a warning look.

She lifted a shoulder, but appeared unrepentant.

Mrs. Chalmers, as tall and thin as her husband was plump and short of stature, walked in with a tray of glasses and a pitcher of water in her hands. Emma, Colley, Wade, Peter, and Ned all hurried to help themselves. Adam waited until all were served before taking the last glass.

Once the thirst was slaked all around, and Peter was satisfied that Robby's condition hadn't worsened, even if it hadn't improved, Adam went back to business. From the way he shot question after question at Ned, Wade, Colley, and himself, Peter gathered the marshal was trying to narrow the field of those he considered suspects. Clearly, the man didn't think Emma had done the dreadful deed.

Neither did Peter.

Then again, he didn't see either of his employees harming another soul, and he knew he hadn't killed anyone.

Before Peter knew what had happened, Adam aimed his questions almost exclusively at Emma. At one point, she fell silent. The room's thick hush became awkward, uncomfortable. Adam did nothing to change the atmosphere, and Peter felt like shifting in his chair. He refrained.

Instead, he kept his gaze fixed on her face. Her expression made clear she was thinking back over the events of that awful night.

"It's occurred to me," she said after a bit, her voice quiet and thoughtful, "there are others we haven't considered as possible culprits."

"Really, now?" Adam leaned forward. "Do go on and tell me what you mean, Miss Crowell."

She met his gaze with a direct look, no hint of avoidance or trickery in her expression, just concentration and intensity. "Well, sir," she said. "Ned and Sawyer weren't alone when they held up the carriage. From what I understand, they'd been rustling alongside two accomplices, who were with them at the hold-up. I never saw those men, since I was in the woods attending to my dog. By the time I came back to where the carriage had been before, they had evidently run off with the spoils of their crime. I only heard Ned and Sawyer talk about their partners."

Hope rose in Peter.

"Accomplices, you say?" Adam asked.

Ned bounded up from his chair before Emma could answer. "Oh, yessir! Wouldn't surprise me none if they come back and kilt Sawyer. They told us they'd be back, and they weren't too friendly-like with Sawyer. Why, even a bothered rattler's friendlier'n the two of 'em."

"Who are the two?" Adam asked Emma.

"Why, I don't know, sir. I never did meet them. You'll have to ask Ned."

Adam turned to the young outlaw. "Who are these men, Ned?"

"Tobias and Dwight, Mr. Marshal."

The lawman narrowed his eyes. "Do you mean Hal Tobias and Dwight Smith?"

Ned shrugged. "I reckon that's their names, sir. Always heered 'em called Tobias and Dwight. One of 'em's tall and black-haired. Right big hulking fella, he is. An' th'other one's stumpy, an' limps right bad on one leg. One of his eyes turns right to the corner, too. Looks right odd."

"Sounds just like the two fellas I have me down to the jail right now," Adam said. "Neither one of 'em coulda done it. They been locked up since two days after the holdup. They tried to rob the Bank of Bountiful. Didn't get nowhere right quick, I tell you."

The lawman returned his attention to Emma, asking her the same questions over and over again. Each time he shot one at her, his voice grew sharper, more convicting. The urge to protect her hit Peter hard.

"She swooned, Adam," he said, struggling to keep his voice as calm and even as possible. "She was laid out cold on the ground. She couldn't have seen what happened to that swine."

"Swine, huh?" the marshal said, his steady stare now on Peter.

He opened and closed his fists, trying to keep his wits about him. "What else do you want me to call a man who'd do what he tried to do to her?"

Adam leaned back in his chair, arms crossed over his broad chest, eyes narrowed and fixed on Peter. "Tell me again everything you can remember about that day. And I do mean everything, Peter."

With all the patience he could muster, Peter started at the beginning and went straight through to the end. When he was done, Adam came at him with more of his pointed, irksome, and repetitive questions.

"What started the argument between you and Miss Crowell?" Adam asked.

Peter called on all his patience. "Birth of a lamb."

Adam slapped his small notebook against his thigh. "What did you do when she ran off?"

Apprehension tightened Peter's middle. "Ran off right after her, once I was sure Colley had everything under control at the barn."

"How long did it take you to find her?"

He looked at the graceful walnut clock on the fireplace mantel to his right. "Felt like years, but I didn't think to stop and check a pocket watch."

Adam tapped his notebook with a pencil. "What did you do when you did find her?"

"Grabbed Sawyer by the collar and pulled him off her."

"All right, then. What exactly did you see when you first walked up?"

The image burst into his memory, kicking up the quality of his anger. "That animal was attacking her, Adam. He was sprawled out all over her body, wriggling himself against her, being indecent, trying to...well, you understand."

The lawman scribbled. "What did you hear?"

He remembered her fear. "She was scared and crying, and he was...was breathing hard, and grunting."

"What did you say to Sawyer?"

Peter frowned. "Don't know that I can remember whether I said anything."

Adam looked up from his notes. "What did he say to you?"

He shook his head. "Don't know if he said anything, either."

"Who was with you?"

Peter gestured toward the two other men in the room. "Wade and Ned were somewhere near in the woods looking for her, too."

"What did Miss Crowell do when you found her?"

He couldn't bear to look at her right then. "She wept. What did you want her to do, Adam? She was scared. She'd been attacked."

"When did she swoon? When did she come to? How did she look?"

Peter's patience began to fade away. "Aw, Adam. I've told

you all this over and over again. It's not getting us any farther ahead than when we started."

Adam looked up, met his gaze. "I have me my reasons. Just answer, Peter. It's best if you do."

He let out a frustrated burst of breath. "I'm not sure. It all becomes a blur after I grabbed Sawyer."

"How long were you out of commission?"

"Not long, but I reckon it must have been for a handful of minutes. Maybe ten at most."

Adam rocked his chair onto its back legs. "How do you know how long you were out?"

The last bit of patience Peter had left now hung on by a thread—a fraying thread. "I can't know for certain, but it was just a mite lighter gray when I came 'round as it was when I went out."

"Where was Wade?"

"In the woods."

"Where was Colley?"

"At the cabin with Robby."

On and on and on the questions came at him.

All of a sudden, Colley stomped a booted foot. "All right! That there's enough, young man." She glared at Adam and bolted to her feet. "I did it, you hear? I kilt that skunk, and I ain't one bit sorry I did it. Would do it all over again, if I had me another chance at him."

Adam crashed his chair down onto all its four legs. Every hint of his usual casual attitude vanished. His eyes narrowed, his lips tightened, his body stiffened, and his hand went straight to his holstered gun. "Do you know what you're saying, ma'am?"

"Don't you ma'am me none!" She strode right up to him and met his gaze full on. "I knew something was wrong that night. Peter left me to watch Robby, who was sleepin' like a bear in wintertime. The feeling in me got so bad, I couldn't just sit and wait for 'em to turn up with Miss Emma."

"And how did that turn into you killing him?"

Colley shrugged, then crossed her arms, her expression defiant. "I came up on 'em, and the boss were all out on the ground. So was Miss Emma, but the skunk was standing over her, hands on his belt, fixin' to—to...well, you know."

Emma let out a mewling cry.

Peter shuddered.

Adam glared. "And you just up and took it upon yourself to kill the man? You didn't think to just wrassle him off the girl? You look right strong enough to me to do it, ma'am. Did you have to go and kill the fella?"

Colley seemed to lose all her strength. She took a pair of stumbling steps back to her chair, where she collapsed. All color drained from her face.

Peter grew alarmed. But before he could react, she spoke again.

"I'm fine," she told him, her voice firm if quiet. "I couldn't just let him get away with it, just so's he could go and do it again to another girl." She drew a deep breath, and sat straighter in the chair. "I reckon I best be getting all this out. Ain't no good to keep on keeping it to myself."

In a dull, emotionless voice she told a tale that chilled him to the bone. Years earlier, she and her husband had worked side by side to build a ranch on the raw ground they'd chosen to settle. Bountiful was little more than a building or two, and other farmers were few and far between. Once a quarter, the family would travel to Pendleton to shop for the ranch's necessities.

It was during one of those trips, while her husband attended to the business of packing their purchases on their wagon, and their girls were at the milliner's, choosing fashionable new hats, that she found herself walking down the street with only her son at her side. As they turned a corner, a strange man came up and started a conversation with her. Eventually, it turned inappropriate, and he made it clear her looks and feminine manner appealed to him. Too much so.

Colley did everything she could to discourage the stranger, but he wouldn't be put off. She'd hissed to Charles to go for help, but in the end, her attacker dragged her into a darkened doorway and forced himself on her.

By the time the youth returned, the scene that greeted him was one no woman should ever experience, an attack no child should see committed on his mother. Still, he fought the beast with all his strength, giving Colley the opportunity to gather her wits about her. The two of them did battle with the foul creature, determined to seek justice. When the law showed up, the attacker lay on the sidewalk, his head split in a bloody mess from where it had struck the wall on his way down. A smear of blood on the sharp brick corner told the tale of the injury as well as mother or son could. Better even, perhaps.

Months later, unable to deal with his failure to protect his mother, Charles had left home. His father had fared no better. Consumed by the guilt of having left his wife and son alone while he worried about the ranch more than about them, he let his political conviction take over, and he joined the war effort. He lost his life on a battlefield, leaving Colley to fend for herself for the rest of her life.

"Oh, yes, Marshal Blair," she said, her voice now as strong as ever. "I killed that Sawyer fella, all right. Wish only *I* coulda kilt the man what did me wrong all them years ago. He stumbled and fell trying to run away from Charles and me. Hit his head as he went down." Satisfaction bloomed on her worn features. "But it was *my* bootlace what I wrapped around Sawyer's neck. Pulled right hard, and it got tight on his neck. Dragged 'im off Miss Emma, too. Weren't gonna let her go through what I went through. It ain't what-all a woman can get past just like that. And I would do it again, if I found 'nother like 'im going after her—or any other lady."

The horror of Colley's experience turned Peter's stomach. His pride in his ranch manager grew only greater. "Well, folks, it would seem our mystery's solved. We can all go back to work now, and Emma—Miss Crowell can get on with her trip back to her father. She's worried he's suffered enough, thinking her dead."

The day she left, Peter would suffer, too. But for different reasons.

He had no right to ask her to stay. And she'd given him no suggestion she'd even want him to. She had spoken time and time again about her father, the pain her disappearance had to have caused, and the joy father and daughter would experience when they reunited.

Sure, he'd struggle once she left. He refused to think much about it. He would use his internal strength to make sure his every thought stayed fixed on his son's well-being, something that mattered greatly to him. And he'd think about his ranch.

But he'd never forget what Colley had just said. Her husband had suffered unspeakable regrets because of his extreme attention to his ranch, not only on the day she was attacked, but also the day he gave his life on a battlefield, leaving his family to fend for themselves. Emma had been right on that matter.

"Not hardly likely," Adam said, rising. "I don't rightly know just what I'm gonna do 'bout Missus Colley here, seeing as she's just told us she's a killer, and all. Maybe twice over, even. I'd be one sorry excuse for a marshal, don'tcha think? 'Sides, who's to say she didn't up and kill the first fellow, then turned around and said he'd done her wrong and stumbled himself to death? See how that sounds?"

Although he waited, no one dared to speak. Emma looked furious, and Peter felt outraged. He couldn't come up with the words to tell Adam how stupid his argument sounded. Before he got himself under control enough to talk, Adam went on.

"Can't just go 'round saying 'good job there, Missus Colley' and letting her walk all over the law. That ain't right, folks."

Colley marched right up to him, stared him in the eye, standing toe-to-toe and nose-to-nose, and wagged her index finger at him.

"Now, you listen to me good, young man. I ain't no killer like you're wantin' to say. Sure, I did kill that Sawyer, and I'm getting myself happier 'n happier about the whole awful thing every minute here with you. What did you want me to do? Give 'im a whack or two, and then let 'im fight me, kill me, even, so's he could have his filthy way with Miss Emma? That would just leave 'im to go off and do it again and again. He wasn't giving up, I tell ya."

When Adam didn't answer but kept his expression blank and his gaze on Colley, she shook her head. "Oh, no. Not at all, son. Not when I could have me a say-so in the whole ugly matter. And the future, too. I had to do something, stop him, keep him from ruining anyone else's life."

"Thank you, Colley," Emma said. She stood, walked over to the older woman's side. "I'm nowhere near as strong as you are. I wouldn't have survived it had Sawyer...if I'd had to suffer what you did. You didn't take a life that night, you saved mine. Thank you."

The two women embraced, tears pouring down their faces. Peter had never seen strong, capable Colley show so much emotion, much less weep. His throat tightened and his eyes burned. An impressive pair of ladies, indeed.

And one of them was about to ride out of his life.

And Robby's.

Could he stand by and let it happen?

What should I do, Father? What would you have me do?

Chapter 20

"Do tell. Just what kind of idiotic fool is that sorry excuse for a marshal?" Emma asked, furious. She paced back and forth across the now-empty parlor at the Chalmers' home. "Who would insist on jailing Colley? Especially after being told quite clearly why she did what she did?"

Peter didn't answer, but sat in the sturdy maple chair, arms crossed, a bemused expression on his lean, tanned face.

"And you! Are you simply going to sit there, sir, let the fellow lock up a woman as wonderful as Colley is? For nothing more than saving my life?"

He unfolded himself and stood in front of her, his gaze steady and clear. "I'm going to trust the Father's got the whole situation under control—"

"Under control! Your son is lying on a doctor's table, still unconscious, and your wonderful ranch manager is behind bars for doing something good. What do you see under control there?"

"I didn't say the circumstances were under control. I said God has the situation under control—His control. Those two things are completely different."

Emma felt her anger drain away. "I suppose it's another of those Bible things I need to study more carefully. I just...I can't stand to see Robby like that, and the thought of Colley locked up is more than I can bear."

Peter came to her side. "Believe me, Emma, I know exactly how you feel. I feel the same way. But it won't help Robby or Colley for me to get all in a state, will it? It won't help them if you do, either."

"But I'm supposed to head home soon. I can't leave with things all unsettled."

He took another step closer, a smile tipping his mouth up a bit. "Then don't leave until things are resolved. No one's chasing you away."

She pursed her lips and gave him a narrow-eyed look. "That's not what you said up on the mountain. You said you were bringing me to town to send me home to Papa."

Something in her words caused Peter to react, and it showed in the widening of his eyes, in the additional step that brought him only inches away, in the slight but measurable widening of his smile. For some reason, it made Emma's thoughts fly back to the kiss they'd shared. Her cheeks heated, and before she knew what she was doing, her palms were pressed tight against her cheeks.

Peter donned a questioning look. "I thought you were in such an all-fired hurry to get yourself back to all your parties and your 'regular' life. It was right near all you could ever talk about."

Emma's cheeks felt ready to burst into flames. "When I first came to your camp, yes, that would be true. But that was then. None of that matters anywhere near as much as Robby and Colley do."

The questioning look turned into a frown. "But what about your father?"

Oh, dear. There was Papa....

"Well, now," she said, searching her heart for a way to express the feelings she didn't fully understand. "Papa's a different matter, of course. I do need to let him know I'm not dead, somehow."

Peter rubbed his unshaven, sandpapery chin with a long, work-roughened finger and thumb, his expression full of confusion. "You'd have to go to Milton or Pendleton to find a telegraph machine. Bountiful's still too small, even though a telegraph line is due here soon."

"How long would it take to get to either town?"

He shrugged. "They're both about the same distance away, in slightly different directions. I'd say about...oh, eight hours by horseback—with almost no stops, that is—and maybe twenty to thirty hours by wagon, depends on what stops you do make."

Disappointment knotted her middle. "Oh. I see."

Peter took a deep breath and squared his shoulders. He seemed to come to some kind of decision. The change caught Emma's attention.

"There is something else you could consider," he started. "You seem to have grown quite fond of your life out here, wouldn't you say?"

"Oh, yes." She smiled, thinking back on her experiences at

the camp. "There's so much to learn. A woman would never grow bored out here."

He grinned. "Does that mean you were bored in your other life?"

She'd never thought so before. "I daresay, sometimes."

"I know you're fond of Robby and Colley, and you enjoyed the challenges you faced while with us. You could decide... well, what I mean is that you don't have to leave...at all."

"But—"

"Please hear me out." He ran a hand through his hair again, this time smoothing the rumpled waves. "This is awkward, and I'm not very good at speaking of these kinds of things. But...well, I would hope you've grown to tolerate me enough that after you let your father know how you are you might consider a life with us here—"

"You're asking me to become your housekeeper?"

"Well, yes, but—I mean, no...um...maybe." He shoved his hands in his pockets, looking as awkward as Ned ever had—and almost as young, even though he was more than a few years older. "Let me say this. I...I've grown...um...fond of you, and Robby does need a mother, and the ranch and cabin do need a woman's touch, and I reckon I need some civilizing, myself, and you seem to fit the bill better than anyone else I've met."

Emma's eyes widened in surprise. "Do you mean...are you asking me—"

"I'm asking you to consider marrying me, Emma. I'm sorry this isn't the most romantic, lords-and-ladies, King Arthur and his Roundtable type of proposal, but..." He shrugged.

The knot her nerves had become tightened further. An odd battle began in her midsection, a tussle between a foreign excitement and a queasy anxiety. "Oh, dear." She twisted and wrung out her fingers. "I'm afraid I—I'm in no position to even consider your offer, Peter."

"What do you mean?"

How to tell him something she couldn't understand herself? She drew in a deep breath. "I...ah...am not at liberty to consider any gentleman's proposal. At least, not at this moment."

"Why on earth not?"

"Be—because I'm...betrothed."

"Betrothed?" he echoed as though he didn't know the word.

"Yes. Engaged. To be married."

His eyes widened in a snap. "Engaged!" Anger tightened his jaw. "And it didn't cross your mind to let me in on the secret?"

"It never was a secret." She tipped up her nose in indignation. "The matter just never came up in our conversation, now did it, Mr. Lowery?"

"Not even when we were on the ground kissing?"

Oh, dear. Now she felt a scalding blush from the very tips of her toes to the roots of her hair. Blast her redhead's complexion!

She too, took cover in anger. "I'm not some flighty girl who flits from man to man to—"

Emma stopped, chagrined. All the women she'd known had indeed thought of her that way. And in truth, she had been more than a touch flighty. But that felt so very foreign to her now, as though she were looking back at someone she once knew. Not as a memory of her actions.

She had changed. She'd become a different woman.

"I'd only accepted the gentleman's proposal that morning before I left Denver, and more because my father, my aunt, and my uncle wanted me to so badly. I didn't object to Joshua, but I can't say I was ever madly in love with him. So, as you see, it wasn't the kind of promise many other women would have made to their future husband. It had been more of an expected transaction."

"I'm mighty glad I don't live in your kind of world. A body's word is something precious, Emma. One doesn't go giving it unless one does mean it."

She looked down at the tips of her pathetic boots. "I never gave my word before, and I believed I meant it. I'm sure you can understand how foreign it all was to me when I left Denver right afterward. It was such a very new thing for me, and you must admit, since the carriage reached the foot of these mountains, I've suffered a series of dreadful upheavals. They overtook my memory in the most absolute way. I must be forgiven, if not excused, for not remembering my new and very recent change of estate in the midst of it all." She gave him a reproving glare. "At any rate, you, sir, are hardly a gentleman—"

"We agreed on that a while back," he ground out through clamped teeth, a formidable frown on his face, arms crossed tight across his broad chest, feet planted wide on the floor. "Very early on, if I recollect. I suppose, then, you'll be the sort of woman who takes her promises lightly if something should come to upset your day shortly after you've made those promises."

She gasped. "I most certainly am not. I just explained to you what happened. Were you not listening?" She ticked off fingers as she continued. "A holdup, being held captive by outlaws, being stowed away in a cave, a new captivity in a rustic cabin—which I'm expected to keep with the help of a book or two—sheep, sheep, and more sheep, a surly rancher, a debauched attacker—dear me! The list could go on. Those details might have shoved a new circumstance out of my mind—as I already said."

He sighed. "Look, Emma, I am no fussy frou-frou lord-this-or-that, and I reckon I can't compete with some fancy-pants man with money and a house in town, so I won't. I'm a rancher, and I look at what needs to be done for the ranch. It's what pays for our food and the roof over our heads."

She blinked and shook her head. Nothing changed, how-ever. He still stood before her, looking much like the solid mountain where he'd built his camp and as enigmatic as the dark forest that surrounded it. But . . . he was arguing food and roofs. After proposing. While his son lay in poor shape at a doctor's clinic.

Could Robby's dire condition explain his lack of coherence?

But then, as she turned it all over in her mind, it began to make a strange kind of sense. "And you believe I'm what needs to be done for the . . . ranch?"

"Yes! You're just a part of the whole." Then he frowned, as if he realized how unappealing his response had been. "Not exactly. Not the ranch, that is. I think you're what we need. We need you here more'n the city man who asked your hand in marriage does." He gave her a narrow-eyed scrutiny that made her squirm. "From the looks of it, you gave the poor soul your word, but not your heart."

She didn't respond; she didn't know how without making a bigger mess of things than she already had.

Peter continued. "You know Robby needs a mother, and you love him—it shows every time you look at him—and he loves you. Colley needs a friend, and I need say no more there. Me? Well, I need a—a partner for my future, a companion for all those lonely days to come, and you'd certainly provide more than enough challenge to keep a man on his toes, and fill his days with...with—oh, I don't know! But you'd be the one to do it, all right." He shook his head and rolled his eyes. "Besides, you said I needed civilizing...or some such nonsense."

"Nonsense? Your last few minutes, sir, reveal better than anything I might utter how truly desperate your need of civilizing is."

"I meant no offense, Emma. I just meant to offer what I reckon is best for everyone. Well, except for your papa, sure, but you can visit him anytime you wish, and as soon as you want. I'll make sure you get word to him that you're quite all right straight away. I'm sure Adam will help."

"Pfft! The marshal? The one that's jailed Colley? I'm not sure that man can see a hole in the road, even if it were big enough to swallow his horse."

"Adam's a decent fellow, and a solid lawman." He drew himself up to his full height and then looked down to meet her gaze, a determined expression on his face. "But that's for you to learn when you get to know him better. What I need to know is if you'll consider my proposal."

Her turn to sigh. She was sorely tempted, but she couldn't. Not in good conscience. "I told you, Peter, I'm already promised to another. He's part of the reason I really can't just send Papa a telegraph message. Papa would be here at a moment's notice, just by saying the word. But, Joshua…I must go to Portland as soon—" She glanced toward the examination room. "As soon as Robby regains consciousness."

Peter gave a sharp nod. "Very well. We will never speak of this sorry matter again. You can, of course, stay at Robby's side that long, and then I'll make certain you reach Pendleton safely. From there, I'll send you to Portland, your father, and your real life."

The biting tone of his words spoke of more behind his proposal than his words would have her believe. Or perhaps that was her hope, in spite of everything. Just as the kiss back at the camp had revealed more than just…just—oh, who knew what. But she knew what she had to do.

Peter turned without another word and limped into the room where his son lay. He was the kind of man who would, indeed, keep his word. And he'd just spoken. Something inside Emma felt as though it had died. No, as though he'd killed it off.

Her real life.

What did that mean? She didn't know anymore.

But she supposed she must be on the verge of finding out.

No matter what else happened, only two things mattered: Robby's health and Papa's broken heart. She would see to them in that order. Joshua she would worry about after the first two. There was nothing more she could do for Colley. Not at the moment.

And Peter…well, she would have to think and pray about him. And his proposal.

Dear Lord…she began when a shaky voice called out.

"Papa…?"

Joy sparked to life in Emma's heart; tears sprang to well in her eyes. Through the small space of the partially open door she watched Peter bend down over the boy, a tremor in his shoulders. Robby had awoken. By God's grace, he should recover now, as the doctor had hoped. But the moment soon turned bittersweet. Her time in the Lowery men's world had come to an end.

As the carriage wheels beneath her rolled over the road that was to bring her home, Emma could hardly bear the anticipation, much less all the other sensations that roiled inside her. She would see Papa again at last. She had sent a telegram as soon as she was able, and he had rushed home from a business trip to New York. Her heart pounded and emotions filled her throat. In spite of the blessings she'd found on Peter's mountain, many times she'd thought she'd never see her home again. Or her father.

The carriage driver who had brought her from the Portland train station opened the carriage door. As Pippa bounded out with a short, excited bark, Emma stared at the large white house through a veil of tears. Its tall, elegant façade was graced with a generous porch that swept from side to side, and the numerous windows had shiny black shutters to frame and highlight them. The door, embellished with a substantial brass knocker, opened inward as she watched.

Her breath caught in her throat, and she sprang down from the vehicle. In her rush, she caught the heel of one new boot on the steps the driver had set out for her. She nearly crashed down onto the dusty road. "Oh, no!"

"Emma!" Papa cried out, his voice rough with emotion. "It really is you..."

A moment later, strong arms wrapped around her, sheltering her as they always had.

"Papa...Papa...Papa..."

The flood of feelings made it impossible to utter another word, but she didn't have to speak at all. Her father seemed as overcome with his own emotions and simply held her close, rocking her gently from side to side. "Princess..."

The pet name he'd used for her since her earliest memories brought up another swell of tears, and Emma gave herself over to the moment. She relished the joy of seeing her father again, regretted the new lines she saw etched on his dear face, fresh since she'd last seen him. Her disappearance had surely carved them there.

She reached up and cupped his cheek. "I'm sorry. I'm so, so sorry you had to go through all this—"

"Hush, dear heart." He shook his head. His voice came out as ragged and ravaged as it had after Mama's death. Emma's heart squeezed tighter with guilt and anguish. "You were right. I was too stubborn to listen to reason. I should have gone with you and Joshua—"

She stopped herself. No, that wasn't quite right. While she should have considered Papa's concerns more carefully, she couldn't bring herself to regret her experience. If she'd gone with Papa and Joshua she never would have found herself on Peter's mountain. More important, she never would have met Robby, and would have missed learning what it meant to love a child with all her heart. Still, as meaningful as that experience was, it didn't compare with what had filled her thoughts and dreams all the way from Bountiful to Portland.

If she'd gone with her father she never would have met Peter.

She never would have fallen in love.

There! She'd admitted it.

Even if only to herself.

Papa held her at arm's length and studied her. "Are you truly well? And will you listen to me in the future? Have you learned anything from this awful, dreadful disaster?"

Emma clasped the hands on her shoulders. "Well, Papa. I daresay you won't believe me when I tell you it was no real disaster, even though it was as difficult and painful as you imagine. I learned more than either you or I in our wildest imaginations ever could have envisioned." She drew a deep breath, more certain of who she was and what mattered most to her than at any other time in her life. "I'm not the same Emma you kissed good-bye in Denver—not one bit. But it's not something to tell on the front stoop of the house. Let's go inside, shall we? Then I'll tell you everything."

As she slipped her arm through his, he slanted her a skeptical sideways look. "Everything, right? You won't skip anything or color tidbits with a rosier wash?"

Her thoughts flew to the moments in Peter's arms. To the kiss...

Surely that didn't count. That was only for her and the man she loved.

The man who'd sent her away.

A different sharp emotion stabbed her heart, and she fought the instinctive wince. Aside from that one precious and private moment, she could answer her father with complete honesty.

"Everything, Papa," she said, her voice serious and strong. "I'll tell you everything that happened to me."

They stepped together toward the wide-open front door. He slipped his arm around her waist, held her close to his side. Emma laid her head on his shoulder.

"My dear, dear child. I thought I'd never see you again this side of heaven…"

"Oh, Papa…"

"You've done what?" Papa asked ten days later in response to her declaration. He bounded up from where he'd sat in his favorite leather armchair, a gossamer cloud of his trademark cherry-scented pipe smoke all around him. "Here I thought I'd recovered you, all of you, but now it appears you've left your mind behind."

Not just her mind, it would appear. "I've decided, Papa," she repeated firmly. Emma shook her head. Then she softened her tone. "It's lovely to be here with you again, and with Ophelia and Jedediah. But… now you know I'm not the same person who danced with Joshua in Denver, bought mountains of frocks in New York and London and Paris, and thought of nothing else. I'm not the same person who accepted a proposal because Joshua was the nicest man I'd met and wouldn't be dreadful to see day after day, year after year. Now I know that was the saddest thing I could have done. It was wrong, Papa, and I must see him to make things right. I can't marry him."

Her father frowned.

She went on before he could come up with further arguments. "I—I just can't marry Joshua because I never loved him. I liked him, and there was never anyone else I truly cared for. I just didn't know a thing about life."

Papa puffed on his pipe, then jabbed the mouthpiece in her direction. "And a handful of weeks up on a mountain with outlaws, sheep, and a peculiar, manly woman has taught you all about life?"

Outrage filled Emma. "I'll have you know, Colley is not peculiar! Not one bit. Why, if it weren't for her, I might not be here." She drew herself up to her full height, and fought down the fear that now lived so close to the surface. After all, Peter had sent her packing.

But she intended to fight him on that. As she had on other matters before. "I now know I don't belong in a ball gown for the rest of my life, doing nothing more than learning the newest waltz. There are many other more interesting things to learn about and do in the world. And I've grown quite partial to...to...um—well, to sheep ranching, and Hope County is the loveliest of places—a bit rough, but that roughness is its beauty. And then, I've come to love Robby." She smiled. "He needs me, Papa. I must go back."

Standing, her father paced before the empty hearth. The weather was quite warm and the evening pleasant with no need of a fire. "I suspect there's more to this than Robby and sheep ranching, Emma. What do either of those have to do with Joshua?"

"I can't marry a man I don't love."

"But you can marry a rancher you've just met."

"Of course—er...no! That's not it at all."

"Too late, my girl." His frown returned, deeper this time. "An infatuation is a dangerous thing."

"I don't believe I'm infatuated, Papa. But I'll never know for certain unless I return, will I?"

She watched him struggle with the value of her words. Still, his love and concern seemed to win out. "No self-respecting father would let his daughter go back to a wild mountain man who runs sheep in the middle of nowhere," he said in a stern voice. "That would be negligent and irresponsible of me. I love you too much to do that to you."

"It would, perhaps, be all those things if you were to let me go back just like that." She snapped her fingers. "But I have reason to return. You see, Papa, I'm also learning to listen to God. That's where He's led me. He had a reason for me to wind up there. There were many things I had to see before I could learn. I was a silly girl before I found myself in those woods, at that camp—I didn't lose myself out there, I found myself. Do you understand the difference?"

"And all that because you met a crude man unlike any you'd met before."

"No, it's because I saw life being born. I came to love a child who needed me. I made a true friend who would have given her life for mine—and who is sitting in a filthy jail because of what she did to save me. It's because I learned to spin wool into yarn. I learned to bake biscuits and beans, to cook bacon and tinned chicken and make a loaf of regular bread. Oh, Papa, I learned to be a woman who was worth something, a woman you could be proud of."

"I've always been proud of you, dear."

"I know. But this is different. *I'm* different."

He fell silent as he evaluated her words. "We'll see."

She tipped up her chin. "Indeed we will."

The next morning, she had Jedediah deliver a message to Joshua, inviting him to tea. The event was not the most pleasant one of her life, but she did what she had to do. In the end, she repeated over and over how, while she had been sincere in Denver, she truly hadn't known herself then. She tried to explain how much she'd learned during her time on the mountain, and how wrong she would be for Joshua now. But she didn't think she succeeded. Only time would prove her right in his eyes.

After she dealt with that unfortunate matter, she set about gathering her belongings. Then she had to face Ophelia. To her surprise, it was much easier than she'd thought.

"Child," the older woman said, "I knew something was different 'bout you, right from the very minute you walked in that kitchen door. Then you went and showed me how good and fluffy you'd larnt to make biscuits. M-hm...Emma Crowell making biscuits. Next thing a body knows, a man'll be setting himself on that moon up in that sky, I tell you. Stranger thing ain't happened yet. You're different now, all right."

They packed all of Emma's sturdier garments, and they shopped for adequate shoes and boots. Stockings and petticoats and warm cloaks and coats, cotton dimity nighties and flannel ones, too, all went into the vast steamer trunk that had come ahead of her from Denver. Now, it would return to Bountiful, but with different contents, indeed.

As a side parcel, Emma purchased every children's story book she could find on short notice, and she also gathered an assortment of history texts, a Latin grammar, a French one, and books on art, European architecture, mathematics, and a collection on scientific subjects she found at the last bookseller she visited. *Le Morte D'Arthur* was marvelous, of course, but Robby needed much more than that to become a well-educated man. She also bought him a sturdy leather-bound Bible of his own. The time had come for the boy to begin his own devotions rather than be subjected to his father's impertinent lectures. Or hers.

She bought a lovely bolt of navy-blue floral chintz for Colley, since she would not let herself believe the marshal would remain obstinate about the woman's freedom. In the case of the worst scenario, she would make sure Papa investigated what kind of legal assistance they could provide. Emma was not going to let Colley suffer because of her any longer than she was forced to. She would see to it right away. And then maybe the older woman would let herself soften back to the woman she always should have been, before life and a brute had stolen that part of who she was.

"Well, Papa," she finally said on the night she'd been home for three weeks. "I'm packed and all set to return. Remember. You promised to do something so I can help Colley. She does not deserve the dreadful treatment that horrid Marshal Blair has subjected her to."

"I have made inquiries, dear. Just as I told you I would."

She flew at him, hugging him around the neck. "Thank you, thank you!"

"Easy there, my girl. We'll do everything possible, but you must understand it won't necessarily be up to us."

"I do understand, Papa. But I also understand now how great our God truly is. And He is in control of this—"

Emma drew up short when she realized she'd been about to quote Peter. How much she missed him! She couldn't wait to see him in a few days, to accept his proposal, to become his wife and partner for the rest of their lives.

That was her plan. She prayed it lined up with his.

She stood up straight. "What I meant to say is that I'm not a child any longer. I understand the situation quite well." She stepped back, and tried to remember what she'd been talking about before concern for Colley had distracted her. "Oh, yes. I was about to tell you how Peter insisted I'd always be able to visit you whenever I wanted, and I will do just that, quite regularly, too. I could never do without seeing you for very long, Papa. And you must come see us, too."

"Oh, I think I'll satisfy myself with your visits here. I'm truly not the sheep-ranch sort, you know."

Although his words disappointed her, she knew he was right. He'd always be a businessman, more at home in his office or in a bank, completing his latest transaction, than he'd ever be in the outdoors. Once upon a time, she'd thought the same of herself. Maybe Papa could be persuaded...

That night, she fell asleep with a smile on her lips and sweet dreams in her head.

Chapter 21

All through the journey on the train that rolled down the tracks to Milton, and then on the carriage she took from there to Bountiful, Emma's stomach tightened into ever more tangled knots. Her head filled with what-ifs, and she experienced anxiety unlike anything she'd known before.

What if Robby hadn't recovered as well as she'd hoped? What if that horrid Marshal Blair had done something dreadful with poor Colley? What if Peter's flock had suffered because of the lawman's obstinacy? What if Peter had changed his mind about her?

Would he still be in Bountiful when she arrived?

By the time the driver slowed his team and Emma noticed the outlying buildings from her window, she'd gnawed her fingernails down to the quick, not something she normally did. Then again, she'd never traveled to persuade a man to marry her after she'd first turned him down.

And she'd never had a friend behind bars.

The carriage drew to a stop. The door opened and the tall man in a worn leather vest and faded dungarees stuck his head inside. "Sure and you want me to leave ya here, miss?"

No! her innards cried. "Yes, sir. I know where I am, and I know where I'm going. Thank you very much for your safe driving and for your consideration."

He shook his head, but then withdrew the wooden steps he kept under one of the two benches and set it up on the solid-packed dirt of Main Street. Emma's stomach lurched with the anxiety, and she trembled. Hoping the driver didn't notice the tremors in the hand he clasped to help her down, she placed one foot then the other on the steps, and found herself back where she belonged—well, almost there. She did have some matters to resolve before she could return to the camp.

With renewed resolve firmly in place, Pippa in her basket on her arm, and her steamer trunk precariously plunked on the rough boardwalk next to the jailhouse door, Emma strode in, her bravado leading the way. "Marshal Blair," she said when she saw the lawman seated at his desk. "Are you still holding Colley behind bars?"

"Well, now," the marshal said, looking up from his papers. "I reckoned we'd seen us the last of ya, Miss Crowell. Surprised to see ya, I must say."

"How could you think I'd walk away from the woman who risked her life and her freedom for my sake?"

He stood, crossed his arms, and the faintest hint of a smile threatened the corners of his mouth. "You did strike me as the sort who'd shake off the dirt of our small town the minute you found yerself back among yer kind."

Emma's temper began a slow boil, but she made herself

tamp it down. It was far more important to see to her friend's well-being than to make a point with this dreadful brute. "Well, I'm not that sort, and I'd like to see your prisoner, please."

His shoulders shook some with what Emma suspected was amusement, but she again kept her focus on the truly important. In the end, he gave a sharp nod. "Reckon it can't hurt to let ya go on in and spend a while with her. Might do her some good and perk her up a mite. I hear the judge won't make his circuit here until fall at the soonest. That didn't sit right well with her."

"Of course it didn't!" Emma shook her head in disgust. "What kind of monsters are in charge of our laws and courts? Holding a brave woman like Colley like some wild, dangerous animal in a cage. You should be ashamed, sir."

Again, the marshal seemed amused, but this time, he took a huge ring with a large collection of keys attached, and then gestured toward a door behind his desk. "Best leave that dog here. I'll watch her. This way, please, Miss Crowell."

They walked down the dreariest, most drab corridor Emma had ever seen, or hoped to see again. On either side, cages lined the way, the steel bars formidable indeed. The two men she saw contained within made her both shudder and pray for their condition. Finally, at the end of the grim hall, the lawman stopped and aimed a key into the lock in the cage's door.

"Here ya go, Colley," he said. "You've a visitor I reckon you'll welcome. Can't give you long to visit, but it should do ya good."

Emma flew into the cell, dismay and grief flooding her heart at the sight before her. Strong, confident Colley had been reduced to a shadow of herself in only weeks. She'd clearly lost weight, lines on her face had deepened considerably, and the pewter-colored hair Emma had so admired now sported new streaks of white. On the other hand, the blue eyes shone with their usual vibrancy, and Colley's embrace was as warm and welcoming as Emma remembered.

"You poor thing!" she cried. "So many things about all this are wrong. You should not be here, you know."

Colley led Emma to a narrow cot outfitted with a thin blanket and dingy sheet. Although neat and smoothly spread, the bed looked as dreary as everything else Emma had seen since she walked into the jail.

"Don't know I can rightly say I don't belong here, Emma," Colley said. "I did kill Sawyer, and the Good Lord is the one what has that right."

"B-but he would have...have"—she gestured to fill in her lack of words—"gone ahead and done his dreadful deed. And then, who knows who else he would have harmed? You're a hero. When we didn't have a policeman or—or a marshal anywhere in sight, you did what had to be done. I doubt the high and mighty Marshal Blair would have done any differently in your position."

"But that's his job, and it ain't mine. That's the difference."

"You shouldn't be here, anyway. And I'm going to see you're set free to go back home to the camp immediately."

Colley's blue eyes twinkled for the first time since Emma had walked into the jail cell. "And how're ya thinkin' to do that, missy?"

Emma went on to tell her friend of her plans and her father's efforts on Colley's behalf. She told of the lawyer she suspected would arrive soon to advocate for immediate release. "Understand, Colley, Papa will send the finest lawyer in the West to help you. You will be free again, and soon. We're determined to see this happen. And I will make certain it does. Believe me. I'll make sure you don't spend a moment longer here than necessary."

Although Colley's expression revealed her skepticism, she thanked Emma for every effort she was making for her sake. Then she started in with questions of her own, about Emma's trips, about Portland, about the father she was sure had been overjoyed to be reunited with the daughter he'd been sure he'd lost.

Emma answered it all. Well, almost. She did dodge the older woman's questions about the reasons for her return, and in the process she learned Robby had made a quick and good recovery after he woke.

"He cain't go playing all wild-like all over the mountain for a while yet," Colley said, "but he's fine, and Doc's said many a time he'll be finer'n frog's teeth from this. Won't ever be any more'n a memory—bad memory—for us all. Don't think I've ever seen Peter so happy as when they came to see me 'fore they left for the camp."

Aha! So now she knew where they were. She wouldn't have to resume her vigil at Doc's house, waiting for Robby to be ready to go back home.

Home…funny how that rough camp had become so appealing and welcoming to her, how it beckoned her more than Papa's fine house, how it felt like home to her. She said her good-byes to Colley, who banged a navy-blue-and-white-speckled chamber pot against a bar on the cell's door. The marshal showed up right away.

As Emma walked behind the lawman toward the front of the jail, it occurred to her to ask after Ned. "What have you done with him?"

He barked out a laugh. "Ain't done a thing with the fella. You want to see 'im? He's right here."

To Emma's horror, he stopped before the cell of one of the two prisoners she'd noticed before. The man inside appeared to awaken from a nap when he heard the sound of keys outside his cell. "Wha—what?" His eyes grew wide when he saw her. "Miss Emma! You're here. Why...how can that be?"

"I've come to visit," she said around the lump in her throat.

The marshal opened the cell and Emma stepped inside, again irked by the situation. Ned didn't belong behind bars any more than Colley did. What future did the young man have there? Instead of being locked up, he should be up at the camp, working hard, helping Wade, learning from Colley and Peter how to make something of great worth of his life. She couldn't wait until that lawyer fellow of Papa's arrived in Bountiful. She'd told her father how the man might have more than one client who deserved to be set free.

After a quick farewell, she stepped outside the jail and came to a complete halt on the boardwalk beside her enormous trunk and her smaller travel satchel, as well as her two hatboxes. She had no idea what to do next. She knew nobody in town. Nobody besides the marshal.

And the doctor...

A short while later, she was in the Chalmers' parlor, recounting her experiences to the doctor's wife. After a peaceful night in their extra room, they helped her find someone to take her to the camp, and before long, she was on her way.

Excitement and nerves tangled in her gut. Prayers kept her sane on the way there. Peter...Peter...Peter..., the wagon wheels seemed to say.

It was all in his hands now. She prayed he'd welcome her back.

"Lady Emma, Lady Emma, Lady Emma!" Robby cried when he saw her descend from the wagon in the shadowy dusk. Then the child burst into tears. "Are you really real? And you're back again?"

Heedless of the dirt, Emma dropped down onto one knee and opened her arms wide. The boy threw himself against her, his sobs touching a deep corner of her heart. With tears soaking her face, she scanned the clearing in front of the cabin, looked toward the barn, out to the meadow, but saw no sign of the man she sought.

She patted Robby's back. "Hush, now, honey. I'm real— see? You're hugging me, and I'm hugging you right back."

"But you left!" he cried, his words a painful reproach. "I thought...well, you were gone." He looked up, and Emma saw her worst fears drawn in the agony he revealed. "I thought you'd left me like...like my mama did."

Her heart squeezed painfully tight. "Oh, Robby..." She wished there was more she could say, but she had to content herself with a weak, "I'm here now."

And if I have anything to do with it, I'm never leaving you again.

For long moments, as the burnt-orange sun in the far western horizon crept lower down the sky, she held the child close and satisfied her maternal hunger with the sturdy reality of his presence at her side. Clearly, he'd recovered, as both Colley and the Chalmers had told her. But it was one thing to hear about it. It was quite another to see it, touch it for herself. She ran shaky fingers across his forehead, over the still-red scar where he'd bled so much.

"Miss Emma!" Wade called out, approaching from the meadow. "What brings you here?"

She stood, but kept Robby's hand tightly tucked into her own. "I...well, I had to come back. There is...there were things I needed to do here." She looked down at the still-teary child beside her. "I just couldn't stay away."

"How long will you be staying with us?" the young man asked, his eyes bright with appreciation as he stared at her. "Do you have your things with you?"

She avoided his first question, since she had no idea how to answer. "My trunk and travel bags are in the wagon." She indicated them with a quick wave. "Could you please see to the driver and that my things are brought inside? Pippa's in her basket, as well." She hoped he'd hurry off to find Peter before unloading the wagon.

Her stomach, however, leaped with misgiving at the upcoming encounter. She sent up a silent prayer for God's blessing. The thought of Peter's rejection made her queasy. Would he reject her? Or was there hope yet? Her breath caught in her throat, and she grew lightheaded.

"Fellas!" Wade cried out in the direction of the barn. "I'm needing your help out here." He faced her again. "Won't be but a minute, miss."

Then he looked down at Robby, who'd begun to scuff the

dirt beneath his feet. "And I thought you'd agreed to stay inside and rest this afternoon. Remember? Doc said you can't go tiring yourself too often. Go on inside. Miss Emma will likely want to rest a bit, so you'll have her for company."

Fellas. And she'd be the one to keep the child company inside. Something was off.

"What is...?" She stopped, unsure how to word her question. Aside from needing to see Peter, what exactly did she want to know? "Who...?"

But no one paid her weak attempts any mind. Emma tamped down her curiosity and worry long enough to guide Robby back inside. The condition of the cabin took her aback. A stack of dishes sat on the shelf near the back door. A variety of items covered the top of the table, not the least of which was a saddle and three unidentifiable—to her—tools. The bunks dripped bedding down the side, and Mrs. Lowery's rocker still sat before the hearth.

"What is this, pray tell?" she asked Wade when he walked in.

The ranch hand blushed. "I'm sorry, Miss Emma. I'm not much for housekeeping an' all that. Been busy out with the flock these past few days." He dropped her satchel and hatboxes as though they were embers searing his hands—unlike the evidently cold hearth—and backed toward the door. "The Moore boys'll bring in yer trunk in a minute. Driver said he'd be heading back now. Honored to see ya again."

With a tap to his brow, he grasped the door latch behind him and scurried away. Two young men trooped in then. "Where'd you want us to leave this?" the taller of the two asked.

"Over there." She indicated the corner where the spinning

wheel and Mrs. Lowery's trunk still sat. Where she'd dredged up the gumption to order these two, she'd never know, but something was certainly wrong. It would appear no one was minding the cabin.

"There you are, ma'am," the shorter ranch hand said. "Pleasure to meet you, Miss Emma, but we have to hurry. Wade'll be after us to finish out in the barn before suppertime."

She glanced at the hearth. "Supper?"

The young man shrugged. "Bread, leftover mutton roast, and a can or two from the shed." And then he left.

Before she could catch her breath, Robby tugged at her hand. "See? We need you here, Lady Emma. Please don't ever, never leave us again. Promise?"

At his words, she released his hand and stumbled to the table. She drew out a chair, and shoved an implement out of her way. She plunked an elbow on the space she'd opened and pressed her forehead against her palm. This was not the welcome she'd expected.

But she couldn't sit there, feeling sorry for herself. She'd come back to take her rightful place in this camp, and she evidently had done so not one minute too soon.

"I came back, Robby, because I want to be here. I didn't want to leave, but I had to let my papa know I was fine after getting lost in the woods. As soon as I did that, I returned." *Dear Lord, give me the words to do this right.* "I do want to stay and never leave without you again. But I don't know if I can promise that. It's not up to me this time. It's up to your father, and I don't know what he wants."

The boy gave a tiny giggle, then covered his mouth, his eyes twinkling with mischief.

Emma's nerves stretched to the breaking point. While Robby might think her plight humorous, she surely did not. What did Peter want? Did he still want her? And what would she do if he didn't?

There was at least one question the child surely could answer for her. "Where is your father, Robby? I expected to see him the moment I arrived. Surely this...this mess in the cabin tells me he's gone."

Another giggle, followed by a rapid series of nods. "He's gone."

Now she knew she'd truly fallen through that fictional Alice's rabbit hole without a doubt. Peter had insisted he'd never leave the camp before the fall. He'd left when his son's life hung in the balance, but now? No. He'd never willingly leave again.

Fear slammed into her. "Is he well? Did he hurt himself? Has he caught an illness of some sort?"

Robby danced from foot to foot, his eyes bright with hidden knowledge. Emma wanted nothing more than to reach out and hold him still until he gave her the answers she wanted. But she couldn't make herself stop his enjoyment. Even if it came at her expense.

"Nope," he said, then giggled some more.

She searched her mind for any plausible possibility, landing on the only one left. "Did he go to town to help Colley?"

The boy's chortles of laughter rang in the room. "Nuh-uh-uh!" He spun and swirled his arm through the air, and then, in the grandest gesture a child of his size could manage, he dropped into a deep, deep bow. When he stood again, the grin lit up his face with the purest of joy. "King Peter," he declared, "has gone to fetch us his queen!"

Emma's knees went weak. Her throat tightened. "Queen? What queen?"

He let out a resounding cheer. "You! Papa went to find you!"

While a part of Emma wanted to believe what Robby said, another, more sensible part feared his imagination had gotten the best of him.

After she'd donned a simple cotton blouse and calico skirt, she went to work on the mess in the home. She scrubbed the dishes and pans, and she put Robby to separate the random objects on the table into distinct piles while Pippa sat at his feet. On the one pile, he placed everything that belonged outside, and on the other the tools that never should have landed on the table in the first place. She opened tins of vegetables to go with the mutton and bread, put a pot of coffee to brew, and set the table for the three men, Robby, and herself.

Everywhere she turned, every time she looked at the child who refused to leave her side, all that filled her mind were thoughts of Peter. He surely would return soon, since she wasn't anywhere he might think to search for her. The thought of his arrival at the camp set off a flurry of flutters and feelings of nervousness utterly unfamiliar to her. She wanted him there, at the camp, with her and the others, but she didn't know what would happen once he saw her running the home on her own.

She knew what Robby had said, but what if the child had persuaded himself that was where Peter had gone because he'd wanted her back so badly? Worse yet, what if Peter had gone after her to bring her to the cabin as a housekeeper and a mother to his son? What if he didn't love her as she loved him?

No. That couldn't be. There had been that kiss...

She was sure Peter loved her. He might not know it yet, but she was here now. She might just need to help him see how much he loved her.

But what if...?

And so the days went, three of them, full of joy and full of nerves. The evening of the fourth day, when the beans she'd prepared were about perfect for serving, Emma measured out the ingredients for the evening's biscuits and dug her fingers in to work the dough. When it reached just the right soft, puffy consistency, she shaped the rounds and put them to bake. As she went to clean her hands, the sound of hoofbeats entered the clearing outside. Pippa, who these days divided her time between following Wade wherever he went and shadowing Robby, set off a volley of yelps and yaps. Emma's heart picked up its beat.

She rinsed and dabbed off the dampness on a towel, then hurried to where she'd stowed the few belongings she'd unpacked. Since Peter had only seen her at her worst for the longest time, she wanted to change that first impression she'd made. She looked at herself in her hand-held mirror then ran her hands over her hair, smoothing away the stray strands that refused to stay off her forehead.

Giving up on making them obey, she crossed to the door, but before she got there, it opened wide and her father strode in. Shock froze her for a second, but then she shook her head. "Father! Papa? What are you doing here?"

He harrumphed, his cheeks turning ruddy and a smile curving his lips. "Why, is there something wrong with a father visiting his daughter these days?"

She blinked furiously, only to realize this wasn't a dream. "No, no! Of course not. But why are you here? I thought you said you'd never come, that you were a businessman at heart, not a mountain man at all."

He shrugged and opened his arms. "A man can change his mind, can't he? Come give me a hug, Princess."

She ran to him, took a deep breath of his familiar scent of bay rum and cherry pipe tobacco, and then looked up again.

"I'm so glad to see you. I didn't expect to so soon." She stepped back and gestured him inside. "Please come in, you must be tired and—Colley!"

"Thought ya'd never see me outta that there jail of Adam Blair's again, didn't ya?"

Emma flew into the older woman's arms. "I'm so happy to see you free again. Are you well? Did he hurt you? If he did, I'll make sure Papa's lawyer—"

"You don't have to do a thing, dear child," her father said. "I'm here to see this through."

Emma clasped her head between her hands. "I must be dreaming. I just left you behind in Portland. Colley in jail..."

Papa strode around the cabin, stared in all directions with his usual curiosity. After a moment or two, he gave a slow, satisfied nod. "Interesting place, this. And I gather the boy built it himself, too. Quite a feat, I must admit."

Emma batted at her father's shoulder. "Never mind the cabin, Papa. What are you doing here? I would expect you back at the hotel in Bountiful."

Papa's eyes twinkled when he looked at her. "Don't you think you can trust me? I needed to come see a few things, learn more about all this."

She could only stare.

Her father went on. "Shouldn't a man get to know the fellow who's asked for his daughter's hand in marriage? I can't very well do that when he's here and I'm in Portland. Besides, you were right. This dear lady"—he gestured toward Colley—"was in great need of help. I brought Hubert so he could see to it the marshal understood the pertinent law in no time. She's been released into your Mr. Lowery's supervision—in a probationary kind of arrangement. Hubert's now seeing to Ned's release."

Colley huffed. "That Adam Blair says if I don't behave he'll be haulin' me back to that jail faster'n your biscuits're gonna burn there, missy. See to 'em quick. I reckon all these fellers are gonna be right hungry here."

"Oh, no!" Emma ran to save the bread, her heart beating like a big kettledrum. She was thrilled to see her father, and it was a joy to know he and Hubert Merritt had managed to set Adam Blair straight about Colley's situation, but...where was Peter? The man Papa said she was about to marry...shouldn't he be the one in a hurry to see her again?

"I did bring you a surprise from Portland," Papa added. "And I know how you love surprises. But you'll have to fetch it in here. I'm much too old for this kind of travel these days, my dear. And I had no idea it would be such an arduous trip..."

Emma called on every bit of her decorum, fought down the urge to run as Robby might do. Instead, she made herself walk calmly outside. The sun had begun to set in the western horizon. The sky glowed a rich russet scattered with stray ribbons of plum and purple. It nearly took her breath away. Yet another glorious painting by the Master's hand.

She couldn't believe she'd once hated this mountain. She didn't think she would want to leave it again anytime soon.

"I'm back," Peter said close behind her.

She spun around and found herself only inches away. His eyes searched her face, and she felt his glance as though his fingers had touched her skin. She drew in a deep breath, savoring the piney, clean scent of him. She'd missed him. She couldn't believe how much.

"You have nothing to say?" he asked, his mouth quirking up in a grin. "You're never silent, Emma, you know that? This is a first." His eyes twinkled with mischief. "Are you ill?"

"Oh, you." She made a face and shook her head. "Of course, I'm fine. I can't believe you chased off after me."

"I can't believe you turned right around and came back."

"I told you I was a different person."

He ran the tip of his finger down her nose. "A floured one, I would say."

She shrugged. "Someone had to make the dinner biscuits."

He grinned wider. "I believe Wade's been here the whole time. He could do it."

She sniffed. "Did you think I would sit around all day and let him wait on me?"

"I didn't know what to think."

"And now?"

"Now, I think I'd like an answer to my earlier question."

Her heart pounded so hard she could scarcely draw a breath. "And what question would that be?"

"Well, I have a few, now I think on it." He crossed an arm over his chest and tapped his nose with the index finger of his other hand. "Hm...don't you reckon Robby might be in need of a new mama these days?"

"That could be."

"And what about those lessons we talked about? He might need help with those again, right?"

"Perhaps."

"There is that cabin over there, and the woman's touch I mentioned it might need. Do you think you're up to the task of taking it on?"

She gave him a superior stare. "With my right hand tied to my back."

His lips twitched as he clearly fought a laugh. "Well, then. I reckon we've come to the most important question of them all."

"Which is?" She held her breath.

He slowly dropped down on bended knee, his expression more intent than the light tone in which he spoke. "Are you ready to start in on civilizing me?"

Her breath burst out in a peal of nervous laughter. He chuckled with her, took her hand in his, and then grew serious. "I've grown to care a great deal for you, Emma. I think... I reckon I could say I'm most of the way to loving you forever already. I'm ready to wed you when you say the word. Would you be willing to give me the time so you can be sure of your feelings for me?"

She smiled, covering their joined hands with her still-free one. "I was afraid I'd ruined my chances. And I thought you'd never ask me again if I let any length of time go by. That's why I came back right away."

"I didn't want you to have too much time on your hands in Portland. After all, there is that Joshua fellow to consider."

She shrugged. "He didn't stand a chance." She gave him an impish grin. "What was that question again, Mr. Lowery?"

A damp gleam appeared in his eyes. "Will you marry me, Emma? Be my Mrs. Lowery?"

A tear dampened her cheek. "Yes, Peter. Very, very soon."

Peter told her how he felt about that with a kiss.

Reading Group Guide

1. When Peter and Emma first meet, each one comes with an expectation of the other based on their lives up until that encounter. Do you think either one was unreasonable? Were they reasonable? Have you ever found yourself in a similar situation, and how did you respond?

2. Have you ever met a "Colley," someone who was absolutely anything but the person you believed you saw? What impact did your Colley make on you once their true nature was revealed?

3. What spiritual lessons was Emma learning early in the story?

4. What do you think of the father-son dynamic between Peter and Robby? Have you ever found yourself unable to relate to someone you love? How did you overcome the situation?

5. Has there ever been a time when you've let emotions blind you to reason? Emma's experience had calamitous results. How did your experience affect you?

6. Given the various characters who had reasons to commit the murder, who did you suspect? Why?
7. Was there anything in Emma's character at the opening of the book that might have led you to expect the woman she'd become by the end?
8. What part did Robby play in the spiritual growth of the adults around him?
9. What have you learned about yourself in view of Psalm 31?
10. What did Peter and Emma learn about themselves? About each other?

Turn this page for
an excerpt of Ginny Aiken's

For Such a Time as This

Available now from FaithWords.

Chapter 1

Olivia Moore swiped the back of her hand across her cheek. She slapped away a trickle of tear, the only moisture visible as far as she could see in all directions.

Drought.

Such a simple word, but, oh, how complicated its reality was to her family. And not just to her family. All the other farmers and ranchers scattered across Hope County were suffering as much as Mama and Papa, with no hint in the cloudless sky of any relief to come.

"Oh, I hate this," Leah Rose, Olivia's youngest sister, complained. "I hate it, I hate it, I hate it!"

Olivia hitched the willow basket more securely onto her hip, crammed down another one of their father's shirts with the rest of the laundry, and prayed for patience. "Nobody likes to fight the wind when they're trying to work. But we must get the clothes inside before they get dirtier than before we washed them. You don't want to scrub them again, now, do you?"

Leah rolled her eyes then yelped and rubbed her nose, her eyelids, and her mouth.

Another blast of hot air buffeted Olivia right then, its texture rough and sandpapery with the tiny grains of dry dirt it picked up as it gusted across her family's ravaged land. She wrapped her arm tighter around the tree limb where Papa had tied one end of the wash line. The bark rasped her skin.

Not ready to go back inside the house quite yet, she propped the basket between her hip and the bare trunk then shielded her eyes with her free hand. The wind whipped her calico skirt into a froth against her legs, the flapping another unwelcome irritant.

Leah Rose muttered something, but the rising wind carried away the words. Olivia suspected it was just as well. More grumbling that echoed her own misery didn't appeal just then.

She didn't want to gather still-damp laundry any more than Leah Rose did. Still, Olivia couldn't be too hard on the girl. She, too, wished things were as they'd always been, that the old rhythm of their pleasant lives still determined their daily schedules. In previous years, that late in the summer, nearly September, had meant days filled with the mad busyness of preparing for winter. Olivia had always worked with her mother as Elizabeth Moore canned, dried, salted, and helped her husband smoke the results of their efforts, the fruits of their land. The hardworking couple had made certain their family would have enough provisions to see them through the dark, cold months ahead. Olivia admired her parents' diligence.

That year, however, diligence would not be enough.

"Oh, Livvy, I can't stand it another minute!" Leah Rose threw a petticoat at Olivia, but before she could catch it, a gust of wind snatched it and turned it into a tumbleweed, rolling and bouncing just out of her reach.

She sighed and hurried after the voluminous white garment. "Go on in, then. I'll be right behind you. When I'm done with the wash, you understand. Let Mama know for me."

Leah Rose bent against the wind, dramatizing a bit more than necessary, and ran to the house. Once on the porch steps, she glanced back over her shoulder. "I will. And do hurry, Livvy. I want to show you my latest project."

Leah Rose had the ability to turn needle, fabric, and thread into exquisite things of beauty. Olivia, while a competent enough seamstress, couldn't come close to producing the fine needlework at which her youngest sister excelled. "I'll be happy to see what you've accomplished so far as soon as I've finished out here."

She chased after the elusive petticoat, the willow basket on her hip hampering her steps. But if she set it down, the contents would likely capture the swirling dirt. With every step she took, her irritation rose. Just as she came within a finger's length of the renegade piece, the wind caught it, tossed it up and over, and then flung it against a large rock that in previous years Elizabeth and her girls had ringed with cheery blossoms. This August the flower bed around the boulder lay bare, the soil as dry and dusty as everything else.

Olivia rushed the garment, but the next blast of wind snatched it away again, whirling it across the rear of the house. Finally, when she was about to give up on ever capturing the infuriating piece of clothing, it slammed up against the privy wall and sagged in a pile onto the dirt at the base. Olivia grabbed the petticoat, shook it out, grimaced at the dirt stains it had gathered, and finally stuffed it in her basket, resigned to another session with hot water, lye soap, and the washboard.

Her temper didn't tamp down as easily as the fabric did. Frustrated by her family's situation, and aggravated by the rebel slip, she squared her shoulders and marched back over to the clothesline, her every step propelled by her resolve.

With renewed vigor, she yanked a pillowcase off its mooring, reached for a pair of socks, and then an old towel. In moments, she had stripped the rest of the wash from where she'd hung it not so long ago. When she reached the post at the end of the line, she leaned on it and paused to catch her breath, a difficult endeavor as the gritty air continued to batter her face. Through narrowed eyes she looked out over the Moore property—Papa's pride and joy.

Olivia's heart constricted, and she fought again for breath. As awful as the scorching, dusty wind was, she knew it wasn't wholly to blame for her misery. Her distress stemmed from watching her dear parents work, work, work, and then, by virtue of a twist of nature's fickleness, see all their efforts come to nothing.

In the years since they'd come to Oregon Territory, her father had plowed and planted his fields as soon as spring deemed the land ready. For the last two years, however, the plants had battled to drink what little moisture the land provided, and when the sturdy shoots had broken through to the sunshine, they'd been ravaged by the sudden arrival of swarming airborne beasts that descended on the young crops. The ravenous grasshoppers had left nothing behind.

Despite the weather, Olivia lingered outside. She couldn't bear to see the worry that drew deep lines down either side of Mama's mouth again, nor hear the strain in her mother's voice. She didn't know what she would do in an hour or so when Papa dragged himself inside for whatever Mama put together and passed off as that night's supper. The ruts etched across his forehead and those that fanned out from the corners of his eyes made her heart ache with futility.

Mama and Papa hadn't meant for Olivia to overhear their late-night conversations. But she had. At the age of nineteen, she was no child. By all rights she should have been married already, and maybe even a mother, as well, like her friends Adelaide Tucker and Rosie Thurman. But so far she hadn't been tempted to take that step with any of the very few marriageable men in town, and her parents hadn't pushed, to her great relief. She'd yet to meet the man who appealed to her enough to make her consider the momentous change.

She'd been happy to stay home. She helped Mama with the younger children, and with the never-ending work around the house. She also helped her father and the boys with whatever she wheedled Papa into letting her do out in the barn.

But even those welcome chores had vanished with the last of the grasshoppers. Papa had been forced to sell Olivia's sheep when he no longer could provide properly for them. There was little feed anywhere, and whatever could be found came at a dear cost indeed. Faced with the choice of feeding animals or feeding his children, Stephen Moore hadn't even blinked. He'd sold a fair number of the Moores' prized cattle as well.

The small sum Papa had realized from that sale hadn't stretched far enough. Olivia wasn't supposed to know what her parents had resorted to, but she'd struggled with sleeplessness during the last couple of months as their circumstances had worsened, seemingly by the day. Papa's anxious words during the late-night conversations had confirmed her unsettled feeling.

He'd been forced to mortgage the property.

"Livvy!" Leah Rose called.

"Coming—" Olivia tried to respond, but her dry mouth turned the word into a croaked rasp. She ran her tongue over her parched lips, grimacing when she tasted the dust there. She started toward the house and gave her answer another go. "I'll be right there."

At the top of the porch steps, she cast a final glance down the long brown drive. It was as dry and dreary as it had been the last time she'd looked that way, scant minutes earlier.

"Well, Lord," she said. "I trust you will show me what I'm to do at a time like this. I'm not a child anymore. Surely you have something for me to do. I refuse to be nothing more than another mouth for them to feed here at home. Show me, Father, but please don't take too long. Our situation is dreadful. Winter isn't far off now. And when it comes..."

She couldn't let herself think of that right then. She had to focus on solutions rather than the frightening what-ifs. There had to be a way for her to help her father and mother. Even if she had to leave the home and family she loved.

"Livvy!" Leah Rose cried again, impatience in her voice. "You said you were coming."

As Olivia closed the front door behind her, a sharp pang crossed her chest. She was going to miss her little sisters...her brothers...her parents...their home...Once she discerned the Lord's leading, of course.

Until then, she'd relish every minute she was blessed to spend with them.

"Here I am, silly!" she answered, drenching her words with more enthusiasm than she felt. "Let's see that needlework of yours."

Sunday morning, Reverend Alton delivered a thought-provoking sermon on 2 Corinthians, third chapter, third verse, where he exhorted his congregation to be living scriptures for the lost world, flesh and blood illustrated lessons on God's abundant blessings. After the final hymn, Olivia followed her family outside the church, her Bible hugged close against her chest, her soft drawstring leather purse slung from her right elbow. The fierce winds of the past week had finally calmed, and the fine dirt that had roughened the air had settled down once again.

While the sky remained as relentless in its clear blue brightness and the ground as persistent in its dusty brown dryness, the temperature had dropped enough to make midday almost bearable. Olivia had dressed in her best slate-gray serge skirt, white blouse, and fine blue fitted jacket. She appreciated any chance to dress up, since at home, with work always needing to be done, simple cotton calicos made the most sense.

Before the Moore family left home for the service that morning, Olivia had told her mother and father that Adelaide Tucker, her dearest friend, had invited her for lunch—and, of course, for Addie to show off three-month-old Joshua Charles Tucker, Jr., her pride and joy. Olivia missed Addie since her friend had become a married lady. As much as there was at home to keep Olivia busy, Addie had far more on her plate, what with all her responsibilities as wife and new mother.

"You'll meet us back here by three, right?" Papa asked after Olivia's two brothers had left to find their friends. Mrs. Alton approached Mama and the younger girls, since the pastor and his wife had invited the remaining four members of the Moore clan for the noon meal.

"Oh, yes," Olivia said. "I'm sure Addie will be tired by then. She's told me Baby Josh keeps her up for hours most nights, and she must steal naps whenever he sleeps. She and Joshua have been trying to teach their sweet little one that nights are for sleeping, but that lesson seems to hold no interest for him."

Mama traded glances—and knowing smiles—with the pastor's wife. "It does happen with some little ones. I suppose you might have been too young to remember, Livvy, but your sister was like that, too. Marty took almost a year to figure out what sunset meant."

"Poor Addie!" Olivia shuddered. While no one could accuse her of laziness, she did enjoy crawling under her blankets, and most nights she dozed off right away. "I won't tell her about Marty—"

"Hey!" the Moore family's tomboy yelped. "I learned, didn't I?"

Olivia fought a laugh. "Of course you did, Martha Jean. And, I'm sure, not a moment too soon for Mama and Papa."

Chuckling at Marty's glare, and aware of the time passed as they'd visited with Mrs. Alton, Olivia set off toward Addie and Joshua's neat clapboard house. While the church sat on the eastern edge of Bountiful, Joshua's parents had built their home in the center of the small town, next to their thriving livery stable. Now that the elder Tuckers were in heaven with the Father, Josh ran the business, while Addie ran their household with easy efficiency and good humor.

Olivia enjoyed any opportunity to catch up with her friend as much as Addie did playing hostess.

Her stroll from the church to Addie's place had her crossing the road a few houses down from Reverend and Mrs. Alton's home. A final glance back showed Leah Rose and Marty standing to a side while Papa helped Mama up the front steps and into the generous-sized white house. Her younger brothers were…well, Olivia hadn't heard where the boys planned to spend the afternoon, but she suspected they might be with the Carters, since that family abounded in high-spirited boys.

As she hurried down the wooden sidewalk toward Addie's home, a burst of children's laughter at Olivia's left caught her attention. A chorus of shrill girlish cries followed, as they evidently headed toward her.

The loud guffaws grew more raucous.

The frantic screams grew more frenzied.

The commotion resounded from the alley up ahead. She quickened her pace, curiosity piqued. Before she reached the mouth of the alley, a trio of little girls, around the age of eight or nine, burst into the street, white-faced, their wails near to hysteria, their shoes kicking their Sunday dresses into a froth of skirt and petticoat.

Seconds later four boys, in their Sunday best as well, darted out from the alley and surrounded the girls, fencing them into a huddle in the middle of the street. Fortunately, Sundays saw little traffic once churchgoers left for home.

"We got 'em now, Luke!" a freckle-faced, red-haired imp

yelled as he ran circles around his anxious victims. "Hurry up afore they get away."

The towheaded boy with chocolate eyes joined in with his own taunt. "Fraidy-cats."

All four closed ranks around the girls, their laughter destroying the afternoon's peace. The high-spirited quartet made for a lively, if frightening, cage for the captives.

As Olivia marched toward the children, a new sound joined the cacophony. Grunts and snuffles grew louder, ushered in by a dusty dervish that stampeded past her. A dervish otherwise known as . . .

"A pig!" Olivia backed up flat against the front window of Mrs. Selkirk's charming new millinery store. She was not about to step into the swine's path.

A fifth boy, this one with jet-black hair tumbled down over a pair of brilliant blue eyes, followed on the heels of the monstrous hog.

"Go on, go on, *go on*!" He yelled, stomped his feet, and smacked two sticks against each other, urging the filthy creature along.

His cronies laughed so hard that the red-haired one fell in a heap onto the dusty road. The little girls tried to flee through the opening his fall created, but the hog went for that exit route at the same time. As the girls ran past, three pretty Sunday dresses picked up dirt from the pig's coat.

The girls' wails multiplied.

The boys' laughter did as well.

The hog tore off between two buildings, his hooves kicking up a dust storm all their own. "I'll get him!" hollered the black-haired boy as he chased after it around the corner.

She'd seen enough. Olivia tucked her Bible between her elbow and her ribs as she hurried toward the children before the other boys ran off as well.

When Eli locked the door of the bank, the usual thrill at the sight of the gold-foil letters on the pane of glass sped through him:

BANK OF BOUNTIFUL

ELIJAH WHITMAN, JR., PRESIDENT

He breathed a prayer every single day, thanking his heavenly Father for helping him save the enterprise he and his late father had worked so hard to build. He'd come too close to losing everything two years earlier.

As he pushed away the memory of that painful time, he heard children's squeals and laughter from not too far away. Then, a clear feminine voice called out, "Gentlemen."

Silence descended.

He wished he had that kind of effect with his two youngsters every time he spoke to them. He slipped the key into his pocket, sighing. Things were fast approaching a desperate stage at home.

He stepped down to the sidewalk and glanced down the street. A young woman marched toward a group of children gathered in the middle of the road. The picture they painted piqued his curiosity. What parent would allow youngsters to run wild in the middle of town in their Sunday best?

Eli headed toward the group.

"Gentlemen," the lady repeated in a firm, stern voice as he approached. "Which one of you would care to explain what this"—she gestured to encompass the entire scenario—"is all about?"

The boys grew mute.

The girls rushed to the lady's side.

"Oh, Miss Livvy!" cried a petite blonde with bouncy curls. "They're horrid, these boys. Look. Just *look* at what they did to my lovely new dress."

The young lady—Miss Livvy as the girl had called her—dropped down to the child's level, clearly more concerned about the besieged girls than about the possible soiling of her gray skirt.

"I saw what happened, Melly," she said. "Go home now, girls. But as you do, would you please stop by Mrs. Tucker's home and let her know I'll be late? I might not even make it today after all."

All three nodded and stepped away. Before they left, however, Miss Livvy seemed to have another thought. "If any of your mamas is upset with the state of your clothes, please have her speak to me. I'll vouch for you."

With a chorus of agreement, the girls scampered away. The young lady then turned to the tight knot of boys. "Now, gentlemen, what do you have to say for yourselves?"

"Ah..."

"Um..."

"Er..."

"Hm..."

When none of them responded, Miss Livvy prodded, "Well?"

Silence reigned on Main Street.

She went on. "Aside from the apologies you owe the three young ladies—"

"Aw..."

"Nah..."

"Really?"

"But..."

"Aside from the apologies you owe the three young ladies," she repeated, "there is still the matter of that runaway pig."

Eli stifled a laugh. A pig? He crossed his arms, enjoying the moment.

"Oh, no!" the red-haired boy cried. "Pa's gonna kill me if he sees Rufus's not back in his pen."

Rufus. Eli smiled, he couldn't help himself. Albert Brown, a friend of his son Luke, would soon be facing a dressing down, if not a switching, from his father. Mr. Brown put a lot of stock in his pigs.

Miss Livvy seemed to agree with his assessment, as her lovely features brightened with her own smile. "Perhaps you should have thought of that before you decided to torment the girls," she told Albert.

"Uh-huh." He took a step away from the gathering. "Reckon so. Yes, ma'am, I do."

Miss Livvy crossed her arms, Bible and purse hugged close. "Not so fast. You have some friends here, don't you?"

With a lingering look in the direction of the offices of the *Bountiful Scribe*, the town's weekly paper, and the school-house, Albert stopped. He wiped the dusty toe of one shoe on his other trouser leg. "Yes, ma'am."

The other boys donned differing levels of worry.

"And did your pa say for you and your friends to chase his swine around town?"

He blushed under his freckles. "No, ma'am. He don't rightly know Rufus's gone."

"Then it would seem that you gentlemen could well be called thieves. You took a hog that didn't belong to any one of you. After all, Rufus wasn't *given* to you."

"Oh, but—"

"That ain't how it happened—"

"Not so—"

"Nah—"

"And," she said as though they hadn't argued, "thieves are fair game for Marshal Blair, don't you think?"

Four pairs of eyes opened wider than ever. The boys began to argue, their statements indecipherable since they spoke one over the other.

She went on in her calm, even voice. "So. What'll it be, gents? Shall I send for the marshal or will you set things to rights again?"

"SOOO-oo-eeyyy!" shrieked the aforementioned porker as it reappeared, galloping back down Main Street toward Miss Livvy and the boys.

"There!" the lady cried. "A chance to do your duty, gentlemen. Catch him—Rufus—and return him before I'm compelled to fetch Marshal Blair."

The boys pelted off after the squealing swine, each determined to beat the others to their quarry.

Eli caught sight of the three girls peering out from around the corner of Metcalf's Mercantile. Apparently they'd stayed to watch the boys get their just deserts.

The hog darted toward them.

The girls squealed.

The pig did as well.

The boys pursued the animal, one of them managing to get a hand on its ear, but the creature changed direction, and the would-be captor fell to the dirt.

The girls laughed.

Jonathan Davidson, another of Luke's friends, bounded upright and dusted off his clothes. "That's not funny."

"Neither was chasing us, Jonny!" said the small blonde. Her headful of ringlets bobbed with her indignation.

Miss Livvy donned a slight smile and seemed to settle in to observe.

Eli followed suit.

Young male glares flew toward the girls as they tried to capture the pig who, after his taste of freedom, did not intend to be caught. He darted and weaved from street-side to street-side, the boys in hot pursuit. The girls found the situation hilarious.

No matter how hard the boys tried, each time any of them came close to laying hold of the animal, the pig wriggled out of their clutches. The would-be trappers grew grimier with every pass, as the girls giggled and cheered on the elusive prey.

"Miss 'Livia!" Albert bellowed after he, too, landed face-first in the dust. "It ain't funny. Make 'em stop laughing!"

Miss Olivia arched a brow. "The young ladies didn't find being chased by runaway livestock particularly humorous, gentlemen."

The pig turned back toward the way he had come, but a fifth boy, dirty and breathless, blocked his escape.

Eli recognized the fifth trouble-maker. In a flash, he stomped down the street, anger and frustration burning in his belly.

"Lucas Andrew Whitman!" he roared from just behind Miss Olivia. "What is the meaning of this?"

If you liked SHE SHALL BE PRAISED,
be sure to pick up award-winning author
Ginny Aiken's novel REMEMBER ME WHEN.

"In this engrossing second installment of her Women of Hope historical series, Aiken delivers a beautiful, inspirational slice of life set in 1880s Oregon...Rich with detail, the events unfold very naturally."
—*Publishers Weekly*

Marriage has been difficult for Faith Nolan. Her husband Roger, Pine Ridge's mercantile owner, likes his liquor and turns mean when he indulges. However, it is his unwillingness to help others that grieves Faith's tender heart the most.

Faith decides to drive a wagonload of critical supplies to a remote logging camp owned by Nathan Bartlett, while Roger sleeps off his latest bender. When Roger realizes what Faith has done, he violently confronts her, and she is knocked unconscious. When she comes to, she finds her husband nearby, dead in a pool of his own blood. Soon the primary suspect, Faith finds surprising support from the women in the town of Bountiful, and handsome Nathan Bartlett. But it is her trust in God that will see her through.